I0716539

CROWN
OF
SLUMBER

R.L. PEREZ

CROWN OF SLUMBER

A SLEEPING BEAUTY RETELLING

CROWNS OF THE FAE

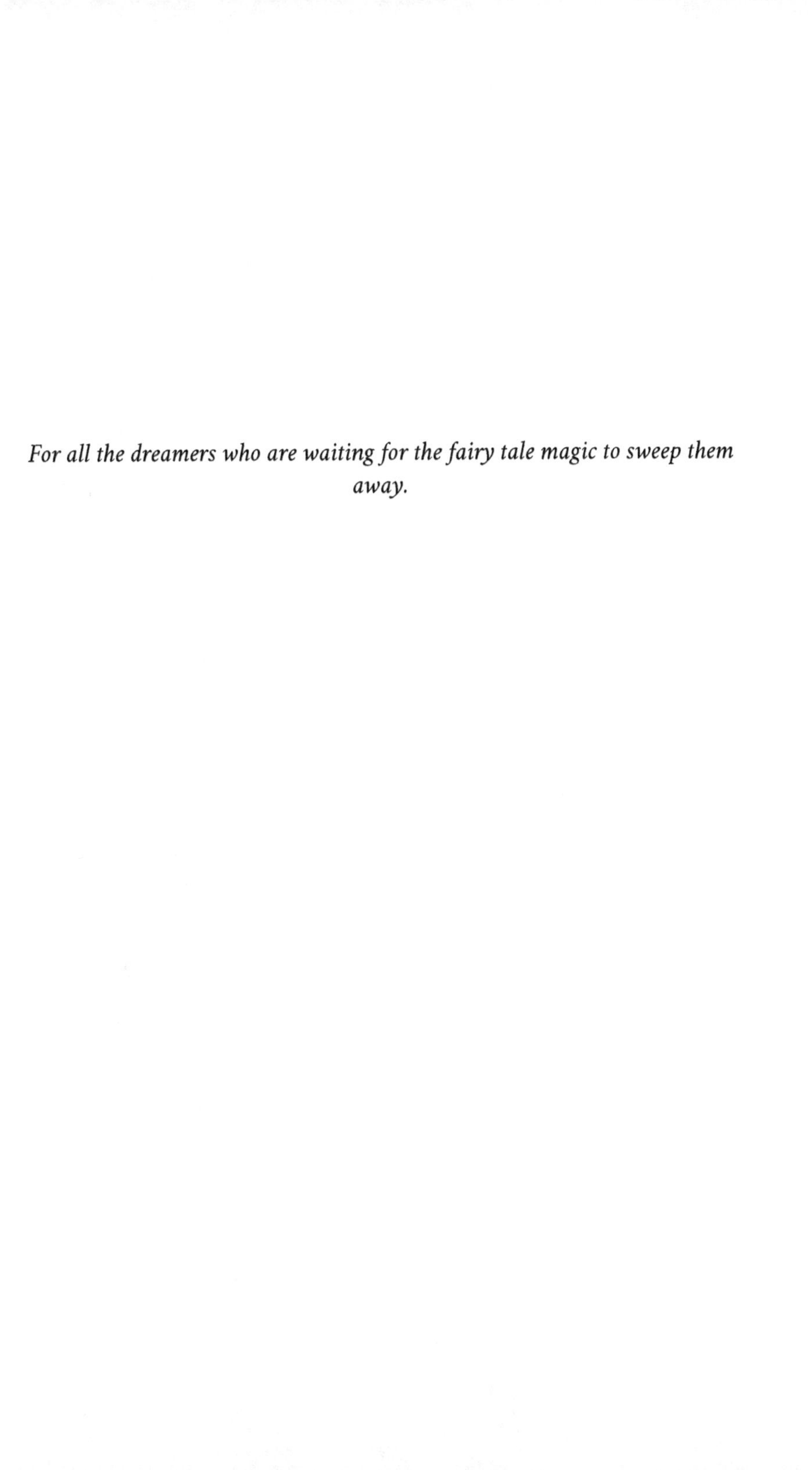

For all the dreamers who are waiting for the fairy tale magic to sweep them away.

Star Court
Winter Court
Lunar Court
Fire Court
Wind Court
Autumn Court
Summer Court
Sea Court
Spring Court
Earthen Court
Sun Court
Shadow Court
THE TWELVE FAE COURTS OF VALORA

ANDROMEDA MOUNTAINS
CELESTIAL RIVER
COURT OF MIDNIGHT
THE WILDS
WINTER COURT
STAR COURT
COURT OF TWILIGHT
MISTWOOD HILLS
FIRE COURT
AUTUMN PALACE
AUTUMN COURT
FELLSPAR INN
SUMMER COURT
MIRROR LAKE
KELLEN FALLS
JEWEL RIVER
WITCH CLANS
SUMMER PALACE
SEA COURT
THE NORTHWESTERN REGION

AUTHOR'S NOTE

This novel contains elements of sexual assault. Nothing graphic is described on the page, but a character who was assaulted recounts the event to another character and works to overcome the trauma of the incident.

There is also graphic violence, imprisonment, and graphic sexual content (consensual).

Please be mindful of your triggers and mental health before you read.

The Summer Princess

Dragons made much better company than fae nobles.

The familiar smell of sulfur and pine and earth filled my nostrils as I strode down the path to the nesting grounds.

It smelled of home.

A small smile lit my face, in spite of the exhausting ordeal I would face today. For this moment, I could relish the respite from court affairs.

I was the eldest daughter and next in line for the throne of the Summer Court. Father would be stepping down soon. In truth, he was quite healthy; but I knew Mother was anxious to retire with him. He was reluctant, but he knew it was best for the kingdom.

I couldn't blame my mother for wanting to step back. I wanted the same thing, after all. To live in the forest with my clan of dragons was my fantasy.

I didn't mind court politics. But solidifying my position as queen with a union with another fae court sickened me. I had to pretend to be flattered by the suitors who only saw me as a pretty ornament attached to their arm when in reality, I wanted to retch.

News of Father's abdication had spread quickly. Already, suitors from other kingdoms had come to seek my hand.

Not for me, of course. But for our dragons. Every kingdom wanted them.

My fingers curled into tight fists at the thought. Every king and queen would use our dragons as weapons, would enslave them, would butcher them for gold.

I would never allow it. Never.

As queen, I could protect them. Better than my father ever could.

Heat swirled around me as I drew closer to the nesting grounds, a warm and comforting presence. I never minded the sweltering temperature. In the Summer Court, the sun blazed for sixteen hours every day. Add the dragonfire, and it made our court seem like a furnace.

But I longed for it. My pale, rosy, and freckled skin craved the heat as if it had been siphoned from me at birth. My sister, Gigi, often joked about it; that the witches cursed me with fair skin in a kingdom forever punished by an overbearing sun.

A row of hydrangea bushes marked the entrance to the grounds. I stopped to smell them, allowing another smile to spread across my lips.

The dragon clan loved the smell of hydrangeas. It kept them at ease. Especially the younglings.

My fingers brushed against the soft blue petals as I entered the grove. Large pine trees speared toward the sky, providing a cocoon of shade. As soon as I reached the cover of trees, my skin pebbled from the absence of the heat. The dragons liked their privacy, and the younglings, who were often skittish during their early years, preferred the isolation from our people.

Except for me. They were all comfortable around me.

I was their guardian, after all.

A low, gentle thrumming noise filled the air, making the ground rumble. Some would call it a growl, but I knew better; it was a purr.

I grinned widely. "It's nice to see you, too, Mal."

A black dragon with midnight scales inched forward. He stood taller than our grandest carriage, with sharp silver talons and fiery golden eyes. A long, white scar ran down one eye, making it look milkier than the other. A battle scar, courtesy of the Midnight Court.

All the fae courts sought after our dragons. But the Court of Midnight had been the most ruthless in their pursuit. Mal had fearlessly defended our kingdom against the threat ten years ago, but the price had been steep. We'd almost lost him that day.

Mal rumbled a low sound and drew closer to me, his hot breath warming my body. He pressed his long snout into my arm, and I scratched underneath his chin.

"I missed you, too." I leaned my forehead against his, and he purred again.

Mal was fearsome, but he certainly wasn't the biggest of our dragons. He was a Darkener, which was our rarest species. The biggest and most fearsome was Kade, our green Bloodmare; she was as large as our castle. But, due to her size, she was often in hibernation. It took a great deal of energy for her to emerge from the nesting grounds. We often let her be.

What I loved about Mal was that he was big enough to intimidate but small enough to cuddle. A laugh escaped me as he nuzzled further into my shoulder, proving exactly that. My arms wrapped around his scaly neck as I drew him close.

His low whine rumbled in my ear, and I sighed, understanding his intention. I wasn't sure how, but I could easily communicate with the dragons. Even if I didn't know exactly what they were saying, I could read their intonations, deciphering meaning from certain sounds and inflections.

Gigi, my sister, often called me a witch for it. "Aurelia is a dragon witch!" she would shout, while I, in turn, would ruffle up my already unruly strawberry blond hair and cackle wickedly while chasing her around the castle.

"I'm sorry, friend," I lamented, withdrawing to run my hand down Mal's snout once more. "We can't go riding today. There are more suitors to see." I wrinkled my nose.

Mal snorted, lifting his chin. I imagined if he could, he would be rolling his eyes.

I chuckled. "I know. Believe me, I'd much prefer riding. But I have duties to attend to."

He let out another questioning rumble, his head tilted as he scrutinized me.

I shook my head. "I don't know what I'll do. I must marry eventually, I suppose. But none of these suitors are..." I trailed off, unable to find the words. Truth be told, they were all terrible. Handsome, sure, but they were vile, conniving, conceited, and downright boring. They wanted to speak of armies and battle strategy, or how much price a tract of farmland could fetch, or how many heirs I could produce. If I brought up horticulture or literature, which were two of my greatest interests, they would either laugh as if I made a joke, or they would smile blandly and change the subject.

A few years ago, I'd had an arrangement with the Autumn Prince.

For a while, I was planning to be his bride. And he hadn't been *completely* terrible. Not until…

No. I shoved the thought from my mind before it soured my mood even further.

"Whoever I do choose to marry will have to pass your inspection first," I declared, and Mal lifted his chin again, all smugness and satisfaction. "If you don't like him, I will turn him away at once."

Mal huffed in amusement, and I grinned, scratching under his chin again. "How is Azure doing?"

Mal's answering hum had a distressed edge to it, and the smile slipped from my face. "Can I see her?"

He dropped his head, turning to lead me farther into the grove. Anxiety had my fingers clenching into fists at my side as I hurried after him. The slope descended to a bumpy crater the dragons had dug to protect their eggs. Only a few large gray ones hadn't hatched yet; the rest of the hatchlings were nestled close to their mothers.

All except for one.

As blue as her namesake, Azure was draped along the soft soil, her scales reflecting the shimmering light of the sun that filtered through the canopy above. Her long, slender body seemed serpentine, with a curling tail and narrow snout buried in the earth. She wasn't much bigger than a calf at birth. Her lungs rattled with each breath she took, her eyes closed tightly in pain.

She was sick. And there was nothing I could do for her.

A few days ago, she had seemed to be improving. She drank the milk I offered her, even nibbled at the fish I brought.

But now she seemed worse than before. Even her blue scales lacked their usual luster.

Beside me, Mal stiffened, then let out a low growl.

Only then did I notice a cloaked figure was crouched by Azure's side.

"Get away!" I barked, sprinting forward, prepared to strike whoever dared to come near my dragons.

When the figure removed their hood, I faltered at the familiar white hair and silvery eyes.

Samiria. She was a fae witch, the sage of her coven. The only one bold enough to come near the dragons because she was the only one they would allow. It was said that sages had a special kinship with the beasts. I hadn't believed it until I'd seen the dragons settle under Samiria's gaze like they did mine.

Despite her familiar presence, my body was still tense with apprehension as I approached. I had never found her among the hatchlings before. Generally, she tended to the older dragons. "What are you doing here?" My tone was gentler, but still commanding. I didn't like how close she was to Azure.

Samiria straightened, bowing her head in respect. "Your Highness."

I frowned. The witches rarely acknowledged royalty. I was accustomed to being addressed as "Lady Aurelia" by the coven. It was why they didn't get along too well with my family. They operated under their own set of rules, believing the fates to be the true rulers of the land. The witches had pointed ears like we did, which meant there was some fae blood in them. But that was where the similarities between us ended.

"Samiria, what are you doing here?" I said again.

"I was under the impression my presence was permitted in the nesting grounds," she said, her voice low and raspy. "Is that no longer the case?"

"Why are you with Azure?" I snapped. I wasn't in the mood for her cryptic games today.

"She is weak. She needs sustenance you do not have here."

My eyebrows lifted as I glanced from Samiria to the sick dragon. "Do you know what ails her?"

"She needs her mother."

"Her mother is not here."

Samiria was quiet for a moment. Then she said, "Tell me what you know of her."

I bristled at the command in her voice but obeyed. "I only caught a glimpse of her. Blue scales, just like Azure. Wherever the mother is, she's been badly wounded."

"And how do you know that? Did you see her get hurt?" Samiria's silver eyes glinted as if she knew something I didn't.

"No, but I heard her scream. Felt her pain."

Samiria's eyes seemed to burn with intensity. "You felt it?"

"Yes." I couldn't explain it. But hearing the shriek of that poor dragon filled me with a devastation so potent I couldn't breathe.

Samiria nodded slowly. She was the only person who fully understood my connection to the dragons. "How long ago was this?"

"Two weeks ago."

Her wrinkled lips pressed together in thought. "The hatchling doesn't have much time left then." She looked at me, her gaze sharpening. "Azure is a Blue Amethyst. They are a rare species I have only encountered once. The hatchlings can only survive by feeding on droplets of the mother's blood for the first year. Only then can their powers manifest."

My eyes widened. "Powers?"

Samiria nodded. "Yes, Blue Amethysts have magical powers. Some can share visions of the future. Others can read minds. I believed all the Blue Amethysts had perished long ago, but…" She trailed off, gazing sadly at Azure. "Clearly, I was wrong."

"There must be something we can do for her." I knelt to the ground, bringing my palm to Azure's small snout as she whimpered in pain. "Can't another dragon's blood suffice?"

"Sadly, no. Other dragons do not possess the same magic she does. A Blue Amethyst is tethered in life and death to the magic flowing through their veins. Much like the fae. Much like us witches. If her magic dies, so does she."

Tears burned in my eyes as I stared helplessly at the small dragon, who arched her neck and moaned. "Please," I begged, turning to Samiria. "Isn't there some kind of spell you can cast? Some magic you can give her?"

Samiria stared at me, her otherworldly eyes drilling into me as if trying to convey some hidden meaning. After a long moment, she said, "Blue Amethysts are born of the Star Court."

My head whipped toward her in shock. "The Star Court? I thought all dragons came from here."

"Oh, child, the dragons once were *everywhere*. Long before fae kind came into being, they were the dominant species. You would be surprised to learn just how many dragon species originated from the Star Court." Her shrewd eyes seemed to glimmer at me, as if she knew something I didn't.

"If she is from the Star Court, then how did she end up here?"

"That I do not know. But a dragon feeds on the magic of its ancestral land." She leveled another significant look at me.

My stomach hollowed. "You're saying… she needs to be in the Star Court?" The Star Court was the home of two kingdoms: the Court of Twilight, a place where humans and fae coexisted, and the Court of Midnight, who had already tried to take my dragons once before. The same court who had blinded Mal's eye. "Samiria, they will *kill* her."

"The sage before me spoke of a magical substance called stardust," Samiria continued as if I hadn't spoken. "It is rumored to be found in the rivers of the Star Court." She looked at me again, her eyes heavy with an emotion I could not place. "If such a substance exists, it is likely the only thing that can save this dragon."

I swallowed around the lump in my throat, glancing down at Azure once more. A single tear leaked from her eye, and my heart twisted with agony. "If I enter the Star Court without invitation, that is grounds for war," I said softly. Even entering the Court of Twilight would be risky, as they had openly declared their alliance to the Court of Midnight. The Summer Court and the Court of Midnight had been feuding for centuries. After their attack ten years ago, we had reached an armistice, but it was fragile. One wrong move, and battle would commence once more.

Mother and Father would never allow it.

But… perhaps, as queen, I could find a way.

Samiria's mouth quirked as if she'd sensed the direction of my thoughts. "I am only conveying to you what I know. I bid you farewell, Your Highness."

Without another word, she lowered her hood and withdrew from the crater, retreating into the woods until her cloaked figure vanished completely.

The Midnight Prince

I braced my hands along the stone balcony of my chambers that overlooked the winding river below, lined by braziers emitting silver flames. The light cast an eerie glow on the water, making it appear like a shimmering snake that rippled in the night. Below, the chatter of townsfolk milling about during the kingdom's Nightfire fete echoed, filling the air with a delightful babble that mingled with the rushing waters.

Ordinarily, the sound would bring me joy.

But not tonight.

Tonight, my gaze was pinned on the flickering embers of three of our braziers. The Nightfire was dying, and we didn't have the oil or the magic to start it up again.

Thankfully, the people were unaware. There was enough light for them to continue with their festivities. But it wouldn't be long before the dying fires would bring panic to our people.

"Sire," Gorrick, my guard captain, said from behind me. "We've lost the Nightfire in the southern sector."

My fingers clenched the stone railing so tightly my knuckles turned white, and the cold and unyielding surface bit into my palms.

We were out of time.

"Have the citizens evacuate to the western sector," I said.

"Yes, sire." Gorrick's feet shuffled with his movement, but I stopped him.

"Double the guard," I told him. "Once those fires are out, we have no idea what manner of beasts will emerge."

"Of course, sire." Gorrick bowed, pressed his fist to his chest, and exited the chambers.

With a heavy sigh, I ran a hand through my hair and turned to face the scene below once more. My eyes were drawn to the darkness in the south, where our Nightfire had just gone out.

I watched, waiting.

After several moments, the bobbing light of torches appeared, but they were faint compared to the blazing beacon of our Nightfire braziers. They wouldn't hold off any unseelie beasts, that was for sure.

And here I stood, their prince and monarch, with no solution for them.

Soon, our entire kingdom would be plunged into darkness. And I could do nothing to save it.

"Fennick."

I turned to find my mother, Queen Sonara, standing at my open door. She wore a silver gown that shimmered with each movement as if it were made of the stars themselves. Her silver crown rested atop her head of raven black hair, and a faint glitter lined her olive toned skin. It was a Nightfire tradition, to adorn one's body like the stars. And Mother looked like the brightest star of them all.

A soft smile lit my face as I turned to inspect her. "Careful, Mother. You'll outshine everyone. Even the stars."

She grinned and waved her hand at me, stepping farther into my chambers. Her midnight black hair was pinned atop her head with several curls resting against her cheeks. She tucked one behind her ear as she joined me on the balcony.

"I have just spoken with Cressida," Mother said, her voice soft. Cressida was the court mage. "She says there is nothing we can do."

My expression sobered. I had expected this. But it didn't stop my stomach from dropping.

"This may be our last Nightfire fete for a while," she went on. "We cannot hide this from the people for much longer. If they notice before we tell them, we could lose their trust. I plan to make an announcement at midday."

I nodded. "What of the other kingdoms? Can we ask our allies for assistance?"

"The stardust we use in our oil is unique to the Star Court," Mother said. "Ordinary oil can only burn for so long. But stardust keeps ours burning all night."

I nodded with a grimace. Stardust was our most precious commodity. We used it for currency, medicines, enchantments, and, of course, Nightfire.

And we were running out of it.

I sighed, bracing my forearms on the edge of the balcony. Here in the Midnight Court, the sun rarely made an appearance. Only during the summer did it peek out for an hour or two before retreating behind the horizon once more. We were Night Fae, after all. Our souls were made for the night.

But to be plunged in utter darkness was far too dangerous. We were accustomed to darkness, yes, but so were other less civilized creatures. All manner of unseelie beasts roamed these lands, and the Nightfire was the only thing keeping them from preying on our people.

"Cressida did say there was one other substance we could use," Mother said slowly.

At the wariness in her voice, I turned, eyebrows raised. "Well, don't keep me in suspense, Mother."

Mother's lips pinched, as they always did when I joked. "Dragonfire."

I stiffened at that, my body coiling in anger. *Dragons.* Of course. Another reason to despise the Summer Court. Gritting my teeth, I turned to face the scene below once more, trying to ignore the rippling rage coursing through me. "Summer will never help us."

"I know."

"Then, why even bring it up? There is nothing we can do." My eyes narrowed as I thought of the rumors floating among our guards. "Wait a moment... I've heard people whispering of how we captured a dragon. Mother, is that true?"

She scoffed and waved a hand. "Pay no attention to idle gossip, Fennick. Don't you think if I had a dragon somewhere, we would be using its fire by now?"

I sighed. I supposed it was too good to be true.

She placed a hand on my arm, and I met her gaze. A fierce intensity burned in her eyes that matched the anger pulsing through me. "We've received word that King Stefan is abdicating to his eldest daughter. She is young. Inexperienced." A serpentine smile spread across her face.

My eyes narrowed. "What are you suggesting?"

"We are desperate, Fennick," she said, her tone sharpening. "We cannot simply sit back and watch our people suffer. The time for pleasantries is over. If Summer will not assist us, then we will take what we need by force."

Alarm shot through me, cooling my anger. "Mother, you speak of war. Our kingdom cannot support a war on top of the stardust shortage."

"What are our other options?" she snapped. "What else would you have me do, Fennick?"

I fell silent at that. I had no other possible solutions. Enchanted fire was already hard to come by in the Realm of Valora. No other kingdoms had easy access to it.

Except, it seemed, the Summer Court.

Mother was right. We had no other options.

"I know you can… *convince* her," Mother continued, her tone full of meaning.

I whipped my head to look at her in accusation. "You mean use my gift?" My fae magic allowed me to persuade others to agree with me. But it only worked if their minds were amenable.

I doubted the Summer Princess would be an easy target.

Mother seemed to read my apprehension. "I hear the Summer Princess is quite beautiful. And you are always *so* charming with the court ladies."

I fixed a flat stare on her. "Not with ladies from an enemy kingdom."

Mother shrugged. "You do love a good challenge, don't you?"

I glanced down at the braziers along the riverbank. Another one was fading, its dying embers floating into the night.

Could I charm the Summer Princess? Even with my charismatic personality and fae magic, it would be difficult to erase centuries of hatred and tension between our kingdoms.

"What can I offer her in exchange for her help?" I asked. "Gold? Steel?"

"You can offer her safety. A promise that we will not invade and seize what belongs to us."

I stared at her. "You wish me to go to their kingdom and charm the princess only to turn around and threaten her people if she does not comply with our demands?" I loved my mother, but she was known for being a brutal queen for a reason. Some called her heartless. And while I understood why she made the decisions she did, it didn't mean I wanted to be the same kind of ruler as she was.

The idea of entering an enemy kingdom uninvited and demanding they surrender their most precious resource to us did not sit well with me.

Mother leaned closer, her gaze sharpening and her smile cold. "As I said before, Fennick. The time for pleasantries is over." She withdrew and stepped away from the balcony. "I know you will not fail me." The threat lining her words made me stiffen as her heels clacked on the marble floors. I didn't turn to look at her as she left my chambers.

My jaw was taut as I faced the balcony once more, my eyes upon the darkness of the southern sector. Faint torch lights still bobbed in the distance. My arms grew tense as the tree branches quivered, and bestial roars echoed.

The unseelie creatures had come.

My eyes crammed shut as screams filled the air. The screams of my people.

Despite my mother's callous nature, she was right; I would do this for our people.

And I would not fail.

THE SUMMER PRINCESS

"The weather today is lovely, Sir Levin," I said, my hands clasped demurely in front of me. I resisted the urge to fidget with the blue fabric of my dress. "It would be perfect for a ride. We have forest trails the horses particularly enjoy."

Sir Levin, a fae lord from the Sea Court, wrinkled his nose, his thick brown mustache quivering with the motion. We sat in the receiving room in the castle, sitting on opposite sofas with a tray of tea and scones on the table between us. The wide octagonal window next to us boasted a view of lush green pine trees and rolling hills. I ached to be outside to enjoy it.

"Ah, no," Sir Levin said. "I'm afraid I'm not much of a rider. And all these trees make my nose itch." He sniffed as if to emphasize the point.

My eyebrows lifted. "You… do not like trees?"

"Well, not *pine* trees. From my court, we are accustomed to beech trees and palm trees. Much less stuffy."

I forced a smile. "I see."

He was not the only noble to complain about our woodsy terrain. And he certainly wouldn't be the last.

"We do have the Jewel River that winds through our forests," I continued. "You would be surprised how cool the air is there. And the pebbles at the bottom of the river glisten like jewels, which gives the river its namesake. Would you like to see?"

Sir Levin grimaced and rubbed the back of his neck. "Actually, I was hoping to catch a glimpse of your dragons."

I stiffened. "Dragons?"

Sir Levin's dark eyes lit up with excitement, nearly bulging from his rotund face. "Yes, they are legendary! I hear you have one that is the size of this castle!"

"My dragons are not an attraction for public display, Sir Levin," I said coldly. "And at this time of year, many of them are hibernating and wish to not be disturbed."

"Ah, yes. I understand. But… surely you have one or two I could sneak a peek at? A union between our courts could bring great things to both kingdoms. I would have to be comfortable around the dragons eventually."

I lifted my chin. "You speak as if our negotiations are complete, Sir Levin. I must remind you that nothing official has yet been decided."

His face reddened, and he scraped a hand through his short cropped black hair. "Forgive me. You are right, of course. Well, perhaps you can return to your embroidery and I can speak with King Stefan instead?"

My eyes narrowed. "The king is otherwise engaged. As you may have heard, he is abdicating to me in a few days. So whatever you need to speak with him about, you can discuss it now. With me." I offered a humorless smile.

Sir Levin fidgeted, shifting his weight from one foot to another. "Ah. Right. Of course. Well…"

I raised my eyebrows expectantly, waiting.

"I merely… wished to discuss commerce," Sir Levin mumbled after a moment. "The treasury and tithes and other financial decisions your kingdom makes. Surely a dull topic for a lady like yourself to worry about."

"Our lumber mills provide our main source of revenue," I said, my voice brisk. "We keep them well maintained and staffed throughout the year. We do not take tithes from our people, but we do tax them, which pays a comfortable wage for our soldiers and armies, should we have need of them. As of right now, our people live well and have few complaints." I cocked my head at him. "What specific financial questions did you have, Sir Levin?"

His cheeks turned even redder, making his round face look very much like a ripe tomato. He stammered something incoherent about *conversing with women,* and I'd had enough.

My hands fell on my thighs and I fixed him with a glare. "If you are not here to converse with women, as you say, then why *are* you here, Sir

Levin? Merely to gawk at our dragons? To size them up for your own use? I was under the impression you wanted to get to know me to see if a union between our courts would be amenable. But I am sorry to say I am not impressed in the slightest. May I recommend, in the future, that should you seek the hand of a bride, you should show an interest in *her* and not her assets? Oh, and be sure not to belittle her with talk of embroidery and the assumption that financial discussions are too complex for her fragile mind to understand."

I stood and smoothed my palms along my skirts. "Captain Huxley will show you out. Good day to you."

Sir Levin babbled something that sounded like an apology, but I wouldn't hear of it. I'd swept from the room before he could even rise from his seat. My steps were quick and purposeful as I made my way down the hall and toward the staircase.

"Aurelia?"

I stopped with my hand on the bannister, turning to find Mother emerging from the opposite hall. She glanced from me to the receiving room, a question in her blue eyes. "Where is Sir Levin?"

"I dismissed him," I said shortly.

Mother huffed a laugh. "Burning suns, Aurelia, you have to make a match eventually. You can't dismiss *everyone* simply because they look silly when they chew."

"Sir Belefort's beard was *oozing* with stew! It was repulsive."

Mother leveled a hard stare at me. "Aurelia. Be reasonable."

"I don't see why I must choose a husband *now*. Surely, it can wait."

"Surely not. The instant you take the throne, you will be targeted as a young and naive monarch. You need a strong and capable king to rule by your side, and a kingdom to ally with. I am sad to say we have few allies because..." She trailed off, her lips clamping together.

"Because of what?" I prompted, my eyes narrowing.

"Because of how sensitive you are about the dragons."

My head reared back. "You would prefer we trade the dragons like... like *cattle*? They will be weaponized! Enslaved. Tortured for sport!"

Mother sighed and waved a gloved hand. "You don't know that. And it's careless of you to assume as much without even being willing to negotiate about it. What if there is a court out there who would treat the dragons with as much care and kindness as you? But you refuse to see it because you won't even entertain the idea, Aurelia. You must think of our kingdom and our people as you do the dragons. They are not your subjects. And when you take the throne, you will have an entire population to consider."

"I know that," I snapped.

"Do you?" Mother stepped closer, her blue eyes flaring wide. "Your father did not make this decision lightly, Aurelia. But if you prove to us you are not ready, then we will delay the abdication. Show me you will sacrifice for this kingdom."

"Sacrifice the dragons?" I asked, my heart plummeting to my stomach. If Mother forced me to choose between the dragons and the throne, I wasn't sure what I would say.

Mother sighed. "No. I'm not asking you to give them up. But please be more open. It is natural for other kingdoms to be curious about them. Surely, there is no harm in showing them to your suitors? You did say that a dragon is the best judge of character. Perhaps they can help you make your decision." A small smile lit her face.

I opened my mouth to object, but before I could, a figure bounded toward us, her tight blond curls bouncing with the movement. "I saw Sir Levin leaving in a carriage," said Gigi, my younger sister. "That must have been less than five minutes. A record for you, Aurie!"

"Hush, Giselle," Mother chastened. "It's no laughing matter."

"It is a *bit* of a laughing matter," Gigi protested. "The man looked like a walrus."

I snorted, then covered my mouth as Gigi's giggles rang in the hallway. Mother swatted at her arm, but a smile tugged at the corners of her lips.

"And what does your ideal suitor look like, Gigi?" I questioned. She was sixteen, and it wouldn't be long before she would be looking for a match, too.

Gigi stroked her chin in contemplation. "Well, he must be handsome. If he looks anything like a walrus, I will turn him away at once. He must also have a sense of adventure. And he must be kind to animals."

I gestured to Gigi with a pointed look at my mother. "I have similar requirements. Although it isn't necessary for him to be handsome."

Gigi elbowed me. "But it would be nice, yes?"

Ignoring her, I turned to Mother. "Sir Levin was complaining of our pine trees and refused my offer to go riding. And I saw the greed in his eyes when he asked of the dragons. It was not out of curiosity or kindness. It was purely for his own gain."

Mother cast her gaze to the ceiling as if praying for strength. "And you are using your sister's judgment as your defense?"

"I resent the implication that my judgment cannot be trusted," Gigi said with a huff.

"I am merely stating that regardless of my... overprotective tendencies toward the dragons, Sir Levin was *not* an ideal match. But I promise that, in the future, I will try to be more open to others." I nodded to reassure myself I could do this.

When the next suitor asked about the dragons, I would not downright refuse. I would entertain the idea.

If only for a moment.

Desperate to escape after Sir Levin's departure, I decided to forego wearing my riding leathers. It wouldn't be as comfortable, but at least I was wearing a simple cotton dress instead of a stiff ballgown. It had been days since I'd taken Mal riding, and I knew he was restless.

He wasn't the only one.

I was making my way to the entrance doors when I rounded a corner and ran straight into Father. He grunted, and I stumbled backward, barely catching myself before falling over. With a sniff, he adjusted his royal blue tunic, surveying me with irritation brimming in his dark eyes.

"I know I taught you better than that, Aurelia," he said. "Do watch where you're going."

"Pardon me, Father." I bowed my head submissively.

He sighed. "Why are you in such a hurry? Aren't you meeting a suitor today?"

Gods, the last thing I needed was another reprimand for turning Sir Levin away. I cleared my throat. "He... left. Sir Levin did not stay long. I don't think he likes our court very much."

All true.

Father arched a single doubtful eyebrow, and I resisted the urge to squirm under his scrutiny. He was far more stern than Mother, and I always had the sense that I never lived up to his expectations, especially as next in line for the throne.

To convince him to abdicate to me had not been an easy feat. And every day, I held my breath, expecting him to change his mind and keep the crown from me.

"Things were much simpler when you were engaged to the Autumn Prince," Father said with a scowl.

I stiffened, trying not to dwell on what had transpired between me and the Autumn Prince. Those were memories I actively strived to forget.

But our engagement had been broken. I would never marry him, no matter what.

"You have a sacred responsibility to this kingdom, Aurelia." Father's voice was low and grave.

"I know that," I said quickly.

"Do you?" he challenged. "Because I often feel you are more concerned with prancing through the forest than running the kingdom."

Prancing. I bit back my ire and said in a steady voice, "I do care about running the kingdom, Father. I assure you. I am taking this seriously. If you have something pressing I must attend to, I will, of course, see to it."

I stood straight, hands clasped in front of me, eyeing him expectantly. Inside, my chest coiled with a tightness that longed to be loosed, to be freed in a way that only flying through the sky could accomplish.

But I wasn't lying. If Father had need of me, I would force down the urge to ride my dragon and do what the king asked of me.

I needed to prove myself to him. I was determined to show that I could be a worthy queen.

A long, tense moment passed between us. Father continued to eye me with doubt and disapproval while I held perfectly still as if a predator were sniffing me.

At long last, he waved his hand. "Go. I have nothing for you. But do return quickly, will you? It is unseemly for the future queen to be roaming the woods like a hag."

I wrinkled my nose at the word *hag.* Burning suns, was that really what he thought of me?

Instead of replying, I curtsied low and bustled away before he could chastise me further.

Even after I entered the nesting grounds, my insides still burned from my encounter with Father, reminding me of my constant shortcomings. But then I heard Mal's low rumble of anticipation before I even reached the grove. I broke into a run, a smile already spreading on my face, my worries forgotten.

The moment I set foot under the canopy of trees, Mal bounded forward like a puppy, slamming into me and sending me careening toward the forest floor. His wing wrapped around me, cushioning my fall so the roots and hard earth wouldn't scrape my elbows. I burst out laughing as we tumbled to the ground together.

"Easy there," I said between chuckles. "If I break my neck from your violent displays of affection, we'll never be able to go for a ride."

Mal responded by licking my cheek. I retched, wiping the sticky saliva off my face. Dragon saliva was thick and pasty and certainly *not* my favorite substance to have coating my face.

"All right, let me up so I can saddle you," I groaned, shifting against his weight still pinning me to the ground.

Mal grumbled but inched backward so I could rise.

"I don't want to hear it," I told him as I fetched the saddle and my riding boots from the tree hollow where I'd stashed them. I used to keep them in the stables but it was much easier to keep it among the nesting grounds. It also made for a quicker getaway when I wanted to escape my court duties. "I've ridden without a saddle before, and your scales *hurt.*"

Mal huffed and lifted his snout as if affronted by the idea that anything about him would cause me discomfort. I hauled my saddle over to him and tapped his snout lovingly.

"You're still my favorite," I murmured. "Don't you worry."

I slid off my high heels and slipped on my boots, sighing with relief at the flexible comfort of the leather compared to the tight straps I'd been wearing earlier. I hoisted the saddle atop my dragon and fastened the leather straps underneath his belly and on either side of his wings. Mal obediently knelt, lowering his head to the ground so I could climb on. With practiced ease, I swung one leg over and secured the harness around my legs and lower back to keep myself from falling mid-ride.

"To the skies, my friend," I said, patting the side of his long neck.

With an eager roar, Mal reared back on his legs and shot forward. We started at a gallop, the ride much bumpier than any horse I'd ever ridden. We had to clear the grove first or risk crashing into the tree branches and shattering my skull in the process. The wind whipped at my hair, tugging loose strands of hair free from my braid. I laughed, my eyes burning from the intensity of it as we darted down the path, Mal's claws digging into the soil and leaving a spray of dust behind us.

When we cleared the grove, his wings spread on either side of me. His legs continued pumping while he flapped his wings, and slowly we rose into the air. I let out a whooping laughter as he soared higher and higher. The cloud moisture tickled my arms and face, and the air stung my eyes, but burning suns, I didn't care at all. I felt nothing but pure, untethered freedom as we arced through the sky. My gaze fell to the treetops below. They were so small, so insignificant now.

I laughed again, closing my eyes and enjoying the sensation of gliding effortlessly through the sky. I felt Mal's low rumble of satisfaction as his pace slowed and we coasted, his wings stretched and keeping us afloat as he sliced through clouds with grace and ease.

Mal and I were one. We both yearned for the open skies, for the freedom to fly where we wished. To break free of our confinements and follow wherever the wind took us.

Nothing mattered but the open sky. Nothing but me and Mal.

THE MIDNIGHT PRINCE

The Summer Court was sweltering. I truly didn't understand how anyone could tolerate it.

From the moment I entered the borders, the heat and humidity pressed in on me, making it difficult to breathe. A thin sheen of sweat immediately formed on my brow and neck.

Not to mention the blazing sun. Stars, it was unbearable. We never used carriages in the Star Court, but it made me yearn for one, just for respite from the unforgiving and blinding light.

I paused often to drink from my waterskin, unaccustomed to being so thirsty. But, if I was completely honest with myself, I was stalling. I wasn't eager to march into the Summer palace and demand for something that didn't rightfully belong to me.

So, I took my time. I brought an envoy with me, only for pretenses, but I was planning to negotiate with the princess on my own. Mother made it clear the matter was to remain discreet.

Which meant she didn't want anyone blabbing to the other kingdoms about our hostile negotiations.

I gritted my teeth as I took another swig of water. Stars above, I *hated* this.

But it couldn't be helped. As Mother said, we were out of options.

If I had to choose between my kingdom's safety and maintaining pleasant relations with the Summer Court, I knew which one I would pick.

When I urged my horse to continue onward, the cobbled road curved slightly, and I sighed with relief. A canopy of overhanging trees stood over us, providing merciful shade from the sun. Under the cover of branches, the air actually felt quite cool, and were I not already over-heated from the ride, it would indeed feel pleasant.

But my patience was gone, and I was past feeling appreciative of this wretched kingdom.

Peeking through the trees were the tall, gleaming spires of the emerald Summer Palace, the sun reflecting off its glistening surface and sending rays of green light streaking through the sky.

Beside me, Horace, the envoy, rode stoically, his eyes fixed ahead. Not even his bushy mustache twitched.

I cleared my throat, fidgeting in my saddle. Horace always made me uncomfortable. He was so quiet and so *serious*. I often wondered if Mother assigned him to be my envoy on purpose, to dissuade me from joking so often.

It wouldn't work.

"Well, I'm convinced," I said, adopting an air of false solemnity. "This place must be Hell. It's the only explanation for this heat. There must be a fiery pit of despair somewhere, right?"

I cast a sidelong glance at Horace, who merely grunted in acknowl-edgement but said nothing more. Gods, I yearned for my friend Marek, who had once been my personal guardsman. Now, he was married to the queen of the Court of Twilight. Less than a day's ride away from me, but still farther than I was accustomed to.

Mother had urged me to bring a formal guard with me, but I didn't think that would be received well. Then again, me demanding the use of the dragons of the Summer Court wouldn't be received well, either. And if the princess ordered me to be arrested, I would have nothing but my own strength and wits to protect me.

Even so, I intended to be forthcoming with the princess. More forthcoming than Mother would have wanted me to be. Perhaps if I explained the dire situation of my people, she would be more amenable to lending us her dragons.

I wanted to project an air of humility. So, I left my guards behind.

"When we arrive," I said to Horace, "I'd like you to ride ahead of me to announce my presence. Allow the princess time to prepare. I'm sure my unexpected arrival will not be welcome."

Horace merely nodded, keeping his gaze fixed ahead.

"Are you married, Horace?"

"I am, Your Highness."

"What's her name?"

"Judith. We've been married for fifteen years."

"That's lovely. Any children?"

"No, Your Highness."

I nodded, unsure of what else to say. I didn't know much about the man, but perhaps I could amend that. "When you aren't busy, ah, *envoying*, what is it you like to do?"

Horace finally blinked and turned his dark gray eyes on me, his thick eyebrows knitting together in confusion. "Your Highness?"

"If you had the day off, what would you spend your time doing?"

His mustache puckered with his frown. "My wife enjoys baking."

My eyebrows lifted. "Ah. That sounds nice. And do you enjoy baking as well?"

"Not particularly. But I do enjoy eating the food she bakes."

I barked out a laugh. The man's hobby was *eating*. "Well, give me a delicious slice of buttered bread, and I'm in heaven. I can't blame you there, good fellow."

I could have sworn his eyes crinkled slightly with a smile that was hidden by his mustache. But it was gone in an instant as he fixed his gaze ahead once more.

We had nearly reached the palace when my horse stiffened and snorted, tossing his snout this way and that in agitation.

"Easy, Romulus." I patted his neck to try to soothe him. But he reared back with another snort, stomping his hooves.

My eyes narrowed as a tendril of heat coiled around me. My head snapped up and I glanced between the trees lining the road.

In the distance, something growled.

My hand went to the sword belted at my waist. "Horace?"

"I heard it, too, Your Highness." Horace sat up straighter in his saddle. Somehow, his horse was unaffected by whatever lurked in the forest.

I sniffed the air. It smelled of some kind of sweet flower and... charcoal.

A roar echoed, but it was faint, as if from miles away. I cast my gaze skyward, and my heart lurched in my throat.

A black dragon soared above us, wings spread wide and a roar pouring from its snout. It was a roar of *delight*. It coasted back and forth, arcing through the sky.

And on its back was a woman with long, blond hair, her arms spread just like the dragon's wings. I sat and watched for a moment, mesmerized by the sight. The woman released a whoop of excitement.

I wasn't sure why, but I found myself grinning.

"Heavens," Horace said, following my gaze. "That looks quite dangerous."

I laughed again. "It looks *incredible*." I couldn't deny it. Regardless of the animosity between our kingdoms, I was in awe. I had no doubt that if I possessed dragons, I would want to do the same thing.

My horse lurched again, still in distress. I looked to the trees once more, frowning at those distant sounds. Leaves crunched. Branches twitched. And more coils of heat snaked forward, twining around me like strands of magic.

I slid off my saddle and lowered to the ground.

Horace stiffened. "Your Highness?"

"Ride on without me," I said. "Romulus is nervous and can't take much more of this."

"Your Highness, I don't think you—"

"There are dragons nearby, Horace," I said, leveling a meaningful look at him. "It's what we came here for. I just want to take a look before I meet with the princess."

Horace's mustache seemed to curve downward in displeasure. "The queen would not like this."

"The queen is not here." I winked at him.

He grumbled something unintelligible but took the reins from me and urged the horses onward while I strode into the forest, following the tendrils of heat still beckoning me closer.

A strange, sulfuric smell filled the air, making my nose itch. The deeper into the forest I went, the louder the animalistic sounds became. Growls. Snorts. Huffs. Cracking branches. Faint screeches.

Oh, yes. This was definitely a dragon nest.

Every muscle of my body went stiff with awareness. A bead of sweat trickled down my face. My heart raced with anticipation.

Strangely, it was more curiosity than fear that overcame me. My pulse spiked, the excitement making me tremble.

Yes, the dragons could certainly eat me alive. But this was an opportunity I might never again experience, provided the Summer Princess denied me, as I was almost certain she would.

But more importantly, this offered a unique possibility I had not considered: could my fae magic work on dragons? I had tried it on the wyvern I had encountered in my travels, but they were not sentient. My magic did not work on mindless beasts—as was proven by my restless and stubborn horse.

But dragons? Could I convince one of them to come with me? To save my kingdom?

I had to try.

The air grew warmer as I approached, the soft earthy ground sloping downward into a sort of crater. My breath stuck in my throat as I took in the first creature, a magnificent silver-scaled dragon roughly twice the size of my horse. Despite the canopy of trees overhead, his scales shimmered in the faint sunlight, sparkling like diamonds.

"Stars above," I whispered.

The dragon whipped his head toward me, nostrils flaring. His amber eyes surveyed me, narrowing in suspicion.

I slowly lifted my hands in placation, my steps slow and careful. "Here now," I murmured. "I mean you no harm." My magic, which often remained buried deep within me, rose to the surface. I squashed the instinct to shove it down and instead coaxed it forward, allowing it to coat my tongue as I said softly, *"You know I am a friend."*

Wisps of energy swirled around me, tickling my skin. The dragon's head tilted to the side, almost in curiosity.

I wasn't sure if that meant the magic had worked or not. So, I kept going. *"I am your friend. I do not wish to harm you."*

More energy poured from me as I continued inching closer to the dragon.

He merely huffed, but he did not flinch away from my approach.

"Gods, you are magnificent," I said as I finally came within reaching distance. My hands, which were still raised, edged closer to the beast.

He did not stir. He did not even blink.

"May I?" I wasn't sure if he understood me, but I felt like I should ask permission all the same.

The dragon arched his long neck, then bowed his head toward me. I sucked in a gasp at the gesture. Somehow—miraculously—this dragon had accepted my presence. A stranger. A potential threat.

And he was bowing to me.

He grumbled softly, as if impatiently demanding me to… what? Pet him like some domestic canine?

I exhaled a laugh of disbelief and closed the distance between us, allowing my fingertips to brush his scales. They were sharper than I expected, like steel with a harsh edge that could slice through my flesh. I almost jerked my hand away for fear of cutting myself. My movements were delicate as I swept the pads of my fingers along the smooth, razor-sharp edges of the scales. They seemed sharper than the tip of my sword.

The dragon lifted his head, and my hand curled under his chin, finding a soft spot just underneath that was smooth, leathery flesh. I curled my fingertips, scratching, and his throat rumbled with pleasure.

I laughed again. "You are nothing but a kitten with claws, aren't you?" I scratched again, and he seemed to sigh with pleasure.

Delight soared through me at this unexpected friend I'd found. Would he be willing to help me? If I asked, would he come with me?

Perhaps I wouldn't need to bother the princess at all…

"Who are you?" demanded a voice.

I stiffened, glancing up. I had been so captivated by the silver dragon that I hadn't noticed several other dragons had come to investigate, including the black one I'd seen roaming the skies… with the blond woman still atop him. Her wild and unruly hair had a tint of orange to it, and her bright blue eyes were blazing with accusation as they fixed on me. Her freckled nose wrinkled with disdain.

Well, shit.

THE SUMMER PRINCESS

I wasn't sure how long Mal and I flew—it felt like only minutes, but I knew it had to have been an hour or more, judging by the violent shivers I couldn't escape. Even if my mind didn't notice the cold, my body still did. If I flew for much longer, the chills would make me sick.

With a sigh I nudged Mal's belly with my leg. "Time to descend, Mal."

He growled with displeasure but arced to the left, pitching downward. We'd flown too far once before, and I'd been ill for two weeks. Mal wouldn't risk it. Not only because he cared for me, but because I was his only rider; he couldn't bear to be grounded for that long.

Dragons didn't necessarily need riders, but they preferred it. It made them feel safer, knowing we were on their backs. Samiria had once told me that, long ago, there had been fae beasts that roamed the skies, hunting dragons. The dragons had bonded with the fae who possessed the strongest magic and were best suited to protect them. Generations later, it was still their instinct to bond with a rider before taking to the skies.

Which made little sense to me. I had yet to manifest any fae magic, much to my confusion and frustration. I also had no memories of my childhood, which led me to believe some kind of horrible magic had manifested itself early on, and I hadn't been strong enough to handle it.

Perhaps I was just broken.

I once tried to teach Gigi how to ride. I managed to secure her on a mild-tempered Greyback named Jorey. But once she was harnessed in the saddle, Jorey refused to move. I wasn't sure how, but I could understand his intention: he would not ride with someone who didn't trust him.

So, for now, I was the only rider. I tried to ride as many of them as I could to keep them content. Most often, it was just me and Mal; he was the only dragon restless enough to demand a ride every day. The others were satisfied with weekly rides. Sometimes even less frequently than that.

Mal smoothly glided through the sky, sinking lower and lower until he landed just in front of the grove. I stayed atop him as he clambered into the forest, both of us breathless from our flight.

"That was incredible, Mal," I said with a grin, patting the side of his neck. "Your wing movement has improved. That was the smoothest ride yet."

Instead of purring with delight, Mal's entire body went tense and rigid. His claws dug into the soil, and his back arched with a growl. I stiffened, my legs tightening in the saddle as I scanned the forest for the threat. My skin prickled with awareness, my heart thundering.

It didn't take long to notice the stranger. He was tall and muscular, adorned in riding leathers and polished boots. His burgundy coat was finely crafted and worthy of a high lord, at the very least. He stood by Jorey, his hand outstretched to pet the Greyback. To my surprise, the dragon lifted his head, eyes closing as he allowed this stranger to run his fingers down the silvery scales.

My eyes narrowed. "Who are you?" My voice was harsh and echoed in the forest.

The stranger turned. He had chestnut hair that swept over his forehead, mussed and untidy. His green eyes surveyed the woods with part amusement, part curiosity. His tan skin was only a few shades lighter than his hair.

"Apologies," he said lightly. "I was on my way to the palace and found myself here. These creatures are beautiful. Quite breathtaking."

"Step away from him," I snarled, dismounting from my saddle and storming toward Jorey.

The man lifted his hands and withdrew from the Greyback. "Forgive me. The dragon seemed to like it. If he'd recoiled, I would have stopped."

I faltered at that, glancing down at Jorey. His eyes had opened, his snout lifting as if searching for the warm hand that had been stroking him moments ago.

My mouth opened, then closed.

The dragon *liked* the stranger.

This had never happened before. The dragons were only ever comfortable around me and Samiria. Gigi, they tolerated, but begrudgingly.

So how had this stranger calmed them so effortlessly?

Who the hell was he… and why was he here?

My eyes swept over his belted leather tunic and vest and polished leather boots. Nobility, most likely.

My heart sank. "You are here to court the princess, then?" He was just like Sir Levin, trying to catch a glimpse of the dragons. Only this one was bold enough to sneak into the hatching grounds. Why the dragons hadn't roasted him, I had no idea. My hand absently began stroking under Mal's chin. He stood stiff and alert, his eyes pinned on the stranger.

"No," the man said, straightening and placing his hands behind his back. Nobility indeed. "I'm in the Summer Court on business."

My eyebrows lifted as I turned to face him. "Really? What kind of business?"

A wide smile spread on his face, the gesture so natural that it seemed perfectly suited to his features. As if a smile belonged there and always would. His eyes crinkled, the green in them seeming to deepen with his amusement. "Ah, well, I can't just share all my business dealings with strangers, now, can I? Who are *you*?"

"I—" I faltered. The words *I'm the princess* had almost escaped me, and I was prepared to tell him off for venturing too close to the dragons. But for the first time, here was a nobleman who *didn't* know who I was. Someone who wasn't seeking my hand.

The notion was oddly freeing. Almost as freeing as my ride with Mal.

I cleared my throat, turning to Mal to remove my saddle. "I am only here to tend to the dragons."

The man arched an eyebrow. "So you are like a stable hand."

I scoffed. "Hardly. The dragons mostly care for themselves. I am only here to ensure the restless ones go flying as often as they need to, and that the hatchlings are protected." I thought of little Azure, who would die without the nourishment of her mother. Was the stranger here for her? Had he stolen the mother and returned for the offspring?

But no, he wasn't anywhere near the hatchlings. And I didn't dare look over to the crater where Azure was curled up, lest the stranger follow my gaze and investigate.

The man frowned and nodded, scrutinizing Jorey with interest now. His eyes sharpened with a shrewdness that made my stomach twist.

"What?" I demanded, placing my hands on my hips.

"I am merely surprised that the royal family takes such measures," he said.

"You think we would cage them like wild beasts?" I said hotly.

The man raised his palms once more. "Gods, no. I pictured a beastly dragon who guards the castle to fend off wayward men like myself. These delightful creatures are... much more magnificent and affectionate than I had imagined."

"Oh." I dropped my arms by my sides, feeling foolish. "My apologies."

The man laughed. "*I* am the one who wandered into the forest, my lady. It was only justified the Keeper of the Dragons accosted me."

I chuckled at the title. "If you are here on business, then why are you roaming about the woods?"

The man was extending his hand to Jorey once more. When I didn't stop him, and the Greyback nudged closer with excitement, the man began stroking him once more, a soft smile gracing his handsome face. After a moment, he said, "I often come to the forest... to dance."

A loud and rather unladylike laugh burst from my lips, followed by an obnoxious snort. I immediately clapped my hands over my mouth, but the damage was done. The man straightened, his eyes going wide and a half smile curling along his lips. "Good gods, what was *that*?"

Still chuckling, I shook my head, my face on fire as I turned away from him.

"No, no." His light footfalls came closer as he approached. "I *distinctly* heard you make a sound, fair maiden. Please repeat it for my delicate ears."

I laughed again, softer than before. "Stop that!"

"I will not! Whatever is so funny about the thought of me dancing in the forest?"

More giggles poured from my mouth. Tears streamed from my eyes. "You are a liar. You must be a human, then?"

He smirked, then brushed his hair away from his ears. His *pointed fae* ears.

My jaw dropped. Fae could not lie. "You are in earnest? You truly go dancing in the woods?"

He crossed his arms, a look of indignation on his face. "I am affronted and, quite honestly, offended that such an idea amuses you, my lady. I am known as one of the finest dancers in my kingdom."

Though my lips twitched, I straightened, my head only coming to his shoulder as I gazed up at him. "Are you, now?"

"Yes. My dancing skills are renowned."

"Well, then. Prove it."

His mouth opened, and pure shock flitted across his face.

Burning suns, that was satisfying.

My smile only grew as I lifted my chin. "Show me your renowned dancing skills, good sir."

He cleared his throat, then rubbed his chin. "I, ah. Well, my dancing skills are only appreciated with a partner."

"Oh, forgive me! Where are my manners?" I unlaced my boots and stepped out of them, my bare feet pressing into the soft soil. I drew closer to him and extended my hand.

His face slackened in surprise. "What are you doing?"

"Well, offering myself as your partner, of course."

Half his mouth quirked upward. "You, the mighty dragon tamer, can dance?"

"Why so surprised? Is it so shocking that a lady such as myself would know how to dance?" I mimicked his air of offense and sniffed haughtily.

He laughed and removed his coat, then tossed it to the ground next to my boots. "Very well then, fair maiden. Prepare to be dazzled by my grace and finesse."

His hand came around me, his fingers splaying along my upper back. My arm rested against his, my palm to his shoulder. His other hand clasped mine, our fingers interlacing. His skin was warm and smooth. Certainly not the calloused hands of a tradesman.

He seemed to notice the same about me. His eyes darted to my hand in his, his eyes narrowing slightly. I watched his calculating expression take in everything about me, from the cotton dress to my bare feet to my stiff and elegant posture.

I was a walking contradiction. My authoritative tone and poise suggested royalty, but my muddied dress and lack of propriety suggested otherwise.

"You are an enigma, my lady," he murmured, his voice soft as he drew me close.

"As are you, good sir." Like him, I was scrutinizing my dance partner, noting the smooth and clean shaven chin, the unruly hair, the fine clothes. He smelled of pine and mint and something that reminded me of waterfalls; the rushing waters and the cool forest air. The scent momentarily transported me to Kellen Falls, where my parents had often taken me.

My thoughts dissolved as he stepped forward, guiding me in a swift waltz. His feet moved with grace and ease, each step gliding us backward, then forward. My skirts swished with the movement. I allowed my arms to relax in his as he led, a wide smile of surprise spreading along my face.

"There now," he teased. "You seem utterly shocked that I am capable of such an accomplishment."

"You cannot blame me," I said. "A strange man comes into the forest and pesters my dragons, then claims he ventured into the woods to *dance*. Would you believe it, if you were me?"

"Probably not," he admitted. He didn't even miss a step during our conversation. We continued spinning as I followed his lead. "Then again, you are not exactly what I expected, either. This feral dragon keeper—whose bark is far more vicious than that of the creatures she tends to—can dance just as well as I can! How unusual indeed."

I threw my head back and laughed, my chest feeling lighter as delight coursed through my body. This dance, this moment of anonymity and amusement, was the most unexpected and enjoyable encounter I could have imagined. "So you admit it, then? My skill equals your own?"

"I would not say *that*," he hedged. "After all, I am leading, am I not?"

"Then, allow me."

This time, he did stumble, and another bloom of satisfaction spread through me. Burning suns, I did *love* catching him off guard.

"I beg your pardon?" he sputtered.

"Allow me to lead you and show you my own skills."

He raised a single eyebrow. "What exactly are you proposing, fair maiden? For you to lead as a man does?"

"And why is it that only men get to lead? Why should they be expected to bear this responsibility entirely on their own? Wouldn't *you* like to be led for once? Wouldn't that be nice?"

He frowned as he considered this. "Well, that's certainly a unique notion." His steps slowed, and he dropped my arms. "Very well, then, feral dragon keeper. Show me what you can do."

I laughed, then repositioned our arms. I had practiced leading with Gigi before, but she was much shorter than I was. This was a struggle, as the stranger stood more than a head taller than me. Even so, I wrapped my arm around his waist, resting my hand against his back. He placed his own hand along my arm, his fingertips tickling the exposed flesh of my collarbone. Despite the ridiculousness of our pose, his nearness brought heat to my face, and I found I couldn't look him in the eye.

Gods, if Mother could see me now... Dancing with this stranger, our bodies so close. I didn't even know his name.

My mouth turned dry as I took a deep breath and started us off in the same waltz as before. Truth be told, my steps were clumsy, but the stranger did not mock me as I expected. He followed my lead, and we spun around the forest clearing once more. Eventually, once I had a handle on our movements, the dance was just as smooth as before.

The man's eyebrows lifted as he gazed at me with awe. "By the gods," he said softly. "You *can* lead."

I laughed. "Perhaps you should not underestimate a lady, good sir."

"Perhaps you are right." He grinned widely, his eyes crinkling again, and I found myself returning the smile. His palm was warm against mine as we stepped forward, then back. He surprised me by twirling me once, then bringing me back in. After that, he led the dance, and I allowed him to. Our positions changed effortlessly, switching hands and arms, before we slid back into the dance. The forest filled with our laughter. Even some of the dragons ventured closer, their eyes curious. Mal had curled up on the ground, wrapping his tail around himself and resting his chin on the tip—a sign of his contentment. Clearly, like Jorey, he had accepted this stranger.

When we were both out of breath, we finally stopped and released one another. I was near dizzy from the constant motion, and I sank onto a nearby stump to reorient myself. The man clapped his hands together twice. "You are a rare gem, my feral maiden."

I laughed. "Stop calling me that!"

"Are you not feral? I saw you riding that dragon, your hair untamed and wild like some creature. Almost as if you belong here with them instead of whatever grand manor you were likely raised."

My face fell at that reminder. I hadn't been raised at a manor at all, but a palace. And I had no doubt my mother was wondering what was keeping me.

"I should be returning," I said, rising to my feet.

The man straightened. "So soon?"

"Do you not have your own business to attend to?"

He grimaced. "Ah, yes. It was nice to forget about that for a moment, though."

"It was indeed," I agreed solemnly. I retrieved my boots and stroked Mal's chin affectionately.

"Will you not tell me your name?" the man asked.

"Will you tell me yours?" I challenged.

He fell silent at that. Perhaps he, like me, relished the anonymity. It made our encounter all the more exciting.

But it also meant we might never see each other again.

"Do you often come to the Summer Court on business?" I asked.

"I'm afraid not."

I nodded, trying to hide my disappointment.

"But perhaps if my business proceedings go well, I can change that."

I looked up at him, daring to hope. He tipped an imaginary hat to me, that same mischievous smile lighting his face. "Until next time, fair maiden."

I couldn't find the words for a response. All I could do was watch as he made his way out of the clearing, his steps echoing in the wood.

THE SUMMER PRINCESS

 checked on the hatchlings before returning to the palace. Azure's condition had worsened; she hardly lifted her head at my approach. She wouldn't last much longer.

Was I bold enough to enter the Star Court in search of a cure for her? Would I risk a war, all for one dragon?

I couldn't let her die, though. She was tiny and helpless, a glorious, majestic creature worthy of life. It was my duty to do what I could for her.

Wringing my hands together, I quickened my pace, circling around the path to the back of the palace. The grounds were oddly quiet, but I counted this as a blessing; maybe my extended absence would be overlooked.

I thought of my dance with the stranger and stifled a grin. Mother would be affronted, but Gigi would love the story. I resolved to tell her once we had a private moment. Perhaps she could speculate with me about where the stranger came from and if I would see him again.

I eased open the gate to the gardens, passing by hedges and shrubs. Fresh jasmine tickled my nose, along with Mother's famous rose bushes. Ordinarily I would stop to admire them, but I was in a hurry. My gaze flicked to the sun, which was dipping low in the sky. Gods, how had it gotten so late? Why had no one come for me?

I hiked up my skirts and climbed up the trellis against the wall, my movements quick but very unladylike. Luckily, no one was in the gardens right now.

When I reached the second floor balcony, I dropped down with a grunt, then adjusted my skirts. They were stained with mud at the hem, but that couldn't be helped. After ensuring my hair was at least somewhat tame, I strode forward, prepared to find my mother waiting for me with a scolding look in her eye.

But the palace halls were quiet. No sound but the scuffing of my bare feet broke the silence.

My skin prickled with unease. What was going on? It was as empty and lifeless as a grave. Even if my parents and sister were preoccupied, there would still be servants and staff flitting about.

"Hello?" I called uncertainly. My voice bounced off the walls, resonating down the empty hallway.

No answer.

Was there a formal gathering I'd forgotten about? I chewed on my thumbnail, thinking hard. No, I was sure I hadn't missed anything. I knew there was nothing else on my agenda when I'd taken Mal flying.

The tea room. At this hour, Mother and Gigi often took tea together. I gathered my skirts and practically sprinted down the hall, my bare feet slapping against the cool marble.

I rounded the corner and choked on a horrified scream, covering my mouth before it pierced the air.

A servant lay prone on the floor, a tray of biscuits surrounding him. He must have dropped it when he'd fallen.

"Gods!" I crouched to the floor, sweeping his long blond hair out of his face.

I knew this man. It was Hastings from the kitchens. He often brought us our tea and refreshments. My hands shook, my breaths coming in sharp gasps. Burning suns, what had happened to him? Was he dead?

"Breathe, Aurelia," I whispered to myself, inhaling through my nose, then exhaling deeply. "One step at a time. Check to see if he's breathing first." I swallowed hard, then leaned close. After a moment, I heard deep, slow breaths coming from his chest.

Thank the gods. I pressed a hand to my chest, trying to calm my skittering pulse.

Then, Hastings uttered a loud snore.

I jumped with a yelp, scrambling away from him, eyes wide.

He snored again.

I blinked. What the hell?

With slow and careful movements, I drew closer to him, lifting his arms and searching his tunic for injuries. But he seemed perfectly fine. No blood. No bones jutting out at odd angles. No bruises.

And he was *snoring*.

Was Hastings… asleep?

I poked him uncertainly. "Hastings?"

He didn't rouse.

I shook him more forcefully. "Hastings!"

Still, he continued to snore.

With a frown, I climbed to my feet, glancing down the hall to see if anyone approached. I needed to inform our medic about Hastings' condition. Perhaps he drank a tonic that made him extra sleepy? I knew he often took a special medication for his heart.

Yes, that was all. Surely, there was no reason to panic.

But I couldn't stop my legs from sprinting down the hall, my mind frantic. *Someone, anyone, please...* The hall was eerily empty as I raced past the library and the study, only stopping when I reached the tea room.

Gasping for breath, I braced one hand on the open door frame before going utterly still at the sight before me.

Soft snores filled the air. The room was full of sleeping figures. On the chaise sofas were Mother and Gigi, their bodies sprawled along the cushions with an informality that would make the queen blanch. Two servants lay on one end of the room, next to the tea cart. On the opposite end was Pearl, Mother's lady's maid.

I clutched my chest, which was tight with anxiety. I couldn't make any sense of this. Why was everyone asleep?

I approached the sofas, checking my Mother first. Like Hastings, she had no visible injuries. Her face was smooth and free of worries or concerns.

I shook her shoulders. "Mother."

Nothing.

I shook her more violently. "Mother, wake up!"

Still nothing.

I tried Gigi next. I jostled her, pinched her, even slapped her across the face—knowing she would forgive me for it later—but nothing would wake her.

I sank to my knees, choking on a sob. What was going on? Was *everyone* in the palace asleep?

I had to know for sure.

I raced down the halls once more, passing by sleeping servants along the way. When I reached my father's study, I barged in without knocking, which ordinarily would earn me a stern scolding.

There he was, fast asleep, his head resting on a stack of papers on his desk.

Oh, gods.

My stomach roiled as I left, darting down the spiral staircase before heading to the servants' quarters.

"Hello?" I shouted as I strode down the hall, barging into room after room. Most were empty, but a few housed snoring subjects. I descended to the kitchens and sucked in a gasp.

More than a dozen figures were lying on the floor, including the chef. On the hearth, several pots were bubbling over. With a yelp, I hurried over, using a cloth to protect my hands as I eased the still steaming pots of stew onto the countertop.

The kitchen staff had fallen asleep in the middle of preparing supper. How in the hell had this happened?

After ensuring the hearth was doused—I didn't want to inadvertently burn down the palace—I left the kitchens, my body quivering with exhaustion and fear.

What was I to do? I didn't have any magic. I didn't know *anything* about powerful spells, but I had no doubt this was the result of an enchantment. But what could I do about it?

My thoughts turned to Samiria and the witches. Surely, they would know something! I had to find them.

With renewed purpose, I made my way to the entrance doors, easing them open to reveal the courtyard bathed in the amber glow of the setting sun.

I froze when a shout rang out from the other end of the courtyard.

My body went stiff with awareness. Someone was awake!

My feet were moving again, careless of the concrete biting into my bare skin with each step. I hastened down the steps and rounded the corner, then faltered at the portcullis separating the palace from the main road.

A man stood on the other side, banging against the metal bars. "Hello!" His voice was hoarse as if he'd been shouting for hours.

My eyes narrowed as I came toward him. He straightened at my approach. "Thank the gods!" he said. "Are you all right? What's going on?"

I descended the final steps, then felt my blood run cold.

It was the stranger from the woods.

My mouth fell open as I took him in, still wearing the same fine tunic as before. His eyes grew wide, his face turning pale as he recognized me, too.

"You," I said, stopping before I got too close to him. "Did—Did you do this?"

His head reared back. "What? No! I came here straight from the forest and found everyone asleep! Even my envoy can't be roused."

"Your envoy," I repeated. I glanced over him with more scrutiny. I'd thought him to be nobility before. But what if...

"Who are you?" I demanded, my voice sharpening.

He stood a bit straighter, his chin lifting. "I'm Prince Fennick of the Court of Midnight, here to see Princess Aurelia to negotiate on behalf of my kingdom. The matter is urgent."

The world seemed to freeze for a full beat as I processed his words. Then, a harsh bark of laughter burst from me. "Oh, this is just wonderful, isn't it? The prince of an enemy kingdom—*my enemy*—has arrived at the precise moment my people have fallen under an enchanted sleep. A little too convenient, wouldn't you say?"

"It's not convenient at all. As I said, I didn't do this. And—Wait, did you say *your people*?" Fennick staggered back a step, his eyes wide with horror. "Who are you?"

"I'm Princess Aurelia," I said coldly.

He went deathly still, his eyes wide as saucers. Then, he exhaled, running a hand through his brown locks. "Well, shit."

"You said the matter is urgent?" I said, spreading my arms. "Do tell what trouble ails your kingdom, good sir! It's not as if I have anything *pressing* to attend to at the moment."

"Princess—Your Highness, please..."

"I don't have time for this," I spat, turning and striding back up the steps to the courtyard. I was planning on taking a horse to the witch coven, but I refused to open the portcullis and let in that deceitful bastard.

He had to be behind this. This couldn't be a coincidence.

My fingers curled into tight fists of rage as I stormed back into the palace, taking the halls to the gardens like the way I'd come in.

He had the gall to flirt with me and dance with me and *charm me*. All the while he brought this dark magic into my kingdom…

A roar of frustration built in my throat, and once I lowered myself from the trellis, I threw my head back and screamed at the sky. No one would hear because they were all asleep.

Well, Prince Fennick wasn't. But I didn't give a damn what he thought.

He deceived me. It had all been an act. He'd probably known who I was the entire time. The dance had only been a farce to charm me into negotiating with him.

I would rather die. I would *never* negotiate with a man like that.

Cursing Prince Fennick to every layer of Hell I could think of, I escaped from the gardens and hurried down the path that led to the nesting grounds.

Mal met me at the edge of the wood, ears perked up in agitation. He could sense something was off. He had my riding boots clamped between his teeth, as if he'd known I would need them.

"You feel it, too?" I asked, stroking his snout, overjoyed to find him awake. So either this enchantment only affected people, or it stopped at the palace grounds. "I need your help. I know you're probably still tired, but do you have another ride in you?"

Mal grumbled his assent, his eyes glittering with excitement. Even if it pushed him far past exhaustion, he would do it. I knew my dragon better than I knew myself.

I slid on my boots, then brought my fingers to my lips and whistled loudly. After a moment, Jorey's silver scales shimmered with his movement as he obediently bounded from the forest, rushing up to me like an overexcited puppy.

He sniffed me, his tongue lolling as he panted happily. I scratched under his chin and said, "I need you to wake the other dragons, Jorey. The castle must be protected. Can you do that?"

Jorey blinked slowly at me, his snout twitching.

I nodded, my expression solemn. "Yes. Even Kade."

Jorey's ears curled inward with apprehension. I leaned close and pressed my nose to his. "You can do this, Jorey. Kade might be grumpy, but she will do what's necessary to protect our people."

Jorey huffed and lifted his chin, his eyes steely with determination. I kissed the top of his head. "Thank you, my brave friend."

Jorey licked my cheek, then turned and darted back into the forest. After a few moments, several twigs snapped, and the massive trees began to shake as Kade was awakened.

I stared up at the shifting trees, my body tense. Only a few times had we woken Kade for our protection. She was quite a sight to behold.

But I didn't have time to stop and watch. Time was not on my side.

I turned to Mal, who suddenly stiffened and sniffed the air. I whirled, biting back a cry of rage at the sight of Prince Fennick on the forest path.

"What the hell are you doing here?" I raged, stomping toward him. "Was my dismissal not clear enough? Get out of my kingdom!"

He lifted his palms, just as he had when we'd met in the forest earlier. "I only came to help."

"I don't believe you." My eyes narrowed. "Why are you in the woods again? And don't try to say it was for dancing, because that was obviously a lie."

He rolled his eyes. "I *can't* lie, remember? It was a hunch. You seemed very protective of your dragons, so I figured you'd come here."

"Of course I'm protective of them, when bastards like you show up under false pretenses."

"I never lied to you!"

"You deceived me," I snarled. "It makes no difference if the words coming from your lips were lies or not. They were misleading. If you wanted to negotiate me, you should have been forthcoming from the beginning."

He huffed a dry laugh. "Would you have listened?"

I didn't answer. Instead, I turned to Mal, prepared to climb on him bareback. I didn't care if his scales would leave me bruised and sore tomorrow; there was no time to fetch the saddle.

"Princess, let me *help*," Fennick urged.

"Go to hell!" I snapped. "You come into my kingdom, put my people in an enchanted sleep, and then expect me to trust you to help rectify the situation? This is your last warning to leave the Summer Court before I let my dragons have you."

Kade would wake soon, and she had a nasty temper. If she found the Midnight Prince lingering by the nesting grounds, she wouldn't hesitate to attack. I almost smiled at the thought.

I lifted one leg before swinging onto Mal's back. He had lowered himself to the ground to allow me to climb on, but the sharp edges of his scales still dug into my legs, even through my cotton skirts.

I was about to spur him into action when a shout from behind stopped me.

"I swear on my blood and the entire Mardion bloodline that I had nothing to do with this sleeping enchantment that has befallen your kingdom, nor did I know it would occur!"

My nostrils flared as I looked over my shoulder at the prince, prepared to tell him just what he could do with his false promises. But when I saw the trickle of blood running down his palm, I faltered.

Fae bargains were binding. But swearing in blood was the holiest and deadliest of vows. It could not be altered. It could not be undone.

My mouth fell open, and I couldn't form a response. Fennick's face was rigid with determination, the sword in his hand still oozing droplets of his own blood.

"And I swear on my blood," he continued, stepping toward me, "that I *am* here to help. Not to deceive."

"You are here to negotiate," I argued. "You said it yourself."

"That was my original purpose in coming here. But in this moment, your kingdom is in dire need of help. Do you deny it?"

I said nothing.

"Right now, I am the only person able to assist you." His eyes burned with intensity.

I swallowed, my throat dry. He was right. And yet… "You are only offering help to earn favor with me for your negotiations."

"Perhaps. But wouldn't you like to end this animosity between our kingdoms for good? All it takes is one act of good faith. Whether or not you decide to discuss terms with me in the future, I am here to help. I will not revoke that help if you decide you still despise me."

I chewed on my lower lip, considering his words, searching for a loophole or a phrase that could be twisted against me. He had a good point. Especially if I hoped to acquire stardust to save Azure. Perhaps if we took this step to smooth things over between our kingdoms, it would be easier for me to ask for a favor to help the hatchling.

"Do I need to slash open my other palm?" Fennick said impatiently.

"No," I said. My gaze slid to the emerald spires jutting out from the other side of the trees. Inside, my entire family lay asleep, unable to be roused. How long before the kingdom fell apart? How long before the other courts noticed and attacked?

Our dragons had been coveted for centuries. All it would take was one whiff that something was amiss in the Summer Court, and our foes would come running.

My eyes narrowed as I looked at Fennick again. He would only need to send word to his ruthless mother, and their armies would be on my doorstep.

"Fine," I said at last. "Come with me."

Fennick's eyebrows lifted. Clearly, he hadn't expected me to agree. "I shall fetch my horse."

"There is no time," I snapped. "There is room for us both on Mal."

Fennick blinked. "On… your dragon?"

"Are you hard of hearing? Yes! Hurry, prince. Before I change my mind."

Fennick sheathed his short sword and bounded forward, withdrawing a handkerchief to wrap around his bleeding hand. In seconds, he had climbed onto Mal's back with ease, nestling behind me. The warmth of another body against mine was jarring. I was used to the windy air and the freedom of no restraints tethering me. To have another solid presence was foreign and uncomfortable.

Not to mention he smelled like pine and mint and waterfalls, reminding me of our dance together. I shoved the thought from my mind before it rattled my brain.

Shifting my weight on Mal's back, I winced at the scales pressing into me. Yes, my legs would certainly be sore tomorrow.

"You'd best hold on to me," I warned the prince. "Mal will not care if you fall off. And nor will I."

Fennick wrapped his arms tightly around my waist. Mal took off, his claws digging into the soil, his muscles coiling underneath us, jostling us with each stride. After a few moments, his wings outstretched, and Fennick yelped behind me.

I couldn't help but laugh. "You'll get used to that."

His wings beat beside us, and even I couldn't stop my legs from sliding. Without the security of my saddle, I was dangerously close to falling off myself. I clenched my legs, tightening my grip around the dragon. Mal seemed to notice my unease, and his wings straightened, allowing me time to secure my hold on him.

After a few moments, we lifted off the ground, and the ride became much smoother. I sighed with relief, wrapping my arms around Mal's neck and holding him closely.

"Take us to Samiria," I murmured in his ear.

Mal grumbled his response, gliding higher into the sky.

Behind me, Fennick muttered several curses, his arms shaking as he clutched my waist.

"Gods above," he whispered. "Bloody burning stars. This is insane. I can't—Good *gods*."

As Mal arced smoothly through the sky, slicing through clouds, Fennick's mutterings halted, and I heard him gasp softly. "Incredible."

Despite the sheer insanity of our situation—the Midnight Prince, of all people, astride my most beloved dragon—I allowed a wide smile to stretch across my face.

No one, not even the prince of an enemy kingdom, could resist the wonder of flying on a dragon.

THE MIDNIGHT PRINCE

In my upbringing, Mother had stressed again and again to *never* swear by my blood. The price was too great.

But the moment I saw Aurelia—helpless and panicked on the other side of the portcullis—I knew I would do anything to assist her.

Even after I found out who she really was.

I am Princess Aurelia.

My stomach had hollowed, like my insides had been jerked free of my body, leaving a shell of who I once was. This lovely young lady who had charmed me in the forest—whom I believed to be nothing more than a caretaker of dragons—was the very princess I was meant to coerce into helping me.

Seeing her disdain, her loathing and rage, was too much for me. I couldn't bear to have her believe I was here for duplicitous purposes. That I was here only to deceive and steal from her.

Even if it was partially true.

And now, I was sitting atop a dragon—whose scales were quite sharp even through my leathers—clinging to the woman who despised me, for fear that if I let go, she and her dragon would let me fall to my death. The wind whipped around me so fiercely my eyes burned and watered. My hair flapped wildly as the dragon swooped and dived with expert precision.

Aurelia seemed relaxed in my grip, though her shoulders were set; the only betrayal of her discomfort. I wondered how often she shared her dragon with another rider.

When the dragon dipped again, my stomach roiled, and I shut my eyes, burying my face in the princess's shoulder.

She smelled of rain and jasmine and embers.

Thinking of her, how lovely she smelled, how warm and perfect she'd felt in my arms while we danced in the forest, certainly wasn't helping matters. But if it prevented me from vomiting all over her, then I would cling to those memories.

I groaned, and her body hummed with her laughter.

"Dragon riding isn't for weak stomachs, I'm afraid," she teased over her shoulder. She sounded a bit too gleeful for my liking.

"If I didn't know any better, Your Highness, I would suggest this magnificent creature is doing this on purpose. Is it his desire for me to spew all over your fine dress?"

Aurelia snorted in amusement, but after my comment, the dragon's ride became smoother.

Interesting. Could the beast understand me?

"May I ask where we're going?" I said.

"To the witch clans," Aurelia said shortly.

I stiffened, my grip tightening on her waist. "You… are on good terms with the witches here?"

Aurelia hesitated. "At times. We do not mingle often, but when we do, it is with respect."

My eyebrows lifted. Well, that was more than I could say. I had no problem with the witches, but Mother was vehemently against the magic they practiced. As such, when I was a child, learning their runic spells had only intrigued me more simply because it was forbidden.

Mother's hatred of witch magic had ignited my curiosity.

But she need never know just how much I had dabbled in that particular brand of magic.

"And you?" Aurelia asked. "I assume you, too, have witches in your kingdom."

"We do," I said carefully. "But… the royal family does not associate with them. Their magic is seen as crude and unnatural."

Aurelia barked a laugh. "How pretentious of you."

"I never said it was what *I* believe," I shot back.

Aurelia said nothing at that.

Truth be told, the few witches I'd encountered had been kind and respectful, albeit a bit odd and unsettling. They hadn't balked at my curiosity at all; rather, they had seemed to appreciate my probing questions.

They had even taught me how to conjure runes myself.

My curiosity got the better of me. "Do you ever... practice witch magic?"

Aurelia was silent for so long that I thought she hadn't heard me. At long last, she said simply, "No."

We did not speak again until the dragon descended, weaving through trees before landing atop a hill overlooking a wide valley where dozens of tents were erected. Several plumes of smoke coiled in the air, creating a collision of colors ranging from pinks and purples to gold and silver. Already, the heady smell of witch magic filled my nose, reminding me of those rebellious years in my youth when I had wanted to explore everything, even the darkest of magic.

I swallowed down my unease as Aurelia slid off the dragon's back. "You wait here," she ordered. "Mal will keep an eye on you."

I huffed. "I will *not*."

From beneath me, the dragon—Mal—grumbled threateningly, his back going rigid.

"Go ahead and try to eat me," I barked at him. "But I'll bet you aren't too keen on the idea of your lady going into witch lands by herself with no weapons or protection."

Aurelia rolled her eyes and slid her skirt up her leg until it reached her kneecap.

My eyes grew wide. "What the hell are you—" I faltered when she showed me the dagger sheathed at her thigh. "Well." I shifted my weight, still atop the dragon. "That won't do much good against their arsenal of spells."

"What makes you think they'll attack me?"

"I may not associate often with witches, but I know they do not take kindly to uninvited guests."

Aurelia fell silent, and Mal pawed the ground.

"I'll be fine," she told him.

He continued to shift in agitation.

Testing my luck, I slid off his back, my movements far less graceful than the princess's. I fumbled my way down and ended up on my knees, wincing from the soreness in my legs.

"I'm coming with you, Your Highness," I insisted, rising to my feet and facing her fully.

She gritted her teeth, then glanced at the dragon behind me. Whatever she saw in his face made her groan with annoyance. "Fine. But do not address them unless you are spoken to."

"I've been around witches before," I said.

She frowned at me. "I thought you said you don't associate with them."

"I said I don't *often* associate with them."

Her cobalt eyes assessed me with cool calculation as she no doubt circled through my words once more, reevaluating what I'd told her.

Before she could make more assumptions about me, I strode past her, making my way down the hill toward the witches' encampment. I heard her murmur something to the dragon before she hurried after me.

THE SUMMER PRINCESS

I HAD ONLY BEEN TO THE WITCH COVEN ONCE BEFORE, AND I OFTEN TRIED to forget the memory. It had been five years ago. I was twenty and desperate for my fae magic to manifest itself.

I had almost gotten myself and Mal killed in the process.

From that point onward, I vowed never to dabble in witch magic again. The risk was far too great.

My skin prickled with anticipation as I made my way downhill, trying to stifle the flow of memories that assaulted me from my last visit.

A blinding flash of green light. A pair of lifeless eyes staring at me. My body convulsing in pain. Mal's wounded cries.

A lump formed in my throat, and I curled and uncurled my fingers into fists, using the motion to distract me from my anxiety.

When we reached the bottom of the hill, a trio of witches were waiting for us. I had no doubt they sensed our arrival from wards surrounding the encampment.

"We are here to see the sage," I announced, lifting my chin to appear as regal as possible.

The witch in front, a dark-haired woman with a hooked nose, grunted in disbelief. "The sage does not see anyone unless she summons them. Intruders are not welcome on our holy ground."

"I'm not an intruder. I'm a friend of Samiria's."

She offered a cold, cruel smile. "If you are a friend, then she will summon you when she deems your presence necessary."

Rage and impatience warred within me. I drew my hands behind my back to hide my shaking fists. "Please," I begged. "It's urgent. Lives are at stake."

"The only lives that matter to us are the lives of witches," she said coldly.

"And what about the lives of dragons?" I challenged. "Do those matter to you?"

The three witches went perfectly still, their eyes shifting from me to Fennick and back again.

"There is an enchantment that has taken hold of the castle," I went on. "If our enemies discover it, they will invade and seize the dragons."

"Then bring them to us. We will protect them here."

"I cannot," I said. "They are bound to the nesting grounds in the forest surrounding the palace. Samiria understands this. Please let me speak with her."

A second witch, with short white hair, stepped forward, her eyes steely. "We have not forgotten the last time you were here, my lady."

My mouth went dry, and sweat coated my palms. My voice was rough as I said softly, "Nor have I. It is not an incident I intend to repeat. We will make this visit brief. I swear it."

"And who is he?" asked the third witch, a shorter woman with flaming red hair. She gestured to Fennick, who stiffened beside me.

"He is my companion, here to assist me in breaking the enchantment," I replied without even glancing his way. I hoped my casual dismissal of him would prevent the witches from scrutinizing him further.

The three witches glanced at one another, their eyes conveying hidden meaning. Given what I knew of their abilities, I wouldn't be surprised if they were communicating with their minds.

After a moment, the hook-nosed witch nodded brusquely. "Very well. You may request an audience with the sage. But if she refuses you, you must leave."

"I understand," I said. "Thank you."

"Follow me." The witch turned on her heel and strode toward the mass of tents. The other two witches stepped aside to let us pass, but the white-haired one shot me a glare that told me she'd be watching closely to ensure I didn't try anything foolish.

I felt Fennick's eyes on me as we weaved through tents, following the dark-haired witch. I didn't look at him, though. Instead, I focused on my breathing, trying not to allow the earthy clove smell to overwhelm my senses.

It smelled so familiar and brought with it a whirlwind of memories I'd tried so hard to forget.

Screams. Broken bodies strewn on the ground. My blood on fire. Mal's shrieks of agony.

"What happened when you were last here?" Fennick murmured next to me.

"That's not your concern," I snapped, blinking rapidly to clear my head of the nauseating images that plagued me.

"It is if I'm your *companion*," Fennick pressed. "If my life is in danger by being here, I'd like to know."

I whirled to face him, my nostrils flared and my eyes drilling into him. "It's not. You are perfectly safe. When I was last here, I was curious and reckless and dabbled in spells I shouldn't have. I assure you, I will not be doing it again."

Before he could reply, I turned away, hastening to keep up with the witch's brisk pace.

Though it had been years since my last visit, I still remembered Samiria's large tent, the smell of rosemary wafting from the flaps. The dark-haired witch raised her hand to stop us before she ducked inside, leaving me alone with Fennick. Around us, several witches bustled about, casting us curious glances, and some outright glaring at Fennick, clearly dismayed by the presence of a man.

I crossed my arms and chewed on the inside of my cheek, trying to control my breathing.

It's not like last time. It won't happen again. You are safe. Everyone here is safe.

I closed my eyes. My heart was racing, thundering mercilessly against my ribcage. My bodice felt too tight, too restrictive. All around me, screams and cries echoed, results of the damage I'd caused.

"Aurelia."

My eyes flew open, and I found Fennick standing before me, his jade eyes searching mine. His hands were on my shoulders, though I hadn't felt or heard him approach. Startled by his nearness, a sudden rush of sensations slammed into me. The warmth of his fingers on my shoulders. His now familiar scent of pine and mint. The whispering breeze in the air, tickling my face.

I exhaled, long and slow.

"Aurelia," Fennick said again, his voice a soft murmur. Belatedly, I realized he had never spoken my name before. It was always "Your Highness." Though it was oddly intimate, I realized I needed to hear my name from his lips. It grounded me.

And perhaps he realized this, too.

"Move your feet," he said.

I blinked. "I'm sorry?"

"Feel the earth beneath you. Plant yourself right here in this moment. You are here and now. Nowhere else."

I swallowed hard, though my pulse still skittered. I shuffled my feet, the toes of my boots digging into the soft earth. Closing my eyes, I focused on the sensation. The smoothness of the soil. The soft scuffing sound of leather gliding along the dirt.

My breathing was shaky, but my pulse was slowing.

"You're safe," Fennick murmured. "There is no danger here."

My eyes opened slowly, my lashes fluttering as I took in the concern etched into his face. Gods, why did he even care? Wouldn't he rejoice if I spiraled into a chaotic fit and collapsed into a heap on the ground?

Shame and guilt coiled within my chest, making it hard to breathe for an entirely different reason. I'd been downright hostile to him, but none of this was his fault. Even after he swore on his own blood, I still had treated him poorly.

I had gotten along with him just fine in the forest when we danced. Perhaps I could try to see him as that handsome stranger in the woods instead of the prince of an enemy kingdom.

"Thank you," I whispered, my cheeks heating. Mother was right; I behaved abhorrently toward other courtiers. And my sour attitude wasn't helping anyone. "Please forgive me, Fennick. I should not be so cruel to you."

Half his mouth quirked into a smile, his eyes brightening. "Think nothing of it, Your Highness. And please, call me Fenn."

Warmth bloomed in my chest, and I nodded. "Very well, Fenn. And... you can call me Aurelia."

His smile widened, and for a moment, he was nothing more than the charming man I'd danced with in the forest.

The tent flaps slid open, and I stepped away from Fenn, my face flushing as I wrung my hands together, suddenly flustered.

The dark-haired witch appraised us both with a sharp look. "The sage will see you now."

The Midnight Prince

Something had happened between Aurelia and the witches, and whatever it was, it still haunted her. As curious as I was about it, I knew she would never tell me. I was the last person in the realm she would trust with that.

Perhaps it had to do with her fae magic. I wasn't sure what her power was. Maybe it was dangerous and volatile. Maybe she had little control over it.

I could understand possessing a power you didn't want.

Yes, my powers of persuasion were convenient. But after years of using them for my own gain and for the benefit of my people, I started to feel exactly like the filthy deceiver Aurelia believed me to be. And it became harder to tell the difference between people who genuinely agreed with me, and those who were coerced into it by my magic.

Aurelia and I entered the sage's tent, and the flaps closed behind us. To my surprise, the dark-haired witch remained outside, leaving us alone with the sage.

The tent was bigger than I'd pictured, spanning the size of my bedchamber. In the center of the space was a bubbling cauldron, though I saw no fire burning underneath it. Shelves lined the perimeter of the tent, filled with ancient books and texts as well as various magical objects such as crystal balls, jars of sinister-looking fluid and body parts, and black candlesticks.

Atop a stool in front of the bubbling cauldron was a petite figure with white hair. Her eyes were closed, her fingers hovering over the steaming contents of the cauldron as she whispered words in a different language.

Beside me, Aurelia shifted her weight on her feet, clearly uncomfortable. I thought of how she'd nearly stopped breathing from her panic earlier, and I stepped forward to speak.

Before I could, the woman said in a low, ethereal voice, "I know who you are, Prince of Midnight."

I stilled at that. Slowly, she opened her eyes, which were a piercing silver as they fixed on me. "Your kind have shunned my people for centuries. And you dare set foot on our holy soil?"

I swallowed. "Whatever animosity exists between the royal family and the fae witches does not extend to me, *Shalani.*"

The sage straightened, her eyes flaring wide. *Shalani* was a term of respect in the witches' holy tongue. Her eyes narrowed as she surveyed me with closer scrutiny. "And yet," she said slowly, "you have done nothing to quell such animosity, have you? A prince of noble breeding such as yourself would have remarkable *influence* on other people, wouldn't you agree? But you choose not to use it."

I frowned at the way she'd said *influence.* As if she knew exactly what my fae magic could do. My spine was rigid, my skin prickling with awareness. I said nothing more, partly because I had no response—she was right, after all—and partly because I was afraid what I would give away by speaking. It already seemed she knew too much about me.

The sage's eyes slid to Aurelia. "Lady Aurelia. I am surprised to see you here, given what occurred the last time you visited our lands."

Aurelia's cheeks flushed, and she bowed her head. "Forgive me, Samiria. I would not intrude if it were not urgent."

"You're referring to the sleeping curse." Samiria slid off the stool, sweeping her emerald cloak to the side as she strode toward us. Though she only came up to my chest, her presence was still commanding.

Aurelia sucked in a sharp breath. "You know?"

"Of course I know, child. When a powerful magical presence enters my domain, I *always* know."

"Then, what is it? How do I break the enchantment?"

Samiria said nothing for a long moment. She dragged a long finger along the rim of the cauldron, seemingly unbothered by whatever heat emanated from it. Finally, she murmured, "I do not know. It is no magic I have seen before."

Aurelia's shoulders sagged, and her breathing turned shaky. "There is nothing you can do?"

"I did not say that." Samiria's eyes sharpened as they fixed on Aurelia. "All I know is it is not normal witch magic. This particular spell bears resemblance to the magic of the Dream Mage."

"The Dream Mage," Aurelia repeated.

My stomach coiled tightly in recognition. *Oh gods...*

Samiria looked at me as if she knew I'd recognize the name.

Before I could speak, Aurelia said, "Did this magic not affect you?"

Samiria shook her head. "It seems the witches are immune. But the entire palace grounds have been claimed by this spell."

Aurelia's hands curled into fists at her sides. "And the rest of the kingdom?"

"Unaffected."

Aurelia's breath rushed out of her, and her hands relaxed. "Well, that's good, I suppose."

"I know you are clever enough to understand the purpose behind such an attack, Lady Aurelia." Samiria's expression hardened.

Aurelia nodded. "To incapacitate the royal family."

"Yes. But they aren't the only ones who reside at the palace, are they?"

Aurelia's face paled. "The barracks."

Samiria nodded slowly.

Shit. I ran a hand through my hair. The barracks were likely located on the palace grounds. Which meant the entire army of the Summer Court was under the sleeping spell.

Anyone could invade and face no opposition.

Aurelia's wide eyes fixed on me, as if she were thinking the same thing. Anger and horror warred in her gaze, and she glared at me in accusation. I shook my head slowly, prepared to deny it. How could she *still* think I was the one behind this?

But could I blame her? Our kingdoms had been at odds for centuries. The Star Court was the most likely suspect.

"How are we unaffected?" I asked, hoping to distract Aurelia before she ripped out my throat.

Samiria lifted her chin, then strode toward me. With a swift movement, she tugged down the collar of my shirt. I jerked away from her, but not before she exposed the witch rune etched below my collarbone.

"What is that?" Aurelia asked.

"Yes, young prince," Samiria said slyly. "Do tell us what that mark is." Her smirk indicated she knew *exactly* what it was.

I fumbled with my tunic, shifting the collar back into place as I tried to find my voice. "It's a protection rune."

Silence followed my words. After a moment, Aurelia demanded, "What does that mean?"

I closed my eyes with a sigh. "It's a mark of the witches, meant to protect me from harmful magic."

"Harmful magic like a sleeping curse, I'd wager," Samiria said, her eyes glinting with amusement.

Aurelia whirled to face me, her eyes blazing. "Tell me again you had nothing to do with this," she snarled. "Perhaps you have another witch rune somewhere that allows you to lie to me. Or to even falsify a blood oath."

"Nothing can negate the power of a blood oath," Samiria said sharply. "If this prince truly did spill his blood and swear something to you, it is binding. Even witch magic cannot counteract that."

"Aurelia, I've had that mark for years," I quickly explained. "I was curious about runic magic and wanted to try it for myself. A witch in my lands made it for me."

Aurelia's nostrils flared, her gaze full of venom. "Whatever explanations you give me, it is still oddly convenient that the instant you show up, this curse takes my family, *and* you have a rune that protects you from it." She frowned, turning to Samiria. "But what about me? How was I not affected?"

Samiria's amusement faded as she fixed a somber look at Aurelia. She said nothing as she approached the princess, then gripped her elbows to turn her around. With a baffled expression, Aurelia obeyed, and Samiria pulled on the cotton fabric of her dress, gently tugging it downward to reveal a black spiral marking on her left shoulder blade.

My eyes widened. Aurelia had a witch rune?

Aurelia wriggled uncomfortably, but Samiria kept a firm grip on her. "What is it?"

"You can't see it?" I asked.

"Of course I can't," Aurelia snapped. "It's on my *back*."

"But you've never seen it in mirrors? Your lady's maid never pointed it out when she does your hair?" My voice was thick with incredulity. And she accused *me* of duplicity.

Aurelia finally jerked free of the witch's grip and turned to face me, her cheeks reddening. "*No.* If there's a mark on me, I was not aware of it, nor have I seen it." She glared at Samiria. "What is it? Did you put it on me?"

Slowly, Samiria shook her head, her expression unreadable. When she said nothing else, Aurelia put her hands on her hips. "Samiria, tell me!"

Samiria straightened, her eyes narrowing. "You do not command me, Lady Aurelia. Remember on whose land you tread."

Aurelia immediately ducked her head. "Forgive me."

Samiria strode to the cauldron, running her finger along the rim once more. "There are many runes of my people. Some are so complex that they can be rendered invisible to the bearer of the mark, along with anyone else not blessed by runic magic." Her eyes lifted to meet Aurelia's. "Rest assured that I have never marked you before, child. Nor has anyone in my coven."

"But... surely, you recognize it?" Aurelia asked. "Do you have any idea what it means? Or who put it there?"

Samiria sighed. "I am forbidden from speaking of it. There are holy laws that I am blood sworn to obey."

Aurelia took several trembling breaths, then shook her head. "I don't understand. How could I have a witch mark on me? And if you or your coven didn't put it there, then who did?" She lifted her hands to her face and massaged her temples. "Gods... What does this even mean? Is there *anything* you can tell me?"

"Only the witches of *this land* are bound by this law," Samiria said, her words slow and measured.

A stunned silence followed her words. I shifted my weight, thinking of the witches in my land. Could they help her? They had certainly been willing to help me in the past.

"As for your sleeping enchantment," Samiria went on, her gaze fixed on the steaming contents of the cauldron, "there are powerful elements that can break curses. One of these is the blood of a Blue Amethyst."

My brows furrowed. A Blue Amethyst? Was that some rare bird species I was unaware of?

Aurelia's breath hitched, and her eyes flared wide. Whatever a Blue Amethyst was, she knew. Her face paled, and she shook her head. "Samiria, I cannot. She's too weak. I don't even know if her blood is potent enough."

"It's not," Samiria said. "You're right; the beast is too weak. But if you can find a way to heal her—or find her mother—then you can break the curse."

I crossed my arms. "What is a Blue Amethyst?"

Aurelia's gaze was fixed on the floor, her eyes calculating. Samiria said nothing; she merely watched Aurelia, as if waiting for something.

"Did you know this would happen?" Aurelia asked in a low voice. Her eyes flicked to the witch, and a hint of suspicion crept into her gaze.

Samiria straightened, her eyes flashing. "No, I did not. I know the Dream Mage has been getting stronger, but I did not know she would strike this kingdom."

Aurelia nodded slowly, and I found myself prickling with irritation that she trusted this witch's word so easily, whereas I had sworn in blood and she *still* didn't believe me. "If I bring the Blue Amethyst to you," Aurelia said softly, "can you break the curse?"

"Yes," Samiria said, her eyes cutting to me and back to Aurelia again. "Do you recall the… substance I told you about yesterday in the nesting grounds?"

Aurelia nodded, her jaw tense.

"The Blue Amethyst needs to ingest this substance first. It will help her heal. And once her strength is restored, then her body will be able to endure the spell."

What the hell were they talking about? What *substance*?

But Aurelia nodded, clearly understanding whatever Samiria was talking about.

Impatience and confusion clouded my thoughts. I blew out an exasperated breath, knowing these two cryptic women would not answer any of my questions.

At long last, Aurelia bowed her head and said, "Thank you for your helpful information, Samiria. I'll be back as soon as I can."

Samiria inclined her head, too. "I will await your return, Lady Aurelia. I wish to protect this land as much as you do."

I opened my mouth to speak, but Aurelia grabbed my arm, all but hauling me out of the tent. The last thing I saw was Samiria's knowing look before the tent flaps concealed her from view.

THE SUMMER PRINCESS

My head was spinning.

The blood of a Blue Amethyst.

Of course the only thing that could break this curse was the blood of a dying dragon.

And some witch had put a rune on me without my knowledge. It could have been recent. Or it could have been when I was a child. But what the hell did it mean? Did it have anything to do with my lack of fae power? Was *that* why I couldn't perform magic? Was it the reason behind the explosive destruction I had caused the last time I set foot on the witch lands?

My thoughts spiraled as I trekked back up the hill to where Mal was waiting. It wasn't until Fenn grasped my shoulder, halting me in my tracks, that I realized he was calling my name. He spun me to face him, his expression uncharacteristically somber.

"Aurelia," he said. "What's going on? What is a Blue Amethyst?"

I sighed. My instinct was to take this secret to my grave. It was my duty to protect my dragons, after all.

But if stardust was indeed the key to healing Azure, then the only way to get it would be to ask for Fenn's help.

"It's a rare species of dragon," I said. "There is a hatchling in our nesting grounds, but she is dying. Without the strength of her mother, she cannot survive."

Fenn was quiet for a long moment, his gaze turning wary. "Where is her mother?"

"I don't know. Captured or killed, most likely."

Fenn's expression turned stony, his brows drawing together.

I continued, "My only hope of saving her is locating her mother... or accessing stardust."

Fenn's head reared back, his eyes suddenly guarded. "Stardust? Why?"

"The Blue Amethyst comes from the Star Court." I couldn't look at him as I spoke, so I kept my gaze fixed on my hands as I wrung them together. "The magic of your land can heal her. Samiria told me that stardust is the only substance that can cure her, besides the blood of her mother."

Fenn was silent for so long that I finally chanced a glance up at him. His brow furrowed, and he frowned, his expression unreadable. "You need stardust," he repeated.

"Yes."

He shook his head and huffed a dry laugh. "You need something from me."

My eyes narrowed. "Yes."

The smirk that filled his face made my blood boil. "How *convenient*." With that, he strode past me toward Mal. The dragon lifted his head, his golden eyes fixed questioningly on me. His back was rigid, no doubt from the tension between me and Fenn.

The prince moved toward Mal as if to climb atop him, but Mal growled, the sound a low rumble in his throat, stopping Fenn in his tracks.

"Fenn, wait," I said, hurrying after him. Fenn was eyeing Mal with apprehension, but the steel in his eyes told me he'd probably try something stupid, like climbing on an angry dragon.

I tugged on his shoulder, whirling him to face me. His eyes were hard and unyielding.

He wouldn't help me.

But I had to try.

"Please," I whispered. "*Please.* This is my kingdom. My home. I need your help."

"You are asking me to give up our most precious resource when you have done nothing but fling accusations at me since you found out who I was."

"I know," I said quickly. "And I apologized for being unkind to you. It has been... a stressful day, as you can imagine."

He grunted at that.

"You swore you would help me!" I argued. "Was that not in earnest? Now that it requires a sacrifice on your part, you're going back on your word?"

His nostrils flared, and he leaned closer to me, his green eyes blazing. "I swore to help you *here.* To try to find out the problem and a possible solution. I came with you to the witch lands. But to travel to my kingdom? To convince our treasurer to give up our already dwindling supply of stardust, for our enemy kingdom? They will laugh in my face. My mother would have me imprisoned for such audacity." He leaned back, shaking his head. "I'm sorry, Your Highness. I can't help you."

So now we were back to formalities. There was something very final about that. He was dismissing me.

"You need something from me," I blurted.

He stilled, eyeing me with apprehension.

"That's why you're in the Summer Court, right?" I went on.

Slowly, he nodded.

I stepped closer until we were almost nose to nose. Or rather, nose to collarbone.

"If you need something from me, and I need something from you, then can't we strike a bargain?" My voice was low, like we were sharing a dangerous secret.

In a way, we were. Making a fae bargain with my enemy was more dangerous than riding the wildest of dragons.

His eyes flared wide. After a moment, one corner of his mouth lifted. "My, my, Aurelia. You surprise me. You would bargain with the likes of me?"

I swallowed, my throat dry. "If it saves my kingdom, then yes. I would. Wouldn't you do the same?"

His smirk vanished, and his jaw went rigid with determination. "Of course I would."

"Then, you'll do it?" I held my breath, not daring to hope that he would agree.

He released a long, slow breath, then rubbed the back of his neck. His eyes flicked from me to the encampment down the hill. After a long moment, he said, "Yes. But not here. This air is thick with witch magic, and I don't want it interfering."

My heart lurched, and I exhaled a short laugh of disbelief. He'd agreed. He'd actually agreed.

His eyes burned with amusement. "Don't rejoice yet, little ember. We still need to accept the terms of the bargain. And I'll wager it will be *very* difficult for us to find common ground."

He was right about that.

My brows furrowed. "Little ember?" I repeated. How very patronizing.

He smirked again. "Yes. Because of your fiery temper and diminutive stature."

I rolled my eyes and shoved past him to climb atop Mal. The dragon had relaxed now that Fenn and I had reached an agreement.

"I am *not* diminutive," I said as Fenn climbed up behind me, his arms circling my waist. "I'm nearly as tall as you are."

"'Nearly' being a generous term."

I jerked my elbow into his gut, and he grunted, then laughed. With a nudge of my feet, Mal took off, racing back toward the nesting grounds.

THE MIDNIGHT PRINCE

I STILL COULDN'T WRAP MY HEAD AROUND THE CONCEPT OF FLYING ON top of a dragon. Yes, the scales were immensely uncomfortable, and it was clear Mal would chew my head off if Aurelia asked him to.

But the way the wind whipped at me, dancing along my skin and singing in my ears… It was otherworldly. Mal expertly arced through the sky, dipping high and low. Like before, it seemed he was trying to make me ill. But unlike before, my stomach was ready for it. Perhaps I just needed to orient myself with the dragon's movements. Either way, I couldn't stop a whoop from escaping me, and I heard Aurelia's loud laugh follow after. She stretched her arms wide as if she, too, were a winged creature floating through the sky.

I wasn't quite brave enough to loosen my grip on her waist. I still had my doubts that Mal would catch me if I fell.

"Perhaps *little ember* isn't the right name for you," I said in her ear. "Perhaps I should call you *little sparrow*. Because you belong in the sky."

"Why must I be a *little* anything?" she asked, glancing at me over her shoulder. Despite the challenge in her tone, her eyes were alight, burning brighter than the sun.

She truly belonged here in the sky.

"Firebird," I said. "You're a firebird. It accounts for your flaming temper *and* your need to fly."

She grinned at me, the motion lighting up her whole face. It pierced through me, igniting something low in my belly. I cleared my throat and slid my gaze away from her glowing features before the sight of her undid me.

I could never resist a beautiful woman.

It didn't take long for the gleaming emerald spires of the castle to come into view, but that wasn't what snagged my attention first. A massive form rested next to the palace. I would have mistook it for a mountain had I not distinctly remembered there being no mountains this close to the palace.

"Is that… a *dragon?*" I asked, my voice weak.

"Her name is Kade." Pride laced Aurelia's voice.

My mouth hung open as I stared, wide-eyed, at Kade the dragon. Her gleaming jade scales were just as luminous as the castle, but a few shades darker. A large, rotund belly protruded from her torso and rested against the ground. Sleepy black eyes blinked in our direction. Her enormous wings were tucked against her chest, and as we arced lower, I realized she had *two* sets of wings. No doubt they were necessary to keep such an enormous weight airborne.

Mal gave her a wide berth, swooping to the other side of the castle. I noticed several trees were felled, likely from Kade getting into a comfortable position.

A small price to pay in order for the castle to be protected.

Once we were under the cover of the trees, Mal landed and ran the rest of the way, returning us to the nesting grounds. Aurelia dismounted immediately, rushing over to a fenced-in area I hadn't noticed before. She leapt over the fence and crouched to her knees, muttering words I couldn't hear.

I slid off Mal's back, nearly falling on my face in the process. As I drew nearer to the fence, I noticed a small, blue creature curled up in the soil like a snake.

I stopped short. This must have been the Blue Amethyst. My throat turned dry, my stomach sinking with dread. The creature was so small. Her wings were translucent and frail; certainly not strong enough to carry her. No scales covered her thin membrane of flesh, and several bones were visible underneath, as if she was starving and wasting away.

I swallowed hard, guilt and concern wrestling within me. This creature was dying. And she was the only key to saving Aurelia's kingdom.

Meanwhile, my mother fought vehemently for access to these dragons, even going so far as to threaten war if our demands were not met. I had come here in her name, prepared to use my fae magic if necessary.

My stomach soured. What kind of person was I? Aurelia was not the vicious princess I thought her to be. And she was certainly not as heartless as Mother claimed.

After a few moments, Aurelia stood, brushing the dirt from her hands and climbing over the fence. "Mal can fly us to the border, but any further and he will be outside the protection of our land," she said, striding past me to where Mal waited, his head lifted and his golden eyes shrewd as they watched Aurelia. "Besides, we'll need his help defending the castle. It's too risky to take him with us, and Kade will only last a week before she needs to enter deep sleep again."

"You forget, princess, that we have yet to strike our bargain," I said softly.

Aurelia turned to face me, her expression wary. "The dragons need their orders. Can't you see how restless they are?"

Mal's wings twitched. Behind him, three dragons pawed the ground nervously. The silver one who was so fond of me kept turning his head back and forth as if expecting enemies to appear on either side of us.

"Jorey, go catch some fish for Kade," Aurelia instructed. "She'll need as much nourishment as we can give her."

Jorey, the silver dragon, grunted in acknowledgment before bounding down the forest path and disappearing. My heart gave an unexpected twist at his departure.

"They can understand you?" I asked.

"Yes," she said shortly, making her way to a pair of auburn dragons. "I need you both to look after Azure while I'm gone. Can you do that?"

Both dragons inclined their heads and shuffled toward the fenced-in area where the Blue Amethyst rested. I frowned after them, remembering how Aurelia had mentioned the Blue Amethyst's mother had been taken or killed.

I remembered the rumors in my court that we had managed to capture a dragon. But I hadn't believed them, especially since there was no proof. Seeing the tiny Blue Amethyst, helpless and frail from the loss of her mother, made me reconsider this...

But no. It couldn't be. Mother had told me it was nothing more than idle gossip. And besides, if Mother *had* managed to capture a dragon, she would not have sent me on this mission. We needed Dragonfire, and if my court somehow had a dragon hidden away, they would have used her fire by now.

I was certain of it.

Aurelia wrung her hands together and chewed on her lower lip, her gaze fixed on the emerald spires of her castle. "I wish we had more time. I don't like leaving everyone… like that."

I thought of the stable hand and various servants I'd seen lying prone on the ground, dozing blissfully. Aurelia's family were likely in the same position. If I were her, I'd want to hide them just in case invaders came in my absence.

She drew in a breath and faced me, her chin lifted and her eyes hard with determination. "State your terms."

I blinked at her abruptness. "Ah. Well…"

She sighed and crossed her arms. "Time is of the essence, Fenn. Tell me what your price is."

I rubbed the back of my neck, feeling like the biggest bastard in the realm. Clearing my throat, I muttered, "I need one of your dragons."

Her eyes bulged and she took a step away from me. "I beg your pardon?" Her tone was icy.

I shook my head quickly. "Listen, I have a plan. But first, you need to understand something. We have unseelie tribes surrounding our kingdom's border. Only light can keep them away, and, as you are well aware, in the Court of Midnight, we do not see much sunlight throughout the day. Only Nightfire can provide enough light to keep us safe. Stardust is one of the substances that keeps the Nightfire burning continuously. But… we are running out of it. And with the Nightfire dying, the tribes are hunting down my people."

My words came out in a rush as I continued, "Apart from stardust and Nightfire, only Dragonfire can produce a strong enough flame to match it. Please understand that I am not simply here because we want dragons for weapons or entertainment. My people are *dying*, Aurelia. And this is our only option."

Aurelia's eyes had narrowed into slits as I spoke, and her jaw worked back and forth as she assessed me. After a moment, she said, "You said you had a plan."

"Yes," I said, encouraged by the fact that she hadn't outright refused my plea. "The witch mentioned someone who is called the Dream Mage. I've heard of her."

Aurelia's eyes grew wide. "Her? The Dream Mage is a woman?"

I nodded. "She tried taking over the Court of Twilight a few years ago. I wasn't there, but I know someone who was. She possesses the same magic, and I guarantee she will help us if we ask."

"The Court of Twilight," Aurelia repeated. "The human kingdom?"

"Yes. They rule the eastern part of the Star Court. But it's not just a human kingdom anymore. It's populated by fae and humans alike."

"You want me to travel to the Court of Twilight?" Aurelia asked incredulously.

I shrugged. "It's on the way to my kingdom. Don't you need to go there for stardust anyway?"

She frowned. "And that's your plan?"

"Not entirely," I hedged, shifting my weight from one foot to the next. Behind Aurelia, Mal perked his head up, eyeing us with curiosity. "Aurelia, if we go to the Star Court, it will arouse suspicion. Especially if we are without any dragons." She opened her mouth to argue, but I raised a hand. "Let me finish, please. My mother has instructed me to seize your dragons by *any* means necessary. She is willing to declare war on your kingdom to get them. Rest assured that I am *not* so willing. But if I return with you and we don't have dragons, she will go after your kingdom. She won't believe we are working together, unless..." I hesitated. This was the part of my plan I knew Aurelia would hate. I wasn't too fond of it myself.

"Unless what?" she asked impatiently. "Out with it, Fenn."

"Unless we claim we are engaged to be married."

THE SUMMER PRINCESS

All I could do was laugh in that arrogant prince's face.

He was insane. He had to be. There was no other explanation.

I laughed and laughed, my voice ringing out in the forest. The other dragons continued to twitch and fidget, and even Mal cocked his head at me in concern.

When I was wiping tears from my eyes, my breathing leveling out, I finally said, "They said you were a rake and a jester, but I never expected a joke like *that*."

Fenn stared at me, his expression flat and unyielding. "It's not a joke. I'm completely serious."

I shook my head, refusing to believe he could even entertain the idea. "Then, you're not a jester, you're an idiot." I turned away from him, striding toward Mal. I wasn't sure what I planned to do, but taking off into the sky seemed like a good idea. Perhaps we could go to the Star Court and extract stardust ourselves.

Fenn tugged on my arm, whirling me to face him. I bared my teeth, prepared to shove my dagger into his gut, but the plea in his eyes stopped me. He released his hold on me, lifting his hand in a placating gesture.

"Just let me explain," he said, his voice eerily soft. "Please."

My nostrils flared, but I offered him one stiff nod.

He exhaled with relief. "Both our kingdoms are weak, Aurelia. We need allies. We need defenses. You need stardust, and I need Dragonfire. The only *logical* reason for us to acquire both is through a union of marriage, where our kingdoms can share resources."

"Or we could sign a treaty," I interrupted.

He arched an eyebrow. "After centuries of animosity, what would prompt this treaty?"

I scoffed and crossed my arms. "What would prompt a marriage contract?"

"Well..." Fenn drew out the word, offering me a lopsided smile.

I scowled. "You expect the entire realm to believe you *seduced me?*"

"No one knows you. Even my mother didn't know what to expect from you. And it's safe to say you completely caught me off guard when we met in the woods."

I let my arms fall, my chest loosening at his words. Yes, he had certainly caught me off guard as well. For one brief second, I allowed myself to yearn for that stranger, that dashing man who had swept me into the most glorious dance of my life.

But he was an illusion. He wasn't real. Because the man standing before me was not the same person at all.

"It will be easy to let other people believe you are prone to my... irresistible charm," he said, still grinning, his eyes glinting with amusement. "Even if you very clearly aren't."

I shot him a glare that told him exactly how much I loathed this idea. "What do *you* get out of this? You seem a bit too fond of the notion of pretending we are courting."

He laughed. "Don't flatter yourself, princess. I'm just presenting an opportunity for our situation."

"Bullshit." I crossed my arms. "Why are you pushing this? Be honest with me, or the deal is off."

He sighed and ran a hand through his hair. "We need strong allies right now. With my court under attack from unseelie tribes, it's the perfect opportunity for our enemies to swoop in and take the city while we are defenseless. If the realm knew that the Midnight Court allied itself with the only court who possessed deadly dragons..." He trailed off.

"Then, they would leave you alone," I continued.

"Exactly."

I couldn't fault him for this. It was similar to my own situation; we were weak and under attack, too, if in a different manner. To have a strong ally would deter our enemies from moving in as well.

Which was strange, considering the court I was *most* worried about invading was the Court of Midnight.

"You are about to take the throne," Fenn went on. "It's the perfect opportunity. I couldn't very well seduce your father, now, could I?"

At the mention of my father, my gaze flicked to the emerald spires of the castle—my home—just visible between the trees. I thought of Father, asleep at his desk, and Mother and Gigi, unconscious in the tea room.

I could do this. If it meant freeing my family and my people, I could pretend to be engaged to this bastard.

"It's also the only reasonable explanation for why we are traveling alone," Fenn added in a low voice.

My gaze shot to his, my heart lurching. "What does that mean?"

"You know what it means," he said in exasperation.

I swallowed. "Even if we are engaged, it would still be highly improper to be traveling without a chaperone."

"Not with me. I have a reputation for being... well, as you said, a rake."

"Oh, really? So, you're notorious for escorting highborn royals without an envoy, guard, or chaperone?"

He winced. "Not exactly." He drew closer to me, his smirk returning. "But it won't be hard to imply that we were so enamored with one another that we couldn't keep our hands off each other, and we had to dismiss our escorts." He tilted his head at me, his eyes darkening with a fire that made my stomach clench. He wasn't even touching me and my skin felt hot from his nearness.

He lifted a hand, brushing his knuckle against my cheek. My breath hitched.

"Ah, see?" he said. "That's all we need."

I cleared my throat. "What?"

"This blush right here will tell the lie for us." He stroked my cheek once more.

I slapped his hand away. He was only pointing out my blush. Nothing more. "Even if I *did* go along with this ludicrous plan, what about my dragons? You really expect me to just give you one?"

"Not me," Fenn said. "My kingdom. And I'll be safely escorting you to my court, introducing you as my bride, deceiving my people and my family, all to give you your precious stardust. Not to mention I'll be bringing you to the only person who has connections to the Dream Mage. I will need quite a big favor in return for all this, Aurelia."

My gaze slid to Mal, who still stood behind Fenn, his golden eyes fixed on me as if asking if I was all right. A hard lump formed in my throat, and I found it hard to breathe.

Not Mal. I couldn't give him up. I *couldn't*.

"Which one?" My voice was strained, and I couldn't take my eyes off my dragon.

Fenn's eyes softened. "We need whichever dragon has the strongest fire."

My chest swelled with relief, though I hated myself for it. I loved all my dragons. I really did.

But Mal held my heart.

"That would be Jorey," I said. "His silverfire is the most powerful flame."

Fenn's eyebrows lifted, and the corners of his mouth tilted up in a genuine smile. Not a teasing smile or an arrogant smirk, but a soft, gentle smile that seemed to transform his features into someone else.

Into someone who resembled that stranger I met in the woods.

"Good thing he already seems quite fond of me, then," Fenn said.

I nodded once. Yes, I could do this. Jorey *did* like Fenn. He could be happy with him. I straightened, squaring my shoulders. "You need to swear that you'll protect him. No chains. No cages. No whips."

Fenn's expression sobered. "Yes, of course. I will ensure he is protected and looked after."

I chewed on my lower lip, my stomach in knots. This still didn't feel right.

"Aurelia."

Fenn had his hands on my shoulders, forcing my eyes to meet his. "I will swear by my blood if I have to. Not one of your dragons will be hurt. Not on my watch."

I exhaled, my breath shaky. Tears blurred my vision, and damn, but I didn't want to cry in front of this man. I blinked rapidly to clear the fog in my gaze, trying to focus on mundane things to distract myself. The lush leaves of the trees. The smell of hydrangeas around us. The shuffling and groaning of Kade as she shifted her position, making the ground rumble.

"All right," I said at last. "Let's strike our bargain."

Fenn released my shoulders and took a step away from me. "Very well. In blood?"

I nodded. Verbal bargains were binding, but I wasn't taking any chances. Blood was the only guarantee. A bargain in blood was the most dangerous kind of magic because it resulted in instant death if broken.

Technically, a verbal bargain also resulted in death. But it was slower, and it began with a burst of pain in the mind, slowly increasing with every passing second.

If Fenn betrayed me, I didn't want him to have any time to save himself. I wanted him to die immediately.

Fenn drew his short sword from his belt and offered it to me, but I shook my head.

"I'll use my own." I pulled it from the sheath at my thigh.

Fenn dragged his blade along his palm, and I did the same. Then, we clasped hands together. Already, warmth bloomed along our hands, making my skin tingle.

"I'll go first," Fenn offered. He took a deep breath and said in a steady voice, "I, Fennick Mardion of the Court of Midnight, swear by my blood to uphold this bargain with Aurelia Perdis of the Summer Court. I swear to escort her to my kingdom under the pretense of our royal engagement, to protect her to the best of my ability, and to supply her with as much stardust as she needs. I swear to assist her in locating the Dream Mage. I also swear to do everything in my power to protect the dragons of the Summer Court, and to ensure that whichever dragon is given to my kingdom lives the most comfortable life my people can offer."

I mentally sifted through his words, ensuring they were to my liking, before I said my part. "I, Aurelia Perdis of the Summer Court, swear by my blood to uphold this bargain with Fennick Mardion of the Court of Midnight. I swear to travel with him to his kingdom as his intended and to play the part of his future bride... at least until I acquire the stardust I need or the Dream Mage is located. I—I vow to gift the Midnight Court one of my dragons..." I stopped to clear my throat, finding it difficult to breathe again. "...to gift the Midnight Court the dragon with the strongest flame, only after his part of the bargain is fulfilled."

Fenn frowned for a moment. "I'd also feel a lot better if you swore you wouldn't try to kill me."

I scoffed. "Really?"

"I mean, I swore to protect you, so it's only fair."

With a groan, I added, "And I swear not to hurt, maim, or attempt to kill Prince Fennick. I also swear not to instruct my dragons to hurt or kill him, at least until our bargain is fulfilled." I glared at the prince. "There. Satisfied?"

He smiled. "Very. Consider our bargain struck."

"Our bargain is struck," I echoed.

Heat burned between our palms, singeing my skin. I hissed in pain but clenched his fingers more tightly in mine, knowing it was only sealing our bargain. Steam rose from our clasped hands, and the blood between us scorched my flesh. I bit down on my lip to keep from crying out, and Fenn's grip tensed in mine as he fought the pain as well.

At long last, the heat subsided, and I dropped his hand, lifting it to inspect my palm. I'd never struck a blood bargain before, but I'd heard of marks appearing when the bond was solidified.

Sure enough, as I flipped my hand around, I saw a small black swirl circling my middle knuckle. My breath caught in my throat as I inspected it. It was so faint it almost wasn't visible. But it was there, forever etched into my skin.

A permanent reminder of this dangerous agreement between me and the Midnight Prince.

The Midnight Prince

I knew this bargain was a terrible idea. But it was the only sure way to get what we both wanted. What we both *needed* for our kingdoms.

Mother was no fool. She would see right through our ruse.

But the kingdom wouldn't. To them, it made sense for a royal to accept a marriage contract with a princess from another kingdom. Even if that kingdom had been our enemy for centuries.

I did this for them. It would improve my image to my people. And perhaps one day they would refer to me as the prince who saved them instead of the prince notorious for seducing women.

Aurelia kept shooting me scathing looks as she packed our belongings, attaching them to a clip on the saddle strapped along Mal's back. I'd managed to grab my saddlebags from the stable. Somehow, Romulus, my horse, was still awake—clearly, the sleeping enchantment only worked on people, not animals—but Aurelia insisted flying would be faster.

"We'll need horses once we reach the border," I pointed out, remembering her claim that the dragons had to stay in the Summer Court.

"Yes, and I have a contact in Florien who can get us horses," Aurelia said in a clipped tone.

My eyebrows shot up. "You have contacts in the Autumn Court? I thought you hated the other courts."

She snorted. "No. Just your court."

Fair enough.

"Here." She shoved a warm, lumpy towel into my hands. When I glanced down at it, I saw several slices of fresh bread wrapped in a small cloth.

I blinked at her. "What's this?"

"You know, for a royal, you aren't very smart." She smirked. "I would have thought you'd recognize bread when you saw it. Unless you don't have that in your kingdom."

I rolled my eyes and bit into the warm, soft bread before groaning in satisfaction. My stomach rumbled in acknowledgment.

"I figured you were starving," Aurelia muttered, her gaze fixed on the ground.

"Why would you care?" I asked between mouthfuls of bread.

"I may not like you, but I'm not heartless," she snapped. "Besides, it was going to waste anyway. The kitchen staff had just baked it before... well, before all this happened."

"This is warm," I pointed out, my tone accusing. Between our visit to the witch lands and our blood bargain, there was no way the loaf had stayed warm for that long.

A blush bloomed across her cheeks. "I might have put it in the hearth for a few minutes. But it was purely selfish. I wanted it warm before I ate my share."

"Hmm." I tore into another bite of bread, enjoying the way the buttery softness dissolved on my tongue. "Well, it's very good. Your staff are quite talented."

"I know." Sorrow crossed her features, and her brows knitted together. "Are you ready?"

I swallowed the last bite of bread and nodded. Aurelia climbed atop Mal, but when I moved to join her, she shook her head. "You'll be flying Jorey."

My eyes widened. "What?"

A loud, indignant snort sounded to my left. I turned and found the silver dragon pawing at the ground, his sharp talons piercing the soil. On his back was a saddle identical to Mal's.

I felt the blood drain from my face as I gaped at Aurelia. "You can't be serious."

"If he's to be your dragon, you need to learn how to fly on your own."

"Not *now!*" I said weakly. "I thought we needed to move quickly!

How do you expect to travel to the border at a decent pace when you have to coach a bumbling idiot to fly on his own?"

She arched an eyebrow at me, clearly amused. "Bumbling idiot? You? Never."

"I know. I'm normally the picture of charisma and grace. So you must know that if I'll go so far as to say I'm a bumbling idiot around dragons, then I mean it."

The corners of her mouth twitched, but she wouldn't look at me. Instead, she focused on tightening the straps of the buckle on Mal's saddle. "What did you mean when you said you came into the forest to dance?"

I was silent for a moment, still fixated on the horrifying notion of riding a dragon on my own. "What?"

She finally looked at me, her eyes solemn. "When we first met, you said you came into the forest to dance. Clearly, that wasn't true, but I can't figure out how you were able to say it if it was a lie."

"Oh." I swallowed around a tight lump in my throat as I was reminded, once again, of the deception of our first meeting.

Except it *wasn't* a deception. Not on my part. As much as she wanted to believe in my duplicity, I hadn't known her identity then.

Perhaps I could demonstrate as much with a kernel of truth.

With a deep breath, I said, "I didn't say that was my purpose for being in the woods. I said I often went into the forest to dance. Which, in my kingdom, is the truth. Every week we hold a Nightfire fete, which involves food and dancing and merriment. It's a celebration of stars and the resources that make it possible for the fire to burn brightly."

Aurelia's brows knitted together in confusion. "And you do this... in the forest?"

"The entire event takes place outdoors. On the balconies, the verandas, the gardens, and, yes, the forest. It's a celebration of nature and nightfall, so it's best enjoyed where we can see the stars. The Crescent Glade is my favorite place to dance during the fete. It's just outside my castle."

She made a small sound in the back of her throat, and it wasn't until I looked at her and noticed her lips twitching again that I realized it was a small laugh. "I'm sorry," she said quickly. "I'm just having trouble picturing you dancing on your own in the forest. It seems rather silly."

"Well, of course it would be silly to dance alone. But I always have a partner."

Her expression cleared, and she nodded, ducking her head as she continued fiddling with the saddle. "Right. Of course." She cleared her throat. "And, with your dwindling resources, what does your court do now? Do you continue with these Nightfire celebrations?"

My stomach twisted at the reminder that my people were suffering. The last I'd seen, one of the Nightfire braziers had gone out, and the southern sector had been attacked by unseelie beasts.

How many other sectors had lost their Nightfire? How many people had we lost to the unseelie tribes?

"No," I said at last. "No, I believe my mother would have discontinued the fete for the time being. But I'm hopeful that our arrival can start it up again." Something warm tickled the back of my hand, and I jumped, my heart lurching in my chest. Jorey had drawn closer and pressed his snout into my hand as if searching for treats. His warm breath tickled my skin.

Aurelia laughed. "Saddle up, prince. It's time for your first flying lesson."

Even though Aurelia had instructed me on how to tighten the saddle, I still felt like I was about to fall off.

But, to his credit, Jorey was a smooth flier, and, unlike Mal, his movements were slow and careful, as if he knew how nervous I was. My body was rigid, my arms wrapped around Jorey's neck as his silver scales dug into my flesh, but I didn't care. It kept me more securely on his back.

"He can sense your distress," Aurelia said as she and Mal glided alongside me. "He won't fly so fast if he thinks you are uneasy."

"I *am* uneasy," I snapped. "I can't just turn off the emotion, Aurelia."

She chuckled. My terror amused her. "Relax, prince. I wouldn't have put you on my dragon if I thought he would kill you. That would go against our bargain."

I frowned, mulling over her words. She was right. She wouldn't risk allowing the blood bargain to claim her life. Not over this.

I took a deep breath and loosed my hold around Jorey's neck. He grumbled softly as if to reassure me. I patted the top of his head. "You're a kind creature, Jorey. I think we'll get on splendidly."

His right ear twitched, and his body jerked as his tail swished back and forth. He truly was just like a playful canine.

"You dig in your heels when you want to slow," Aurelia said. "Otherwise they will take off at their own speed. Generally, you can trust their pace, but… with some of the more unruly dragons, you have to be more careful." Her mouth quirked in an endearing smile, no doubt as she fondly recalled this experience with some of her other dragons.

"Dig in my heels," I repeated. "So, like, the opposite of riding a horse."

"Yes."

"Perfect," I grumbled. "That's not confusing at all."

"If you put your trust in Jorey, he will take care of you," Aurelia said. "He is the tamest of all the dragons. I even let my sister ride him once."

My eyebrows lifted. "Really?"

"Really."

I nodded, focusing on a steady exhale before dragging one finger along the smooth surface of Jorey's scales. The silver sparkled in the sunlight, momentarily distracting me from my fear. "All right, then. Off we go, Jorey. My life is in your hands."

Jorey let out a sound that seemed a lot like an excited bark. A laugh bubbled in my throat, but before I could react, Jorey jerked forward, taking a nosedive straight for the ground.

A scream tore through me, the wind lashing my body as we descended. Just when I thought we would crash into the treetops, Jorey leveled, arcing smoothly in the air, his wings folded back as we gained speed. The momentum carried us, the trees a blur beneath us. My eyes burned, and tears streamed down my face. The scream still felt lodged in my throat, and my chest felt ready to burst from the tension coiled within me. Jorey's muscles pumped from under my legs, and his wings flapped once, giving us another burst of speed. My heart raced, thundering against my rib cage as I waited for the inevitable fall, for my body to slide easily off the saddle and into oblivion.

But it never happened. I stayed atop the dragon, secured by the saddle. A whoop sounded from behind me. I shot a quick glance over my shoulder to find Mal swerving and spinning in the air with Aurelia laughing, her arms spread wide.

Like the firebird she was.

A grin formed, and I found myself wanting to laugh along with her. But Jorey flapped his wings again, and the movement jostled me. Startled, I faced forward again and scrambled for purchase, my hands instinctively searching for reins that weren't there. Jorey seemed to sense my disorientation; he leveled out, angling his body so I was perfectly lined up with the saddle. Somehow, he could sense which direction my body was wobbling. He knew exactly how to tilt himself so I could right my balance.

A single, surprised chuckle burst from my lips. Jorey's ears twitched as if he, too, were laughing.

"Amazing," I murmured, patting his head again. I noticed there were three triangular ridges along the back of his neck. When I poked at one, a low, rumbling hum vibrated through him, almost like a purr. "Are you ticklish there?" I teased, then nudged the ridge more firmly. He stiffened, his left wing twitching, and flicked his ear in agitation.

"Probably best not to do that when he's focused on keeping you steady," Aurelia said from my right.

Despite her teasing, I couldn't help but shoot her a wide grin. "This is incredible."

She smirked. "I know."

"How much farther until we get to the border?"

But Aurelia was frowning, her gaze distant. Her hand stroked the side of Mal's neck, and only then did I notice the dragon was flexing his talons, his nostrils flaring wide.

"What is it?" she murmured to him.

Mal made a low growling sound, and Aurelia's head jerked upward, her eyes scanning the trees below us.

"What did he say?" I asked, unease trickling through me. From beneath me, Jorey's muscles flexed, his head turning slightly to the left. One ear perked up as if he heard something I couldn't.

Aurelia shot me a dark look. "There's a clan of goblins waiting for us at the border."

THE SUMMER PRINCESS

I COULD SMELL THEM, EVEN FROM HERE. I'D ONLY ENCOUNTERED GOBLINS once before, but their pungent odor was unforgettable.

Mal detected them first, of course. His head whipped back and forth, his nostrils flaring wide as he growled in response to the threat.

"It's all right." I patted the side of his neck, even though panic coursed through me. "Take us to the falls. Hopefully it will mask our presence from them."

Mal grumbled his assent and dipped lower, his claws brushing against the tallest tree branches. Jorey followed his lead. Fenn was rigid in his saddle, his face pale, but he said nothing as the dragons descended.

Mal weaved expertly between trees. Even before he landed, the sounds of rushing water surrounded us, reminding me of past summers and simpler times.

Before Mal had finished landing, I was already unbuckling the saddle and dismounting. Beside me, Jorey slammed into the earth, the waterfall's roar masking the sound of the impact. Fenn was staring, wide-eyed at the massive waterfall attached to the mountain. We didn't have tall, snow-capped mountains like the Winter Court, but we still boasted a few modest mountain ranges. This was one of my favorites— a sprawling expanse of grass-covered peaks with rivers and waterfalls sprinkled throughout. The falls ran into a wide pool that filtered into the Jewel River, which cut directly through the Summer Court.

"What is this place?" Fenn asked, his voice full of awe. His head tilted backward as he took in the full height of the mountain. "I didn't know your court had mountains."

"They're covered in trees, and they're quite small, so it's easy to mistake them for large hills," I said with a shrug. "This is Kellen Falls. I used to come here all the time. I think."

He shot me an incredulous look. "You *think?*"

I frowned, my brows knitting together. "No. I mean. I don't know. I don't have very many memories of my childhood." When I sensed Fenn looking at me in curiosity, I went on, "I don't remember it, but my parents told me I had a terrible accident as a child. I almost drowned. It affected my brain, and ever since then, I have trouble accessing some of my long term memories. They are a bit… foggy."

The gaps in my memory were frustrating, to say the least. My parents speculated that was why my fae magic hadn't been able to properly manifest itself. Perhaps it never would.

Fenn said nothing, his gaze wistful and somber. Something akin to regret flashed in his eyes. "I'm sorry."

I dropped my gaze, uncomfortable with his sympathy. "It's fine."

Fenn gazed around, his expression turning thoughtful. "It feels… cool. The air is cooler here."

I smirked, grateful for the subject change. "We're more than just a kingdom of unbearable, scorching heat, you know."

He winced, as if he had been thinking exactly that.

I couldn't blame him. After all, his kingdom—a place of complete and total darkness, lit only by the stars and, apparently, Nightfire—seemed rather miserable, too.

Mal nudged me with his snout, his golden eyes wide with concern.

"I'll be fine." I pressed my forehead to his. "Protect the castle. Take care of Kade. We'll return as soon as we can."

"They aren't coming with us?" Fenn asked.

I shook my head. "I can't risk the goblins finding them, or worse, following them back to the castle. You'll get Jorey when our bargain is complete. Say your goodbyes now, prince."

Fenn turned to Jorey, whose ears perked up hopefully. The prince's mouth turned down in an uncharacteristic frown, his brows knitting together. "Well. Goodbye, my silver friend. If all goes well, I'll see you soon, and you can come home with me."

Jorey opened his mouth, his tongue lolling out happily. In a swift movement, he licked Fenn's cheek. Fenn made a retching sound and wiped at his face, but he was laughing, the delight in his eyes betraying him.

I busied myself with the packs attached to Mal's saddle, trying to ignore the stinging burn behind my eyes. This would be the longest I'd go without Mal. I didn't often travel outside my kingdom, but when I did, it was only a few days at a time.

This journey to the Star Court would take several days. It would be a miracle if we made it back before Kade had to return to her deep slumber.

Mal nudged my hand with his head again, and I scratched underneath his chin. He grumbled something low and mournful.

I sighed. "I know. But we can do this. You and I are strong." I placed my hands on either side of his face, then ran a fingertip lightly along the scar that cut through his eye. "Promise me you'll be careful. Take care of yourself. I don't know what I'd do if something happened to you."

He cocked his head and let out a soft whine.

I kissed the top of his head. "Enough of that. You have a job to do. We both do."

He dipped his head with a soft huff, then turned away from me. Tears filled my eyes as I watched him and Jorey take to the skies, their forms vanishing from view.

I wiped my nose, avoiding Fenn's gaze. Parting from Mal, and reminding myself how he got his scar in the first place, only made me despise the prince even more. It wasn't his fault, and it wasn't fair—I knew that—but I couldn't help but resent him. It had been *his* kingdom that had nearly killed Mal.

And now, I was traveling to that same kingdom in search of a way to save my people.

"So, the goblins," Fenn said slowly, taking his pack from me and slinging it over his shoulder. "What are we going to do?"

"We'll keep to the Jewel River, using the water to mask our tracks and our scent," I said. "With any luck, we'll avoid them."

"But if they're by the border—"

"It's a long border, Fenn," I snapped. "We can go around them if necessary."

Fenn's mouth clamped shut, his eyes flaring with irritation. "Stars, you're grumpy without your dragon."

"Get used to it," I muttered, shoving past him to make my way toward the river.

He trailed after me, and an uncomfortable silence fell between us. He matched my pace easily, following as I led us downhill along a trail adjacent to the riverbank. The waters shimmered in the sunlight that filtered through the treetops.

After an hour, I dropped my sack on the ground and crouched near the river's edge, cupping my hands to bring the water to my face. I washed the sweat off my cheeks and forehead, then drank deeply. The water was cold and brisk, and I greedily gulped it down. The fresh taste was so much better than the water from the well by the castle.

Beside me, Fenn followed suit, running his wet hand through his hair and down his neck. Water trickled along his throat and collarbone, and as he tugged down the front of his tunic, I caught sight of the witch rune etched into his skin. My eyes snagged on the sculpted muscles of his tanned shoulders and chest.

I blinked and quickly turned away, my heart racing. *Stupid,* I chided myself.

Fenn was handsome. There was no doubt about it. But that was exactly why I needed to be careful. He had charmed many women, making fools of them, coercing them to his bed only to discard them afterward.

I refused to fall prey to his seduction.

"We're close," I said, keeping my gaze fixed on my pack as I tightened the strap. "Keep a sharp eye. I can already smell the goblins."

"You can?"

I looked at him then, and he was arching a dubious eyebrow at me.

"Goblins let out an awful stench," I told him. "It's one of their only weaknesses."

"I know that," he said. "I've fought goblins before. But normally I can't smell them until they're right next to me."

I shrugged. "Maybe the goblins here are different."

"Maybe." But he eyed me with a scrutiny that made me fidget.

I stood and shouldered my pack before resuming my trek down the trail, not bothering to look back to ensure Fenn was following.

Before I knew it, he was hiking alongside me, his lengthy strides matching mine. "I've studied witch runes for a while, you know."

I cast a sidelong glance at him. "What?"

"I know a lot of runes."

I frowned. "Why are you telling me this?"

"There's one rune that's meant to reveal spells and enchantments on a person. If you want, I could cast the rune… on you. To figure out what *your* rune is for."

I stopped in my tracks, turning to face him to discern if he was mocking me or not. But he merely blinked innocently at me, his face betraying nothing. After a moment, I continued walking. "No."

"Why not? Don't you want to know what the rune means?"

"Of course I do. But I don't trust you to cast a witch spell on me."

"So you'd rather keep living in ignorance? You'd rather do nothing?"

I stopped again, whirling to face him, anger rising up inside me. "What do you know? You're a stranger to me, Fenn. Don't think you can pass judgment about my life. You're still my enemy. The ruthless prince from a vicious family who continuously tries to take what's most precious to me. It's because of you that Mal—" I stopped short, my mouth snapping shut as more tears burned in my eyes. Gods, I already missed my dragon so much. How could I ensure he was kept safe? What if I came back and found out something had happened to him?

Clearing my throat, I turned away from Fenn. "No. I don't want your runes, Fenn. The only thing I need from you is what was outlined in our bargain. Nothing more."

To my surprise, he chuckled. "I find your sour attitude quite endearing, little firebird."

I rolled my eyes, choosing to ignore him as I made my way down the trail, keeping close to the river so its sounds would drown us out.

When the roar of the waterfall behind us had almost faded completely, I raised a hand to stop Fenn, my nostrils flaring as a familiar foul stench filled my nose.

"They're close," I whispered.

"How do you know?"

"I told you I can smell them."

Fenn inhaled deeply. "I don't smell anything."

"Well, I can."

"I'm not sure I believe you."

I suppressed a groan and shot him a glare. "Are you calling me a liar?"

"No. I'm simply questioning whether it's the goblins you're smelling or… something else."

"What else could I be smelling?"

He shrugged. "Maybe you soiled yourself."

I closed my eyes, rubbing my temples to ward off the headache of enduring this prince's insufferable presence. "I loathe you more intensely than a thousand burning suns."

"So what you're saying is… you have strong feelings for me?" He cocked his head and offered me a roguish grin, his hair flopping on his face so it covered one eye.

I made a retching sound and let my hands fall against my thighs. "Fine. I warned you. If you get eaten by bloodthirsty goblins, it's your own damn fault." Muttering a string of swear words under my breath, I unsheathed the dagger at my thigh.

Fenn chuckled softly. "So grouchy." But he followed suit, drawing his own blade, which was a short sword.

"You have to strike them at the throat or the heart," I told him. "Any other wound will not stop them."

"I'm aware. Like I said, I've fought goblins before."

"Well, you've proven to be rather unintelligent so far, so I wouldn't be surprised if you'd forgotten."

He grinned at me. "I love it when you flirt with me, little firebird."

Burning suns, this prince would get us killed. I resisted the urge to run him through and crept along the riverbank, my heart drumming an erratic rhythm in my chest.

I'd only fought goblins once before, and I'd had Mal to protect me. Right now, I could only rely on this moronic prince. I didn't even know how many goblins waited for us.

To my left, a twig snapped, and I whipped my head in that direction, my skin tingling. But nothing was there.

Leaves rustled. With a jolt, I glanced upward and found several shaking tree branches. Another twig snapped from behind me.

My blood ran cold. *Oh, shit.*

"Fenn—"

Three sharp twangs rang out.

"Down!" Fenn shouted as he crashed into me, tackling me to the ground. My shoulder and hip screamed in pain as they caught the brunt of my fall. With a *thunk,* an arrow embedded itself into the earth mere inches from my face.

An almighty roar erupted, and more than a dozen goblins poured from the trees and descended on us.

THE MIDNIGHT PRINCE

Searing, blinding pain exploded through me. My awareness homed in on that singular point of agony—a white-hot fire burning in my shoulder.

I'd been struck.

But I couldn't dwell on it. Enemies were closing in on us, and Aurelia was shouting something.

Gritting my teeth, I rolled off her and staggered to my feet, my shoulder screaming in protest. I caught sight of the arrow shaft protruding from my flesh.

No, I thought. *Do not dwell on it.*

I'd been in battle before, but it had certainly been a while. I inhaled deeply, and that familiar metallic tang of blood filled my nose and mouth.

My blood.

It reminded me of the battlefield. Of loss and rage and nothing but pure bloodlust.

The horde of goblins drew closer. They were gray-skinned, with small white horns and leathery flesh that stretched thin over their bony frames. Their inky all-black eyes were dark and full of a vicious hunger that only fae blood could satisfy.

Beside me, Aurelia held her dagger, poised to strike. Only the slight tremor in her hand betrayed her fear.

"Can you fight?" I asked, my voice a low rasp.

"Of course," she snapped. "I wouldn't carry a dagger if I didn't know how to use it." She cut me a glare, and then her gaze snagged on the arrow embedded in my flesh.

Her face paled, making her freckles stand out starkly against her cheeks. "Fenn—"

"No time," I muttered, tossing my blade to my left hand to avoid exacerbating the wound in my shoulder. I couldn't fight as well left-handed, but I could make do.

When the first goblin came within striking distance, I slashed my blade, opening his throat. Black blood poured from the wound, and he made a horrible gagging sound, but I was already moving on to my next target. I plunged my dagger into another goblin's heart, then stabbed straight through the neck of another, slicing his head clean off.

As he fell, his head rolling, I glanced quickly at Aurelia, and my mouth fell open. She whirled, slicing her blade with precision and grace. When she fought, she used her entire body. Her legs moved, her feet gliding back and forth as she danced away from her opponent. She used the force of her kick to weaken a goblin before burrowing her blade into his chest and twisting hard.

Brutal, yet elegant. She hadn't been bluffing when she claimed to be an adept dancer. And she was using that skill to fell her enemies, one by one.

A sharp pain sliced through my arm, and I jumped backward. In my surprised stupor, a goblin had dragged its claws straight through me. I bit out a curse and slashed my sword, but he leapt out of reach. I advanced, but two other goblins closed in on me, entrapping me.

I stilled, assessing my options. Blood dripped down my arm, and my tunic was drenched from the arrow still lodged in my shoulder. Dizziness clouded my mind. I wouldn't last much longer.

The goblin nearest me flashed his sharp canines in delight.

Aurelia cried out and sank to her knees. My head whipped toward her, shock jolting through me. She fought one goblin, but she hadn't noticed another as he pounced on her, his sharp teeth digging into her shoulder and drawing blood.

"Aurelia!" I roared. With a burst of energy, I aimed a high kick, slamming my boot into a goblin's chest and knocking him down. Before he could recover, I slashed open his throat.

Aurelia screamed, her voice echoing in the forest, and the very trees seemed to quiver from the intensity of it. When I glanced her way, I could have sworn her eyes glowed green.

Another goblin came for me. I tore my gaze from Aurelia and blocked his attack. But another cut his claws across my shin. My leg buckled, and I sank to one knee.

A bright blue flame ignited next to the riverbank. Somehow, the goblin attacking Aurelia had caught fire. His screeches split the air as the flames consumed him. He turned and raced toward the river before plunging himself into its depths.

Fortunately, this distracted the goblins surrounding me. I beheaded two more.

But, unfortunately, several goblins swarmed Aurelia, marking her as the bigger threat.

"No!" I shouted, my blade singing with each stroke as I killed one goblin after another, trying to make my way to her. But there were too many of them.

"*Stop!*" I bellowed, channeling all my remaining energy into that one word.

I didn't think it would work. Fae magic normally wasn't strong enough to overcome the bloodthirsty rage of the unseelie.

But the goblin closest to Aurelia froze, his black eyes going wide as he looked between me and Aurelia. The princess narrowed her eyes at me, only hesitating a moment before she stabbed the goblin in the heart.

"*Leave her be,*" I said, allowing my magic to flow through me. The force of my power drained me, and the blade fell from my hands. Black spots hovered in my vision, and I swayed, falling to my other knee. I would pass out soon, and the goblins would devour me.

But I could save Aurelia.

Another goblin burst into flames. Then another. Soon, every creature was consumed by this strange blue fire. Their anguished screeches made my ears throb. One knocked into me, and I fell backward, the sleeve of my tunic catching fire. I hastily patted it down to quench the flames, then stared, awestruck, as the goblins dived into the river one by one, leaving a cloud of billowing smoke behind them.

"Up," Aurelia hissed in my ear. "*Now.*"

She tugged on my uninjured arm, but I still groaned in pain. Every inch of my body throbbed in an agony that speared through my head like an axe in my skull. Gods, it was unbearable. My head slumped as I yearned for unconsciousness.

"Oh, no, you don't," Aurelia chided, tugging more forcefully on my arm.

"*Shit*, Aurelia," I barked as a fresh explosion of pain coursed through me. I staggered to my feet, allowing her to guide me into the cover of the forest. The river still gushed smoke from the goblins attempting to put out the fire. But it wouldn't kill them. They would come for us again, more enraged than ever.

"We're almost there," she muttered, still half-dragging me.

"Almost where?" I mumbled, my voice slurring. Darkness crowded my vision, and I welcomed it.

A pinch in my arm brought sharp clarity to my mind, and I winced. "Gods, you are violent."

"Good thing, otherwise we'd be a meal for the goblins right now."

I blinked hazily at her. Her jaw was set with determination as she stared forward, guiding me toward a destination I couldn't see. A long, bloody gash ran along her jaw, and another smaller cut bled from her forehead. The back of her dress was soaked in blood from when the goblin took a bite out of her.

"Did you do that?" I whispered. "Did you set them on fire?"

Uncertainty flashed in her blue eyes, but she said nothing. She didn't look proud or smug. If anything, she looked *afraid*.

"Aurelia," I said, my voice gaining strength. "Was that you? Or something else?"

After a long moment, she said softly, "I don't know."

Aurelia kept me awake, pinching and prodding me until I was certain she would leave bruises. But it worked. By the time we reached the small inn nestled in the forest, I was on my feet, instead of being partially dragged. Granted, I was still leaning heavily on Aurelia, but with her arm laced through mine, it wasn't as obvious.

Nothing could cover up our injuries or blood-soaked clothes, though. There was also an arrow sticking out of the front of my torso, which was quite alarming.

A shimmering, rippling fog hovered in front of the inn, and when we passed through it, the air seemed to rumble.

Was I hallucinating?

"What was that?" I asked.

"Protective wards surrounding the inns," Aurelia said. "It keeps out the unseelie, like those nasty goblins."

Ah, now I remembered... Something similar happened on my journey to the Summer Court. I squinted through the fog clouding my vision as the familiar cottage came into view. "I know this place. I've been here before."

"It's Fellspar Inn," Aurelia said.

I stopped in my tracks. "Damn."

Aurelia stared at me. "What is it?"

"I stayed here on my way to your kingdom."

"So?"

My eyes closed, shame and irritation washing over me. "So... I did not sleep alone for the night." I leveled a meaningful look at her.

Her cheeks flushed, but she glared in response. "Really? You couldn't restrain yourself for one night?"

"The journey here was *several* nights, thank you very much, and I did restrain myself for the better part of the trip."

She only rolled her eyes. "Regardless of your proclivities, they will still shelter us for the night. I know the owner." She urged me forward.

I tugged on her elbow to stop her. "That's what concerns me. Aurelia, we need to appear as if we are betrothed. If this owner knows you, he will likely share this information with others, and we need the news to spread quickly. Not only will it help our story, but it will also keep your kingdom protected if people are aware the Star Court has allied itself to you."

She stilled, her eyes calculating as she considered my words. "And your court would be safer, too, I'd wager."

"Well, yes. Not only that, but, I have... rather regrettably made a reputation for myself. If we truly want this lie to be believed, then we must share a room."

She whirled to face me, her eyes blazing. "*What?* Absolutely not!"

"Aurelia," I said.

"I am not sharing a room *or* a bed with you, you foul, twisted—"

"Stars above, I do not want to bed you!" I snapped. "It's only for appearances. I will sleep on the damn floor if I have to. But no one will believe that I am courting someone with chaste intentions."

She shifted her weight. "Royals court like that all the time. It wouldn't be proper, and people would know that."

"Yes, but you and I cannot lie. If we declare we are sharing a room for the night, that will spread the rumor for us." I paused, eyeing the cut that still bled freely on her forehead. "Not to mention it will give them something else to gossip about besides our horrifying state."

She sighed. "Fine. But if you try anything tonight, I will gut you."

I chuckled. "I don't doubt it."

Aurelia gripped my arm firmly, leading me toward the front door of the inn. Truth be told, it was a rather charming venue, the three-story cottage looking more like a secluded home in the woods than a place of business. Perhaps that was the appeal.

A row of neatly trimmed rose bushes lined the stone walkway. The windows were adorned with vines of ivy and jasmine, the smell tickling my nose. The cottage was built with thick, wooden slats and had a thatched roof on top. Had I been a commoner in the Summer Court, this would certainly have been my ideal profession: an innkeeper of a pleasant place such as this.

Aurelia pushed open the door and guided me through it. In the small foyer, a plump woman, her messy gray hair coming out of her bun, bustled behind a desk, muttering to herself. Her cheeks were pink as she glanced up at us, her face paling. "Burning suns, I knew it! I've already sent for the healer. Your Highness, what happened?" She hurried around the desk and helped us into the sitting room.

"No, no," Aurelia said quickly. "We don't want to leave blood on your beautiful furniture. We'll just need a room for the night."

"Your Highness, you both need medical attention. The healer should be here any moment."

Aurelia nodded. "That would be helpful, thank you. But we do need a room. We must change and clean up if we are to present ourselves to the Autumn Court in a few days."

I shot an alarmed look at Aurelia before schooling my features into a neutral expression. The Autumn Court? We hadn't discussed this. I knew we would be making a few stops in this kingdom, but I wasn't aware we would be making a formal introduction to the royal court.

"I have your usual room prepared, Your Highness," the woman said.

"And I already have another room available upstairs for this gentleman as well."

"No," Aurelia said quickly. "He can share my room."

The woman's eyes grew wide as she glanced between us. Familiarity flickered in her expression as she gazed me up and down.

Oh, yes, she remembered me. I flashed her a dazzling smile and fixed an adoring look at Aurelia.

"One room?" the woman repeated. "For the two of you?"

Aurelia's eyes sparkled with delight as she leaned closer to whisper, "We haven't officially announced it yet."

The woman uttered a shocked squeak before covering her mouth. "By the gods! It cannot be! You and the Midnight Prince?"

Aurelia arched an eyebrow in my direction, and I shrugged. Yes, I had made my presence—and my title—known during my stay here. There was nothing to be done about it now. If anything, my notoriety might help us spread the word.

"It is true," Aurelia said, and the shy smile on her face looked so genuine it made my heart stutter. Her eyes shone, and the rosy glow in her cheeks made her look positively radiant. "Unfortunately, we were attacked by a clan of goblins along the way, but our injuries are minor and we should be fit to continue our journey after a healer tends to us."

The woman cast an uncertain glance at the arrow protruding from my body, no doubt questioning the *minor* aspect of our injuries.

I forced a smile. "It's merely a flesh wound."

"Of course." The woman wiped her hands on her apron, then stretched her hand toward the foyer. "Let me fetch your key for you."

"I can pay you—" Aurelia said quickly, but the woman shushed her.

"Nonsense. Consider it a gift. And, if you feel so inclined, I would be *honored* to be invited to the royal wedding." The woman curtsied slightly and dipped her gaze.

Aurelia faltered. She blinked, then swallowed hard, regret filling her eyes.

"Of course," I said at once, my voice smooth and inviting. "Any of my beloved's acquaintances would be most welcome to our wedding."

The woman beamed, then ducked behind her desk. After a moment, she resurfaced with a large, brass key and handed it to Aurelia. "Room seventeen on the first floor."

"Ah, Dreya, you always take such good care of me," Aurelia said with a wide smile.

Dreya curtsied again. "Of course! I keep the room ready for you. It is yours and yours alone."

Aurelia flushed. "You are too kind. I wish you would let us pay for the trouble."

"Think nothing of it, Your Highness. You are welcome here anytime. Come, let me help you with your belongings." She scooped up Aurelia's sack and lifted it to her shoulder with surprising strength before leading us down the hall toward the room.

THE SUMMER PRINCESS

IF MY SISTER COULD SEE ME NOW, SHE WOULD HOWL WITH LAUGHTER, I thought as I followed Dreya down the narrow hallway toward the room I usually stayed in. *Pretending to be engaged to the prince of my enemy kingdom... and sharing a room with him, no less.*

I knew exactly what Gigi would say. *Aurie, he's gorgeous! Who cares what kingdom he comes from? I'd share a room with the most vile, ill-tempered man in the world if he looked like* that.

The corners of my mouth twitched as I thought of my sister's response. But sorrow soon took over, dragging my heart down to my stomach as I remembered where I'd left Gigi.

Frozen, unconscious in the tea room.

A hollow feeling settled in my chest as I was achingly reminded of how alone I truly was. Fenn was technically on my side, but our alliance was precarious at best, and I still expected him to try to alter our bargain or betray me in some way.

I couldn't be myself. I had to constantly be on guard. And there was no one I could talk to in earnest.

Sudden exhaustion tugged at my body. I was so very, very tired. The bone-weary fatigue clouding my body was not only physical; an emotional weight bore down on me, threatening to pull me under.

When Dreya helped us into the room, I mumbled a quick thanks to her before shutting the door and sagging against it, my eyes closing as I slid to the floor.

"Was she expecting you?" Fenn asked, his voice full of curiosity.

I opened one eye and found him frowning at the tub of steaming water on the opposite end of the room.

Ah, yes, I'd forgotten. There was no separate bathing chamber. We would have to wash in front of one another.

Perfect.

And yet, I was too tired to care. My eye closed once again. "It's fae magic."

"Come again?" Fenn asked.

"Dreya has a connection to the earth and the land where this cottage was built," I said, my voice barely a mumble because I was too weary to properly articulate. "She can anticipate the needs of others, and the cottage responds to that need."

"That explains how she knew we'd need a healer before we arrived," Fenn said.

"Didn't you stay at this place before? How did you not notice?"

"I was a bit preoccupied." Smug amusement laced his tone. I heard him shuffling around the room, opening drawers and wardrobe cabinets.

I opened my eyes to peer at him, inspecting the room with fresh eyes. I'd stayed here once a year every year for a long time. Mother and Father had expected me to marry the Autumn Prince, but that arrangement had ended when—

I shut down the thought. I didn't want my mind to go there. Not now. I didn't have the energy for it.

Instead, I focused on the cozy bedroom. Plum drapes framed the large window. A matching purple rug covered the left half of the room. On one end was a large bed with four posters and delicate white drapes. On the other end was a wide, copper tub with steam rising from the depths. Next to it was an open wardrobe, through which Fenn was shuffling.

"It's furnished with clothes exactly my size," he said with a laugh of disbelief. "This is incredible! I've never experienced fae magic like this."

I smiled slightly. "The witches bound her to the land. I'm sure that connection helps to strengthen the magic."

"Bandages, ointments, and poultices," Fenn said as he continued searching through drawers. "Yes, this room definitely has what we need. Although with your shoulder wound, I think we'll need a healer."

"There's an arrow still protruding from your body," I shot back. "We *both* need serious medical attention."

Fenn closed the wardrobe and leaned against it, rubbing his face with one hand. "What happened back there with the goblins?"

I cocked my head at him. "I could ask you the same thing." When his brows knitted together, I added, "You told them to stop—to *leave*—and they did."

"That's what you're concerned about? Not the fact that they spontaneously burst into unholy blue flames?"

The incredulity in his voice made me drop my gaze. In truth, I couldn't explain what had happened.

But I had a hunch that I wasn't keen on sharing.

I cleared my throat, refusing to look at his probing gaze. "Did you do something to those goblins, Fenn?"

"Did *you?*"

"Will you just answer my damn question?" I barked. "I asked you first."

He smirked at me. "And if I answer, will you do the same?"

My lips clamped together tightly. After a moment, I said, "Yes."

He laughed. "I don't believe you."

"I can't lie."

"No, but you can dodge my question. So I'll do the same. Yes, I *did something* to those goblins. I fought with all the strength I possessed in order to keep myself—and you—alive. You're welcome, by the way."

My nostrils flared, my blood boiling as I climbed to my feet, ignoring the shooting pain that seared through my body, my cuts and scrapes throbbing. "Fine. You want me to answer honestly? The truth is, I don't know what the hell happened or what caused the fire. All I know was that goblin bit off a chunk of my shoulder and suddenly, he caught fire."

Fenn straightened, then winced and cradled his right arm. "Your shoulder?" he repeated.

"That's what I said," I snapped.

He took a step toward me. "Can I see?"

Frowning at the note of curiosity in his voice, I turned to show him the bloody gash of my flesh wound, still bleeding profusely through my dress.

Fenn sucked in a breath. "Aurelia, that's exactly where your rune is located."

My heart jolted as I remembered Samiria pulling down the fabric to expose my shoulder blade and the witch rune I had never known was there.

A goblin bit my shoulder—in the precise location of the rune—and then caught fire. That couldn't be a coincidence.

My breathing turned ragged, and I suddenly felt dizzy. Gods, I was so tired and confused and overwhelmed by all of this—the sleeping curse, the mysterious rune, and the insufferable prince in front of me.

A warm hand pressed on my uninjured shoulder, grounding me in place, and I found myself leaning into that warmth. Fenn had drawn closer without me realizing, but I didn't mind it. The warmth of him at my back was strangely comforting.

"Aurelia, does this mean—" he said.

A loud knock sounded at the door, and I took a step away from Fenn.

"It's the healer, Your Highness," came an old, wiry voice on the other side of the door.

"You may enter," I replied.

The door opened, and a tall, thin man with wide-set eyes and a full beard of wispy white hair entered. He wore long, emerald robes that reminded me of the wizards I'd read about in storybooks. He glanced between us, his gray eyes impassive. After a moment, he gestured to me. "Greetings. My name is Healer Warren. Lie on the bed please, Your Highness."

"You really should tend to the prince first," I objected. "The arrow—"

"I was told that the Summer Princess was the priority," Healer Warren said, his voice low and soft. He had a soothing tone, which I imagined was quite helpful in his line of work.

Before I could argue, Fenn said loudly, "That's absolutely correct. Please tend to my fiancée first."

I resisted the urge to roll my eyes as he flashed me a roguish grin. I made my way to the bed, then sank onto it.

"On your stomach, please," instructed Healer Warren.

With a nod, I rolled face-down into the sheets, wincing when the movement tore at the gash in my shoulder.

Healer Warren hummed with interest as he drew closer. "I will need to cut through your dress, Your Highness."

I thought of Fenn standing behind me, and my face burned. I was grateful to hide my blush in the pillows. "That's fine," I said, my voice slightly muffled.

Fabric ripped, and cool air tickled my upper back as the cotton was swept away. I closed my eyes, willing my stomach to stop coiling with anxiety. I'd just been attacked by goblins—one of them had taken a large bite out of my shoulder—and I was worried about being half naked in front of the prince? It was absolutely ridiculous. I forced the thought from my mind and focused on keeping my breathing steady.

"This will need stitches," the healer said.

I frowned. "You won't be using magic?"

"I will. But my magic only speeds up the healing process. I must do the mending by hand."

"All right."

I waited for Fenn to say something witty or sarcastic, but he remained silent. My eyes stayed shut as Healer Warren did his work. A numbing agent spread across my shoulder blade, and the slight tug of my skin as he knitted it back together was jarring, but not painful. Whatever ointment he'd applied was truly miraculous.

After he was finished, he pressed his hand into my injury. I hissed in pain, but after a moment, the wound began to burn, and warmth spread through my body. I gasped, my body stiffening in response as his magic washed over me.

"It's done," he said.

I sat up, then reached over my shoulder to touch the wound. The stitches were there, but there was no longer a gaping hole in my shoulder. Now, it was nothing more than a puckered ridge, still held together by the stitches.

"Now, your face," Healer Warren said, his expression still as stoic as ever, as if he was merely reading a mildly interesting book.

I scooted to the edge of the bed, and he dabbed some ointment on the cuts along my face, then pressed his fingers into it to infuse his magic. Each cut burned, like before, and the same warm flood of awareness shot through my body, making my blood sing and my bones rattle.

When he was finished, he gestured for me to rise, and I stepped around him. Fenn stood in my path, still leaning against the wardrobe, his face a touch paler than before. His green eyes were dark with an unreadable emotion, his jaw taut and his nostrils flared.

Before I could ask him what was wrong, the healer said, "Your turn, prince."

Fenn pushed off the wardrobe, his steps steady despite the arrow still lodged in his flesh.

"Lie on your good side, please," said Healer Warren.

Fenn nodded, his gaze steely with determination. With a grunt, he eased himself onto the bed, his right side up. Blood gushed from the wound, staining the sheets.

I swallowed hard, unease churning in my gut. But I forced myself to watch. If he could witness my healing, then I could do the same.

"I will need to break the shaft first," the healer explained. "Then, I will remove it entirely and stop the blood flow before you bleed out."

"That would be much appreciated," Fenn said with a snort.

In spite of the situation, my mouth twitched into a smile. Trust Fenn to make light of his dire circumstances.

The healer ignored his joke and continued, "It will be quite painful, but I urge you to remain as still as possible while I stitch the wound. Once the wound is closed, I can quicken your healing, but if you are dead, my magic can do nothing."

"Noted," Fenn muttered.

"If you wish, your fiancée can hold your hand."

I choked on a laugh, then disguised it as a cough. Fenn uttered a low groan that sounded a lot like a wheezing chuckle.

I cleared my throat. "Ah, I don't—I'm sure he's perfectly capable—"

"Oh, but dearest, I *want* you to be by my side," Fenn said, his eyes sparkling with mirth. "With your hand in mine, I know I can endure this. In sickness and in health, remember? This will be great practice for us."

I covered my mouth, but I couldn't stifle the loud and unladylike snort that erupted from me. Healer Warren wrinkled his nose in disapproval, but Fenn buried his face in the pillows, his shoulders shaking. He tensed, then turned his head to swear loudly as the motion no doubt exacerbated his injury.

My face was on fire as I came to the opposite side of the bed and knelt next to it, taking Fenn's clammy hand within mine.

With labored breathing, Fenn turned his weary gaze on me, his eyes hooded. "I hope you don't have a weak stomach, *beloved*."

"I just had a chunk of my flesh torn out by a bloodthirsty goblin and endured the healer stitching the wound back together," I said dryly. "I think I can handle it."

"Ah, but my bride has such a delicate constitution," Fenn said, patting my hand as Healer Warren approached, leaning over Fenn to inspect the arrow.

My grip on his fingers became a tight vise, and he sucked in a sharp breath. "Oh, forgive me," I said in my gentlest princess voice. "I am only preparing you for the intense pain you are about to experience." I squeezed tighter.

"Very thoughtful of you, dear one," Fenn said, his voice strained.

With a loud *snap*, the healer broke the arrow shaft, and Fenn howled in agony, his grip on my own fingers tightening.

"Brace yourself, prince," Healer Warren said in a brisk voice, then yanked the shaft from Fenn's shoulder.

Fenn cried out, his body jerking violently.

"Hold him still!" Healer Warren bellowed over Fenn's screams.

Fenn started thrashing on the bed. Blood gushed from his wound, pouring onto the sheets. All I could do was stare, the blood draining from my face in horror.

"*Now*, Your Highness!" Healer Warren barked.

His sharp tone jolted me from my stunned stupor. Without thinking, I climbed onto the bed alongside Fenn and wrapped my leg around his to hold him steady. I clutched his face between my hands, forcing his frenzied eyes to meet mine.

"Look at me, Fennick," I said. "*Look at me*, dammit!"

His green eyes found mine, and his body went still, but I could feel him quivering beneath me.

"You are stronger than this," I told him. "Focus on me. My leg is wrapped around yours in quite a scandalous manner. I know you will tease me relentlessly for it later. And I snorted earlier. I have no doubt you will enjoy tormenting me over that as well."

Recognition stirred in his gaze, but his face was still clammy, his expression slack with shock.

"I have freckles," I blurted, knowing I sounded absolutely insane. But I uttered the first thing that came to mind. "Can you count them all? Gigi tells me the number changes every day. One day she counted fifty on my face. Another, there were only twenty."

Fenn's breath hitched. He grunted, his body twitching as Healer Warren worked on sewing the wound up. Fenn licked his lips, then said hoarsely, "Gigi?"

"Giselle. My sister. She's sixteen. And I miss her terribly."

Fenn's eyes remained fixed on mine. I wasn't sure why, but I kept talking. I needed to distract him, so I babbled the first things that came to my mind. "She would adore you. Her greatest ambition is to marry the most gorgeous royal in the realm."

"Are you… calling me gorgeous?"

"I'm saying she would overlook your appalling behavior and rakish reputation in favor of your good looks."

His eyes crinkled with amusement. "So you *do* find me handsome."

My cheeks heated. "Perhaps. Not right now, though. Right now you look like a corpse."

He wheezed, but I touched his good shoulder to keep him still. "No laughing. You'll ruin Healer Warren's hard work."

"I didn't know you had a sense of humor, little firebird."

"Of course I do. You just never give me an opportunity to show you everything I have to offer."

"Or perhaps you're too busy hating me to find my jokes funny."

The words were playful, but his tone was serious. He held my gaze, and I couldn't look away. I was painfully aware of my hand still pressed against his cheek.

I swallowed. "I don't hate you."

He huffed in disbelief.

I rolled my eyes. "All right, I *strongly dislike* you." Healer Warren tugged on the thread, and Fenn's body twitched again. My eyes flicked to the healer, then back to the prince, and I remembered we were supposed to be engaged. I quickly added, "Well, I did before. But of course, now that we are betrothed, it would only be appropriate for my feelings for you to… change."

"And have they?" Fenn's eyes burned into mine.

My throat was so dry. I considered my words carefully. "Regardless of who my fiancé was or what kingdom he came from, yes, I would strive for fond feelings to ensure an amicable marriage."

To my surprise, Fenn chuckled. "You make marriage sound so *boring.*"

"Well, we hardly knew each other when we got engaged," I said. "We still hardly know each other."

"I've done scandalous things with complete strangers," Fenn said smugly. "So you can only imagine what unspeakable things I could do to you, fair princess. Especially on our wedding night. That is anything but boring."

Now my face was on fire. "And what if I said I wanted to wait until then?"

"Then I would laugh, because I certainly can't wait. Your body is too irresistible to me. To wait the duration of our engagement would be torture for me. And you wouldn't want to torture your dear fiancé, would you?"

Your body is irresistible to me. Fenn couldn't lie.

My heart twisted in my chest, but I forced myself to respond. I doubted Healer Warren was paying much attention, but just in case he was, we had a ruse to maintain. "I certainly wouldn't."

THE MIDNIGHT PRINCE

I wasn't sure when, but at some point, I lost consciousness. The last thing I remembered was Aurelia, with that endearing blush tinting her cheeks, flirting with me.

The ruthless Summer Princess… flirting with *me*.

Surely, I was delusional.

When I woke, darkness surrounded me, save for a dying oil lamp in the corner of the room. With a groan, I sat up, blinking to allow my eyes to adjust. The mattress dipped from my movement, and I ran my hand along the fresh sheets. Someone had changed them while I was unconscious. Which was a good thing, since I had thoroughly stained them with my blood.

"Aurelia?"

From across the room, a soft grunt sounded, followed by shuffling and the creaking of floorboards. I squinted as a dark shape rose from the floor and hobbled toward me.

"You're awake." Aurelia's voice was groggy from sleep.

I frowned. "Stars, Aurelia, were you sleeping *on the floor*?"

She groaned and rubbed her face. Her hair looked burnt orange in the fading light, a tangled mess around her head. A blanket was wrapped around her shoulders. "I wasn't about to climb into bed with you when you were unconscious from your injuries. What kind of person do you think I am?"

"I think you're a princess who isn't accustomed to sleeping on hard wood floors."

She rolled her eyes. "You were the one who insisted we share a room."

I sat up, then instantly regretted it as a rush of dizziness clouded my mind. I raised a hand to my head to steady myself and closed my eyes.

"What are you doing?" Aurelia snapped, pressing down on my uninjured shoulder to guide me back down on the mattress. "You need to rest."

"I'm fine. The healer sped up my recovery. It only aches a little bit."

"Right," Aurelia said doubtfully. "So, if you stand up right now, you won't sway at all? I won't have to catch you before you collapse into a pathetic heap on the floor?"

I let out a short laugh. "Gods, you really know how to flatter a man, Aurelia."

"Go back to sleep, Fenn."

"I can't sleep if you're just going to lie down on the floor. I'm a gentleman."

She snorted. "Not from what I've heard."

My eyes snapped to hers. "What have you heard?"

"The staff is whispering about you. They remember your… proclivities from the last time you were here."

A crooked grin spread across my face. "Ah, yes. Well, we were not very quiet when we stayed here."

Aurelia wrinkled her nose. "You are disgusting."

"Hmm, that's not what the barmaid thought."

Aurelia tugged the blanket more securely around herself. "Well, if you're all right, then I'm going back to sleep. Stay awake, if you must, but I'm tired."

She turned away from me, but I caught her wrist. "I'm serious, Aurelia. Take the bed."

"You can't sleep on the floor!"

"Why not?"

"Because you're injured."

"*Was* injured. Besides, you sustained injuries, too. I could make the same argument for *you* to take the bed."

"You may call yourself a gentleman, but I am a lady, and I would never—"

"Fine," I said, scooting to the other side of the bed. "Then we'll share."

Her mouth fell open. "I will not—"

"The bed is big enough for us both."

"Gods, do you ever stop? Does it ever exhaust you, this constant need to lure women into your bed?"

"I'm not trying to lure you. I'm in too much pain and far too tired to try, even if I wanted to seduce you."

She shook her head. "This would be completely inappropriate."

"Aurelia."

She exhaled in exasperation. Even in the darkness, I could make out a faint blush creeping into her cheeks.

"We're sharing a room," I said slowly. "Everyone will presume we'll be engaging in... certain activities. I'm not asking you to do anything with me tonight. Despite what you might think of me, I *am* a gentleman, and I would never try to coerce someone who wasn't willing. We both need the rest. This will be completely innocent. I swear it."

She hesitated, her lips pressing together tightly. After a long moment, she said softly, "Very well."

I scooted farther until I was curled up on the edge of the bed. The mattress dipped as Aurelia sank onto it, still rolled up in her blanket. She positioned herself on the very edge, lying on her back and staring at the ceiling. The bed was so large that we didn't even touch. I inched closer to the middle.

She stiffened. "What are you doing?"

"Ensuring I don't fall off the edge in my sleep."

She nodded, but her form didn't relax. I looked her over, noting the set of her jaw and the way her arms were tucked tightly against her chest.

"You know I would never hurt you, right?" I asked. Something twisted in my gut at the sight of her like this, and I couldn't bear it. This fierce, stubborn, infuriating princess seemed as helpless as a child right now.

She licked her lips. "I don't know you, Fenn. So, no, I don't know that."

"I swore in a bargain."

"Yes, well, that wouldn't stop you from trying, would it?"

"Trying to hurt you?"

"Trying to..." She trailed off, her mouth clamping shut.

A knot formed in my throat. Oh, gods. "Aurelia, did someone—"

"Good night, Fenn."

"Aurelia."

Her head whipped toward me, her eyes blazing. "I said good night. We don't know each other. And I sure as hell don't owe you any explanations. Now stop talking so I can fall asleep."

Well then. The feisty princess had returned. In truth, it was a relief to see her like this because she seemed more like herself when she was angry with me.

"Did you know we have a glowing river in the Star Court?" I asked.

Aurelia's brows furrowed. "What?" Her tone was still clipped.

"It's called the Celestial River. It glows because over centuries, stardust has collected at the bottom. We've harvested much of it, but over the years, the substance has embedded itself in the rocks and soil within the ground."

"Why are you telling me this?"

"Because the waterfall you took me to—"

"Kellen Falls."

"Yes, that place. I felt a sense of peace while I was there. Something I've only ever felt next to the Celestial River. I thought it was a connection between me and the land. *My* land. The home of my blood and my ancestors. It felt right to be bonded to the place of my heritage. But when I saw that waterfall, the river surrounding it, the canopy of trees, and the mountain… Well, it startled me how much it felt like home. Even though your court is completely different from mine."

Aurelia was silent for a long moment, but I noted that her shoulders had relaxed and her breathing had slowed. After a long moment, she said, "Maybe you are just very fond of rivers."

I laughed. "Maybe. But I wonder if you'll feel something similar when you see the Celestial River."

Her eyes turned contemplative, her gaze still fixed on the ceiling. "It does sound rather incredible," she admitted. "A glowing river, I mean. I'll bet it looks even more enchanting at night with all the stars."

"Why do you think we have a weekly celebration? It's our opportunity to express our love and gratitude for the land the gods have given us."

She took a deep breath. "We don't have anything like that."

"You don't?"

"No. We have the Summer Solstice ball, and the occasional festival, but that's it."

"Then however did you become such a terrific dancer?"

She laughed lightly. "So, you admit it? My skills are impressive?"

"Better than many of the ladies I've danced with," I said. "Though still not quite as impressive as my own skills."

She snorted. "Of course not."

"If you don't have very many balls or celebrations, then how did you learn to dance so well? And how have you maintained those skills?"

She shifted, nudging closer to the center of the bed. When her elbow brushed my arm, she sucked in a breath and drew her arms over her chest again. I hurried to think of a question to ask to distract her, but then she spoke. "My father wanted a son. He was a soldier, trained from birth to protect his kingdom and fight the enemy no matter the cost. He wanted to train a son in the same way, to teach him to wield his sword alongside his people. When he only had daughters, he sought to teach us in the same way, but it wasn't what he expected. It was... difficult at first. For me and Gigi. We did not like the training exercises he put us through. And we often begged for Father to relent, to stop trying to mold us into the children he wanted us to be."

She swallowed and took a shaky breath. "It was harder on my sister, I think. She so desperately wanted Father to love her. For me, though, I could tell Father would never love us the way we loved him. He is distant. Not unkind, but not affectionate either. Not like Mother."

Aurelia shifted again, and her shoulder pressed into mine. But this time, she didn't move. And neither did I. I held my breath, waiting for her to continue.

"Eventually, Mother stepped in," she continued. "She urged us to find an aspect of training that we could enjoy. Gigi chose archery. She loves the bow and arrow, and Father couldn't have been more proud. But I could never find a weapon I liked. So, I turned to dance. I found an instructor who taught me how to move my body with fluid grace, and then our trainer utilized those movements so I could use them in battle.

"Father wasn't pleased at first. I think he was disappointed that I couldn't share his interest in weaponry and military training. But, after a year, I showed him my skills, and we sparred." A slow grin spread across her face. "And I bested him for the first time."

I huffed in surprise. "You bested the *king*?"

"I did," she said smugly. "After that, he realized the benefit of my training. It caught him off guard, and it would likely do the same for my opponents in battle."

I frowned and nodded. "That's… rather admirable."

She turned to look at me, her eyes glowing in the lamplight. "What is?"

"You. Finding something you love and incorporating it into what you're expected to do. Knowing what I know about you, I would have predicted you would dig in your heels and downright refuse to train if it was something you didn't want to. But instead, you found a different way. A unique way. Something that could please both sides. It's… very diplomatic."

Her eyebrows lifted, her lips parting in surprise. After a long moment, she forced a laugh and said, "Prince Fenn, are you saying I'll make a good queen?"

I blew out a breath through my lips. "Well, let's not entertain such outrageous thoughts. You are still a feral dragon keeper, after all."

She chuckled, and a strange sense of warmth filled my chest at the sound.

"Can I ask you something?" I said.

"You just did."

I barked out a laugh and rolled on my good side to face her. "You said to Dreya that we would be announcing ourselves to the Autumn Court."

Aurelia sighed, her gaze still fixed on the ceiling, her hands clasped atop her stomach. Ever the demure princess, even when sharing a bed with her enemy after sustaining severe injuries from a goblin attack. "I don't know why I said it," she admitted. "It seemed like a good idea at the time. We need people to believe our engagement is real, and two neighboring royals traveling through a kingdom would announce themselves in other circumstances. I didn't want Autumn to be offended if they found out we passed through their domain without paying respects."

I hummed, my eyebrows raised. Impressive. "Like I said—very diplomatic. But we didn't plan for this."

"I know. But it will be good practice for us. For when we must put on a show for your court. We won't know as many people here, so if we slip up, the consequences shouldn't be too severe."

I snorted. "You don't know Autumn Court, then. Bunch of nasty gossips."

"I know Autumn Court just fine," Aurelia snapped, her tone icy.

I stilled, then looked her over. Her shoulders were rigid once more, her arms wrapped around her chest.

Oh, shit. What had happened to her? Had it been someone from the Autumn Court? "Aurelia…"

"Good night, Fenn." She rolled on her side away from me.

"*Aurelia.*"

She switched off the oil lamp, plunging the room in complete darkness. I huffed in part amusement, part frustration. But the princess had blocked me out. After a few moments of tense silence, I rolled onto my back and muttered, "Good night."

THE SUMMER PRINCESS

MY DREAMS WERE PLAGUED BY MEMORIES I HAD BURIED DEEP, HOPING TO never have to face again.

First, my encounter with the witches. Now, the Autumn Court. I couldn't escape my past, no matter how much I tried.

And Fenn... Gods, he was insufferable. And far too curious for his own good. He noticed my discomfort. It wouldn't take him long to figure it out, especially once we announced ourselves at court.

What a stupid, foolish decision I'd made. The *last* thing I wanted to do was visit the Autumn Court.

But relations with them were delicate, especially after ending my engagement with their prince. If they heard from someone else that I was getting married, it could drive a wedge between our kingdoms and shatter our precarious alliance.

When my eyes opened, registering the faint fuchsia and amber glows of sunrise filtering through the curtains, I found myself encased in warmth. It pressed close to my skin, wrapping me in a cocoon of pine and mint and the fresh scent of waterfalls.

"Mmm." I burrowed further into the warmth.

Only to realize it wasn't a blanket or fur.

It was a person.

Fenn.

My eyes flared wide, and my breaths turned to sharp gasps. The foggy remnants of my mind now burned with sudden, blinding clarity.

Fenn's arm was wrapped around me, tucking me against his chest. One leg had draped over mine.

I was effectively trapped in his embrace.

Oh, gods. This couldn't be happening. How had I allowed this to happen?

Damn Fenn and his bedmates. He was likely used to curling up with another woman in the middle of the night. I gritted my teeth and carefully grasped his fingers, then lifted his arm and placed it gingerly along his side.

He didn't even stir.

I exhaled, then wriggled closer to the edge of the mattress. His leg shifted, and he grunted in his sleep, turning his head to bury his nose in my hair. He inhaled, then hummed something incoherent, his breath tickling me and sending prickles dancing over my skin. His leg tightened over mine, pressing himself directly into my side.

Pressing something *else* directly into my side. Something hard.

Closing my eyes, I felt a blush creeping along my cheeks. Burning suns, now was not the time.

Ignoring Fenn's legs—and other parts—I rolled until I flopped off the bed, barely catching myself before I collapsed in a heap on the floor. I straightened and faced the bed, my face on fire, as I expected Fenn to wake from my movement and berate me with ridicule and flirtatious remarks.

But he didn't. He murmured something in his sleep, then clutched a pillow against his chest in the same position he'd had me in.

In spite of my embarrassing situation, I found myself smiling. In his sleep, he seemed like nothing more than a lovable puppy who wanted to cuddle.

And he talked in his sleep. I couldn't make anything out, but I logged that information away for later.

Once I'd escaped the bed, I allowed myself to study the prince a bit longer. He had the thickest eyelashes I had ever seen, and they fanned out against his tan skin. His jaw was slack, his mouth slightly open as he breathed deeply.

He seemed so peaceful. Blood still stained his chin and neck, and most of his clothes. His shoulder was bandaged heavily. But with the way he was stretched out so carelessly, one would think he hadn't been injured at all.

Shaking all thoughts of the prince from my mind, I made quick work of peeling off my blood-stained garments. The copper tub on the opposite side of the room was already filled with steaming water, and I slid into it with a sigh of contentment. I kept glancing at Fenn on the bed, but he didn't stir, so I took my time detangling my hair and washing the grime from my body.

It took me the better part of an hour to scrub the blood out of my hair, but thankfully Fenn snored through the entire ordeal, and I hadn't had to worry about him seeing me naked.

As soon as I stepped out of the tub, it refilled itself with steaming water in preparation of Fenn's needs. Water gushed in as if from an invisible spigot, steam floating above it. The sound of the water hitting metal made me think of Kellen Falls again, and I recalled how Fenn had confessed the place had felt like home to him.

The thought was both comforting and alarming. I was touched that this man felt so at peace in a place I loved. But at the same time, I was unsettled by the fact that we had something in common. He was the Midnight Prince. My enemy. A royal from a kingdom that rarely saw sunlight.

We were so different. Opposites, in fact. We couldn't—*shouldn't*—share a common interest. It made no sense.

I dressed myself in a simple gown of elegant burgundy silk, courtesy of the magical cottage that anticipated our needs. It also somehow knew I didn't have a lady's maid to help me dress, and the thin fabric was easy for me to button myself, despite my injuries.

The healer's magic was indeed astounding. There was only the dullest ache in my shoulder, as if I had pulled a muscle while training with Father weeks ago. I rolled my shoulder, marveling at the ease with which I could do so. Then I found myself staring into the mirror on the wall by the wardrobe. My skin was still pale, my freckles standing out starkly on my cheeks like sickly spots. My strawberry blond hair was finally clean, and it fell in wavy tresses down to my ribs.

Swallowing hard, I turned and slid my sleeve off my shoulder. A pink, jagged scar cut through my shoulder blade. I couldn't see it, but I knew the witch rune was there. I ran a finger over my scar, waiting to feel... something. I wasn't sure what. Warmth? Ridges over my skin? Some kind of indicator that there was magic infused in my flesh.

But there was nothing. Whoever had put the rune mark on me had been skilled. The spot didn't look or feel different from any other part of my body.

With a sigh, I slid my sleeve back into place, then twisted my hair into a messy braid that draped over my injured shoulder. The gown was sheer, and though the sleeves draped past my elbows, the neckline cut low, and the dress exposed a large portion of my back. If I shifted a certain way, the scar would be visible.

And so would the rune. At least, to anyone who was able to see it.

Like Fenn.

I frowned, glancing at his unconscious form still sprawled on the bed. His untidy chestnut hair had flopped over one eye, and one small point of his fae ear was visible from underneath.

The Midnight Prince was an enigma. He was a flirt and a rake, that was for certain. But he also dabbled in witch magic and befriended dragons and had enough compassion to distract me with anecdotes of his home when he noticed I was in distress.

I wasn't sure what to make of him.

Fenn groaned and rolled over in his sleep, and I quickly turned away before he caught me staring. He grunted, then swore loudly, hissing in pain when he no doubt exacerbated his wound.

I smirked and faced him once more. "Good morning, dearest."

He blinked sleepily at me, his green eyes clouded and incoherent. "Morning, little firebird." His voice was low and throaty and made my stomach do dangerous things. I clasped my hands behind my back, reminding myself that however handsome he was or however delicious his husky voice sounded, he was still… well, Fenn. Nothing but trouble.

Fenn squinted at me, looking me over slowly and deliberately. "You are dressed."

"I am."

He groaned again and sat up, then winced. "And I am not."

"Excellent observations. You are quite astute."

Half his mouth quirked in a devilish grin. "And you are quite lovely. Especially in that… stunning gown." He looked me over again, and I was painfully aware of how much of my chest was exposed. I resisted the urge to cross my arms over myself once more.

He seemed to realize he was staring, and he dropped his gaze and cleared his throat. "I mean to say… you look the part of a princess and a devoted fiancée."

"Thank you."

"I should probably dress as well." He lifted an arm and sniffed, then recoiled. "Gods, that's foul. I apologize for subjecting you to my filth all night."

I chuckled and waved a hand. "We were both filthy, Fenn. I've already washed."

"Well, I must… I should…" He sighed, then rubbed his eyes.

I found myself grinning. "Why, Prince Fenn, are you *bashful* in the mornings?"

He rubbed a hand down his face. "It just takes a moment for my brain to wake up, that's all." He dropped his hand with an exasperated sigh. "As soon as I get out of this bed, I will completely undress so I can bathe. Either you can assist me, or you can make yourself scarce, but the choice is yours."

Dammit. My cheeks heated, and I dropped my gaze, unable to find my voice. Now *I* was the bashful one.

I inhaled deeply, trying to clear my head instead of focusing on the image of Fenn naked.

Naked and wounded. Recovering from severe injuries.

Injuries he sustained from fighting by my side. Protecting me. All with an arrow embedded in his shoulder.

I thought of how he had ordered those goblins to stop attacking me, and they had. How the very ground had seemed to shake from the power of his words.

An image of the blazing blue fire that consumed the goblins filled my mind.

We still hadn't discussed what had happened. And I wasn't sure I wanted to. I didn't want to consider what kind of volatile power flowed through my veins—lethal enough to incinerate a clan of goblins.

But Fenn was keeping secrets, too. He had some kind of magic that had stopped the goblins from feasting on my flesh.

I needed answers. I had to find out what his fae magic could do, and I had to know the extent of my own powers as well.

One thing was for certain: I wouldn't get any answers by hiding.

Lifting my chin, I looked Fenn straight in the eye and said, "I'm not going anywhere."

He blinked at me, his eyes flaring wide for a moment before a smirk spread across his lips.

Before he could say anything scandalous that would likely make my cheeks turn even redder, I strode toward him and whipped the blanket off him. He jerked from the motion, then winced, rubbing his shoulder.

"Why do I get the feeling you will *not* be gentle?" he grumbled.

"Oh, does the poor, pampered prince want someone to coddle him?" I teased. "You're stronger than that, Fenn."

His head whipped toward me, his eyes narrowing slightly. Confusion, surprise, and some other emotion I couldn't place flitted across his features. "Perhaps you're right," he said, his voice soft and contemplative.

I looked at him, assessing the rigid set of his jaw and the determination blazing in his eyes. I had only been joking, but perhaps there was a truth to my words that he didn't often let himself see. Despite his flirtations and romantic exploits and cavalier attitude that aggravated me so, he did have a strength about him that I hadn't expected. And perhaps those around him were so used to him making light of situations that they didn't often see it.

Perhaps he didn't see it too often, either.

Fenn eased off the bed, letting his legs dangle off the edge. He groaned, his face paling as he shifted. I extended a hand to help him up, but he ignored me, rising from the bed and swaying slightly before striding toward the tub.

"Do you want me to—" I offered, feeling uncomfortable.

"No," Fenn said, his voice uncharacteristically stern. "I'll do it." With his good arm, he unbuckled his trousers and let them fall to the floor.

Burning suns, my face was on fire. His tunic covered most of him, but his bare, muscular legs were on full display. My mouth felt like sandpaper as I watched him step out of his trousers and tug at the hem of his tunic.

Oh gods, oh gods. I swallowed hard and found myself moving toward him, desperate to help, to busy myself with something other than gawking at this injured man as he undressed in front of me.

"I don't need help," he argued.

"Shut up," I snapped. "I'll still let you do it, but I'll wager getting your wounded arm through your sleeve will be more difficult on your own."

He scowled but made no further objections. His good arm was free first, and I carefully eased it over his other arm, avoiding the injury as best I could before freeing his body from the stained, bloody garment. I let it fall to the floor, then turned away from him, refusing to let my gaze stray toward his bare chest. Instead, I bustled through the drawers of the wardrobe and found various healing balms and ointments, plus lavender-scented bathing soap.

"Are you going to bathe me?" Fenn asked, and I was relieved to hear a mocking lilt to his voice. It meant he was more like his normal self again.

"Would you prefer I call an attendant?" I asked. "I'm sure Dreya has someone available."

Fenn was quiet for a long while before he muttered, "No. But I'm perfectly capable of washing myself."

I snorted. "Are you? With that wound in your shoulder, it will be hard for you to use both hands."

"The wound is healed."

"No, the healing has only been quickened. It still hurts, doesn't it?"

His silence was answer enough.

I pretended to keep looking through the wardrobe for supplies as I heard him move behind me. Then, a light splash sounded, indicating he'd gotten in the tub.

I exhaled, my chest loosening, before I turned to him with several bottles in my hands. He was fully submerged, and he groaned in pleasure as he slid so low that only his head and the tops of his shoulders were visible.

"Gods, that feels good." His voice was low and husky again, and gods above, I couldn't *think* knowing he was completely naked under that water and making sounds like that.

"You have blood in your hair," I blurted.

He raised an eyebrow at me. "Yes. I fought goblins yesterday, you know."

"I can wash it out for you."

He chuckled. "You are quite hospitable today, aren't you, darling?"

I rolled my eyes and moved closer to him, setting the bottles down on the small table next to the tub. I squirted a bit of lavender soap on my palm before running it through his hair. Despite what we'd been through, his hair was still soft and thick. It was matted and tangled and sticky with blood and sweat, but it was still soft.

Fenn cleared his throat, fidgeting as I weaved my fingers through his hair. "You know, this is ridiculous," he said, the words coming out in a rush. "You had a goblin take a bite of your shoulder, and *you* still managed to bathe yourself."

I found myself smiling. "Yes, but I didn't have the goblin's teeth pierce all the way through my shoulder to the other side and then continue fighting through the injury, making it worse."

He scoffed. "Are you scolding me? If I *hadn't* kept fighting—"

"I know," I said softly. "We both would have died. As much as it pains me to say it… you saved my life yesterday, Fenn. I couldn't have fought them without you."

He said nothing. For a few moments, silence fell between us as I worked my fingers gently through the tangles in his hair. The act was so intimate that I felt my face burning again. I was *bathing* this man, this prince. He was naked in a tub in front of me and I was lathering soap in his hair.

I abruptly dropped my hands, letting soap drip onto my skirts. "Should be ready to rinse now." My voice was strained, and I cleared my throat.

Fenn didn't seem to notice. He took a breath, then slid into the depths of the tub. He lingered for so long underwater that I worried I would have to pull him back up. At long last, he resurfaced with a gasp and shook his wet tresses out of his face with a grin. "That was quite pleasant."

I rolled my eyes. "You are a child."

"Will you be applying soap to my *entire* body, little firebird?" He cast a dark and heady glance my way, which I dutifully ignored.

"I will wash your right side, but that is all. The rest you can reach with your uninjured arm."

He chuckled, and I forced my thoughts to distance themselves from the task at hand. Instead of dwelling on the fact that Fenn was naked in this tub, and my fingers would be roaming across the expanse of his skin, I thought of the last book I had read. It was a mystical tale of a dark plague that had befallen a kingdom of elves.

After a steadying breath, I poured soap onto my hands and knelt by the tub. I felt Fenn's eyes on me, but I stared at the soap as I rubbed my palms together, forming bubbles.

The elven king sought out the help of the wise enchantress to banish the plague from the land, I recalled, focusing on the words from the pages I'd read last week. Gods, had it only been last week that I was reading in the library, with Gigi pestering me to go riding?

Knots formed in my stomach, but I pushed them away and dived into the elven kingdom I had been so eager to read about.

All magic has a price, the enchantress told him.

"Aurelia?" Fenn asked, jolting me from my thoughts.

I realized I was kneeling next to him, my soapy hands poised mid-air. I must have looked quite foolish, sitting there utterly frozen.

"Raise your arm, please," I said quietly.

Fenn obeyed, lifting his uninjured arm out of the water. I methodically began scrubbing the grime and blood from his skin while recalling the details of my book.

Name your price, the elven king had said. The enchantress had told him the plague had been created by a dark curse enacted through a blood sacrifice. A life had been given to bring about the plague. And a life would have to be given to end it.

"This is the most serious bath I've ever taken," Fenn said.

I looked at him and found his amused eyes fixed on me. Only then did I realize my brows were furrowed, my jaw set with determination. I probably looked ridiculous, so stoically focused on keeping my mind clear of distractions.

"My thoughts are elsewhere," I said, which was entirely the truth.

"Oh? What are you thinking of?"

My soapy fingers glided up his arm, and he tensed when I reached the tender spot underneath his shoulder.

"A book," I said.

"What kind of book?"

"Something I read last week. It's about elves and curses."

"Oh."

I arched an eyebrow at him. "What kind of book were you thinking of?"

Fenn grinned. "Something scandalous that you would only be reading in the privacy of your own bedchambers."

"Gods, do you ever stop? You are utterly incorrigible."

"Incorrigible? Or irresistible?"

I only sighed, working the soap into his shoulder and then down the left side of his chest. When I reached just below his ribs, he jerked wildly, then snorted.

I stilled, my eyes growing wide. "What was that?"

"Sorry." He snickered again. "Ticklish."

My mouth quirked into a smile. "You're *ticklish*?"

"What's so unbelievable about that?"

"Oh, nothing… if you're ten years old."

"You mean to tell me there isn't a single spot where you are ticklish?" He gave me a flat look of disbelief.

I swished my soapy hands in the water to rinse the soap off and met his stare with my own. "That is something I never intend for you to find out."

His eyes glittered. "Mmm, good. I do love a challenge." His pupils flared, and for a moment, the vibrant green of his eyes seemed to burn, making my skin boil and my blood sing. Heat flooded my face, and my lips parted. He was sitting up in the tub, leaning toward me, so close I could see the droplets of water running down his throat and disappearing down his chest.

I stood so abruptly that my hands splashed water onto the floor. "Your left side is clean," I muttered quickly before wiping my wet hands on my skirts. "I'll see about getting us some breakfast while you finish up."

"Aurelia—"

Before he could say anything else, I slipped out the door, letting it snap shut behind me. For a moment, I leaned against it, focusing on calming my erratic pulse and steadying my breathing. My eyes closed, and my thoughts returned to the book I'd been thinking about.

I will do it, the elven king said. To save my people, I will give my life to end this plague.

The enchantress had nodded solemnly. So be it, she said.

My eyes opened, and I set my lips into a grim line. For a moment, I'd forgotten why I was here—why I was tethered to this infuriating prince in the first place.

My people were in danger. And just like the elven king from the story I'd been reading, I would do whatever it took to save them.

Nothing—not Fenn or his naked body or his lewd jokes—would distract me from that.

The Midnight Prince

I couldn't shake the feel of Aurelia's soft fingers weaving through my hair or dancing over the tenderest part of my abdomen.

As I finished bathing and dressing, my movements clumsy as I avoided stretching my right arm too much, all I could think of was how I yearned for her to return. If she saw me half dressed, it would rattle her, and that endearing blush would spread across her face.

I didn't know why I enjoyed it so much. Over the years, I'd been with plenty of women. Aurelia hadn't shown the least bit of interest in me.

But perhaps that was why I craved it so much. As I said to her, I enjoyed a challenge.

I shook my head, cursing under my breath as I fumbled with the buttons of my shirt. This was foolishness. Once our bargain was complete, we would likely never see each other again. Our kingdoms would be on better terms, but that didn't have to mean anything.

We would part ways. Because, to her, I would always be the enemy prince.

I exhaled a harsh breath through my teeth, turning to inspect my appearance in the mirror. The tunic and coat were simple; certainly not the elegance I was accustomed to. But the soft fabric was soothing against my skin, and it was surprisingly comfortable.

I would take comfort over elegance. With a smirk, I glanced at the wardrobe. This cottage *did* seem to understand exactly what I needed. The belt at my trousers even had a strap for my short sword.

When I was fully dressed, I left the room and made my way down the hallway. Voices echoed, and a woman's high-pitched laugh rang out. I followed the sounds until I found Aurelia and Dreya taking tea in the sitting room. A plate of biscuits and scones sat on the table between the two sofas.

"Your Highness!" Dreya immediately rose and fell into a quick curtsy.

"Please," I said, lifting my hand. "You have taken such good care of us in our time of need. You don't need to curtsy, and you certainly don't need to refer to me as *Your Highness*. Fenn will do."

Dreya blushed and wrung her hands together, then shot an uncertain glance toward Aurelia, who lifted her eyebrows. "Oh, I couldn't possibly…" Dreya mumbled.

"Then Prince Fenn."

Dreya nodded once, her lips pressing together in a thin line.

"Don't stop on my account," I said, gesturing to the plate of pastries before sliding onto the cushion next to Aurelia. The sofa was small, and my arm and leg pressed against hers.

She stiffened for a brief moment, then relaxed against me as she no doubt remembered our ruse. She placed a hand on my knee and said, "I've sent word to the Autumn Court of our upcoming arrival. They should be expecting us before dusk."

"Excellent." With my uninjured arm, I reached for a blueberry scone and took a bite. Warmth flooded my tongue, and the sugared fruit tasted divine. I took another bite and groaned with satisfaction. "This is quite good."

"Hallie is the best baker in the realm," Dreya said proudly.

Aurelia nodded her agreement. "She certainly is."

"Well, be sure to give her my compliments," I said, licking the sugar from my fingers. With my other hand, I clasped Aurelia's fingers in mine, then brought the back of her hand to my lips and brushed a kiss against it.

Aurelia's cheeks flushed, her eyes flashing with irritation. I only smirked at her. "Did you sleep well, my love?" I murmured, my lips still on her hand.

She took a slow, deep breath before batting her eyelashes at me and offering a simpering smile that was anything but genuine. "How could I not? I was with you the entire night."

She turned away, withdrawing her hand as she took a biscuit. I frowned at her, noting that she hadn't answered my question. Would it have been a lie if she had said she had gotten a restful sleep? Had she been kept up by memories of whatever had happened to her to make her fear sharing a bed with me?

Dreya glanced uncertainly between us, and I smiled again before she suspected anything was amiss. "The room was lovely, Dreya. Thank you for your hospitality. I will tell everyone in my court that this is the inn to stay at."

"That's assuming anyone in your court will venture this way," Aurelia muttered between bites of her food.

"Why wouldn't they? With our union, the two courts will be allies. I'll wager we'll have many correspondences between our kingdoms."

Aurelia's lips tightened, and she lifted her teacup to her lips before taking a long sip. "We'll see," she whispered.

I scrutinized her, the rigid set of her jaw, the dark anger brewing in her gaze. Did she not believe that relations between our kingdoms would improve? Granted, once our false engagement ended, there would certainly be a strain. But she would get her stardust—and her people would be safe—and my kingdom would get a dragon. Surely, the benefits of our bargain would finally end the animosity between our courts.

Dreya cleared her throat, her shrewd eyes missing nothing. "Is there... a date set for the wedding?"

I leaned forward conspiratorially. "Between you and me, we haven't officially announced it yet. But rest assured that news of a royal engagement like ours will be shouted from the rooftops, and you'll be sure to know once arrangements have been made." The deception rolled easily off my tongue. I wasn't certain how deeply into our ruse we would go. Aurelia and I hadn't agreed to officially announce a wedding date, so I didn't want to make false promises. Not when my fae blood prevented me from lying.

Dreya's face fell, and Aurelia leaned over the table to clasp her hands. "You will be more than welcome to attend. Perhaps we can even arrange for Hallie to bake something delicious for the ceremony."

Dreya's eyes lit up. "Oh, Your Highness, that would be the greatest honor!"

Aurelia smiled and took another sip of her tea, the icy rage in her eyes dimming slightly.

. . .

Dreya had Hallie bake us an extra batch of scones and biscuits for the road and insisted we take a pair of horses as well. Aurelia would only accept the kindness if Dreya allowed us to reimburse her for them. The innkeeper stammered her thanks, but she took the gold, and the relief on Aurelia's face told me just how guilty she felt about taking advantage of the woman's hospitality. Before midday, we set off, each saddled on our own horse. We kept to the main road, keeping a light, easy pace as we rode in silence.

I watched Aurelia as her distant gaze remained fixed ahead, as if she was trying not to look at me. She absently traced the marking on her knuckle from our bargain. I had an identical one on mine as well, but it was difficult to see on my tan skin.

"Why do you often come to that inn?" I asked her.

Aurelia took a moment before answering. "Wouldn't you want to return to a cottage that can anticipate your needs?"

"That doesn't answer my question."

"I'm not obligated to answer your question."

My eyes narrowed at her. "What's the matter with you? Did I do something to offend you?"

She scoffed. "*Everything* you do offends me, Fenn."

"I don't understand why you're being so hostile after—"

"After what? We shared a bed? I tended to your wounds? I scrubbed your injured body?" She shook her head, her lip curling in derision. "Don't think that just because we shared a few amicable moments together that that makes us friends. I just didn't want you bleeding out or slowing us down with an infection."

My stomach soured, and I found it difficult to swallow around the lump in my throat. "If there is something specific I have done that has caused you genuine pain, I'd like to know."

Aurelia exhaled, then turned to look at me, her blue eyes cold. "Why did you say that to Dreya? About relations between our courts?"

I frowned. "Why shouldn't I say that? Isn't that the point of our ruse?"

"Do you know what she could do with access to stardust? She could enhance the magic of the cottage. She could expand her business so that she isn't scraping by to make ends meet."

I snorted. "She hardly seems to be *scraping by*. I saw several other patrons there during our stay."

"Dammit, Fenn, that's not the point! Do you have any intention of sharing your wealth with other kingdoms, or is this all just a game to you?"

I glared at her. "That's rich, coming from you. How many dragons have you shared with other courts?"

Her nostrils flared. "That's different. Dragons are brilliant living creatures who don't deserve to be caged or—"

"And do you think we are merely sitting on a pile of unused stardust, laughing idly while the kingdoms around us waste away?"

"Of course not, but—"

"I *told* you stardust is scarce, and yet you still accuse me of hoarding it from other kingdoms? Gods, it's no wonder your court has no allies."

"What is that supposed to mean?" she snapped.

"It means your people have isolated themselves from other kingdoms for years, Aurelia. You've only brought this on yourself. You accuse me of not helping anyone, but what are *you* doing for the Realm of Valora? Have you done anything to assist another fae court besides your own? Anything at all?" I raised my eyebrows at her in a challenge.

Her cheeks reddened, and her nostrils flared. She opened her mouth, no doubt to argue with me, but then faltered. "I—" She stopped again, her mouth clamping shut. The blush on her face spread to her ears. "That's not—"

I only continued to raise my eyebrows at her, and though I tried not to look smug, the glare she threw at me told me I was failing.

At long last, she found her voice. "All anyone cares about are our dragons, Fenn. We tried to be civil. We tried inviting other kingdoms. But all they wanted was to steal from us."

"Are you sure it was theft? And not just kingdoms trying to barter?"

"Dragons are not *goods* to exchange!" she said hotly.

"Then trade them for other animals!" I shouted. "Other *people*, even, since you seem to care more about your damned dragons than anyone else. Offer to give a kingdom a dragon in exchange for a powerful fae warlock. Or in exchange for livestock that your people desperately need."

She scoffed and fixed her eyes on the road ahead, her gaze full of fire. "This is what's wrong with Valora, Fenn. Making exchanges as if these aren't intelligent beasts with souls."

"What the hell is the matter with you?" I couldn't hold in my rage any longer. How could this woman be so naive? *"That is how court works. Everything is an exchange. Even lives, even intelligent beasts with souls.* Gods, aren't you supposed to be a princess? Shouldn't you know these things? Haven't you been raised your entire life to make a marriage contract that would benefit your kingdom? You *are* a good to be exchanged. That is what you do for your people. How is it that you can auction off yourself to the highest bidder but you wouldn't dare do the same for your dragons? How is this any different? Are you not also a brilliant living creature who doesn't deserve to be caged?"

Her mouth opened, then closed as she looked at me. Her face was still flushed, but the ire in her expression had shifted to curiosity and confusion. For a long moment, nothing broke the silence between us save for the clopping of our horses' hooves.

"It shouldn't be this way," she said, her voice quiet.

"Well, it is," I bit out. "And if I hadn't been in your kingdom when the curse hit, you would have been in deep shit. Because I guarantee that no one in Valora would have bothered to come help you. Not with the way you've cut yourself off from the world."

Her eyes narrowed into slits. "You aren't blameless here, either, Fenn. We may have isolated ourselves, but you haven't done a damn thing to try to smooth relations between us, either. Your kingdom attacked and slaughtered my people, bringing war to both our kingdoms. *You* breached our borders. *You* shed first blood. Why the hell would you risk the innocent lives of your people like that? How selfish are you?"

A storm raged in my chest, and I found it hard to breathe. Red crept into the corners of my vision, and I knew if I spoke, I would say something we would both regret. So I stayed silent, trying to quiet the tumultuous emotions roaring inside me.

Aurelia snorted, as if she'd won the argument. "That's what I thought."

"Maybe we should just not speak to one another," I said, my voice tight. "I would much prefer that."

"Fine by me."

I nudged my horse into a trot, eager to quicken our pace and put an end to this wretched journey alongside such an unpleasant traveling companion.

THE SUMMER PRINCESS

It had been a few years since I'd traveled through the Autumn Court. The chill in the air raised goose flesh on my arms and made me shiver. The leaves shifted from a vibrant, lush green to amber, scarlet, and gold. The forest thinned, the sun filtering through the gaps in the trees left by the bare branches. Our silent journey was punctuated only by the crunching of leaves under our horses' hooves.

After an hour of enduring the brisk air nipping at my skin, I tersely informed Fenn I needed to stop at a modiste in Florien before we reached the royal sector. Although it had been a while since my last visit, I could still be easily recognized. Many people in the Autumn Court knew me. My visits had certainly not been discreet, especially considering that at one point, I had expected to become Queen of the Autumn Court.

The reminder slithered through me, accompanied by vile memories that made my stomach twist into knots so tightly it felt like my body was caving in on itself. Bones collapsing. Muscles shriveling. Blood draining. My body seemed to be disintegrating in that singular, terrifying moment.

My horse gave a loud snort, jolting me from my thoughts. I blinked, forcing myself to focus on the task at hand.

Get to the modiste. Put on my princess persona.

I refused to think about arriving within those palace walls I tried so hard to forget. No, I wouldn't dwell on that yet.

I traced the faint black marking surrounding my knuckle—a reminder of my bargain with Fenn.

But it was also a reminder of why I was doing this. For my family. For my people. For my kingdom. I thought of the laughter in Gigi's eyes, of her youth and innocence. She still had so many years of life left in her. I had to save her. I had to do this.

One step at a time. And right now, the first step was getting to the modiste.

The farther we journeyed, the more tightly I gripped the reins, my shoulders rigid and my breathing coming in short spurts. I felt Fenn's curious gaze on me often, but I ignored him, keeping my gaze fixed steadfastly on the ombre of orange and red leaves before me. The warm colors looked like a burst of flame.

Like a firebird.

Unbidden, a smile crept along my face as I thought of Fenn's nickname for me. But I squashed that thought, too.

Clear thoughts. Nothing but the burning leaves before me.

We reached the center of Florien before noon. The forest path widened to a cobblestone street, filled with elegant square buildings with cream-colored pillars and wrought iron balconies. All around us, people bustled about. Carriages jostled past us. The townsfolk cast us several curious gazes, and I lifted my chin, resisting the urge to fix my hair or straighten the fabric of my dress. At the Fellspar Inn, the dress had seemed luxurious and fine. But here in the center of a big city, it felt nothing short of shabby.

"Try to smile, little firebird," Fenn murmured. "They are watching."

I felt my lips twitch in response.

When we reached the modiste, I took a deep, steadying breath. Fenn and I were here together. This was just another part of our ruse. I could play this role. I could pretend.

For my kingdom. For Mother, Father, and Gigi. Yes, I could do this for them.

My insides squirmed with unease, and I yearned for Mal's comforting presence, for the way he would nudge my hand with his snout, sensing my distress.

But he wasn't here. And the sooner I got through this, the sooner I could return to him and take to the sky.

I squared my shoulders and dismounted my horse. Fenn extended his arm to me, and I had to suppress the urge to slap it away. His smirk told me he knew what I was thinking.

"Fix your face," I muttered. "Keep looking at me like that and people will think you have ill intentions."

He leaned in close, his whisper tickling my ear. "And what if I did?"

A completely new kind of shiver rippled over me, and I swallowed hard.

He chuckled, the sound low in his throat. "I told you, Aurelia. I have a reputation. Even here in the Autumn Court, people know of me and my exploits."

"I didn't," I challenged. "And my court is next-door."

He rolled his eyes. "Didn't we already discuss this? You've isolated yourself. But perhaps our efforts today can remedy that."

I bristled at the implication that I was a problem to be fixed, but I bit my tongue as we stepped through the doors of the modiste. A bell chimed, and a woman with brown skin and thick locks of black hair turned from the mannequin she was gathering fabric around. Her brows puckered together as she looked us both over.

"Ah, darling, you were right," Fenn said, his voice loud and confident as he casually draped his arm around me. "This place is lovely. Purchase whatever dresses you require. You know our coffers are good for it."

I raised my eyebrow at him. The only reason that statement wasn't a lie was because he knew I only required one dress. He flashed me a sly grin in response.

"Don't neglect your own appearance, dearest," I said in my most cheerful, simpering voice. "We wouldn't want to announce ourselves at court looking like peasants."

He snorted and disguised it with a clearing of his throat.

The seamstress uttered a short gasp and stepped around her mannequin to approach us. She was plump, and only came to my chest, but her steely eyes and strong chin revealed her shrewd, determined nature. "Bless my soul, is that Princess Aurelia? I haven't seen you in ages, my dear!" She swept into a curtsy and straightened, her eyes gleaming. "Look how lovely you are!"

I smiled warmly at her. "Thank you, Mera. It has indeed been a long time. This is Prince Fennick of the Midnight Court." I gestured to Fenn, who bowed deeply.

"A pleasure, my lady."

Mera blushed. "Oh my. I've heard things about you, Your Highness. What brings you to the Autumn Court?"

"Our engagement, of course." Fenn flashed a dazzling smile.

Mera's mouth fell open. "*Engagement?* To whom?"

I forced a smile on my face and took Fenn's hand, lacing his fingers in mine.

Mera's eyes grew wide. "To—To Princess Aurelia?" She pressed a hand to her chest. "I—Well..." She took a deep breath, clearly at a loss for words.

This was not the reaction I was expecting. At any rate, I needed to keep the conversation going before things got out of hand. I gestured to a violet dress in the corner. "What about that one, Fenn?"

"Hmm, I'm not sure it's your color, dearest. I think a nice maroon or umber would suit you nicely."

I stared at him. His eyes twinkled with amusement. "Perhaps you're right," I said slowly, then turned to Mera. "Do you have anything available in those colors? I understand you have a business to run, and we can pay you handsomely for the rush order."

Mera smoothed her hands on her skirts, composing herself. "I—Yes, my lady. Of course. Let me see what I can find." She turned, then glanced over her shoulder at us in clear bewilderment before disappearing behind a curtain.

I couldn't help myself. I snorted loudly into my hand, my face on fire. "Gods, that was a disaster."

"Get used to it." Fenn leaned casually against a wooden beam that supported the ceiling. "People said for years I would never marry. And... they seem to know you well here. It will be harder to pull this off if people have a reason to doubt our relationship. Anyone who knows you would laugh at the idea of us marrying."

I nodded absently. "Yes. They would."

I felt Fenn's probing gaze on me, but he didn't ask, and I didn't volunteer the information. It was hard enough returning to this court after everything that had happened. I wouldn't dredge up those memories just to sate his curiosity.

It didn't take long for Mera to bring out several fabrics for me to try. She seemed to have overcome her initial shock and chatted away merrily about the Harvest Festival and the latest gossip at court as she took my measurements. She found a midnight black suit with a hunter green vest that complimented Fenn's eyes. It fit him almost perfectly, though it was a bit short on his legs.

When she took the clothes behind the curtain to make the finishing touches, I slumped against the wall, my head throbbing from keeping up my persona for so long. At least at Dreya's inn, we'd had frequent breaks where we could remove our masks and be ourselves. This was the longest stretch of time I'd had to keep up the charade.

"Can you handle this?" Fenn asked quietly. I hadn't realized he'd leaned against the wall alongside me, his eyes uncharacteristically somber. "We don't have to announce ourselves at court."

My eyes closed. "Yes we do. We've already told too many people, and I've already sent word to the royal family. To not make an appearance would be a grave insult, especially after—" My mouth clamped shut.

"After what?" Fenn prompted.

I said nothing, my brows scrunching together as I tried to ward off memories.

"To hell with this, Aurelia." His voice was low and closer than before. I opened my eyes to find he'd moved directly in front of me, his face inches away from mine. "If I am to play the part of your betrothed, I need to know what history you have with this Court. If I show up and someone mentions it and I *don't know* what they are talking about, it will give everything away."

My stomach was in knots. I swallowed around the hard lump in my throat. "Prince Tyrone and I were once betrothed."

His head reared back. "You and the Autumn Prince?"

I nodded. "Well, the Autumn *King* now. His father recently passed."

"I see." His jaw ticked back and forth. "How long ago was this betrothal?"

"Three years ago. Nothing official was announced, but everyone expected it with how often we were seen together."

Silence fell between us. I couldn't look at Fenn, but I knew he was expecting more. My eyes closed again. "I ended the arrangement. My father smoothed things over. And I haven't returned since."

This time, the silence was thick with tension, a palpable thing drifting between us like smoke.

"That's why we have to maintain good relations with them," I went on, if only to fill the awkward silence. "To travel through the court without a formal announcement would strain things even further, and right now, we can't afford to make an enemy of Autumn."

"Aurelia," Fenn said slowly. "What actually happened?"

"I'm not obligated to answer your question."

"Aurelia." His tone was impatient.

Fortunately, at that moment, Mera returned with my burgundy dress draped over her arm. She beamed at us both. "Some of my finest work, I think. Come, my lady. Let's make sure it fits." She gestured that I go behind the curtain with her.

I followed, then paused and glanced at Fenn over my shoulder. "Prince Fenn should come, too."

Fenn blinked and Mera looked uncertainly between us.

"But I'll be fitting you into your dress, my lady," Mera said hesitantly. "It isn't proper."

I leaned close to her and whispered conspiratorially, "It won't be anything he hasn't seen before." This was technically true, given our state of undress while the healer tended to us at Fellspar Inn.

Mera's blush returned, her cheeks coloring so vividly she looked like her skin had been burned.

"Besides, he will need to dress too, won't he?" I continued. I felt Fenn's amused gaze on me, but I fiddled with the silk fabric of my dress in Mera's arms. "It will be more efficient for us to get dressed together."

Mera shifted her weight and cleared her throat. "Erm. Well. If—If that is what you wish, my lady."

I nodded tersely and strode for the curtain, the heavy footfalls of Fenn following behind me. After a moment of muttering to herself, Mera came along as well.

"Naughty little firebird," Fenn murmured in my ear, making my skin pebble.

"You would have done the same thing," I whispered back.

He merely chuckled in response.

The dressing area was stocked with racks of frilly dresses, and a lengthy mirror stood on the opposite end of the room, flanked by a pair of mannequins. Mera positioned me in front of the mirror and gestured I step out of my travel-worn dress. Her eyes shifted to Fenn, who stood in the corner, arms crossed, not even pretending he wasn't watching.

Mera unbuttoned the bodice, and I slid the straps of my dress down, wriggling until it puddled at my feet. My underthings still covered most of my body, but it was sheer, leaving nothing to the imagination. My curves, my breasts, my thighs, were on full display, shrouded only by a thin, translucent fabric.

My eyes locked onto Fenn's through the mirror. His pupils flared, the green of his eyes seeming to burn as he watched me. Fire coiled low in my belly at the heady lust brimming in that look.

I lifted my chin at him in a challenge. "You look as if you're seeing my body for the first time, darling."

Fenn laughed, the sound low in his throat. "Every time is like the first time, my little firebird."

My cheeks burned at the term of endearment. There was something intimate about the nickname, and to have him utter it in front of Mera made the flush in my face only deepen.

Mera exhaled sharply as she helped me into the corset and petticoat. I sucked in a breath, my rib cage screaming in protest. Ordinarily, we didn't wear corsets in the Summer Court as the stifling heat was already too constraining. But here in the Autumn Court, there were different expectations, and it had been far too long since I'd worn one. My back went rigid, and the breath whooshed from my lungs.

With practiced ease, Mera gathered the mass of burgundy fabric around me and fastened it tightly. I grunted from the force of her movements.

"Everything all right, my lady?" she asked.

"Yes," I said breathlessly. "It isn't painful. It just takes some getting used to."

She chuckled. "Things are far different in the Autumn Court, aren't they?"

I smiled. "Indeed."

"You know, we abhor corsets in the Midnight Court," Fenn said from across the room. "Too restrictive."

"Is that so?" I said. "And are you speaking from experience?"

He grinned wolfishly. "Would you be shocked if I said I'd worn a corset before?"

I laughed loudly, and Mera let out a sharp squeak of alarm. I quickly apologized and fixed my gaze away from Fenn before I snorted and Mera told the entire kingdom about the piglet princess from the Summer Court.

When Mera was finished, she stood back to admire her work, a satisfied smile gracing her face. The heart-shaped neckline scooped low, revealing an ample amount of cleavage. The sleeves were small and capped, cupping along my upper arms and leaving my collarbone and shoulders exposed. The skirt fanned out widely and was studded with tiny golden gems along the edges.

While the fabric looked burgundy on its own, when it was on me, it transformed into amber and gold, shimmering with each movement. This was Mera's specialty—her fae magic brought her designs to life, but only when they were worn by the subject.

"You truly are a miracle worker." I twirled, watching as the fabric shifted color.

Mera blushed and waved a hand. "It's all thanks to the fae magic, my lady. My work wouldn't be half as fast without it."

I looked at Fenn in the reflection again. "What do you think, darling? Is it as stunning as you imagined it?"

His eyes were pinned on me, his lips parted slightly and a look of awe and surprise etched into his face. He swallowed, his throat bobbing, as his gaze roved over me slowly. After a moment, he said in a strained voice, "It's... magnificent."

Mera curtsied. "Thank you, Your Highness." She gathered my hair together, running her fingers through the strands to sort out the tangles. She twisted it into a knot and pinned it to the top of my head. Elegant, but simple. With a smile, she turned to Fenn. "If you'll step in front of the mirror, I'll dress you next."

Fenn obeyed, unbuttoning his shirt as he went. I stepped back, my skirts bumping into the racks of clothing in the process. I caught one dress before it fell in a heap to the floor, then took extra care to replace it on the hanger.

When I turned back to Fenn, he was shirtless, and he was removing his trousers.

My throat went dry. Oh, gods... His tanned skin was a masterpiece. His arms were taut with well-tone muscle that flexed as he moved to loosen his trousers. My eyes dragged over his abdomen and chest, the rune marking below his collarbone, then lingered on the V-shape just above his waistline.

His britches clung to his muscular thighs, and the bulge between his legs...

I dropped my gaze at once, my face on fire.

"What's the matter, dearest?" Fenn teased. "You act as if you've never seen my full body before."

My blush deepened, but I forced myself to meet his smug expression in the mirror. "Your body is a work of art, Fenn. And it disarms me every time."

His eyes heated, and a single eyebrow arched. Half his mouth quirked upward in an alluring half-smile that made my stomach turn molten.

It didn't take nearly as long for Mera to dress him, as Fenn assisted with the buttons and didn't have to don a corset and petticoat like me. The vibrant green vest complemented his olive skin tone and emerald eyes, and the midnight black fabric of the suit made the tawny tones of his hair stand out.

When he was finished, he turned to face me and spread his arms. "Well, dearest? What do you think?"

In truth, he looked elegant. Princely. The type of gentleman Gigi would drool over.

I took a shaky breath and said, "You will make all the ladies swoon, my darling."

His grin widened.

Mera made some last-minute adjustments before declaring our attire perfect. She even gave us two extra parcels wrapped in silk lavender ribbons, claiming they were a gift for giving her the honor of outfitting us. I tried to refuse, but she insisted, and since being at the Autumn Court would require multiple dazzling outfits fit for royalty, I couldn't help but be impressed by her foresight.

As we passed through the curtain once more, I offered my sincerest thanks to Mera for her stunning work. Fenn took her hand in his and pressed a kiss to it. Her blush returned.

"It was lovely to make your acquaintance," Fenn murmured in his most sultry voice.

I turned so Mera wouldn't see me rolling my eyes. Fenn paid her with a pouch of gold coins, and we took our leave, now fully prepared to announce ourselves at the Autumn Court.

THE MIDNIGHT PRINCE

THE AUTUMN PALACE WAS OSTENTATIOUS. THE WALLS WERE MADE OF A reflective glass that mirrored the blinding sun wherever it stood in the sky. As a Night Fae who rarely saw the sun, I found this to be quite bothersome.

As Aurelia and I approached the gleaming castle walls, I had to often lift my hand to shield my eyes from the searing light shooting back at me.

"I'm surprised you aren't hissing in pain," Aurelia remarked from beside me, her gaze stoic as she looked upon the palace walls without even an ounce of annoyance. "Aren't you a nocturnal creature who fears the daylight?"

"I don't know how you fae folk tolerate it," I muttered. The pounding in my temples made it impossible for me to find a cleverer quip than that.

"How does it work, exactly?"

"How does what work?"

"Your Night Fae powers."

I snorted. "We don't have any Night Fae powers. We just have ordinary fae magic like you."

"I don't have ordinary fae magic, remember?" She smiled wryly, but the darkness in her eyes betrayed how much this disturbed her.

It disturbed me, too, to be honest. I was traveling with a woman who held some kind of dangerous power that could set goblins aflame, and she had a mysterious witch rune marking her shoulder.

"Most fae magic is powered by the sun," I said. "But ours is powered by the light of the stars."

"And when the stars go dark?"

I leveled a look at her. "They never go dark, Aurelia. They shine for an eternity. For *us*."

She blinked, her blue eyes full of curiosity as she gazed at me. "You truly believe that?"

I shrugged. "Many fae cultures worship the sun. Ours worships the stars. It isn't that different."

"That must be nice." The words were so soft I almost didn't hear her.

"What is?"

"To have a belief. A purpose. Something to put your faith in."

"You don't?"

"No. I don't."

I was hoping she would elaborate, but her expression closed off, her eyes dimming, and I knew that was the end of our conversation. At any rate, we were nearing the outer walls of the palace, and her grip on her reins had gone so tight her knuckles turned white. I wasn't even sure if she noticed the reaction.

I would be getting nothing from her now. Her mind was on whatever incident had occurred the last time she'd been in this court. Perhaps behind these very palace walls.

A conflicting surge of emotions swept over me—a mixture of sympathy and protectiveness, the urge to shield her from whatever she was hiding from; but at the same time, annoyance and rage rose up as well. I could not defend her if I didn't know what the threat was. If our plan was to work, I needed to know this secret.

Because I was certain there were people in the palace who knew it already.

I gritted my teeth in frustration. This princess was infuriating. And she accused me of being selfish, of needlessly creating a divide between our kingdoms? How were we supposed to be allies when she kept herself closed off like this?

A darker, more disturbing thought slithered into my mind. What if this was similar to what had happened with the witches? I wasn't fully aware of the situation, but I could make assumptions. She had dabbled in a darker power, trying to access her magic. It had gone badly. Judging by what she'd done to the goblins, it wasn't hard to picture the carnage.

Had she caused something similar here in the Autumn Court? Was that why she was keeping it a secret—because she was ashamed?

But no. If that were the case, we would have been escorted with a heavy guard. Perhaps even arrested on the spot.

She had said her father had smoothed things over. Exactly how had he done that?

The questions rattled around in my head as the blinding sun beat down on me from the castle's reflection. It was lower in the sky now, so it wasn't a direct beam of light shining in my eyes. In fact, the amber and fuchsia hues of the setting sun cast a brilliant glow on the palace walls, making it look like a kaleidoscope of flames.

I sucked in a breath, and Aurelia chuckled next to me.

"Yes, that is the appeal," she said softly. Her tone was a mixture of wistfulness and bitterness. "No one can resist the glowing palace of the Autumn Court."

My brows knitted together as I took in the hardening of her expression. Before I could speak, a loud, metallic creak split the air, and the gates to the outer wall slid open to allow us in.

I straightened in my saddle and put my court mask into place; a look of smugness and superiority. The expression that reminded Aurelia how much she hated me.

But it was who everyone expected me to be. Who Aurelia expected me to be. And it was my armor.

A few guards greeted us at the gate and escorted us through the courtyard. I had visited the Autumn Court a handful of times, but always after sundown because of the customs of the Night Fae. Now, the cream-colored walkways and vibrant red-leafed trees stood out to me. So blindingly bright and colorful compared to the dark gleam of the Midnight Court.

A stable boy tended to our horses, and I resisted the urge to stretch my legs upon dismounting. Gods, I was so sore. But I kept my armor in place, with my spine rigid and my expression unchanged. I linked Aurelia's arm in mine as we climbed the steps to the entrance doors. Her hand was trembling, and I gave it a squeeze.

"You are a firebird," I whispered to her. "Magnificent and fierce. No one will quell your flame."

Her gaze slid to mine, surprise and awareness flickering in her eyes for a brief moment, reminding me of the determined creature that she was.

I only hoped she reminded herself of it as well.

This wretched court seemed to remind her only of her weaknesses.

Aurelia remained poised and stiff alongside me, but her steps were sure and steady. Her chin lifted, and a cold detachment settled in her gaze. She, too, was wearing a mask. And I was surprised and alarmed at how easily I could see through it.

How had we become so close that I could tell when she donned a false persona? I wouldn't even call us friends, and yet the idea of seeing through her facade felt... intimate.

The guards led us through a spotless marble hallway lined with paintings of droll bearded kings from the past. Our footsteps echoed along with the clanging of the metal swords of the guards.

We reached the throne room, also flanked by guards, and the doors were thrown open for us. I took a deep breath and squeezed Aurelia's hand once more before we strode inside.

An entourage greeted us. Two rows of armed soldiers created an aisle that led to the dais in front of the stained glass windows, upon which rested three thrones occupied by the royal family. A crowd of nobles filled the space in front of the dais, every pair of eyes fixed on us.

My smirk widened. I did love a captive audience.

The man sitting in the middle throne—the largest of the three—had dark blond hair, a goatee, and a hooked nose. His black eyes were fixed on Aurelia with a hunger that made me clutch her arm more tightly against me. His gleaming gold crown could only mean one thing: he was the king.

He must have recently been coronated. Last I'd been here, the Autumn King had been a white-haired codger who had managed to live a decade longer than anyone expected.

The new king turned and whispered something to the woman sitting on the throne next to him—his mother, I presumed. She had graying brown hair, but her blue eyes were cold as they surveyed us.

The third throne was occupied by the king's younger brother, who had identical blond hair but was clean-shaven, his eyes a warm brown. He glanced between me and Aurelia with a slight frown as he rubbed his square jaw.

"We perplex them, beloved," I murmured to Aurelia.

"Indeed," was her only response. Her eyes remained stoically fixed ahead, her expression betraying nothing as we made our way down the aisle of soldiers. When we reached the foot of the dais, she curtsied and I bowed.

King Tyrone waved his hand. "No need for that. Aurelia and I are old friends, after all."

Aurelia stiffened next to me but replied easily. "That we are, Your Majesty. I understand congratulations are in order for your coronation. Apologies for missing the ceremony, but I had important matters to attend to in my own court."

A carefully crafted deception. She hadn't downright stated she was sorry to have missed it—because she wasn't. And even if it was only a matter of signing a single document, the excuse was still valid.

Clever firebird.

Tyrone smirked as if he saw through the politeness. "I must admit I was… surprised to receive your notice. I would not have believed it unless I had seen for myself. Is it true you are engaged to be married?"

The entire room seemed to hold its breath with anticipation. Aurelia lifted her chin with a smile and said, "That is why we are here. Prince Fenn and I have reached an agreement between our kingdoms and are delighted to announce the happy tidings."

Tyrone scratched his chin, frowning as he glanced between us. "I see."

A tense silence fell between us. Aurelia and I remained perfectly still under his scrutiny.

After a long moment, I couldn't help myself. I forced a chuckle and asked, "Have we passed your inspection, Your Majesty?"

Tyrone's eyebrows lifted, his gaze finally snapping to me with a glare. "I am simply caught off guard. It wasn't long ago that my entire kingdom expected this woman to become their queen. And now you show up to announce a rather abrupt engagement that we knew nothing about."

"It is not my obligation to inform you of my relations with other kingdoms," Aurelia said brusquely.

"It is if you intend to maintain good relations with *my* kingdom," Tyrone snapped.

"Is my fiancée to keep you apprised of *all* of her lovers?" I demanded.

Tyrone's mother choked on a cough, then pressed a hand to her chest as she cleared her throat.

I smiled wickedly. "Forgive me. But if King Tyrone expects my future wife to keep him so informed, then that must mean he expects a missive for every person she takes to her bed. Is that not so?"

Tyrone's cheeks turned red. "I did not—"

"Truth be told, this arrangement happened rather suddenly," I went on. "There wasn't much time to send proper notice. I even had to send a courier to inform my mother, for which I will be soundly chastised. She will be incensed that she did not receive the news in person."

Tyrone's brows furrowed. "Why the rush, then? What led to such a rash development?"

"We wanted to smooth relations between our kingdoms," Aurelia provided. "We had come to a business arrangement, but… it was prudent for something more binding to bring our kingdoms together after so many years of strife. A union of marriage seemed like the best way to bridge that gap." She turned and flashed a rather convincing smile at me, which I returned.

"And, of course, it doesn't hurt that we are wildly attracted to one another," I added with a chuckle.

Aurelia inhaled a sharp breath beside me, the corners of her mouth twitching and her eyes closing in exasperation for the briefest of seconds. It took all my restraint not to bark out a loud and obnoxious laugh.

Yes, I was putting on a show for the Autumn Court. But I was also putting on a show for *her*. And the way her fingernails dug into the skin of my arm told me she was well aware of my efforts.

Tyrone cleared his throat and shifted in his seat, his frown deepening.

"We were passing through your lands," Aurelia said, her voice gentler, "and we knew it would cause grave offense if we did not announce ourselves. Please consider this a gesture of good will between our kingdoms. Your court is the *first* place we have made this official announcement."

"Aside from your own?" Tyrone asked.

Aurelia's expression froze, her body rigid.

Shit.

"Yes, of course," I said quickly. "The king and queen of the Summer

Court made no objections to our announcement. They aren't *exactly* as thrilled as we are, but that's to be expected." I chuckled again as if we were sharing a joke.

Tyrone did not smile. Another tense moment of silence passed.

Aurelia took a deep breath. "Your Majesty, if we are unwelcome, we will take our leave. I understand if things are strained between us because of past circumstances..."

"Nonsense," Tyrone said, waving his hand again. "It is merely a surprise, that is all. Of course you both are welcome, as well as any attendants you have brought with you." He glanced behind us expectantly as if searching for our traveling party, though he likely already knew we traveled alone.

Aurelia's cheeks flushed. "Ah. Right. Well—"

"We have none," I said with a grin. "We thought a more... intimate situation would be fitting. It can get awkward with attendants when we can't seem to keep our hands off of each other. I can't tell you how many of my valets and manservants have had to witness my hands—"

"Fenn," Aurelia said sharply, her fingernails digging into my arm again.

I laughed as if I hadn't expected to reveal as much. "Forgive me. Needless to say, our party consists of only the two of us."

Tyrone's face was beet-red, his brows lowered in rage. I only smiled innocently in return.

"That is highly inappropriate, don't you think?" asked Tyrone's mother. "Not to mention unsafe. What if you encounter robbers? Or the unseelie?"

"You'll find I am a capable swordsman," I said. "And Aurelia is quite impressive with a blade in her hand. She felled an entire clan of goblins on our way here."

Aurelia turned to gape at me, while the crowd whispered frantically in excitement. Tyrone's brother raised his eyebrows, a small smile playing at his lips.

"Well," Tyrone said, sitting up straighter in his throne. "Regardless of how... unorthodox this all is, you two are welcome to stay as long as you wish. We have our Equinox Ball tonight, if you wish to join in the festivities."

Aurelia sank into a curtsy. "That is most kind of you. We would be delighted to attend."

My smile was lethal as I replied, "Indeed we would."

The Summer Princess

I was going to *strangle* Fenn.

If I didn't know him, I would have assumed he was blind. That he was incapable of reading the emotions of the people around him.

Unfortunately, I *did* know him. And he was doing this intentionally. He delighted in setting fires and watching as the world burned around him.

Throughout our introduction to the court, I kept my gaze either fixed on the floor or demurely aimed at King Tyrone. I never let myself glance toward his brother, as much as I felt Callan's eyes searing into me.

And Fenn was doing a spectacular job stoking my ire. By the time we were escorted from the throne room, my fists were shaking with rage.

I held my tongue as a servant showed us to our rooms. Fenn tried to convince the attendants that we would share a room, but they informed us they were under specific instruction to prepare separate quarters. It was also painfully clear the servants would be punished if we did not comply, judging by their pale faces and stammered responses. One young woman seemed on the verge of tears.

Fenn and I exchanged uncertain glances. Our quarters were on opposite ends of the hall. Although I should have been relieved to have so much space between us, a darker part of me presumed Tyrone had done this on purpose.

My insides twisted at the thought.

I was shown my room first, the Golden Room. Every inch of it spoke of its namesake. Gold tapestries, plush gold pillows, a gold and umber rug running from the doors to the open windows that boasted the dark purple rays of the sun's descent.

I'd stayed in this room once, long before Tyrone and I had begun our courtship. I was grateful I hadn't been placed in the Magenta Room —that one held some of my darkest nightmares, and I had no desire to ever return to it. Small mercies, I supposed.

I ran my fingers over the delicate gold embroidery of the comforter on my bed. My eyes took in the grand armoire against the wall and the oval mirror atop the vanity on the opposite end. Wide, frightened eyes met my own in the reflection.

I was unrecognizable. Not the firebird Fenn claimed me to be, but a scared, trembling creature that I did not know. This place turned me into a weak prey, simply waiting to be hunted and devoured.

I squared my shoulders and lifted my chin. I refused to be cowed.

A knock sounded at my door, and I whirled, my heart racing, my breath catching in my throat. Terror seized my heart in the tightest of clutches, squeezing, squeezing, squeezing…

"Aurelia?"

Fenn opened the door and poked his head in, his curious green eyes surveying the room with interest. He chuckled. "This is *much* nicer than mine. I fear they may have accidentally placed me in the servants' quarters."

A sharp breath whooshed through me, and only then did I realize I hadn't been breathing. I sucked in huge gulps full of air, practically gasping. Suddenly dizzy, I grabbed the mahogany frame of my four poster bed, struggling to catch my breath.

"Aurelia?" Fenn said again, stepping fully into the room and shutting the door behind him. I couldn't even muster the strength to don my court mask in front of him. I'd been keeping up the ruse for so long, pouring all of my strength into maintaining my cold and confident persona, that I had nothing left.

A warm hand pressed into mine, and I jerked back, taking several steps away from Fenn. He raised his palms placatingly.

"Sorry," he said quickly. "You look unwell. Should we depart tonight? We do not have to stay here."

"Yes, we do." My voice was clipped. "It would be the greatest offense for us to leave without making an appearance at the ball."

"To hell with appearances," Fenn snapped. "You are paler than death. I'd wager that showing up and spewing your dinner all over their guests would be a greater offense."

"Oh shut up," I groaned, rubbing my temples. "You've already put us in too great a mess. I don't know why I even bother."

"Excuse me?"

I let my hands fall against my thighs. "Your behavior in that throne room was *appalling*."

"No, my behavior was precisely what everyone expected of me."

I let out a dry laugh. "So it never occurred to you that perhaps you should defy those expectations? No, it's far better to just drag me down to your level, isn't it?"

"You're being daft again, Aurelia," Fenn said, his voice low and lethal. "Perhaps I am not simply behaving as a foolish and spoiled prince. Perhaps there is another reason behind my behavior."

"Another reason besides your own sense of morbid amusement?" I grumbled.

Fenn was in front of me in a flash, towering over me, his eyes flashing dangerously. I stared up at him, daring him to come closer. If he touched me, I wouldn't hesitate to ram my knee right between his legs.

"Our ruse isn't foolproof, *princess*," he practically spat. "It has plenty of holes. And we needed a fool to take the blame for that. So I played that part for you. You're welcome, by the way."

"I am *not*—" I said hotly.

"Furthermore," he went on, talking over my interruption. "That king was looking at you like you were a piece of meat he was going to bite into. And I wanted to remind him that you do not belong to him; you belong to me."

My face flushed. "I don't—"

"And lastly," he said, and with each word, his voice did not rise, but it became softer and somehow more dangerous. "My behavior was to remind you that you despise me. That you hate me. That your anger can be more powerful than your fear. Because you were like a stunned gazelle standing before a ravenous lion in that throne room, Aurelia. And I was not going to stand by and watch you wither away."

My breath caught in my throat, and my head reared back in

surprise. My lips parted as I stared at him, too startled to even muster a reply.

He had done those things… for me? He had noticed how Tyrone's very presence seemed to elicit a reaction from me?

Of course he had. Fenn was no fool. He was shrewd, and he noticed far more than I liked.

I swallowed, my throat suddenly dry. I didn't know what to say. What *could* I say? I would wager Fenn wanted some kind of explanation, but I wasn't about to give it to him.

"It isn't hard to guess what happened here." His voice was barely more than a whisper, a breath against my face. "You don't have to tell me. But I know he mistreated you. And it's taking all of my restraint not to track him down and slice off his balls with my dagger. So I am telling you again, to hell with appearances. You don't owe anyone anything, Aurelia. Not me. Not him. If you wish to leave, simply say the word and I will take you from here."

My breaths came hard and fast, and I couldn't seem to get enough air into my body. My skin felt hot and cold all at once. A thick lump formed in my throat, making it hard to swallow or speak. I moistened my lips, but that didn't help. Fenn's eyes darted to my mouth and back up again as if tracking the movement of my tongue.

I felt I should be thanking him. Or shouting at him. I wasn't sure what to feel in this moment. All I knew was his chest was mere inches from mine, his face hovering in front of me, so close I could taste the breath on his lips.

And yet he didn't touch me. His body was angled carefully so it lined up with mine but left space between us. I could feel the warmth emanating from his chest, but we were still not touching. As if he knew I could not be touched right now. As if he knew it would shatter me completely.

He knew. I hadn't told him a thing, but he still somehow knew. He read me in ways my own mother could not. My parents, my sister—they never had a clue what had happened here.

But Fenn, the prince of an enemy kingdom, the most infuriating man I'd ever met, had somehow figured it out.

As much as I loathed to admit it, he was my ally right now. The only person I could rely on.

I exhaled, long and slow. I would need to face this truth eventually.

The time for running was over. I was here, and the past had finally caught up to me.

"Tyrone wanted more than I could give him," I whispered. "At first, he respected the boundaries I put in place. But as our courtship continued, he grew more impatient. He began to pressure me, and I feared our arrangement would dissolve if I could not satisfy him, so…" I paused and swallowed, trying not to dwell on that night. "So I obliged."

Fenn's nostrils flared, his eyes burning with rage, but he said nothing, allowing me to continue.

"It was… Well, it was fine. Nothing spectacular, but it wasn't terrible. I thought it would satisfy him, but he only wanted more. I gave as much as I could, often making up excuses as to why I could not stay in his chambers or why I had to return to my court before sunset." I took a shuddering breath. "And then his brother Callan returned from the war."

Fenn blinked, confusion creeping into his expression. I felt only a sliver of satisfaction at catching him off guard. Clearly, he hadn't anticipated everything.

"Callan was charming and patient and sweet. Everything Tyrone was not. I found myself drawn to him. Yearning for him." My eyes closed, and a tear tracked down my cheek. "It was wrong. But I wanted to *feel* something. I felt nothing for Tyrone. And I longed for just one ounce of passion. Just once.

"We told ourselves it would stop. But it didn't. And when Tyrone caught us, he—he—"

"You don't have to continue," Fenn said quietly.

"I do," I insisted. "This needs to be spoken, or it will fester inside of me until it eats away at my soul. Tyrone took me to his bed. I let him. I did not fight him. He was brutal and violent. He broke me. He destroyed me. I gave myself to him willingly, but he still butchered my soul, carving it from me with such force that I was nothing but an empty shell when he was finished with me. And still… I did not fight him." More tears streamed down my face, and I choked on my next words. "I… did not… fight him."

"Aurelia." There was a plea in Fenn's voice. I had never heard him sound so strained, so devastated. "You did not ask for this to happen to you. Just because you did not physically fight him doesn't make the act any more vile. You were violated. He took from you what you were unwilling to give."

I shook my head, unable to say more. Instead, I succumbed to the tears, allowing them to flow freely.

Fenn shifted, his hand rising and pausing an inch away from my face, as if he intended to touch my cheek but stopped halfway. Even in this moment, he still knew I didn't want to be touched.

The thought only brought more tears. I could not stop them. A dam had burst, and I had no strength left to repair it, to put these memories and emotions back into place.

"We will leave," Fenn murmured. "I will put a healthy portion of iron-laced poison in his tea and we will sneak out into the night before anyone notices we are gone."

I snorted in spite of the situation, then wiped my nose. Gods, my face was a sopping mess. "I don't want to leave." When Fenn frowned at me, I said, "I want to put myself back together, one jagged piece at a time. I want to leave this place with my dignity restored and my soul rebuilt. If I have to depart from here a broken mess once more, I won't be able to survive it." I looked Fenn in the eye, finding my resolve. "I want to put this behind me, Fenn. I want to emerge stronger than I was before. And the only way to do that is to get through this ball, to show him that I am *not* some weak thing he disposed of, but a powerful creature to be feared."

Fenn's mouth curled into a satisfied half-smile. "There's my fire-bird." His eyes warmed as he leaned into me, still not touching, but close enough that if I shifted, my nose would brush his. "I am at your complete disposal tonight, my lady. Just say the word and I will obey."

I found myself smiling in return. "All I need from you is to continue playing your part. Be the handsome rogue who fears nothing and no one."

His grin turned feral. "It would be my pleasure."

THE MIDNIGHT PRINCE

I STOOD DUTIFULLY OUTSIDE AURELIA'S CHAMBERS, HANDS CLASPED IN front of me, looking more like a stoic guardsman than a prince. I would have barged into her rooms and insisted on staying right by her side, but she threatened to run me through with her dagger if I didn't give her privacy, and since I'd seen just how artfully she could wield a blade, I thought it best to remain in the hall.

I would strangle that bastard Autumn King. Ever since Aurelia had confessed her history with him, I'd done nothing but envision all the painful ways I could end his pitiful existence.

Gods, no wonder. *No wonder* Aurelia refused to let anyone into her life. No wonder she closed herself off, isolating herself and her court and turning away any potential allies who came her way. I wasn't sure if she was even aware that she was doing it. But the Autumn King had broken her, and now she was incapable of letting anyone in. No suitors. No friends. No one but her dragons. The only creatures she knew would never betray her.

I blinked several times before adjusting the silk crimson ascot around my neck. I wasn't sure why I was so sympathetic toward her. I owed her nothing. She made her hatred of me abundantly clear.

Even so. No one deserved that. Not even someone as insufferable as the Summer Princess.

After what felt like an eternity, her chamber doors opened, and a maid scurried out, curtsying hurriedly at me before bustling down the hallway. I peered through the open door, catching a glimpse of a wide, sweeping scarlet skirt before Aurelia stepped into view.

My first impression was that her body had been completely swallowed by the dress. I could barely make our her features amongst the scooping skirt that swished with every movement. It was so wide she could barely fit through the doorway. I had to take her hand and all but pull her through.

Laughing, I looked her over. The dress hugged her waist, and delicate ruffles lined the bodice, giving her the appearance of rose petals. The neckline dipped low enough to reveal the curve of her breasts. A smattering of freckles lined her bosom, and the sight of them in such an intimate spot made my mouth go dry. Her capped sleeves hung low on her shoulders, and I found myself following the line of freckles on her collarbone, desperate to run my fingers along it.

"A bit much, don't you think?" Aurelia said with a breathless chuckle.

My eyes snapped to hers, and I cleared my throat. "I—Ah. N-No, I think it's quite—quite—"

Her eyebrows lifted, her eyes sparking with mirth. Her crimson-painted lips curled into a satisfied smile. "Why, dearest fiancé of mine, has my appearance left you speechless?"

I moistened my lips. Damn this woman to the stars… Why was it so hard to speak? I drew in a breath and straightened, throwing my shoulders back and struggling to put my court mask into place. "You are a blossom among wretched thorns, my dear." Her hand was still clasped in mine, and I bent at the waist to brush a kiss against it. When I straightened once more, her breath hitched, and a warm blush spread across her cheeks.

"Thank you. You look dashing as well." Her eyes roved over me, and I couldn't help but smile at the way her pupils flared and her lips parted slightly.

I knew I looked exquisite. The midnight black suit matched the one Mera had designed for our entrance to court, but the crimson vest was new and had an elaborate paisley pattern stitched into it.

I leaned close to her and whispered, "Try not to swoon."

She swatted my arm, which I extended to her with a smirk, and together we strode down the hall toward the staircase.

When we reached the top of the stairs, Aurelia gripped the bannister with a trembling hand, her breath shaky. Below us, the light and chatter of the event filtered up to where we stood.

I glanced at the princess. Her cheeks were flushed, and a few strands of her light orange hair had come loose from the elaborate crown of braids adorning her head. I leaned close to her, using one of my fingers to tuck the hair behind her ear.

"You are a firebird," I reminded her. "And you are magnificent." A sudden boldness took over me, and I pressed a soft kiss to her cheek.

We had never crossed this line before. We weren't in public; there was no reason for the display of affection.

But in this moment, I knew she needed a distraction. And as much as she infuriated me, this lovely creature was frightened, and I had to remind her that I was with her. I was her ally. She had nothing to fear from me. Not tonight.

Her eyelashes fluttered as she turned to look at me, her brows puckering in confusion. Her face was so close to mine that I could count every freckle if I wanted to. There wasn't even an inch of skin that wasn't covered by at least a faint smattering of freckles. The blush in her cheeks deepened, and she moistened her lips. My gaze was pulled to her mouth, which was painted crimson to match her dress. Gods, those soft lips looked so succulent.

Her breath hitched, and she blinked before turning, breaking the connection between us. "I'll be fine," she reassured me, patting my arm.

She was reassuring *me*.

My insides twisted. Was that rejection? Had I been about to kiss her? And… had she denied me?

I wasn't accustomed to this feeling.

I swallowed, my thoughts a dizzying array of confusion as I led her down the stairs. She kept one arm on the bannister and the other laced through mine, clinging to me for support.

The warm glow of the lights grew as we descended. Sconces lined the walls, emitting a vibrant golden glimmer that shone across the entire hall. Below us, hundreds of guests flitted about in Autumn's signature colors: gold, amber, and scarlet. Several waitstaff bustled around with trays of champagne flutes. From down the hall came the echoes of a sweeping melody from the orchestra, and I was certain couples would already be dancing in the ballroom.

"You'll have the opportunity to show off your dancing skills soon, firebird," I whispered to her, and I was rewarded with a slight quirk of her lips.

"Afraid you'll be bested again?"

I snorted. "I would hardly say you *bested* me. Surprised is more like it."

"I think we surprised each other." Her blue eyes met mine and held them.

"Indeed we did." My voice was low and soft.

We reached the bottom of the stairs, and a servant immediately approached and offered refreshment. Aurelia took an apple tart, and I accepted a flute of champagne, bringing the glass to my lips for a sip. The overly sweet nectar was so pungent it stung on its way down my throat. "Gods, I forgot how awful the wine here is." Before the servant left, I gave him back the flute, unable to hide my grimace of distaste.

Aurelia laughed. "You are such a snob."

"You say that now, but once you taste the sparkling fire wine in the Midnight Court, you'll understand."

She rolled her eyes and turned away, her expression brightening as a blond woman in a golden dress that matched her hair bobbed into view, her curls bouncing.

"Aurelia!" she squealed, rushing toward us.

Aurelia dropped my arm to embrace the woman with both hands. "Julieta, it's so wonderful to see you again!"

Julieta withdrew to kiss both Aurelia's cheeks. "It's been far too long! I forbid you from leaving before you tell me every detail of the last three years, including this…" Her gaze slid to me, her brown eyes sparking with a mixture of delight and curiosity. "My, my. You are *not* what I expected the Midnight Prince to be."

I bowed low and offered her my most seductive smile. "Princess Julieta, you are a gem indeed. It's a pleasure to make your acquaintance."

Julieta beamed and curtsied. "I don't suppose you'll save me a dance?" She tilted her head at me, her gaze sweeping over my form, her eyebrows lifting in an invitation.

I almost laughed at her boldness. She and Aurelia could not *truly* be friends, not if she was openly flirting with me in front of my fiancée.

She was beautiful, no doubt about it. In any other circumstance, I would have accepted her offer, perhaps brought her to my rooms for a dalliance afterwards.

Instead, I said, "I fear my dances are reserved only for my

beloved." I took Aurelia's arm in mine once more, and to my surprise, she stood on her tiptoes and pressed a kiss to my cheek. I looked at her, wondering if this was a demonstration of affection in response to the kiss I'd given her earlier, or if it was entirely for show. But Aurelia wasn't looking at me; she was offering a sympathetic smile to Julieta.

"Apologies, Julieta," Aurelia said. "But the Midnight Prince has been claimed for the evening."

Julieta only grinned. "It was worth a shot." She placed her hand on Aurelia's arm. "Let's catch up later, shall we? I know my brothers are waiting for you in the ballroom."

Aurelia stiffened, but Julieta didn't seem to notice as she disappeared into the crowd. I chuckled, shaking my head. "She's brazen, I'll give her that."

"Pay her no heed. She's more flighty than Gigi."

"Your sister is flighty?"

"Oh yes. Her only desire is to find a match with a wealthy and handsome lord, but she has fawned over no less than a dozen different eligible men in the past year."

My eyebrows rose. "How old is she?"

She smacked my arm again, and I laughed. "I am only curious to know if she is close to marrying age or not."

"She is not. She's sixteen." The smile that had warmed Aurelia's face slowly slipped, and I knew she was thinking of Gigi's predicament; lying unconscious, unable to be roused. For a moment, she must have forgotten.

We both had. Here at this festive event, it was easy to slide into the typical court routine we were both accustomed to.

But we were here for a purpose. We had to sell the concept of our engagement. It would benefit us both. I would get the Dragonfire my kingdom so desperately needed, and she would get the stardust required to break the sleeping curse.

I couldn't allow myself to forget that this was a business transaction and nothing more.

We made our way through the crowd, stopping to exchange pleasantries. I was impressed by how many courtiers Aurelia was able to greet by name, as if no time had passed from her last visit. Her smile seemed genuine, and she inquired after their families and affairs, asking personal questions that led me to believe she had known these people quite well.

When we reached the ballroom doors, I leaned in to whisper, "You were truly prepared to be the Autumn Queen, weren't you?"

She glanced up at me, her expression unreadable. "Even if I wasn't, I still care about these people. They are my neighbors and allies."

"You don't have allies, remember?"

"Just because my people are on poor terms with *yours* doesn't mean there aren't other courts I associate with."

My eyes narrowed. She hadn't been associating with other courts in three years, but I wasn't about to bring that up. I now knew why. And tonight, she didn't need that reminder.

Instead, I said nothing, guiding her through the open ballroom doors as the orchestra's music blared louder. Before us, several couples spun in unison on the dance floor, skirts swishing and arms moving with exquisite grace. Garlands of red roses, golden marigolds, and orange dahlias were strung about the room. In each corner of the ball-room, coils of orange flame circled the air, no doubt conjured by magic. I watched for a moment, unimpressed by the faint and feeble attempt to dazzle the crowd. It was nothing compared to the awe-inspiring beauty of our Nightfire.

"Ah, there they are," said a voice nearby. The piercing grip of Aurelia's fingers on my arm told me who it was before the king approached, a gold crown gleaming atop his head. His umber vest was lined with gold lace, and the brilliant shade of crimson on his waistcoat made my eyes throb.

King Tyrone placed a hand on my shoulder as if we were old friends. I went rigid from his touch, tempted to knock him on his ass for it.

"You two look quite the couple," Tyrone said with a smile, looking Aurelia over with that possessive look I'd noticed in the throne room.

I brought my arm around Aurelia's waist, bringing her closer to me. "Thank you, Your Highness. We are honored to be here."

"The ball is magnificent," Aurelia supplied, for which I was grateful. I couldn't truthfully compliment an event with mediocre wine and droll party tricks.

Tyrone beamed. "Only the finest for our equinox, of course! Save me a dance, my dear, won't you? For old times' sake?" He winked at Aurelia and vanished into the crowd before either of us could say anything.

I huffed a laugh. "What an ass. You won't be dancing with him, don't worry."

Aurelia was stiff and unmoving in my grasp, frozen like a stunned creature.

"Aurelia?" I asked.

"I have to," she whispered.

My eyebrows lowered. "You don't. According to these people, you belong to me and no one else. You don't owe him anything."

She turned to me, her eyes flashing with anger. "Don't be a fool, Fenn. To refuse a dance from the king would cause the greatest offense. I *have* to."

"Aurelia—"

She shoved out of my grip, ignoring my outstretched hand as she moved away from me and melted into the crowd.

The Summer Princess

I found myself stepping through the open balcony doors, my feet moving of their own volition. At every festive occasion in the Autumn Court, I often sought out a balcony for respite from making small talk with courtiers. It was a rare opportunity to relax and allow my facial features to sag, providing relief from the constant smiling.

I heaved a sigh, taking in the fresh air, the smell of cool and crisp leaves on the wind. The sun had fully set now, but the faint lavender and fuchsia glows still swirled in the sky, igniting the forest that surrounded the palace. In the distance, I made out the Mistwood Hills that separated the Autumn Court from the Star Court.

We were so close. So close to reaching Fenn's kingdom and getting the answers we needed.

And yet, it still seemed an eternity away. I'd been apart from my family for two days now. Were they well? Was the enchantment that held them dangerous? What if they were in a prolonged, frozen state, and I wouldn't be able to rouse them when I returned?

"Still escaping out here, I see," came a voice behind me.

I whirled, heart pounding, to find Callan with a drink in his hand. His blond hair was smoothed out of his face, which was clean shaven. Last I'd seen him, he had a goatee similar to his brother's. But his eyes were much kinder than Tyrone's. They always had been.

My chest constricted for an entirely different reason. "Hello, Callan."

He moved to my side, bracing one arm on the iron railing while the other clutched his champagne flute, occasionally bringing it to his lips. We stood alongside each other, watching the sky darken bit by bit.

After a long moment, he said softly, "I wasn't sure if I would ever see you again."

I swallowed thickly, suddenly wishing I hadn't come out here. Callan and I had often escaped here together. This was where we shared our most private conversations. Our hopes and fears.

Our secret and most forbidden passion for each other.

My cheeks flushed, and I turned away. "I shouldn't be here."

"Aurelia." He grasped my wrist, stopping me from leaving.

I froze at the sound of my name on his lips. Gods, the way he uttered it like a gentle prayer, a plea…

I hadn't allowed myself to think on how much I missed the companionship of another. *Ached* for it.

But Callan's touch, while warm and gentle, did nothing for me. There was no rush of heat. No jolt of awareness. Not like when Fenn had touched me earlier.

"Please don't, Callan." I could barely utter the words, my throat was so full of emotion.

"I thought—With the engagement broken, I thought—" He broke off with a frustrated exhale, then dropped my wrist. "I suppose I was wrong."

My face crumpled from the note of grief in his voice. Burning suns, he'd believed I'd ended my engagement for *him*.

He had no idea what Tyrone had done. Of course he hadn't. I hadn't told him, and Tyrone certainly wouldn't have.

As far as Callan knew, he and I had been caught by Tyrone, then I'd ended my engagement and left the Autumn Court without notice.

I took a deep, steadying breath and looked at him, bracing myself for the unrestrained emotion I would find on his face. His eyes were tight and full of longing and despair. His brows were drawn together, his jaw taut and rigid. He stood, his back perfectly straight, his fists clenched together.

I cleared my throat. "What you and I shared is over now, Callan. It has been for three years. I'm sorry I did not say goodbye or explain things to you. But it was too complicated between you and me… and Tyrone. I couldn't do it any longer. And now, with the Midnight Prince…" I paused, unable to form a sentence that wasn't a lie. My brain wasn't working properly. Not around Callan. I struggled to come up with the right words to say that would assure him there was no chance of us being together.

Callan's face hardened, his eyes closing off. "Yes. You and that bastard. I can't believe it, Aurelia. Are you truly going to marry him?"

Shit. *I can't lie. I can't lie. I can't lie.* "I… Callan…"

He stepped closer to me. I was achingly aware of the tiny space between his chest and mine. Once, years ago, I might have yearned to close that gap, to wrap my arms around him and remind myself of what his lips tasted like.

But I did not feel that desperation anymore. Whatever feelings I had for him were long gone. I did not love Callan. I never did. He was a means to escape. The release we found was temporary, and I had known that from the beginning.

I had thought he'd known it, too. But apparently, he didn't.

"Things may be different soon," Callan went on, interpreting my silence as hesitation. "Tyrone is—Well, he's not been himself. He's acting rashly, making bold decisions that are angering the court. He's made a lot of enemies." His voice lowered to a whisper. "I have heard rumors that the court will try to have him deposed. If that happens, I will be king, and you and I—"

No. This line of thinking had to stop. I lifted my chin, finding my resolve and meeting his gaze directly. "There is no future for us, Callan. There never was. I thought you understood that. I have an arrangement with the Midnight Prince that I intend to see through. And while I treasured our time together, it is over, and we cannot go back. Please let this go. For both our sakes."

He swallowed, his throat bobbing, and extended his hand, grasping my arm just above my elbow. I froze at his touch, the warmth of his fingers against my flesh.

And, inexplicably, Fenn's face appeared in my mind. That coy smile, the way his eyes darkened with amusement and heady lust when he looked at my body…

Reality jolted through me. I shook my head. Before I could speak, someone cleared their throat behind us.

I stiffened, knowing instantly who it was. Because *of course* he would find us. Of course he would notice we were both missing from the ballroom.

Dread pooled in my chest as I turned to find Tyrone standing at the open balcony doors, fury brewing in his eyes. I stepped away from Callan, cursing myself for allowing this to happen. It wasn't until I put distance between us that I realized how close we'd been standing.

The scene was quite damning. And Tyrone intended to punish me for it. I could see it in the darkness brimming in his gaze.

"Aurelia." The king strode closer, his eyes flicking between us. "I see you and my brother have become… reacquainted."

"Nothing happened, Tyrone," Callan said in a bored voice. "We were just talking."

"Of course you were." Tyrone offered a cold smile, then extended his hand to me. "That dance you promised?"

I bit back a nasty retort. I hadn't promised him *any* such thing. But what I'd said to Fenn was the truth; I could not refuse a dance from the Autumn King at the Equinox Ball he had invited us to. With a deep breath, I nodded, then accepted his hand. He crushed my fingers so tightly I thought my bones might break.

I didn't look at Callan as Tyrone steered me into the ballroom and toward the dance floor. I felt the eyes of the crowd on us as we stepped into formation, my arm against his and his hand at my waist. Revulsion swept over me, and nausea churned in my gut. That was just what I needed, to vomit all over the Autumn King. I took a shaky breath, trying to steel myself. I was not a coward. In this moment, with my fears and memories swirling around me, it was easy to forget who I was.

Firebird, I thought. *I am a firebird. Fierce and relentless.*

My hands and arms were in the same position as when I had danced with Fenn in the forest. When I looked up into Tyrone's face, it wasn't the scowling king I saw, but the playful smirk of a prince. In my mind, I was dancing with Fenn while the dragons watched us, the blue sky overhead and the lush green forestry surrounding us.

A small smile lit my face as Tyrone guided me into the waltz.

"There now," he said, his expression smug. "I knew it would all come back to you."

"What would?"

"How it is to be here with me. To dance with me."

I chuckled. "Forgive me, Your Highness, but my mind is elsewhere."

"On my brother, no doubt." His voice was clipped.

"No, actually. What passed between me and Callan is over. Quite like my arrangement with you."

Tyrone's eyes narrowed, and his grip on my waist tightened. "Don't think that I don't still own you, Aurelia. I've claimed you more than once. Don't forget that."

"I am not your property," I spat. "And you have no hold over me. My father ensured—"

He laughed, cutting off my words. "Your father ensured nothing. Do you know what he promised me? He promised me your *dragons.* He offered a fae bargain, swearing that if you did not grant access to my dragons within five years, then you would be married to me."

My blood turned cold, and my heart dropped to my stomach like a stone in the river. *Oh gods, no.* I would have called Tyrone a liar, but I knew he spoke the truth.

Father, what have you done?

Horror and rage mingled within me, but I couldn't find the strength to utter a single response. Tyrone smirked at me, his face full of triumph.

He'd won. Because he knew I would never surrender my dragons. Not to him.

"Pardon me," said a voice in my ear.

Our dance halted, and I turned to find Fenn standing next to us, his eyebrows raised. "May I steal my beloved from you?"

Tyrone opened his mouth, but before he could respond, Fenn slid between us, easily shifting my arms and gliding me forward to continue our waltz. My steps continued seamlessly, and we spun around the dance floor, leaving Tyrone staring after us.

I was torn between bewilderment and amusement. "Fenn, what the hell are you doing?" I asked through gritted teeth.

He leaned in close, his lips tickling my ear. "You two were making a scene."

My mouth went dry as I cast a quick look around the ballroom. Sure enough, the guests were glancing between me and Tyrone, who was storming off the dance floor, fuming.

Burning suns. Fenn was right. I hadn't been paying any attention to the witnesses of my conversation with Tyrone.

"How bad is it?" I whispered.

He grimaced, then leaned close to murmur in my ear, "Everyone saw you, Tyrone, and Callan return from the balcony. Judging by the rumors I've already heard floating around, it isn't hard to guess what happened."

My eyes closed briefly. "Shit. This is such a disaster."

"I can fix this. But you'll need to play along."

I opened my eyes to glare at him in suspicion. "Fix it how?"

"Do you trust me?"

I stared into his earnest green eyes. There was no trace of amusement or smugness in his face. Nothing but pure affection for me.

Against my better judgment, I found myself nodding. "Yes. I do."

He glanced at the orchestra as the music began to slow. The dance was almost over. "Prepare yourself, princess. I'm going to kiss you now."

My spine went rigid. "What?"

The final note rang out, and he dipped me low with a final flourish. The breath whooshed from me, my stomach dropping from the abrupt movement. Fenn pulled me upright again, our bodies closer than before. His face was mere inches from mine, his eyes dark and seductive as they fell to my lips. I was painfully aware of my breaths, sharp and ragged, the way his chest was flush against mine. I could feel each inhale and exhale in tandem with mine.

Applause followed the song's end, but I barely heard it, barely registered as the couples dispersed from the dance floor. Fenn continued to hold me, his face still hovering close to mine. He brought his hand to my cheek. His fingers were delicate against my skin as he tucked a curl behind my ear.

He waited, his eyes intently fixed on mine. And I realized he was giving me time to push him away, to deny him. Even now, he was offering me the choice to refuse his touch.

But I said nothing. Because this was not like when Tyrone touched me. With him, it was revulsion and despair, helplessness and fear. But now, with Fenn, I felt nothing but heat and longing.

"This will be over soon," he murmured, his breath mingling with mine.

Then he was kissing me.

THE SUMMER PRINCESS

Fenn's lips were smooth and soft and sweet. He tasted of cool mint and the wide open sky. My body soared, something within me unleashing, setting me free—as free as if I were gliding through the clouds on Mal's back, and yet... different. Once I took Mal out for a midnight ride, wanting to see the stars as we flew. It was terrifying and thrilling, and I never did it again. The night sky was so rare in the Summer Court, and it was dangerous as it impaired my vision.

But the thrill... I had yearned for that energy ever since.

Kissing Fenn tasted just like that night. It tasted like a leap off a cliff, a free-fall into the unknown.

His mouth claimed mine with expert precision, prying my lips open as his tongue slid between them. I groaned into his mouth as I tasted him in turn, unable to help myself, unable to stop the growing need pressing between us. His hand traveled up my neck and tangled in my hair. More curls spilled loose, and he tilted my head, angling me so he could more fully devour me. His tongue ravished me, sweeping through my mouth until I could no longer tell where I ended and he began. We were one, our bodies molding together.

His other hand slid along my waist, inching downward until he grazed the curve of my ass. But the heat between us masked all logic and reason. A small part of me balked at the impropriety of this moment, but it was drowned out by his touch, his taste, his tongue.

He broke the kiss only to gasp for air and dive back in, his movements more urgent and desperate, as if he couldn't get enough of me in this moment. As if he would die if he didn't keep kissing me. His hand cupped my ass, squeezing, and I moaned. He grabbed my thigh and hitched my leg up, his fingers dangerously close to my throbbing core. I wanted to scream, to cry out with need. Even through the thick fabric of my dress, I could feel the heat of his hand, his fingers, inching ever so close...

"Fenn," I breathed, before he claimed my mouth again, silencing me, drowning out my whispered pleas.

My fingers curled around the back of his neck, tugging at the soft waves of his hair, bringing his head closer. He broke away from my mouth, but then his lips were on my jaw, my throat, his tongue gliding along my neck. I threw my head back, my eyes closing in complete rapture. I wanted him to taste *all* of me. Gods, his tongue felt so good.

A soft babble of voices echoed behind me. I was prepared to drown them out, but they only grew in volume until one voice cried out, "It's simply atrocious!"

My eyes flew open, clarity slamming into me with painful force. With my neck still arched, my gaze was on the gleaming chandelier on the ceiling. I withdrew, lowering my face to stare at the crowd. Even the orchestra had ceased their playing. The guests in the ballroom surrounded us, gaping at our scandalous display. The skirts of my dress had rolled upward with the movement of Fenn's hand on my thigh, and I quickly adjusted them to cover my exposed legs. My hair fell in messy curls around me, but that couldn't be helped. I couldn't exactly pin them back into place, not without a maid's help.

My heart was already racing, but now it pounded to the rhythm of panic and mortification. Oh gods, what the hell had I just done?

I glanced at Fenn, at his dilated pupils, his lips pink and slightly swollen from our kissing. He, too, was breathless, but he wore a roguish grin that told me just how much he enjoyed the attention. He loved causing a ruckus.

My face burned, and the room suddenly felt too stifling. My chest was in knots as I glanced around the room, searching for an escape.

I spotted Callan, standing by the open balcony doors, his arms crossed and his eyebrows lowered in displeasure. A few paces away stood Tyrone, his face contorted with a mixture of fury and disgust.

I swallowed hard. This was a mistake.

The courtiers continued to murmur, pointing at us with unabashed mockery. One woman laughed, her voice a high-pitched titter. Another sneered at us, her nose wrinkling in distaste.

I was frozen, rooted to the spot. I yearned to flee, to escape from this place, but I couldn't move. I had never been the object of ridicule and mockery, but as the laughter and voices rose higher and higher, it was all I could hear. I was drowning in it. Falling.

"I think we've caused quite a scene, my dear," Fenn said loudly, lacing his fingers in mine. My hand shook, and he squeezed it as if trying to comfort me. But I couldn't be comforted. This was not something I could recover from. "We should retire to our chambers, I think."

He winked at no one in particular and pulled me off the dance floor, guiding me to the doors. The crowd did not part for us. We had to elbow our way through, enduring the askance stares and raucous laughter. My vision blurred as I took it all in, the glares and mutterings, the insults and chuckles. Were it not for Fenn's hand in mind, I would have fallen, my body barely able to hold itself up.

We reached the hall, where several curious figures drew closer to the ballroom, no doubt wondering what all the commotion was about. It wasn't until we reached the staircase that I jerked my hand from Fenn's grasp, finding my voice at last.

"What the hell were you thinking?" I hissed.

"Not here," he muttered, taking my hand again and leading me up the staircase.

I exhaled in exasperation. "Oh, *now* you're concerned with appearances? That didn't seem to bother you five minutes ago."

"*Not here*, Aurelia," he bit out.

My nostrils flared, fury rising up inside me. An array of pent-up emotions surged, fit to burst, and anger was at the forefront. I was ready to explode, ready to unleash it all on Fenn.

He steered me into my chambers, and as soon as the door slammed shut, I whirled on him. "You are a *bastard*. I can't believe you did that!"

"I did warn you." He leaned one arm against the armoire and ran his hand through his hair. I expected a smirk or a smug expression, but he looked worn and weary, as if the incident had drained him.

This only made me angrier. "That was hardly a warning! I didn't give you permission to touch me like that."

His face was uncharacteristically sober. "I know. I'm sorry. The last thing I wanted to do was touch you without your consent. But... my plan worked. I assure you that after tonight, no one will be talking about your deluded love triangle between the two Autumn brothers. They will be talking about how the Midnight Prince and the Summer Princess can't keep their hands off each other."

The heat in my face only intensified. My skin was on fire. "You can't just decide things like that without discussing it with me first!"

"This was the only solution, and it had to be done quickly," Fenn said, pushing off the armoire and closing the distance between us. "Those balcony doors were wide open, Aurelia. You want to talk about foolish actions? *That* was foolish. A private tryst between you and Callan? With Tyrone right there watching?"

"It was not a tryst!"

"And when you came back in, people noticed. *Everyone* noticed. The anger on Tyrone's face. The shame on yours. The longing in Callan's eyes as he gazed on you." He laughed, but the sound was grating and cruel. "Gods, you three are idiots. You wear your emotions plain on your faces for the world to see. You have no sense."

"How dare you—"

"People were starting to talk, Aurelia." His gaze met mine, full of steel and sharp edges. So unlike the carefree and easygoing Midnight Prince I was accustomed to. "There were whispers that Prince Callan would break off another engagement. That he would come between us like he came between you and Tyrone. I had to deflect their attention. That's the point of our little bargain, isn't it? To sell the idea of our attachment. Well, this incident tonight will sell it. People will believe we are enamored with one another."

I stared at him, too enraged to think clearly, to see that everything he said was true. "You still had no right to do that! That was not part of our arrangement."

"Our arrangement was to tell the world we were engaged. To make them believe the lie. This action solidified it. You know what didn't help? Your little tryst with the two brothers. And *yes*, it was a tryst. You might not have intended it to be, but that's what the court saw. That's what they believe." He sighed and shook his head. "If anything, *you* jeopardized our bargain with your actions tonight."

"I was on that balcony first," I said hotly. "I didn't ask Callan to follow me."

"No, but as soon as he showed up, you should have left. You should have known what that would look like if Tyrone caught you. Which he *did*."

"I have history here, Fenn! What am I supposed to do, pretend like none of it happened?"

"Yes! You're a royal! You know how this game is played."

My nostrils flared. "What happened here was messy and complicated and none of us got closure from it. I can't expect a simpleton like you to understand that. But despite what you might think, I am a living being with feelings and emotions, and sometimes I can't always turn those off."

"It was your idea to come here, you know. I told you again and again that we didn't have to do this."

"And *I* told *you* that we didn't have a choice! To not make an appearance would be the gravest of insults!"

"Oh, is that so? And what about after tonight? Do you think that's better, letting them talk like this?"

My mouth clamped shut, my fists quivering at my sides. I was ready to strike him. To pull my dagger from my pack and shove it into his chest. Instead, I jabbed my finger to the door. "Get out."

He blinked. "What?"

"Get the hell out of my room!"

He crossed his arms. "No."

My head reared back. "Excuse me?"

"I said no. I'm not leaving."

I stepped toward him and said through clenched teeth. "If you do not leave right now, I will make you."

Now his smirk was there, his eyes shining with amusement. "Is that so? I'd like to see you try."

For a moment, we stared at each other, my body burning with fury as I glared at him. He stood there, unmoving, looking down at me like I was a child throwing a tantrum.

It was humiliating. Everything about this night was pure humiliation. I couldn't take any more of it. Heat stung my eyes, and I blinked rapidly, hoping to keep the tears at bay before I made things worse. "Why not? Why won't you leave? Do you *like* being here, fighting with me?"

"Of course not. But everyone downstairs believes we are making wild, passionate love right now. And we need to keep up appearances. If

I'm spotted in the hall, everyone will know I'm not with you. And that includes the king."

His words stilled me, making everything inside me freeze. Awareness crept into my angry thoughts, sifting through the fog of my emotions.

Oh, gods. He was right. The last time I embarrassed Tyrone because of my dalliance with another man, he came to my rooms and claimed me. Took me by force.

The sting between my eyes only worsened, my vision blurring with unshed tears. "You—You think Tyrone will try to..." I couldn't finish the question.

Fenn's gaze sobered. "Yes, I do. We embarrassed him tonight. So I'm not leaving your rooms, Aurelia. Not while that bastard is roaming these halls, looking for retribution." He pushed past me and muttered, "I'll sleep on the sofa."

I turned, watching as he sauntered toward the opposite end of the room. He sank onto the cushions of the golden sofa and braced his arms on his knees. He looked utterly exhausted.

I wanted to say something, but I wasn't sure what. I stepped toward him, prepared to apologize or thank him, when a loud knock sounded at my door.

My heart jolted as I whirled toward the door. Shit. Fenn was right.

Tyrone was here.

THE MIDNIGHT PRINCE

I WAS ON MY FEET IN AN INSTANT, ALL EXHAUSTION FLEEING FROM MY body. But Aurelia, her spine rigid and her face drained of color, shook her head sharply at me.

"Let me answer it first," she whispered.

"Aurelia," I growled.

She lifted a hand to cut me off. "If he attempts anything, you have my permission to swoop in and defend my honor with the full force of your lethal charm and unstoppable charisma." Her voice was flat, her tone full of sarcasm, which surprised me. In spite of the situation, my mouth quirked upward slightly, impressed by her delivery of humor.

A fraction of her unease seemed to fade as she met my gaze. Sparks still danced between us, the lingering effects of our heated argument. But the resounding knock sounded again, jolting us both, reminding us that there was a greater danger than our ire for one another.

Aurelia shot me one last warning look before making her way to the door. I ducked behind the door as she opened it, letting the light from the sconces in the hallway filter into the darkened room.

Aurelia stiffened in surprise. "Callan."

I stood up straighter, my back against the wall, the door mere inches away from me. *Callan?* I ran a hand down my face. *Gods, he is such a fool.*

But as I glanced at Aurelia, her light orange hair tumbling down her shoulders in waves, her cheeks filling with color at the sight of her former lover, I could understand how someone would be driven mad at the idea of losing her, of never being able to touch her, or kiss her.

Gods, that kiss… The heat of it still cascaded through my body in a violent rush of awareness. I had kissed many women in my lifetime, but none of those experiences had been as intoxicating as kissing Aurelia.

Which was most unfortunate for me, as her eyes were currently fixed on a different prince. A prince other than me. And the softness in her eyes, the gentle parting of her lips, the creeping blush along her cheeks, told me exactly where her heart lay.

My gut twisted, but I forced myself to focus on their murmured conversation.

"He is unwell," Callan was saying.

"I don't understand," Aurelia said.

"Tyrone. He—He seems quite mad. After what happened tonight, he is not himself. He's paranoid, making wild, outlandish claims that someone is after him, that someone is trying to take his throne. I'm frightened, Aurelia. I really think you should go to him."

"I'm not sure what you think I can do for him," Aurelia said, her voice stiff.

"You were always able to calm him when he wasn't himself. You have a way of reaching him that no one else does. Please, Aurelia. You have to help."

Aurelia scoffed. "I will do no such thing. I owe him nothing. And I owe *you* nothing."

"No, but you owe this kingdom," Callan snapped. "You promised them a queen."

"I did not," Aurelia argued. "No formal engagement was announced."

"You promised with your actions. You promised that you would serve them, that you cared for them. If you care for them now, you'll tend to my brother."

Aurelia inhaled deeply, her chest rising from the movement. Her fists, balled tightly at her side, began to quiver. At first, I worried it was fear that overcame her. But when she spoke next, I realized it was rage.

"Let me make one thing perfectly clear," she said through gritted teeth. "My first and only priority is to my kingdom. The Summer Court. Not your brother. Not the Autumn Court. No one else. Do you understand? I don't give a damn what your brother is going through. He is a beast. A vile monster. And I won't let him near me again, no matter what he is suffering from. Now, if you'll excuse me, I have had an exhausting day, and I must rest now."

She moved to close the door, but Callan shoved his boot in the doorway, stopping it. He crowded her, stepping halfway into her room as he loomed over her.

"He is my brother," he seethed, "and I—"

In a flash, I shifted, sliding between the door and Aurelia and shoving the prince's shoulder, causing him to stumble backward in alarm. I forced a laugh. "Oh, sorry about that! You mustn't linger in doorways like that, or you might get knocked on your ass." I casually draped my arm over Aurelia's shoulders. She tensed under my touch but didn't push me away.

Callan's eyes flashed as he glanced between us, his nostrils flaring. "The king is unwell. He needs—"

"It's not our concern what the king needs. Send for your healers, if you must. We possess no magic to cure any illnesses. Goodbye now."

"You can't—"

I shut the door in his face. Even his obnoxious boots couldn't stop the force of it. The frame rattled from the impact, and Aurelia skirted away from me like a startled rodent.

I turned toward her, but she raised her hands to stop me. "Don't— Don't touch me. Please."

I froze. Her eyes were wide, her pupils dilated in fear. Her face was drained of color once again, making her appear bone-white.

"Aurelia," I said softly. "I'm not going to hurt you."

"I know." Her voice was sharp and frantic. "Logically, I know this. I know you aren't Tyrone. You aren't Callan. But the memories are suffocating now, and all I can think of are those two damned brothers and their damned claims on me and how they think I am just an object to be tossed around, and I... I..." Her voice rose with each word until she was practically screaming at me, her chest heaving as if she couldn't get enough air into her lungs.

I yearned to close the distance between us, to draw her into my chest and hold her until her breathing evened out. But I couldn't. Right now, she needed space. A sense of desperate helplessness filled my chest. I had to help her. Somehow.

"What—What can I do?" I asked. "Aurelia, please. Tell me what to do. What is it you need?"

"I need..." She faltered, considering this. "I need to not feel their skin on mine. Everywhere I look is a reminder of them. Both of them. Tyrone violated me, but Callan... He wanted to *own* me. And I don't think I realized it until now. He wanted me for himself because I was forbidden. Because he wanted what Tyrone had claimed." She shook her head, her breathing ragged. "Gods, I just want to be free of this place. I want to forget. I want something else to occupy my mind. Distract me, please. That's what I need. A distraction."

On instinct, one eyebrow quirked, and a slow smile spread across my face.

She groaned, throwing her hands in the air. "Not that! Are you daft? I said *don't touch me.*"

"I didn't say anything about touching."

She frowned. "I don't understand."

Though every part of me longed to close the distance between us, I forced myself to lean against the heavy oak door, my arms crossing over my chest. "Darling Aurelia, I can unravel you with my words alone."

She went perfectly still, her wide eyes fixed on me, a mixture of curiosity and confusion crossing her features. Her hands clasped together in front of her, her fingers toying with the folds of her crimson dress. A nervous chuckle escaped her lips. "I don't—"

"Do you know what I would do first, if I were to *properly* distract you?" I asked.

She wet her lips, and my eyes followed the movement of her tongue. No, it wouldn't be hard at all to envision how this night would go if things were different—if I were to go about seducing her like I did every other female courtier whose bedchamber I occupied.

I remained silent, waiting for her. My eyebrows lifted.

After a moment, she asked in a strained voice, "Are you really going to do this?"

"Humor me. If it does nothing for you, I'll stop, and you can crawl into that massive bed—alone—and fight your nightmares for the rest of the night."

She winced.

"You wanted a distraction," I reminded her.

She sighed. "Fine." She waved her hand idly and rolled her eyes. "*Unravel me.*" The doubt in her tone was abundantly clear.

But a strange sense of relief and boldness had swept through me from the knowledge that she *didn't* love Callan. It wasn't his body she yearned for. Besides, her doubt only made me embrace the challenge even more. My grin widened.

"Do you recall how my fingers twisted in your hair when I kissed you?"

Her eyelashes fluttered, but she said nothing.

"Your hair is like silk. So soft and lush. First thing I would do is plunge my hand into those curls and pull the last of those pins free. Let it all loose. You're most beautiful with your hair wild and untamed around you. Like the feral dragon queen you are."

Her breath hitched. Her right hand twitched, as if she was about to reach up and touch those tresses I referred to. But she merely blinked at me, her face as stoic as ever.

"Then, I would slide the thin sleeves of your dress down," I continued, my voice low and sultry. "I would count every single freckle on your shoulders. With my tongue."

A strangled sound escaped her. She cleared her throat and swallowed hard.

"Next, I would pin you against that armoire." I gestured to the piece of furniture on the other side of the door. "I would hike up your skirts, exposing those glorious thighs of yours. You would wrap your legs around me and *feel* how hard I am for you."

Her eyes closed and a soft sigh escaped her. Her hands began trembling.

"I would run my tongue along your neck, tasting your delicious skin. Then I'd bite down on your shoulder, and you'd cry out my name."

She wet her lips again. Gods, to see her like this—to imagine what I would do to her—was almost torture.

But it was working. A flush crept into her cheeks, her lips parting as her breathing sharpened.

"I'd tug down on your bodice, sliding it to the side to bear your beautiful breasts to me. And then I would feast on them. Swirl my tongue over your nipples. Close my teeth over them."

"Burning suns," she moaned. Her back arched as if she were living in my fantasy right now, beckoning me to taste her. And gods, how I wanted to.

"My hand would run up your thigh," I continued, my own voice turning raspy from the yearning pulsing through me. "My fingers would reach your slick center. You would be so wet, Aurelia. So ready for me."

"Fenn," she groaned. "Gods, I—I—"

"You what?"

Her eyes flew open, and she suddenly straightened. "Stop."

I stared at her, my heart pounding an erratic rhythm in my chest. Had I gone too far? Was she too embarrassed to continue?

Or had she simply remembered who I was, and that she would never want to do this with me?

"I—" She broke off, then licked her lips. "I need you to touch me."

My eyes flared wide. "I beg your pardon?"

"I want to erase his touches. I want to wipe him from my mind, from my memory. I want *this*"—she gestured between us—"to take its place."

I froze, not sure I was hearing her correctly. For a long moment, I said nothing. "Are you sure? Because only moments ago, you told me not to touch you. I just want you to be certain." My voice was soft and gentle as I tried to assure her it would be fine if we stopped., if we did not do this tonight.

"It will mean nothing," she said breathlessly. "I just need release. Please, Fenn. Can you do that for me?"

A mixture of disappointment and longing filled me. I didn't want it to mean nothing. I wanted to continue what we'd started in that ballroom. I wanted to show her all the ways I could worship her body, to show her just how fierce and beautiful a creature she was. To show her that I could be a man who was devoted to her, as she deserved.

But I was not worthy of her. And I never would be. She knew it, and I knew it.

She just needed a distraction. And I was a rake. This was the perfect task for me.

I allowed a feral grin to form on my lips. It was easy to don the mask everyone expected me to wear. But I had grown accustomed to taking off that mask for her. It felt wrong to wear it here and now, almost as if I was trying to deceive her.

But this was what she needed. In this moment, I would give her anything she asked for.

I pushed off the door and strode toward her slowly, giving her plenty of time to back away. Her hands were still trembling, but she held my gaze, her chin lifting, and did not move away from me.

I didn't stop until her chest was flush against mine, until I could feel the frantic fluttering of her heartbeat. Then, I kept going, walking her backward until she was pressed against the armoire. The doors rattled from the impact, and she gasped.

"Is this what you want?" I murmured.

"Yes." Her voice was only a breath.

I raised a hand and traced the line of her collarbone with my finger, following the swell of her breasts. My finger slid between them, then jerked the fabric of her dress downward.

"And this?" I asked in a whisper.

"Yes."

I tugged until her breasts were free. I took a moment to admire them. They heaved with her frantic breathing, and stars above, they were beautiful. Her nipples were already hard. Gods, she was a masterpiece. A smattering of freckles coated each breast, the patterns unique. I wanted to gaze at each one, to count how many there were, to spot the differences between the two. I wanted to study her for hours.

Instead, I bent over, running my tongue along the tip of her breast. Her moan was loud and full of need as she threw her head back against the armoire, her hips grinding against mine. I closed my lips around her nipple. With tongue and teeth, I sucked and nipped, tugging at it. Her hips rolled in silent demand.

"Gods," she rasped out. "Gods, *please*."

I hiked up her skirts, and she obediently wrapped her legs around my middle, pressing directly against my arousal. It felt ready to burst from my trousers. I wanted so desperately to bury myself inside her, to pound into her until she screamed.

But tonight was for her. Only her.

While I feasted on one breast, I cupped the other in my hand, gently squeezing, then rolling the nipple between my fingers. All the while, Aurelia writhed under me, her body quivering with anticipation. The frantic pace of her breathing only spurred me on, making me harder.

"Please," she gasped. "Fenn, please."

"Please what?" I murmured against her breast.

She groaned, muttering a string of expletives. She knew I was teasing her. I grinned as I continued licking her bosom.

"I need you inside me," she said, her voice hoarse. "*Please.*"

"Well, since you said *please…*"

"You are an ass."

I chuckled, bringing my face up to claim her mouth with mine once more. My tongue collided with hers, and then I drew back just a fraction to lick each of her lips, the lightest of touches. She uttered a sound that was a half gasp, half moan.

My hand sifted through the many layers of her impossible skirt until I found her thigh. I dragged a finger up the inside of her leg. When I reached the moisture collecting between her legs, I hummed in satisfaction.

"Darling, you are positively dripping for me." I leaned in, pressing my mouth to the hollow of her throat.

"Fenn—"

I slid my finger inside her, and she cut off with a gasping wheeze, her hips bucking. I withdrew my finger, my mouth still against her neck, and whispered, "Is that what you want?"

"I—I—"

I paused at the hesitance in her voice. "Aurelia, is this all right?"

Her eyes met mine, and they were wide and frenzied, but a strange sense of vulnerability crept into her expression. "Tyrone never did anything like this with me before."

Pure rage filled me until I saw red, envisioning nothing but the brutal death of that awful, despicable king. I leaned closer to her and growled, "Don't utter that bastard's name when I'm inside you. Think only of *your* body and what *you* want. Aurelia, do you want me to continue?" When she said nothing, I whispered, "I can make you come so violently that your bones, your blood, your very *soul* will tremble. But I will not do anything unless you want me to. So tell me, little firebird, is this what you want?"

She licked her lips then nodded vigorously. "Yes. *Yes.*"

My finger returned to her center, drawing circles around it. She sucked in a sharp inhale. I slowly slid a finger inside, and her head rolled back, her eyes closing as her face went slack. "Oh *gods*," she whispered.

I added another finger, relishing the way her body moved against mine, thrusting and jerking in silent demand. "Fenn," she gasped.

My fingers moved more intently, the motion fervent and

demanding as they pumped and thrust inside her. She moaned, louder and louder, her brows drawing together as the tension built inside her. When my fingers curled inward, brushing against her inner walls, she let out a desperate whimper.

She blindly reached for me, hands groping until they found my waistcoat. She fumbled with my buttons, but I used my free hand to grab her wrists and pin them above her head, pressing them into the armoire.

My mouth found her ear as I murmured, "Not tonight, little firebird. Tonight is only for you."

Her eyes were half crazed as she opened them to gaze at me, her lips parted and deliciously swollen from our kissing. My fingers continued to explore her center, driving into her with more force. Her eyes closed again, her mouth falling open. She thrashed, her body lurching as she rode my hand, whispering, "Oh, yes. *Yes.*"

My fingers were slick with her moisture, but I kept pumping them into her, deeper and deeper. When I inserted a third finger, she cried out, the tendons of her neck straining as she jerked. I felt her insides spasm around my fingers, and I curled them inward again, allowing any fingernails to brush those inner walls once more.

A hoarse cry burst from her as she found her release, her hips rolling against mine, driving me near to madness. The tension coiling inside me was so tightly wound, so close to the edge... Gods, my pulse was pounding, my head throbbing as every ounce of me quaked with need.

"Fenn. *Fenn.*" She whispered my name like a prayer, her face covered with a sheen of sweat. I almost came at the sound of my name on her lips.

For a moment, we were both quiet, my body still pinning hers to the armoire as our breaths slowed. Nothing but our gasps punctuated the silence. I removed my hand from inside her, my fingers slick, and let her legs slide down to the floor. She wilted in my arms, her head leaning against the door of the armoire. I held her there, keeping her upright with my chest. Her eyes closed, a look of satisfied exhaustion on her face.

Somehow, I managed to carry her to the bed and loosen her corset strings. She buried her face in the pillows, oblivious to my movements as I deftly removed her petticoat and slid it off the bed. I turned, intent on relieving myself in the bathing chamber, but Aurelia caught my hand in hers.

I blinked, startled. I had thought she was asleep. And the way she was curled on the mattress, her hair sprawled around her, her eyes tired, I could tell she was halfway there.

"Stay with me," she whispered.

I swallowed hard. "I'm not leaving. I'll be just over there on the sofa."

She shook her head. "No. Right here. Next to me. Please, Fenn."

There was that plea again, and damn if it didn't break down all my barriers. Not that there was anything left after what I'd done to her tonight—what she'd done to *me*.

"I just—I need to—" I cleared my throat. "All right. Let me change first, and I'll come back and sleep here. I promise."

She nodded, her eyes closing again. I extricated myself, fulfilling my needs in the bathing chamber as I thought of her and her perfect breasts. It didn't take long; I was already there.

But even after I'd finished, my body ached for hers. It wasn't the same. I yearned to be inside her, to come as our bodies intertwined. Not like this, alone as I fantasized of a woman who could never be mine.

But there was nothing to be done. Tomorrow would be different. Tomorrow, we would go back to loathing one another. I would become the careless rake, and she the stubborn princess who wanted nothing to do with me.

I removed my waistcoat, vest, and ascot until I was only in my shirt-sleeves and trousers. When I returned, to my surprise, Aurelia's eyes opened and fixed on me. Relief crossed her sleepy features. "You returned."

"I said I would." I slid into bed alongside her, then paused. "Is this all right?"

She wriggled closer to me, nuzzling her nose into my neck. Gods, she smelled incredible. Like jasmine and embers, and the hint of that heady smell after a rainstorm. My arm came around her, drawing her closer to me as I reveled in the warm curves of her body pressed against mine.

Yes, tonight we both had a lapse in judgment. We would succumb to this weakness only once. Tomorrow, things would return to normal.

It was a lie, of course. But my exhausted brain accepted this as I slowly drifted off to sleep.

THE SUMMER PRINCESS

In my dreams, Fenn was hovered over me, his arms braced on either side of me on the bed as he caged me in. His feral gaze swept over me, his teeth flashing in a delighted grin. His mouth was on my throat, his tongue gliding along my skin. I arched into him with a moan, desperate to finish what we started, to feel his naked body, to ravish him as thoroughly as he'd ravished me.

But in the next instant, I was sipping tea in the sitting room of Dreya's inn. Across from me, the innkeeper herself smiled blandly, stirring her spoon in her cup.

"Strange, isn't it?" she whispered.

I frowned, wondering why she spoke so quietly. "What is?"

"This place." She cast a quick gaze around the room, which had shifted. This was no longer the sitting room of the inn, but... the tea room in the Emerald Palace. My home.

And it was no longer Dreya sitting with me, but my sister, Gigi.

She sipped from her spoon, then looked at me, her eyes dull and unfeeling. They were usually a brilliant blue, like mine, but now they seemed more muted and gray. She took another long gulp of tea from her cup, then sighed and glanced toward the window, through which sunlight filtered.

"It's home, and yet... not." Her voice was distant and wistful, as if she were clinging to a memory that was slowly slipping away from her.

I glanced down at my hands folded in my lap. I wore my stained and muddy blue dress from that day I'd met Fenn in the forest. The day my family had fallen asleep, unable to be roused.

The day everything changed.

"I wish you were here with me," Gigi said softly. "I wish you were truly here."

"I *am* here," I said, my voice loud amidst the startling silence of the room. My sister was never this subdued. She was always noisy and boisterous, something we often chided her for. But in this instant, I would rather have my vibrant and energetic sister than this hollow shell of a girl.

Gigi blinked and turned to face me, as if just now realizing I was there. She chuckled lightly. "No, you aren't."

I rose from the sofa, coming to kneel at her feet. I clutched her hand in both of mine as they rested on her lap. "Gigi, I am *here*. I am with you now." Her fingers felt cold, but solid in my grip. I was somehow aware this was a dream, and yet... everything felt so real. The scratchy fabric of her dress. The plush softness of the carpet on my knees. The dampness of my skirts from my morning ride and my time in the woods. Even the smell of the mint tea stung my nostrils. Everything about this place grounded me, drawing me in.

It was real. It had to be.

Slow clarity spread in Gigi's eyes, a more luminous shade of blue bleeding through the gray and showing echoes of the sister I knew so well. Her brows knitted together. "Aurie?" Her voice was hesitant, as if she didn't dare hope that I could really be here with her.

I nodded, my eyes burning with imminent tears. Gods, I had missed her!

She swallowed hard, then squeezed my hands. "You're—You're really here?"

"Yes. It's me, Gigi." I brought her cold hand to my cheek to prove to her I was here in the flesh.

Tears spilled down her cheeks, and she let out a choked sob. "Oh gods, Aurie!" She knocked her teacup to the floor, allowing the contents to seep onto the carpet as she collapsed to her knees to embrace me. I clutched her to my chest, weeping with her as we clung to one another.

"I have so much to tell you," I whispered. "So much has happened."

Gigi suddenly withdrew to look at me with wide eyes, her face paling. "No. *No.* Aurie, you cannot be here." She glanced over my shoulder, her expression stricken as if she expected to find a horrible monster lurking behind me.

I followed her gaze, but all I saw were the open doors of the tea room and an empty hallway beyond. "Why not? I've missed you terribly. All I've wanted to do is talk with you."

She shook her head frantically, dropping my hands as she staggered to her feet. "You can't be here," she repeated. "You—You aren't supposed to be here!" She wrung her hands together and began pacing the room, her eyes wild with terror.

I stood, trying to touch her, to embrace her or hold her hands once more, but she stepped out of reach, still shaking her head.

"No," Gigi was saying as if speaking to herself. "No, you—You're different. Mother explained it to me. You *can't be here.* You're the only one who can—who can—" She brought a hand to her forehead. "Gods, Aurie. Did she find a way to trap you, too?"

I frowned, my heart wrenching in my chest. I had never seen Gigi so frightened. "What are you talking about?"

Gigi looked at me, then closed the gap between us, grasping my shoulders tightly. "You have to wake up, Aurelia. You are the only one who can stop this. The only one she can't reach. If you're here, it means she's close to trapping you. But you have to fight it. *Fight it.* You have to wake up!"

Her voice rose with each word until she was practically screaming at me. Though she stood a few inches shorter than me, she seemed to tower over me with the intensity of her words. My hands began to tremble. "Gigi, I don't—I don't understand."

"Wake up, Aurelia!" she repeated in a shout. Behind me, a strange buzzing filled the air, making the back of my neck prickle. Gigi looked over my shoulder, then made a strangled gasping sound. I turned to look, to see what lurked behind me, but she pressed her hands to my face and screamed, *"Wake up now!"*

With a jolt, I woke, my heart thundering in my chest. Something warm was pressed to my chest. I sat up quickly, the sheets and comforter shifting with the movement. The warmth left me.

Beside me, Fenn grunted in his sleep. His arm had been wrapped around me.

I stiffened, my stomach dropping as awareness flooded my mind.

Last night. The Equinox Ball. Callan and Tyrone.

And *Fenn...*

His hands on me. His tongue. The explosive release that spread through me with violent delight when his fingers moved inside me.

Heat filled my cheeks from the memory. I glanced at him, afraid he would wake. But he remained fast asleep, his long eyelashes fanned out over his cheeks.

I covered my face and found my hands were still trembling. Just like in my dream.

Shit. *My dream.*

I eased out of bed, careful not to jostle Fenn with the movement. When the mattress shifted as I stood, he sighed in his sleep, turning his head and murmuring, "Aurelia."

I stilled, thinking he'd woken up. But he remained still, his slow, soft breathing filling the room once more.

Fenn was dreaming of me. The thought sent an unexpected warmth spreading through me as I strode away from the bed.

Darkness had coated the room, and the faint moonlight shining through the curtains told me it was sometime in the middle of the night. I started pacing the room, my bare feet padding across the floor. I faintly registered that I was still partially dressed in my red gown, though the corset strings were loose and my petticoat had been removed, which made it much easier to walk. My pulse was racing, and I couldn't seem to get enough air into my lungs.

The dream had felt so very real. And Gigi's palpable terror...

It had to have been real. Wherever Gigi's consciousness was right now, I was with her for a brief moment. And there was something in that dream world that frightened her.

The thought of my baby sister so afraid made me want to draw my dagger and lunge into action, to fight off whatever foe she faced. I would die for my sister. I would do anything to save her.

What was it she'd said?

You are the only one who can stop this. The only one she can't reach.

Who was *she*? Was it the Dream Mage?

A hard lump formed in my throat, and I found it difficult to swallow.

You are the only one who can stop this.

You're different. Mother explained it to me.

I suddenly felt warm. Too warm. I wiped my forehead, and my hand came back sweaty.

Different. There was a reason I was immune to the sleeping curse. And it wasn't just because I was in the woods with Fenn or because of the rune on my back. There was something else. Something big. And Mother knew it. Now Gigi did, too.

A frantic desperation roared through me, demanding I take action. I hurried to Fenn's side of the bed and shook his shoulder.

"Fenn," I hissed. "Fenn, wake up."

He groaned and rolled over, draping one arm over his eyes.

I huffed in exasperation and jabbed my fingers into that one ticklish spot beneath his ribs.

He yelped, making a startled, choking sound as he jerked away from me. "Shit! What the hell was that for?" He sat up, rubbing his eyes, then squinted at me, his brows furrowing. "Aurelia?"

"I need your help." Gods, I hated how pathetic I sounded.

Sudden soberness filled his face, and he was on his feet in a flash. "What is it? Has that bastard king come for you?"

"No, no," I said quickly, pressing my hands to his chest to keep him from barging out of the room in search of Tyrone. As much as I would love to see Fenn slice Tyrone to bits, it was nowhere near as important as what Gigi had told me. I quickly filled him in on the details of my dream.

Fenn's frown deepened with each word. I watched for his reaction, holding my breath. I expected him to tell me it was only a dream, that my fear for my family had simply manifested itself into a nightmare.

But he didn't. He remained silent for a long time, his eyes calculating. After a long moment, he murmured, "It's the Dream Mage."

My pulse quickened as he confirmed my suspicions. "You remember what the witch sage said?" I asked, recalling Samiria's words. *"This particular spell bears resemblance to the magic of the Dream Mage."*

That had to be who Gigi had been referring to. The one she was so afraid of.

"The Dream Mage is powerful," Fenn said. "I haven't met her, but I know her name is Rosalina. She's the former queen of the Court of Twilight."

My eyes widened. "You mentioned that a friend of yours in the royal family can tell you where the Dream Mage is."

"Yes. But Aurelia, we have to be careful. The Dream Mage collects her subjects when they are asleep. If she's found a way to get to you, then you're only safe when you're awake."

I swallowed hard. "I—I need something from you, Fenn."

"Anything," he said at once.

His immediate response startled me, and for a moment, I gazed at him in surprise. His expression was filled with determination, his normally playful green eyes appearing more olive in the darkened room. He watched me with such solemness, such concern, that he seemed almost unrecognizable.

But in this moment, I realized *this* was the true Fenn. The one he only revealed behind closed doors. Not the flippant, coy, roguish prince he let everyone believe him to be. Somehow, over the course of our journey, he'd shown me his true nature. It was shocking but also… beautiful. This earnest side of Fenn was kind and loyal and willing to do anything for me.

The thought made my heart twist so painfully in my chest that I forced my mind away from this revelation. I could dwell on that later. But for now…

I looked him straight in the eye and said, "I need you to cast a rune on me. It's time to see what this witch mark on my back truly means."

The Midnight Prince

Thirteen lit candles formed a circle around the bedchamber, one for each of the witch goddesses. When Aurelia asked me if this was truly necessary, I had said it couldn't hurt. Lighting thirteen candles was said to bring the goddess's favor when casting runes.

And I needed all the good favor in the realm if this was to work.

Anxiety tied my stomach into knots. I'd only cast the revelation rune once, and it was when my childhood friend Marek and I had been experimenting with witch runes in our youth. Nothing as serious as this.

I swirled my finger in the saucer of oil and lavender, trying to keep my hand from shaking. Aurelia had changed into her nightgown and now sat on the edge of the mattress, one sleeve pulled over to expose her shoulder, her eyes fixed on me.

"I don't know if this will work," I said for the third time.

"Fenn, I know." Aurelia's voice was soft and patient, but I knew she was likely as nervous as I was.

"I could hurt you." I glanced at her, allowing a moment of vulnerability in that brief look. My fear. My concern for her safety.

Such weakness was so uncharacteristic for me that I couldn't stop myself from quickly adding, "And, you know, that would jeopardize our bargain. I'm not supposed to bring harm to you."

"From what we know, this rune on me is powerful enough to protect me from a sleeping curse," she said. "If anything, I'd be worried it would react to your spell and harm *you*."

I chuckled. "Don't worry about me. I have a protection rune

remember?" I stared at the liquid in the saucer, running the slippery substance over my fingers once more. "This—This will work better with your blood. But I think we should try it first without, just in case. Blood tends to strengthen a spell to its maximum effect, but if this backfires and whatever magical force inside you lashes out, then we certainly wouldn't want to escalate that."

"Right." She sat up straighter, her chin jutting out with determination, eyes blazing. In this moment, she was my fierce little firebird, scared of nothing and no one.

I wasn't sure when she became *my* firebird, in my mind. The thought was so alarming that I pushed it away before it consumed me.

I breathed a long, slow exhale before bringing the saucer with me as I sat right next to Aurelia. She obediently angled the left side of her body away from me to give me better access to her shoulder blade, where the black spiral marking was etched into her flesh. I found myself staring at the exposed skin, the pale rosy complexion and the smattering of freckles I loved so much. Gods, had it really only been hours ago that I'd been running my tongue over those very freckles? And now we were dabbling in witch runes.

I had never been this nervous when conducting experiments with Marek. Then again, we had been young and foolish, heedless of our own safety.

But this was the heir to the Summer Court before me. And she harbored a dangerous magic that we knew nothing about.

If this went badly…

No. I wouldn't allow myself to think it.

Stop being such a fool, Fenn, I chided myself, before dipping my fingers into the mixture once more and painting the image over the marking on Aurelia's skin. She stiffened and inhaled sharply. I knew from experience that, when the concoction was spread on a witch rune, it stung slightly.

"Sorry," I muttered.

"It's fine."

With careful precision, I painted a circle with three dots on one side and a curved arrow on the other. Then, I slowly withdrew my hand and waited.

Aurelia was holding her breath, her body as still as a statue. I wished

I could see her face, to offer her some reassurance. But I couldn't even reassure myself at this point.

The silence in the room was deafening. My pulse thundered in my ears, roaring so loudly I thought she would surely hear it.

Just when I was about to declare the attempt a failure, the spiral on Aurelia's shoulder began to glow a brilliant gold. I stared at it, eyes wide, as a shape took form. It blurred and spread, dancing across her skin like magic light. My brow furrowed as I tried to make out what the image was.

"That feels funny," Aurelia whispered. "What are you doing?"

"Nothing," I said quickly. "It's the rune. It's… making an image."

"An image of what?"

"I can't tell. It looks like a cross between a horse and a bird." I knew it sounded ridiculous, but that was all I could make out.

"Hmm," Aurelia said thoughtfully. "It's definitely an animal?"

"Yes. It has wings."

"A dragon?"

I cocked my head. If I squinted and blurred my vision, then yes, it resembled a dragon. "Perhaps."

"Maybe it's a familiar."

I frowned. "Why do you say that?"

"I—I'm wondering if, perhaps, I have witch blood in me. If that's why my powers are so volatile, and that's why this rune is on me, to protect others from my dangerous power." She paused, then added in a rush, "It's a silly theory, but I've been turning it over in my mind ever since the incident with the goblins."

"So you think your familiar is a dragon?" My eyes grew wide. "You think it's Mal."

She nodded. "It would explain why I feel such a connection with him."

I sighed, absently swirling my fingers in the lavender oil once more. "It's up to you if you want to try the spell again with your blood."

"Yes," she said at once.

"Aurelia, it could be dangerous."

"I need answers. And to do nothing more would drive me mad. Please, Fenn."

There was that damned word again, tugging on my heart, making me powerless before her. I closed my eyes, willing the gods to give me strength to withstand this woman.

"All right." I drew my short sword, and Aurelia stretched out her hand. With the sharpened point, I pricked her finger and allowed several drops to mingle with the oil in the saucer. The mixture sizzled with each droplet.

I swirled my fingers once more, then painted the rune on her shoulder again. The crimson liquid stained her skin, and it glowed gold just like before. But this glow burned brighter and brighter, illuminating the entire room, brighter than the sun at midday. I shielded my eyes from the intensity of it, and Aurelia's back arched, her head thrown back as she cried out. Her body went rigid, her arms stiff at her sides.

"Aurelia?" I asked, panicked.

She said nothing. I set the saucer down and came around the bed to face her.

My heart seized in my chest.

Her eyes were all green with black slits in the middle, like a snake. I had seen her eyes once like this before—when she'd set those goblins on fire. I had thought I'd imagined it, but this confirmed it.

"Aurelia," I whispered, reaching for her hand.

When my skin met hers, she hissed, baring her teeth at me. Long, pointed fangs lengthened from her canines.

I jerked back, afraid she was somehow venomous and would poison me. Like a prey facing a predator, I held perfectly still. All it would take was a single thought to set me on fire, just like the goblins. She was staring at me with those all-consuming eyes, looking at nothing and everything all at once. She cocked her head as if considering me.

Was she going to lunge for me? Was she merely assessing an opponent?

"You know me," I murmured. "You know who I am. I am not your enemy."

She didn't move. Her body remained frozen with preternatural stillness.

"Aurelia," I said again, my voice firm. I had to bring her back somehow. Mustering all my courage, I said in my most cavalier voice, "Don't make me kiss you again, because I will."

Her eyelids fluttered, and for a moment, the usual blue crept into her eyes before the green devoured it once more.

Half my mouth quirked upward in a smile. "You liked it, didn't you? My mouth on you. My tongue. Admit it. You want more."

Her eyes closed, and she shuddered violently, her shoulders trembling from the motion.

"I'm here, Aurelia." I took a chance and brushed my fingers against hers again. She jerked, hissing once more, but when her eyes opened, they were blue and full of confusion.

"F-Fenn?" She shook her head, her eyes shifting from blue to green and back again. "Oh, gods, what—what is happening?"

I stepped closer, clasping both her hands tightly in mine. "It's all right. I'm here. Nothing will happen to you. Come back to me. Come back, and we'll figure this out together. I swear it."

She inhaled a shaky breath, blinking rapidly as if to clear a strange fog from her mind. She wet her lips, and my stomach churned at the sight of her *forked tongue.*

Holy gods.

I forced down my horror and fear, determined to remain stoic and strong for her. She was terrified, and she needed something to anchor her in this moment. I needed to be that anchor for her.

"Come back to me." I raised her hand and brought it to my lips, pressing a soft kiss to her fingertips.

She sighed softly, her shoulders sagging. She swayed, her face going pale and her eyelids fluttering.

I caught her before she fell over. Her skin was cool to the touch, and she trembled in my grasp. I tenderly brushed the loose hair out of her face, and she gazed foggily up at me. "You—You—"

I shook my head, pressing my finger to her lips. "Don't speak. You need to rest.

Her eyes fluttered shut once more, and her head sank onto my lap as unconsciousness claimed her.

I watched her sleep for a long moment, worried the strange beast within her would emerge again. But as the sounds of her slow breathing filled the chamber, it was clear the foreign presence was gone.

But there was no mistaking it. Whatever dwelled inside her was some kind of monster.

The Summer Princess

Black flames consumed my dreams. The heat scorched my skin, melting my flesh away. I tried to scream, but my voice was lost in the firestorm.

Then, amidst the scourging flames, a brilliant silver light shone, igniting the space around me. From within the light came a black-scaled figure I knew well.

"Mal!" I surged toward him, wrapping my arms around his neck and holding him tightly. He nuzzled his snout into my neck and licked me affectionately.

"What are you doing here?" I peered back to look into his golden eyes. "Are you trapped in the dream world, too?"

I am not, he said. *But she is close.*

My mouth fell open. Mal's deep, soothing voice echoed in my head as clearly as if he were another person conversing with me. "You—You can speak to me?"

I always have, Aurelia. You know this.

I shook my head. "No, I don't—You never—"

There isn't time. You must heed my warning. The Dream Mage is waiting for you, and you must be ready. You must unlock the magic within you if you are to save your kingdom.

"I don't understand." Panic rose up inside me. "How am I supposed to do that? The last time I unleashed my powers, I nearly killed an entire clan of witches. I have no control over it!"

You have more control than you think, Aurelia. Think of the level of control you exercise when we are flying through the sky. You put your trust in me to keep you safe, and you must do the same with your magic. Let it go. Let go of the reins, Aurelia.

"I can't!" I protested. "Mal, I could kill someone!"

Aurelia—

His words were cut off by a loud banging. I jolted, my eyes flying open and my heart lurching violently in my chest.

I sat up, finding myself half on Fenn's lap at the edge of the bed. His eyes opened, his body jerking as if he, too, had fallen asleep. "What is it?" he mumbled sleepily.

The banging sounded again, and I jumped, realizing someone was pounding on the door. The candles were still lit, casting the room in a soft amber glow. But the darkness from the window told me it still wasn't morning yet.

Gods, would this night ever end?

More pounding on the door. Then, a horribly familiar voice. "Aurelia, let me in!"

My blood ran cold. It was Tyrone. He had come for me after all.

I was on my feet in an instant, but so was Fenn, his short sword drawn. He gave me a warning look. I darted to the other side of the room, grabbing my dagger from my pack with shaking hands. I would stab the Autumn King if he tried to touch me. Even if it started a war between our kingdoms, I swore I would never let him touch me again.

Fenn casually strode to the door, opening it just a crack. "Your Highness," he said tersely. I tried to peer around him to catch a glimpse of Tyrone, but the door blocked my view. "This is quite an ungodly hour for a social visit, especially in my fiancée's chambers."

"I… I need to… speak with Aurelia." Tyrone's voice was ragged and breathless, as if he had sprinted up the stairs to my rooms.

I frowned. This was nothing at all like the deep, enraged tone I'd expected to hear from him, all authority and fury. This sounded like a completely different person. Someone weak, terrified, and a bit unhinged.

Not Tyrone at all.

"I'm sure whatever you need to speak with her about can wait until morning," Fenn said tersely. "Good night, Your Highness."

He moved to close the door, but, just like his brother, Tyrone shoved his foot in the way, the wooden door rattling from the force of his movement. "I am in *danger*. Do you hear me? Someone is trying to kill me."

I froze, my eyes going wide. My heart lurched painfully in my chest. What the hell was he talking about?

Tyrone was a full blooded fae, so he couldn't lie.

But... he could be mistaken. He had to be. Callan had said he was unwell. Paranoid, even.

Fenn cocked his head. The only betrayal of his unease was the firm set of his shoulders, but his voice was perfectly casual as he asked, "What makes you say that?"

"Someone is following me," Tyrone said in a whisper. "I hear them creeping behind me. All night, I've tried to evade them. But with the household staff asleep for the night, and the courtiers, too, I'm—I'm alone now. And I can't be alone, or I will die. Don't you understand?"

"So, why did you come to Aurelia's room?" Fenn's voice was ice-cold. I knew if I could see his face, his green eyes would flare with intensity, his jaw rigid with determination and fury. This was one of the few moments where, instead of wearing his cavalier prince mask, he was wearing his deadly Night Fae mask. The very room seemed to darken with the authority in his tone. The candles flickered slightly, and I suppressed a shudder.

"Because she is powerful," Tyrone hissed. "I need her power right now. She's the strongest fae in this castle. Only she can fight off whoever is stalking me. Please, Fennick."

I didn't know if I should laugh or cry. Tyrone thought I was power-ful? What in the world gave him that idea? I had never shown my power to him before.

"Aurelia hasn't unlocked her fae magic," Fenn said innocently. "Why do you think she can protect you? Don't you have some kind of strong, elemental power at your disposal?"

"Do you want me to set the entire castle ablaze?" Tyrone snarled. "Fire does me no good. All it does it light the path before me, but whoever follows me is able to vanish into the shadows, even when I burn my flame as brightly as it can go." He groaned, and the door frame creaked as he no doubt leaned on it with his arm. "Our witches have told stories of a princess of the Summer Court who nearly razed their sisters' clan to the ground with her magic."

My blood ran cold, my stomach hollowing as the echoes of screams filled my mind. The faces, contorted with grief and agony. The flames consuming the tents and trees, burning them to nothing but ash.

And people were talking about it. The witch clans were spreading word of a dangerous magic. *My* magic.

Now, the other courts knew about it, too.

I covered my face with my hands, but that couldn't block out the horrors circling my mind. Enemies waging war on our kingdom, not just for our dragons, but for *me.* Either to use me as a weapon, or to end me so I wouldn't be a threat. More screams. More deadly inferno.

Nothing but carnage and destruction and misery.

A sob built up in my throat, and I couldn't stop a small whimper from escaping.

Fenn stiffened, and Tyrone sucked in a breath. "She's awake, isn't she?" the king asked. He pushed forward, but Fenn shoved him backward.

"You are overstepping, Your Highness," Fenn seethed. "Walk away. Now. Before you make yourself an enemy of the Star Court."

My throat went dry. Would Fenn really do that? Would he risk a war with his people, all for me?

"*Please.* I—"

A loud *thunk* cut him off, followed by a roar of rage.

"Shit," Fenn muttered, ducking down low, his sword raised.

I couldn't hide any longer. I surged forward, but Fenn snatched my arm, dragging me to a crouching position beside him, his arms hovering protectively over me. I glanced around, heart thundering, and found an arrow embedded into the door just a few inches above where Fenn had been standing.

No, not an arrow… A bolt from a crossbow.

"*Shit,*" Fenn said again

My wide eyes were fixed on the bolt in the door. A steady stream of blood was trickling from it.

"Fenn," I whispered.

"Stay behind me," he breathed.

"Where is Tyrone?"

A low groan answered me, echoing in the hall. I tried peering around Fenn, but he continued to shield me. "I'm serious, Aurelia! Stay put."

"Why, so whoever is out there can kill us?" I snapped. With all my strength, I pushed against Fenn's back. He stumbled, grunting in surprise, which was all I needed to slide around him.

He swore as I crept into the hallway, still hovering just above a crouching position, my legs moving awkwardly like a crab.

The sconces were burning faintly, barely illuminating the golden rug that ran down the length of the hallway. But even in the low light, I could make out the splotches of blood on the floor.

My heart sank into my stomach. Shit, shit, shit…

Nothing but stillness surrounded me. Whoever had groaned earlier had been silenced.

I didn't want to think about what that meant. But deep down, I knew; Tyrone was dead.

So, why was I creeping down the hallway? Logic meant nothing to me now. All I knew was the quivering in my hand as I wielded my dagger, blade out, so if anyone rushed me, they would get stabbed.

There was no way out if I stayed in my bedroom. Tyrone had been right; someone was after him.

And if they had been stalking him, they would know Tyrone had been speaking with someone. They would come after me and Fenn.

A ringing sounded in my ears, and goose flesh puckered along my arms, making me shiver. I continued following the trail of blood, focusing on taking steady breaths. In this moment, I wished for Tyrone's fire magic; if I could light a brilliant torch that eliminated the shadows in every corner of this hall, I would feel a lot better.

A choked, gurgling sound echoed nearby, and I froze. Someone coughed, and it sounded wet.

Tyrone.

Then, I was running, urgency flooding my veins, my blood pounding. Panic blared in my mind like a warning bell, over and over and over again.

I rounded a corner and found him lying in a pool of blood with a bolt lodged in his chest. The thick liquid surrounding him reflected the light of the sconces and filled the air with a sharp, metallic smell.

Gods, how could one bolt cause so much damage? Tyrone was fae. His body should have been able to withstand the injury easily.

I rushed to his side, ripping a piece of fabric from his tunic to try to staunch the flow of blood.

"Aur—Aurelia," he choked, and blood bubbled from his lips. "Don't."

I shook my head, struggling to stop the gushing blood. But his face was so very pale. He had lost too much blood already.

"The bolt... is iron," he wheezed. "It's too late."

"Dammit, Tyrone! Do you understand what happens if you die? You left a trail of blood from my rooms!" Tears stung my eyes as I tried fruitlessly to save this despicable man's life. Mere moments ago, I had daydreamed of ending him, of letting my blade be the last thing he saw.

And now, there was a killer out there who had made damn sure that there was evidence leading to my bedroom just before Tyrone's death.

"Tell... my brother..." Tyrone coughed again, spraying flecks of blood on my nightgown.

"Be quiet," I ordered, still pressing hard on the wound.

Tyrone's eyes started to glaze over. "So much..." He trailed off with another rattling breath and then went perfectly still.

"Tyrone," I said sharply, then shook his shoulders. "Tyrone!" My voice rang, bouncing off the walls.

From down the hall, a lantern lit. Shuffling noises drew closer.

I stood, my hands and skirt covered in Tyrone's blood.

Oh gods. *Oh gods.*

"Who's there?" called a voice. A servant, no doubt.

I was stunned. Frozen. Unable to move. Terror had me gripped in its vise, and I could do nothing but stare, wide-eyed, as a light drew closer. My mind screamed at my body to move, to hide, to *do something*, but my limbs refused to move.

A warm hand closed on mine. I uttered a soft yelp, but someone was already tugging me forward. A scream built up in my throat, and I waved my dagger, prepared to stab whoever was trying to grab me...

But it was Fenn. His emerald eyes gleamed in the dim light, flaring with intensity.

"Run," he urged.

He tugged on my arm more forcefully, and at long last, I found strength in my limbs. Just as footsteps drew nearer, Fenn and I took off, our steps echoing in the hallway.

THE MIDNIGHT PRINCE

Aurelia's hand was shaking in mine as we sprinted down the hallway. Our feet were bare, our clothes sparse; we hadn't had time to pack our belongings because Aurelia had been a bloody idiot chasing after a dying king.

Luckily, it seemed most of the castle was still asleep. But it wouldn't take long for the staff to discover Tyrone's body and sound the warning bells.

We had to leave this court. *Now.*

We flew down the staircase, our feet padding on the carpet. Inside, my heart beat a roaring rhythm in my chest, panic flooding my veins.

Gods, my kingdom was already in enough trouble. Now, the Autumn Court would be after me…

Shit, shit, *shit.*

Aurelia panted behind me, her breathing ragged. She let out a small cry, and when I glanced over my shoulder at her, I found her face was smeared with blood and tears.

"Are you crying for that bastard?" I hissed.

She only hiccuped, shaking her head, her face crumpling. Stars above, I would never understand this woman.

We flew down the corridor, ducking behind a suit of armor as a servant bustled past.

Instead of heading for the massive double doors that led to the courtyard below, I followed the servant through a door, descending down a narrower staircase.

"Where are we going?" Aurelia whispered.

I didn't answer, making sure to keep a safe distance from the woman who made her way down the stairs. The faint light of her candle cast an eerie amber glow on the stone walls surrounding us, but I was grateful for the light to illuminate the way. I didn't fancy taking a tumble down the stairs when I was running for my life.

We reached the bottom and lingered for a moment as the maid strode down the hall to the servants' quarters. When the door snapped shut behind her, we were plunged in darkness, and silence filled the air. Aurelia's fingernails dug into my palm. Not a single sconce was lit. It was nothing but total and complete blackness.

Aurelia trembled beside me, but I found myself smiling. It was just like home. She likely couldn't see too clearly, but I had the blood of the Night Fae in my veins. Even in the dark corridor, I could make out the lengthy narrow hallway and each door that led to a servant's room.

I squeezed Aurelia's hand to reassure her. "Come on."

We inched down the hall, and for the first time, I was grateful we wore no shoes. Our steps were completely silent.

I paused a few doors down, pressing my ear to the door and listening. The first one had snores coming from the other side. But the second was utterly silent.

Carefully, I inched open the door and peered inside. My gaze swept over the empty bed before I surged inside, dragging Aurelia with me. I softly closed the door before digging through the belongings of whoever once lived here.

"What the hell are you doing?" Aurelia breathed. She stumbled, running into a night table, and swore loudly. "Don't you need a candle or something?"

"Night Fae, remember? Aha!" I grinned as I found a pair of boots and a cloak that looked close to Aurelia's size. Whoever stayed in this room was clearly a woman. I tossed them over to her, then whispered, "Put these on. I'll be right back."

"Fenn—" she objected, but I had already left, gently easing the door shut behind me.

It took me a few more doors before I found an empty manservant's room. The boots were a bit small on me, but they would have to do. As I made my way back to Aurelia, I heard shouts from upstairs.

We were out of time.

Aurelia was pulling the dark hood over her face when I burst into the room. Her face was still sticky with blood and tears, but she looked more resolute and determined, and her eyes were clear. She nodded once, and we hurried through the hall and down another smaller set of stairs. Something banged loudly behind us—a door crashing open perhaps—and we quickened our pace.

At the bottom of the stairs were two doors, and I faltered. I had never been this way before.

But Aurelia had. She shoved past me. "This way." She threw open the door on the left, and we hurried through. It opened to small patch of grass facing a sloping hill. In the distance, I recognized the royal stables.

That was when the warning bell sounded. The chime rang out through the kingdom, blaring against my ears.

Nausea churned in my gut, but I couldn't dwell on it. I couldn't think of how I was now an enemy to this kingdom. Mother would be so furious.

We had almost reached the stables when Aurelia suddenly stopped short.

It took me a few steps to discover she wasn't beside me. I turned to her, my eyes wide with panic. "What are you doing? We have to move!"

"I need to speak with Callan."

I stared at her. "Are you insane? He'll have you imprisoned on the spot!"

"He won't. I know him. I need to speak with him."

I swore, turning away from her and running a hand through my hair. "Aurelia, you are *impossible.* If we linger here, we will be caught and tried for assassinating the king. You know this."

"If we flee, we will only look more guilty!" she argued. "And the Autumn Court will invade *my kingdom.* My kingdom which currently has no defense, no armies, not even a royal family. Fenn, if we leave, we are sentencing my court to death."

I drew closer to her, placing my hands firmly on her shoulders. "Aurelia, listen to me. Even if they did attack your court, you have your dragons to protect it. But I don't believe Callan will let that happen. That foolish prince is in love with you. He won't see clearly, and he will direct his rage to me and my kingdom. He will attack the Star Court first. I am sure of it."

She blinked at me. Clearly, she hadn't considered this. "But… Tyrone was in *my* chambers."

"Did you hear me? Callan doesn't think clearly when it comes to you. And he knew his brother was paranoid, claiming someone was after him. He *knows* it wasn't you. But it would be easy for him to believe it was me. Or someone working for me. He will convince himself that I've poisoned you, turning you against him, brainwashing you into believing you are in love with me."

Clarity sparked in her gaze, her eyebrows lifting. I could tell I was convincing her.

Shouts echoed nearby. Alarm raced through me, and I took her hand. We sprinted for the stables, rounding the corner and nearly colliding with the stable hand.

He was a boy, likely no older than sixteen. He yelped in fright, staggering backward, the bales of hay dropping from his arms.

I stepped forward, but Aurelia grabbed my arm and hissed, "Don't kill him!"

"I'm not going to kill him," I said, shooting her an incredulous look before turning to the trembling boy. *"You didn't see us."* My voice turned low and ethereal, with an echo from my fae magic pulsing around us. *"You fled from the stables when you heard a strange noise."*

The air thrummed with power, making the hairs on my arms stand up. I sensed Aurelia staring at me in horror, but I couldn't meet her gaze.

"Leave now," I said, layering more magic onto my voice.

The boy stared at me with wide, unseeing eyes. After a moment, he turned on his heel and stalked off, leaving the hay strewn all over the ground.

I rolled my shoulders back with a loud exhale, and the thrumming in the air stopped, replaced only by the chill of night and the clanging of the warning bell.

"What the hell was that?" Aurelia demanded. I finally turned to look at her. Her eyes blazed with anger and the hint of betrayal.

My stomach dropped at that look. I knew she was re-evaluating our every encounter, wondering if I had used my powers on her before.

Whatever trust we had established was now broken.

"I'll explain later." I ducked into one of the stables and retrieved a large white stallion. "Come on, he's already saddled. Probably belongs to one of the courtiers from the ball."

I swung atop the horse, but Aurelia hesitated, still visibly shaken by what I'd done to the stable hand.

"Would you have preferred I gut him with my sword?" I snapped. "Get on!"

Aurelia puffed an exasperated breath. She ignored my outstretched hand and swung up, settling in front of me on the saddle. With my arms on either side of her, I flicked the reins and dug in my heels, spurring the horse into motion. In seconds, we were taking off, galloping madly down the road. Behind us, more shouts echoed. I chanced a glance behind us and found flickering lantern lights illuminating dozens of shadowy figures.

Soldiers, no doubt.

I flicked the reins again, and the stallion put on a burst of speed. Wind whipped fiercely at us, and Aurelia's hood fell down, her strawberry hair billowing around us.

"He won't last long if we push him like this," Aurelia said. "Not with two riders."

"We don't need to go far. We just need to make it to the Mistwood Hills and we'll be clear."

"What makes you say that? The soldiers can easily follow us through those hills."

"You'll see," I muttered darkly.

Aurelia glanced at me over her shoulder, brows furrowed and her expression full of mistrust. I had already revealed my fae magic to her. And now, we were about to venture through the deadly Mistwood Hills, which would only further remind her of the despicable nature of my court.

As the horse carried us farther away from the Autumn Palace, my mouth set into a grim line as I felt that impenetrable barrier wedging itself between me and the princess once more.

The Midnight Prince

We rode hard for an hour before the mist began to overtake us. Aurelia stiffened in alarm, her back pressing into my chest, but she said nothing as we slowed to a trot to give the stallion a bit of a rest.

The mist would protect us. I knew that much.

When the fog was so thick we could barely see the path in front of us, I pulled on the reins, and the horse stopped. A sheen of sweat coated his flanks, and he was panting.

I slid off the saddle and helped Aurelia down. She looked around, her eyes wide with fear. "Are you sure we should be stopping?"

"The soldiers won't follow us in the mist," I said, stroking the horse's nose. "There's a stream close by where we can rest and drink."

"Why won't they follow us?" Her tone was sharp. When I said nothing, she grabbed my arm, forcing me to face her. Her expression was hard, her eyes glinting like shards of ice. "Answer the damn question, Fenn."

I looked at her, my expression stoic and blank. "Because the mist is poisoned."

Her face slackened in surprise, the blood draining from her cheeks until she was as pale as a corpse. "*Poisoned?*"

"Yes. It's from a spell cast by my ancestors, meant to protect our kingdom from invaders. It went awry, and spread across the hills."

"I—But we—How are we supposed to cross if it's *poisoned?*" she sputtered.

"Anyone who possesses the blood of the Night Fae are immune to it."

Her eyebrows lowered. "*I* do not possess such blood, Fenn."

My gaze cut to her. "You're with me. You'll be fine."

Her cheeks flushed, her eyes darkening with rage. "Fenn, you'd better—"

With a sigh, I silenced her by placing my hands on her shoulders. She glared up at me. "The spell has loopholes. If someone in a traveling party possesses blood of the Night Fae, the entire party will be protected. And even if that weren't the case, I have a strong suspicion that you would be protected anyway. You aren't fully fae. At least, not seelie."

She blinked, but before she could reply, I turned back to the horse, grabbing the reins and guiding him forward into a slow walk.

After a few moments, Aurelia caught up to me. "What do you mean, I'm not fully fae?"

"When I cast that rune on you, I saw your unseelie form."

She shook her head. "You're wrong. I'm not unseelie."

I turned to shoot her a dubious look. "Are you sure about that?"

She opened and closed her mouth, clearly unwilling to assert her certainty on the matter. Because that would be a lie. After a moment, she stammered, "I—I thought I was part witch! Couldn't that be it?"

"I've never seen witch magic like that before."

"That doesn't mean it's not true," she said hotly. "Isn't there some realm of possibility that there is magic out there you haven't seen before?"

"Of course there is," I snapped, stopping to face her. The rage and unease bubbled up inside me until it boiled over, and I couldn't stop it. "But witches don't have unseelie forms, Aurelia. *You do.* I saw your green eyes. I saw your godsdamned forked tongue. The only explanation is that you have unseelie blood in you. And if you weren't such a stubborn fool, you would see it, too."

Her head reared back, shock, hurt, and anger mingling in her expression. "What the hell do you know? You've known me all of four days, and suddenly you're an expert on my magic? What about *your* monstrous powers? You controlled the mind of that stable hand like it was nothing! Maybe *you're* the one who's unseelie."

"Don't be ridiculous. That's just my fae power."

"Oh, so you don't deny it? You *can* control people. You've probably been controlling me this entire time. That's why I agreed to this wretched bargain with you, it's why I let you kiss me, it's why I let you put your hands all over me—"

I was in her face in seconds, baring my teeth, the fury overflowing within me. How dare she cast judgments on my magic? How dare she look at me with such disgust and horror? "I haven't used my powers *once* on you, princess," I spat. "This is exactly why I didn't tell you—because I knew you would judge me for it. You would think me callous and unfeeling, a vicious savage who forces everyone to do his bidding."

"That's not—" She broke off, her mouth clamping shut, stopping herself before she uttered the lie.

Because it was true. Of course it was.

I gave her a cold smile. "It *is* true." I turned away from her, but she grabbed my shoulder, spinning me to face her.

"If you had just *told* me, I would have believed you. If you had opened up about your powers and told me the truth, instead of letting me find out like that, then I would have trusted you!"

"Oh?" I arched a doubtful eyebrow. "Just like you were forthcoming about *your* magic? About what happened to the witch clans?"

Her face paled once more, and she took a step back.

I smirked. "I thought so. You can't expect me to bare all my secrets to you, princess, if you don't do the same."

"And *you* can't expect me to share absolutely everything with you after only knowing you a few days!" she cried. "Trust comes one step at a time, and I made that first step. I *did* open up to you, Fenn. I told you about—about Tyrone." Her voice quivered, but she pushed onward, in spite of the tears shining in her eyes. "I haven't told anyone about that, not even my own sister. But I trusted you with it."

"Only because you had to! Only because our bargain was at stake! If we hadn't stopped in the Autumn Court, you never would have told me about it, would you?"

Her silence was answer enough.

My smirk vanished, and my eyebrows lowered as I glared at her, taking a step closer so I could loom over her. My nostrils flared as I said in a low voice, "So we're agreed then. You keep your secrets, and I'll keep mine. We only have to pretend for a few more days, and then this miserable bargain will be fulfilled. Then we can finally be rid of each other."

I turned away from her again, and this time she didn't stop me. She said nothing as I guided the horse forward.

It was just as well. I couldn't face her any longer or she would see the devastation in my expression.

Because as much as I had tried not to, I was starting to fall for her.

I needed this reminder. I needed to remember that she saw me as nothing more than a monster. Someone she could never love.

So, this was for the best.

It didn't take long for us to find the small stream nestled in the Mistwood Hills. The path was consumed by fog, but my feet knew the way. The blood within me guided my steps, and with Aurelia following behind me, our journey was unimpeded. After half an hour of walking, the air was starting to thicken, and it was getting harder to breathe.

Just because I was immune to the poison didn't mean it did nothing to me. Sweat formed on my brow, and my lungs strained with every breath.

The trickling of the stream reached our ears before we saw it. Even through the fog, it was almost impossible to make out the sparkling waters in the moonlight. I sank onto a boulder nearby and wiped sweat from my brow. Aurelia collapsed on the ground, leaning back on her elbows and tilting her head toward the sky as she gasped for breath.

The horse made his way to the stream, unperturbed by the mist. I vaguely wondered if ordinary animals were completely immune. Did they feel nothing at all? How blissful that must be. I stared as the horse greedily lapped up the water.

From across the stream, movement caught my eye. Were it not for my Night Fae blood, I might have missed it. My eyes narrowed as I tried to see through the mist.

There it was again. A figure appeared across the stream before the mist swallowed it up again.

I slowly slid off the boulder, making my way to Aurelia, who still sat in the dirt. I squeezed her arm, and she stiffened.

"What?" she hissed.

I hastily brought my finger to my lips in warning, my gaze still fixed on that spot across the stream.

She stilled, her breath hitching, her arm going tense in my grip. I crouched down low, positioning myself in front of her to shield her from whoever watched across the stream.

If they were here, they had Night Fae blood. They could likely see us, too.

Snap. The sound split through the air. Instinct drove me to shove Aurelia to the ground, my body atop hers.

Thunk. The bolt sank into the earth just inches from my face.

"You don't want to hurt us!" I shouted, pouring all my energy into those words. *"Put the crossbow down."* The air quivered from the force of my magic. Dizziness clouded my mind. I was already weak from the mist. I wasn't sure I had any magic left in me.

From beneath me, Aurelia stared up at me with wide eyes, her body trembling. I held my breath, praying to the gods that my magic worked on the assassin, that he would turn and walk away.

I heard a splash, and I froze, holding perfectly still. A rhythmic sloshing sound followed as the attacker waded through the stream.

He was coming toward us.

Shit.

I jumped to my feet, hauling Aurelia behind me. She had her dagger drawn, and I followed suit, wielding my short sword as the figure drew closer.

When the sloshing stopped, he stood right before us, a tall, hulking figure. Gradually, the mist parted to reveal a man with brown hair and a short beard, his dark eyes like steel as he glared at us.

But he wasn't holding his crossbow. Had my magic worked? Had he set the weapon down?

"How did you do that?" he demanded, his voice gruff.

I said nothing, one arm brandishing my sword with the other splayed protectively over Aurelia.

"Tell me," the man growled.

I licked my lips. "Swear you won't harm us, and I'll tell you."

He huffed a dry laugh. "I already can't hurt you because of whatever witchcraft you pulled on me."

I shook my head. "My magic doesn't work that way. I can only influence you if the idea is already there. Which means... you don't want to hurt us. If you did, even my magic couldn't stop you."

I felt Aurelia shift behind me, and I knew she was staring at me in confusion. Yes, there were loopholes to my magic. If she'd stopped judging me for one second, I could have told her that.

The man straightened, his eyes narrowing. "I swear I mean you no harm. My assignment has already been fulfilled."

Slowly, I lowered my arms, but I kept my grip on my sword. Just in case. "You're the Winter Queen's assassin." It wasn't a question. I'd heard stories of the unstoppable hunter who slaughtered at the queen's whim. Thankfully, he hadn't struck our kingdom. Yet. But he was known throughout the Realm of Valora as a bloodthirsty killer who never missed his mark. We likely only crossed paths because he had to pass through the Mistwood Hills to return to his court.

"Yes," he said tightly.

"You killed the Autumn King."

"That was my assignment."

"Why?"

He said nothing. I hadn't really expected him to answer.

"Were we part of your plan?" Aurelia asked. Though I felt her trembling behind me, her voice was sure and steady. Ever the firebird.

The man cocked his head at her, assessing. "No. That was just a happy accident. I had been waiting for the king to put himself in a compromising position, and, thanks to you, he did."

Anger boiled within me. "Do you *want* the courts to be at war? Is that what your queen wants? Because thanks to you, Autumn and the Star Court will be enemies, and the alliance between Summer and Autumn has been shattered."

"It was *already* shattered," the man snapped. "The Autumn Court dissolved their alliance with my kingdom as well. They've aligned themselves with the Dream Mage instead."

My blood ran cold, and Aurelia sucked in a sharp breath. "What do you know of the Dream Mage?" she asked. The force in her voice made it sound more like a demand, and I inwardly winced. The last thing we wanted to do was anger the assassin.

"I have never met her," the hunter said evenly. "But my queen fears her. The Dream Mage has already taken the Lunar Court. It's only a matter of time before she reaches Winter and Star."

THE SUMMER PRINCESS

THE MORE I LEARNED ABOUT THE DREAM MAGE, THE MORE TERRIFYING she seemed. Was she a dark sorceress? A necromancer? A witch? Whatever magic she possessed was incredible and deadly, and I'd never heard of a fae powerful enough to conquer kingdoms on her own.

How the hell were we supposed to stop her? We could use stardust to break the curse, yes, but what would keep her from attacking again? She wanted my court. She likely wanted my dragons. And nothing would stop her. Certainly not us, a broken princess and a wicked prince who couldn't even trust each other.

"Swear to me you will not utter a word of this conversation to another soul," the hunter said, jolting me from my thoughts, "and I will leave you."

"I swear it," Fenn said at once.

"I swear it, too," I echoed. My blood heated from the power of my words, sealing our bargain.

The hunter nodded once and then withdrew. The mist swallowed him up, obscuring him from view. Fenn and I held perfectly still, listening to the water sloshing as the assassin made his way back across the stream. Then, silence fell.

For a long, tense moment, we said nothing. My heart raced, beating uncontrollably in my chest. My thoughts spun in a chaotic whirlwind of terror and uncertainty.

We couldn't do this.

We would fail.

The Dream Mage would conquer our kingdoms, just like she'd conquered the Lunar Court.

We were doomed.

My people would die.

My family would die.

I would die.

I couldn't—I couldn't—I couldn't—

"Aurelia."

Only then did I realize that my breaths had become sharp, ragged wheezes. I was hunched over, my vision spotty, my head spinning. I couldn't get enough air into my lungs. This damn mist... This whole place was affecting me.

Couldn't breathe. Couldn't breathe. Couldn't breathe.

"Aurelia!"

Fenn's warm hands were cupping my face, and the softness of his fingers momentarily jolted me from my panic. I blinked, finding my vision blurry with tears. Gradually, Fenn's concerned face came into focus.

"That's it," he said. "Look at me. Focus only on me."

My pulse pounded, the rhythm roaring in my ears. I struggled to breathe, but I could only choke.

"Feel me." Fenn grasped my hand and placed it against his chest. "Feel my breaths."

I couldn't focus. All I could hear was my raging pulse, my heart thumping louder and louder.

"Up and down," Fenn said, his voice low and soothing. "You feel that?"

I closed my eyes, concentrating on the feel of his hard chest against my fingers. He was warm and solid, and I concentrated on that. He was real. He was here.

His chest rose with his inhale. Long and slow. Then it dropped as he exhaled.

I concentrated on that singular movement. Up and down. In and out.

Eventually, the blaring in my ears settled. My pulse slowed, and my breaths calmed to match his. Tears streamed down my face, but I couldn't even feel the moisture. All I could think about was his chest moving with his calm, steady breaths.

I wasn't sure how long we stood like that—how long he held my hand to his chest—but after what felt like an eternity, I opened my eyes and looked at him. His emerald eyes shone in the darkness, gazing at me with a tenderness I did not deserve.

I had been terrible to him. I had flung unfair accusations at him and cast judgments I was in no position to make.

As much as I hated to admit it, I needed him. Not just for our bargain or for my own protection, but for myself. He grounded me. He understood me.

I needed him.

My mouth opened, and an apology was on the tip of my tongue. I was ready to unleash everything, my sorrows, my secrets, my trust—I wanted to give it all to him.

But instead of an apology, I blurted, "I attacked the witch clans."

His brows knitted together. "I beg your pardon?"

I took a deep breath, my head finally clearing, as I said, "Five years ago, I visited the witch clans to find a solution to my blocked fae magic. Samiria refused to treat me, citing some vague and unhelpful reason—which I now know had to do with my witch rune—but one witch wanted to help me. Her name was Shay." Emotion clogged my throat, and I paused, finding it difficult to swallow. Fenn traced circles along the back of my hand, and I focused on the motion. It pulled me from my chaotic thoughts for long enough for me to continue.

"She cast a spell for me and painted a rune on my hand," I went on. "It was a rune to awaken."

Fenn sucked in a sharp breath. He clearly knew what this rune meant.

I nodded, my eyes closing again. "My magic... *exploded*, setting ablaze all the tents in the encampment. And Shay—Shay—" I broke off with a sob.

"Oh gods, Aurelia," Fenn whispered, using his free hand to stroke my cheek. "I'm so sorry."

"She only wanted to help me," I wailed, my face crumpling with grief. "She was the only one who would help me! She was just an apprentice; she didn't know any better. And I killed her! I k-killed three witches that day, Fenn. So you were r-right. I'm in no position to judge you for your magic. Because m-mine is far worse. *I'm* the monster. You were right. I'm unseelie. I have to be. No one else would b-be capable of such destruction and pain."

"Aurelia," Fenn said. On his lips, my name was both a comfort and an admonishment. He brought me to his chest, his arms encircling me. He continued tracing those soothing circles along my back. The motion was relaxing, but it was far more than I deserved. I shouldn't be comforted right now. I should be punished for my crimes. My magic was volatile and dangerous. I needed to be locked up.

How was I any better than the Dream Mage?

I clung to Fenn's thin tunic, my tears soaking the fabric. I burrowed my face in his firm chest, unleashing all my grief. And still he held me, continuing to rub my back, his cheek against my head as he pressed kisses to my hair.

At long last, I withdrew from him, trying to duck my head to hide my swollen face. But he slid a knuckle under my chin, tilting my face up to meet his. With his other hand, he swiped the tears from my face, his fingers lingering on my cheek.

"Why did you cry when Tyrone died?" he asked.

I blinked. I hadn't expected him to ask that. "What?"

"Why did you cry for him?"

I frowned, struggling to recall the emotions of that moment. "I—I was in shock. A man died in my arms."

"But that man was vile," Fenn said. "He assaulted you. And you probably weren't the only one. He wasn't worthy of your tears."

Not to mention Father made a bargain with him offering either my dragons or my hand in marriage, I thought. Although, it occurred to me that, with the man dead, that bargain had been nullified.

I shook my head. "In that moment, it didn't matter. He was a protector of his people. Despite the mistakes he made, he was a good king. And with his death, his people lost their ruler. I mourned that."

Fenn's eyebrows lifted, a small smile lighting his face. "Exactly."

My brow furrowed. "What do you mean?"

"You mourned a good king. Not a man who had taken something precious from you. *That* is the mark of a good person, Aurelia. You are not a monster. You have a power you can't control, and it just happens to be dangerous. But you didn't know that. You did not go into that witch encampment with the intent to take lives. It was a tragedy, yes.

And those witches who died should be honored. But it was *not your fault.*"

"I was careless! I was foolish, and I should have listened to Samiria."

"You didn't know what you were capable of! Whoever placed that rune mark on you should have warned you, should have been honest about the power brimming inside you. It is on *them*, not you, that lives were lost because of it."

I inhaled shakily and nodded, though I didn't fully believe his words. How could I? My recklessness had cost Shay her life. I would never forgive myself for that.

But Fenn was right. I did not seek bloodshed and conquest like the Dream Mage did. I did not use my powers with the intent to do harm.

That much I could acknowledge.

"What are we going to do?" I whispered. "You heard the hunter. The Dream Mage can't be stopped."

"Do you remember why Tyrone came to your chambers?"

I couldn't stop an incredulous laugh from bursting free. "Do you always ask non sequitur questions like that?"

He grinned but continued, "Tyrone came to you because he said you were the most powerful fae in the palace. And I'm inclined to agree with him."

"But I can't control it."

He leaned closer, his breath tickling my face as he said, "Yet." He stepped back, clasping my hands in his. "Our Nightfire fete has many benefits, one of which is bringing our people together from all classes. Including the witches. My mother might not like it, but to turn away one group of people is to turn away them all. She knows this. So, the witches always attend our revels."

My eyes grew wide as I remembered Samiria's words. "Only the witches in the Summer Court were sworn to secrecy."

"Exactly. I think that, with the help of *my* witches, we can not only unlock your powers, but we can explain who locked them in the first place."

I knew the instant we crossed the border to the Star Court. The air darkened around me, the mist cleared, and thousands of stars gleamed from above. I had expected darkness, yes, but not the beauty of the heavens winking down at me. As we sloped down the last of the Mist-wood Hills, a wide grassy plain stretched before us. No trees marred my view of the starry expanse above us. I craned my neck to take it all in, my mouth falling open in awe.

"Do you know we have a name for each one?" Fenn asked.

"How?" I breathed. "There are too many to even count!"

"For our astronomers, it's their *job* to count them, to study them, to track their growth and movement."

I stared at him in wonder. "The stars move?"

He laughed. "Of course they do. The sun moves, doesn't it?"

I swallowed, unable to keep my gaze off the sky for too long. "Yes, well, we don't see the stars very often. And we don't study them as your court does."

"A shame, because some of the constellations have incredible stories behind them."

"Constellations?" I repeated with a frown.

Fenn grinned, lacing his fingers through mine as he guided us forward. It surprised me how natural and comforting it felt, to have him take my hand like that. Just an unconscious movement. I wasn't even sure he was aware he did it.

He clicked his tongue, tugging on the horse's reins with his other hand to urge him forward. The stallion obeyed, tearing himself from a feast of tall grass.

"See that cluster of stars to the north?" Fenn nodded with his head toward the mountain peaks in the distance, above which rested a triangle of stars.

I squinted, trying to make them out. "Yes."

"That's known as Luna's Hourglass."

"I don't see an hourglass."

"Look harder. Right underneath that triangle is another one that's upside down."

I tilted my head to see it better, and my eyes widened. Sure enough, a faint smattering of stars rested directly above the mountain peak, and it did indeed represent an upside down triangle. "Wow. What does that mean?"

"Our stories say that Luna fell in love with Solus. The moon and the sun. When Miranya, the Star Goddess, discovered this, she punished Luna and Solus for tampering with the natural order of things. She cursed them, binding their fates to this hourglass. When the sands trickled to the bottom, Luna awoke, and the hourglass turned over. When her time was up, she fell into an enchanted sleep, and Solus took over. They were cursed to forever be apart. The sun and the moon."

My heart twisted at the words of the story. *An enchanted sleep.* A week ago, I would have believed it to be a fable. But such an enchantment *did,* in fact, exist. So, who was to say this story wasn't real? "That is… tragic."

"It is," Fenn agreed. "But legend says that Thora, the goddess of new beginnings, took pity on the couple and blessed them with a few days each year where they could be together. You will notice that on some days, you can see the moon even when the sun is shining."

"Yes," I said in surprise. "Yes, that is true. We often see that in the winter."

Fenn smiled. "On those days, Luna and Solus can only glimpse one another in passing. But on the days of an eclipse, they join together for a singular night of passion, reawakening their love for one another."

I stared at Fenn, at the way his emerald eyes darkened as he watched me, the way his full lips parted and his throat bobbed as he swallowed. My skin heated, my stomach fluttering from the intensity of his gaze. Despite the vast and open sky before us, I felt too warm, too close, too stifled here with him. Our hands were still entwined, and he was standing so very close to me.

I wet my lips, and his eyes tracked the movement, making my stomach dip with desire. Gods, I knew exactly how that mouth of his felt on my skin, how his tongue tasted…

I blinked and turned away, thinking of the tale he told. It was romantic, yes, but it was also full of sorrow and grief. The couple could never be together. They were too different. They came from different worlds. And even those few days where they could be together would never be enough.

"We should… keep moving," Fenn said, clearing his throat as his steps continued. I followed, matching his stride, secretly grateful he was still holding my hand, as silly as it seemed.

I thought of the story of the elven king trying to save his kingdom from a horrible curse. In the end, just like the story of Luna and Solus, it was only a fable. A tale to tell one's children at bedtime. But, just like the story of the stars, there was meaning behind it. Pieces of truth that bled into reality.

The elven king gave his life to save his kingdom and break the curse. I would do the same for mine, should it come to that.

Luna and Solus were punished for their love, destined to be apart forever. Did Fenn and I face a similar fate?

But that was ridiculous. I didn't love the Midnight Prince, and he certainly didn't love me.

Even so, my mind kept returning to that tale as we continued onward.

We walked in silence for several minutes, making our way to a forest of spruce trees ahead. Just before we entered the wood, Fenn squeezed my fingers. "I should warn you. We are entering unseelie territory. It's the only way through. And… relations with the unseelie have been volatile."

I nodded solemnly. "You said they've been attacking your people."

"Yes." Fenn's eyes flared with a mixture of sorrow and anger. "We are on the brink of a civil war between the seelie and the unseelie. To enter these woods is to incite an attack from them. So, draw your dagger. And be ready for anything."

I glanced at the stallion, who snorted, one ear twitching slightly. "What about him?"

Fenn frowned, glancing at the horse and then the forest. "I don't want to saddle him just yet. To carry both of us through the entire wood would be too taxing for him. And it's possible we can make it through undetected, if we are silent enough. But if something feels off, we jump on and ride. Understood?"

"Understood."

"Good. Stay close to me."

I took a deep breath, clinging to his hand in mine while drawing my dagger with the other. He wrapped the reins around his wrist and drew his short sword, which glinted in the moonlight. We shared one last look of determination before we stepped into the dark forest.

The Midnight Prince

THE TINY GROVE OF TREES SURROUNDING THE BORDER OF THE STAR Court was unassuming at first glance. But that was exactly what the unseelie tribes wanted.

During the few hours of daylight my court saw every year, the trees were quite pleasant, appearing as nothing more than a simple copse of spruce trees.

But at night, the unseelie emerged from their shadows to prey on unsuspecting victims.

My mother had tried to reason with them. But they only wanted fae blood. And the blood of the Night Fae was particularly delicious to their kind.

This was why they lingered by the border. They knew only Night Fae could pass through the mist. And when the traveling party reached the border, that was when the feral creatures would strike.

But this was the last place we had to travel through before we were safe. Only this forest stood between us and the Court of Twilight.

I felt Aurelia, tense and alert beside me, her eyes betraying no sign of fear. The glint in her gaze was reminiscent of when she fought off those goblins with me.

She was capable and strong. I knew she could handle herself.

But she had never encountered creatures like these. Of that, I was certain. And an intense dread filled me at the thought of her falling prey to the unseelie. If they captured her… If they harmed her…

My heart seized at the thought. My chest tightened with a mixture of fury and panic.

I couldn't let her get hurt. I refused to let it happen.

Even so, I inched closer to her until our arms were touching. She shot me a sharp glance but said nothing.

A deadly silence surrounded us. Not even the creatures of the forest moved. Not a twig snapped, nor a leaf crunched.

The stillness was the most unsettling of all. It spoke of dangers lurking nearby, of silent demons watching from the shadows. My skin prickled, the goose flesh rising along my arms and the back of my neck.

This was a mistake. Why did I think we could creep through these woods undetected? Of course they knew we were here.

I stopped, turning to Aurelia. "On the horse," I whispered. "Now."

Her eyes flared wide. "Why? What is it?" Her head whipped around as if she would be able to see a threat looming.

"You promised you wouldn't hesitate," I growled, placing my hands on her hips. She uttered an alarmed yip as I lifted her and set her atop the horse. I raised a leg, prepared to climb up behind her, when a twig snapped a few yards away.

I stiffened, then froze, my blood chilling.

The forest did not make noise unless someone wanted to be heard.

I swallowed hard, then lowered my leg and drew my sword.

"Fenn!" Aurelia hissed. "Get on!"

My eyes narrowed as several shapes emerged from the darkness.

We were too late.

"They'll catch us," I said in a low voice, not bothering to whisper. The creatures were already here. They lumbered forward, their long arms dragging along the ground. In the moonlight, I caught a glimpse of their fangs flashing. I kept my gaze fixed on the dark figures before me as I said, "When I say go, you go. Do you hear me?"

"Are you insane? I'm not leaving you."

"Aurelia," I warned. One of the creatures stepped into the light of the moon, and I caught a glimpse of his green and leathery flesh. His inky black eyes stared at nothing and everything all at once.

"I can fight with you," she said. Shifting leather told me she was trying to climb down from the horse.

Swearing, I stepped forward and slapped the horse on the rear. With a whinny, he bolted, and Aurelia cried out in surprise. His hoofbeats echoed in the distance, along with Aurelia's shrieks of anger.

She could turn the horse around eventually. But, if she was smart, she would keep going.

I clasped the pommel of my sword with both hands, angling it toward the approaching creatures. Several more passed under the moonlight, confirming my suspicions.

Ogres.

Most people assumed ogres were large, slow, and stupid. But not these. Perhaps it was the magic of the Night Fae, or perhaps these beasts had evolved into something more deadly. I had seen them move so fast they were only a blur to my keen eyes. If they were inching forward like this, it was a choice, meant to intimidate me.

I glared at them, keeping my sword steady. It would not work. I refused to be cowed.

When the closest ogre was only a few feet away, I lunged. My strike was wide and intentional, but the feint worked. The first ogre roared, diving for me, but at the last second, I ducked, ramming my head into its stomach. We crashed to the forest floor, tumbling in a tangle of limbs. Its long arms wrapped around me, and clawed fingers reached for my throat. I nicked it with my sword, and hot black blood soaked my tunic.

The creature hissed in pain, and the hesitation was all I needed. With another swipe of my sword, I opened its throat, barely rolling away before its blood splattered my face.

The remaining ogres screeched in rage before converging. They seemed to blend in with the forest, their movements so swift they were merely shadows streaking forward. My fae sight would not help me here, but I knew what to do.

I closed my eyes, trusting my other senses. Trusting my Night Fae blood.

The disgusting stench of the ogres' skin burned my nose, but it was a telltale sign of their location. Years of training to fight these beasts served me well. My nostrils flared, and the sting of their closeness seemed to singe my insides.

I slashed my sword. An ogre howled in agony. More warm blood oozed, drenching my arms, but I didn't stop. From my left, the foul odor came nearer, and I ducked, dodging the blow of one of their fists, then stabbed one directly in the chest.

He fell, but more were coming. I couldn't fight them off forever. Not on my own.

But I only needed to weaken them. I had a secret weapon at the ready, but I could only use it once. And it would drain me.

I had to save it for the perfect moment.

My body moved, my arm arcing with each thrust of my blade. The ogre's screams filled the air, echoing around me. With each shrill sound, the remaining ogres began to tremble, their bodies quivering.

Silence was their domain. Their safety. It was how they stalked their prey.

Loud noises were distressing to them. And I could use that to my advantage.

I slit the throat of one ogre, then whirled to lop off the arm of another. He sank to his knees with a groan, blood gushing from his stump-of-an arm.

Sharp claws raked over my neck and shoulder, and I cried out, gritting my teeth against the burning fire along my flesh. I staggered back a step, and another ogre wrapped one meaty fist around my throat. I swung my sword wildly, trying to stab any part of him to release the pressure building on my neck. Spots danced in my vision. My lungs strained, and I choked, trying to breathe in.

My arm went limp. The sword fell from my grasp as darkness pressed in on me.

A shout rang out. The ogre released its hold on me, and I fell, gasping. Each breath was like knives in my throat. I gagged and coughed, struggling to clear the fog in my head.

Another shout followed. The ogres roared, and the sounds of a blade slicing through flesh filled the air. I opened my eyes, squinting, and as my vision cleared, I made out Aurelia, her cloak billowing as she twirled. Her dagger flew as she gutted one ogre then stabbed another. She bent over backwards, ducking low to avoid the strike of one, while sliding her dagger along the belly of another. When she leapt, her legs stretched wide, forming a graceful arc, her movements more of a dance than anything else.

Massaging my throat, I staggered to my feet and retrieved my sword, beheading an ogre before it could snatch Aurelia.

"You were supposed to leave," I said, my voice hoarse.

"I never agreed to that," Aurelia said, ramming her blade into an ogre's eye. "Besides, you need me. That beast would have killed you."

Pain flared in my shoulder as I twisted my arm to block the strike of an ogre. Blood ran down my neck and arm, but it wasn't black; it was crimson.

My blood.

I lost my footing, sinking to one knee. I barely managed to roll out of the way before an ogre swiped its claws for me.

"How are they doing this?" Aurelia cried, then swore as one of the beast's claws grazed her shoulder.

"They are ogres," I said. "They can move impossibly fast. You cannot match their speed, Aurelia."

"Then how the hell do we fight them?"

I looked around, my heart racing in my chest. More creatures poured from the trees, converging on us like a swarm of insects.

It was time. I had to act now.

"Like this." I sheathed my sword, stretched my arms wide, and bellowed as loudly as I could. My voice strained against my aching throat, the sound tearing painfully from me. My scream echoed in the forest, making the very tree branches sway.

With all the force of my power and energy, I shouted, *"Leave us! Now!"* The words ripped from me, carving out every last bit of my strength. But I repeated them again and again, drawing power from the earth, the air, and the stars. Pulling from my ancestral home, from the blood of my people.

This was my domain. My kingdom. My land.

And the earth responded to my call.

The air rippled with power, and the ogres were thrown backward from the force of my command and the shrill volume of my voice. Some collided with tree trunks, their bodies lolling into unconsciousness. Others stumbled away, fleeing in obedience to my command.

I sank to my knees but let my voice continue to ring out, scraping against my raw throat. A metallic taste filled my mouth, and I knew I'd pushed myself too far. Blood dripped from my nose and ears.

At long last, the remaining ogres vanished, some skittering up trees, and others disappearing into the shadows, their blurred forms blending into the darkness.

With a groan, I slumped over, my head meeting the earth. Blood pooled from my mouth, and I felt nothing but pain. Pure agony.

Soft footsteps approached, and Aurelia crouched by my side, her blue eyes wide with concern. Her fingers were warm as she swiped a lock of hair from my eyes.

"Fenn?" she said hesitantly.

I mumbled something incoherent, trying to tell her I was fine, but the words came out as more of a gargle.

She chuckled. "I don't know what the hell you just did, but it was impressive. I suppose you'll need me to somehow hoist you atop the horse?"

"No," I said thickly. "I—I can walk. Just… a moment."

But I didn't move. My limbs would not respond. I could do nothing but wheeze, my lungs straining for air as I tried to regain my strength.

Yes. I had definitely pushed myself too far.

"Gods, you are pathetic," Aurelia muttered, rising to her feet and sheathing her dagger. "Hold on."

Her footsteps retreated. I tried to turn my head to follow her movements, but I was in too much pain.

Louder, heavier footsteps thundered nearby. Alarm raced through me, and I managed to lift my head despite the searing agony splitting through my head. "Aurelia!"

Aurelia was gathering up the reins of her horse, and she turned at my shout. But she was too late. A dark shape lunged for her, tackling her to the ground. They rolled and tumbled, and her shrieks filled the forest. With a cry, I pushed myself up on my arms, trying to crawl toward her, but I had nothing left. Every drop of my power had been expended already.

I could do nothing but stare in horror as the ogre wrestled with Aurelia. Grunts and screams followed blows. From the feeble sound of her protests, I knew Aurelia was losing.

"No!" I roared. "No, *stop!*" I tried to summon my fae magic, but nothing happened. The air was still and silent, save for the sounds of Aurelia's struggles. The earth did not respond to my call.

I fumbled with the hilt of my sword, trying to draw it. Perhaps if I could fling the blade at the ogre, I could impale it and help her…

With one last groan, the forest fell completely silent. I froze, horror pooling in my gut as I waited, desperate for a sound, for Aurelia's laugh of triumph, or for the ogre's screech of pain.

I lifted my head higher, trying to make out where the ogre had dragged Aurelia.

But the woods were eerily empty. Nothing but darkness and shadows.

Aurelia was gone.

THE SUMMER PRINCESS

The sudden stillness in the air should have warned me. After Fenn used his strange power to chase away the ogres, the forest cleared, and the feral sounds of the unseelie creatures was replaced by chirping crickets, rustling leaves, and the occasional hooting of an owl. Sounds I wouldn't normally think about.

Until they vanished.

Perhaps one ogre lingered after the rest. Or perhaps another tribe had come to investigate the commotion.

All I knew was, one moment I was gathering the horse's reins, and the next, I was tackled to the ground, my arms and legs scraping on tree roots, my skull connecting with the hard earth. The foul odor of the beast filled my nose and mouth, making me gag.

I tried to strike out with my arm, but it pressed its thick and meaty body into mine, crushing me. One massive hand pressed hard on my nose and mouth, cutting off my air. I managed to bite down hard on one of his fingers, and the toxic blood and stench entered my mouth once more. The ogre roared, withdrawing for long enough for me to bash my head against its own.

That was a terrible idea.

The ogre's skull seemed to be made of steel. A blinding pain rippled through my head, making my eyes water. Darkness pressed in on me, and I felt myself falling.

Fenn screamed my name nearby. But he was too winded, too weak. He couldn't help me.

I was on my own.

The ogre's thick arms surrounded me. I writhed in its grip, struggling to free myself even as the splitting ache in my skull continued to pound, to blind me. He was going to devour me, but I certainly wouldn't make it easy for him. My dagger was sheathed at my thigh, but I couldn't reach it.

I jerked my knee upward and heard a satisfying *crack* as it connected with flesh and bone. The ogre released me, and I tumbled and rolled along the forest floor, twigs and roots and leaves breaking my fall. My elbows were bleeding from the impact, and I tasted blood in my mouth.

But I had to get up. I had to *move*.

I reached for my dagger, but the ogre became a blur of movement, vanishing from several feet away and reappearing inches from my face. I staggered backward with a yelp, tripping on another root.

I waited for the hard, unyielding ground to meet me once more, for more pain to come, but to my surprise, the ogre caught me, its arms circling around me once more.

I stared up at the creature. It blinked back with its all-black eyes. Several large, block-shaped teeth were visible from underneath its thick, black lips. My chest heaved with my terrified breaths as I watched, waiting for the beast to lean in and take a bite out of my flesh.

But it didn't.

Instead, it grunted, the sound low and unintelligible.

Within seconds, several blurred shapes appeared and solidified before us. Three more ogres loomed over me, then sniffed loudly. One of them grunted, pointing at me and looking expectantly at the beast who held me.

I squirmed, trying to free myself, but the three other ogres surrounded me, holding my limbs in place. They continued to communicate with one another until, at long last, the first one nodded, and he stomped forward, flanked by the other ogres.

"No, *No!*" I thrashed and bucked, desperate to free myself, but it was no use. The ogres were bigger and stronger, and I was vastly outnumbered. I tried to scream, to call for Fenn, but one of the beasts clamped a large hand over my mouth to silence me.

I was powerless as they dragged me from the forest.

But I continued to fight, kicking my legs and twisting around restlessly, hoping that one of them would get tired, that there would be an opening I could seize.

Then, the forest began to blur, and I froze, eyes wide. The tree trunks blended together, the sky became a sickening carousel of foggy stars.

The ogres were carrying me away with their super speed. My head swayed, and my stomach roiled from the movement. It was not a smooth ride. I felt each bump and jostle, and after several moments, I lurched, and I couldn't keep myself from heaving up the contents of my last meal.

One of the ogres growled in irritation, jerking his hand away from my bile.

I took my opportunity and bit down on the hand that attempted to cover my mouth again.

The blurred motion stopped as the ogre roared, jerking his hand away from me. I kicked again, managing to free one foot, and slammed it into an ogre's face. One arm was free, and I waved my arm frantically, trying to punch or strike any body part I could find.

One of the ogres grunted something, and a heavy object slammed into my skull. Then, everything went dark.

I awoke to the sound of chanting, though I couldn't make out the words. With a groan, I tried turning my head, and a searing pain shot through my body. I tasted blood in my mouth. The air smelled of stone and embers and the lingering stench of ogre.

Slowly, my eyes opened and made out a low fire burning nearby, illuminating shadows on what looked like a massive boulder. As my eyes adjusted, taking in my surroundings, I realized it wasn't a boulder but a *cave.* I tried to sit up, but restraints pulled at my arms and legs. I managed to lift my head enough to see I was strapped down to a huge slab of stone, my wrists and ankles tethered down.

Oh gods…

I screamed, fighting against the ropes, but they only dug further into my flesh, cutting into me.

The chanting grew nearer, and several ogres appeared, wearing strange brown cloaks, their clawed hands extended and pointing upward.

The ogre in front, a tall, lean beast with thick braids of black hair, drew a dagger from the folds of his cloak. I hadn't seen this one before;

he must not have been in the forest earlier. His eyes were keen and shrewd, and he seemed more... sentient than the others. Like he had a soul, an awareness the others did not.

He dragged the blade along his palm, and black blood dripped to the ground. I stared in horror as he approached, smearing his blood in streaks along my face. I spat at him, turning my head away, but he pinched my chin between two fingers to hold me still.

"What are you doing to me?" I shouted, my voice bouncing off the walls.

I hadn't expected him to answer. He leaned in close, his breath like rotted meat as he growled, "Your power... will feed us."

My mouth fell open as I gaped at him. He could speak? Whoever this was, he was more than just a wild unseelie creature.

But perhaps I could reason with him.

"Please," I begged. "Please let me go. I can pay you. I can—"

But the ogre shook his head. "No gold. Only power."

Horror pooled in my stomach. These ogres weren't going to feast on my flesh. They were going to feast on my *magic.*

Tyrone had said I was the most powerful fae in his castle. Did these ogres agree? Was that why I was tied down to this rock, as if in preparation for a ritual sacrifice?

In a flash, an image appeared in my mind of several figures in blood red cloaks, chanting in a foreign language as blood dripped down their palms. I was among them, my own cloak billowing in the wind as I uttered the ancient and powerful language of the gods. Power swelled around us, magnifying the spell.

Just as suddenly, the image vanished, and I was back on the stone, tied down, forced to accept my fate.

I was delirious. Delusional. Perhaps the ogres had fed me a drug that made me hallucinate.

It didn't matter. I was going to die either way.

"Please!" I screamed, my shrill voice echoing. Several ogres cringed, covering their ears from my outburst. I screamed again, hoping I could weaken them, cause them pain so I could escape. But the ogre who spoke to me shoved a putrid cloth in my mouth, cutting off my cries.

"Be silent," he grunted. "Over soon."

I shook my head, tears streaming down my face. My only hope was for Fenn to find me. But he had worn himself out. He was probably unconscious in the forest somewhere. Meanwhile, these ogres with their supernatural speed could be anywhere in all of Valora by now. They could have taken me all the way to the Shadow Court, for all I knew.

I was utterly and completely alone.

A muffled sob burned in my throat, and I crammed my eyes shut, waiting for the end.

"Let us begin," said the ogre, and the chanting resumed.

The Midnight Prince

Something warm pressed into my face, jolting me awake. My eyes flew open, and the first thing I saw was a pair of bright golden eyes, one of them scarred and milkier than the other.

With a yelp, I scrambled backward, thinking it was some unseelie beast come to finish me off.

Then I realized it was Mal. Aurelia's dragon.

My heart still seizing from panic, I stared at him, uncomprehending. His wings were outstretched, as if he had just landed, his eyes wide, his ears pulled backward in distress.

"Mal," I breathed, rubbing my chest. "What the hell are you doing here?"

He nudged my arm with his nose, then growled low in his throat.

I looked around, surveying the empty woods before me. When the memories came back to me, my stomach hollowed, and my blood ran cold.

Aurelia. The ogres had taken her.

I jumped to my feet, then swayed, my head still fuzzy. Mal stepped in my path, catching me with his head before I fell.

"You can tell she's in danger," I said, massaging my temples.

Mal huffed. I took that as a *yes*.

"Do you know where she is?"

Another huff.

A pulsing urgency filled my veins. Was I too late? Had the ogres already drained Aurelia's blood?

I looked into Mal's frightened eyes. She had to still be alive. If Mal knew where she was, that had to mean she wasn't dead.

"Can I get on?" I asked.

Mal answered by kneeling to the forest floor and bowing his head. I quickly slid atop him, wincing from the sharpness of his scales. There was no saddle, so I had no guarantee that I would survive this flight. My arms wrapped around his neck, ignoring the scales digging into my skin as I held on tightly.

Mal gave no warning before he took off, his great wings beating. Each motion made his torso shift, and I slid, practically falling off. I tightened my hold on him, and once he was in the air, his wings went still, remaining outstretched as he arced through the sky. The stars surrounded us, and under different circumstances, I might have marveled at how close and bright they seemed. Flying during the daytime was one thing, but this… This was incredible.

Aurelia would have loved it.

The thought sobered me, and I leaned forward, trying to make out the details below. To the right, the glittering castle of the Court of Twilight was barely visible. We hadn't been too far before the ogres attacked. I thought of my friend Marek, who was the Twilight King, and his wife, Adira.

Gods, we had been so close. So close to refuge and safety.

Mal veered west, away from the castle and toward the Wilds. My people always stayed clear of this forest, as it was densely populated with all manner of unseelie.

No one who ventured there came out alive.

I swallowed hard, terror threatening to seize in my chest. Instead, I focused on my rage, my determination.

I would get her back. Even if it killed me, I would save her from this terrible fate.

Mal swooped low, descending gracefully until he landed just outside the forest. I moved to dismount, but he growled, his wing twitching as if to hold me in place.

"What?" I asked, confused.

He merely shook his head slowly, then took off at a gallop, his claws digging into the soil with each stride.

I cried out, grabbing his neck once more as he headed into the forest. The branches obscured the stars from view, plunging us into darkness. My breathing came in short spurts as I struggled to maintain my grip on the dragon. The forest passed by in a blur, and I vaguely wondered if Mal's pace was as fast as an ogre's. Hope bloomed in my chest. Perhaps we could reach Aurelia in time.

When Mal slowed, I frowned, glancing around. This particular spot in the forest looked like everything else. Nothing but trees and bushes, and a massive boulder off to one side.

"Mal, she's not here."

He growled again.

"*Nothing* is here. Why did you stop?"

He jostled me until I fell from his back with an ungraceful yelp, my body collapsing to the ground in a heap.

"Dammit, Mal," I hissed, staggering to my feet. "Why are we here? How are we supposed to find her?"

Mal only stared at me, his gold eyes glinting. One of his ears twitched, and I took a moment to look around, wondering if Mal could see or hear something that I could not.

An eerie silence pressed in around us. I should have been more careful. My voice had likely alerted every unseelie creature within a two-mile radius.

Excellent.

I ran a hand through my hair with a heavy exhale, resisting the urge to throttle this dragon. I wished I could communicate with him like Aurelia could. She would know in a heartbeat what Mal was trying to convey.

Frowning, I stepped forward, inspecting the forest with further scrutiny. The air smelled different. The familiar spruce and sage scent filled my nose, but it mingled with something else, something that burned my nostrils.

Ogre. I was certain of it.

But not just that. Other scents were mixed in as well. Something that smelled like charcoal.

My brow furrowed. Charcoal? I inhaled deeply. Yes, it definitely smelled like something was burning.

But what? The forest was clear. Not an ember in sight.

I closed my eyes, trusting my Night Fae senses to guide me. The smoky smell swelled around me, as if guiding me forward. My feet moved, the leaves crunching underfoot as I followed the smell.

Then, I heard it. Faint, almost imperceptible. But it was there.

A scream in the distance.

But it wasn't coming from ahead. It came from *below* me.

I glanced down at my feet, finding nothing but soil and leaves. I stepped forward, then back, then hopped once.

A hollow *thump* echoed.

I gasped, glancing up at Mal, who stared at me, deadpan, as if wondering why it had taken me so long to discover this.

"You could have done something to show me, you great brute," I muttered, crouching to the ground and swiping leaves away. It appeared to be nothing but soil underneath, but as I cleared the area, I made out a faint rectangular groove etched into the ground.

It was a trapdoor.

"Holy shit," I muttered. "These ogres are craftier than I gave them credit for."

I could have sworn Mal snorted in agreement.

Drawing my sword, I wedged the blade in the groove and pushed hard. With a soft groan, the leverage released the latch holding the door in place, and it swung open, revealing a dark staircase below. The gap was huge—big enough to fit even the most massive of ogres. After sharing an uncertain glance with Mal, we both descended.

Despite the broad width of the staircase, Mal had to fold in his wings completely to fit. I had to trust my fae sight to guide us, as no torches or lanterns lit the passageway. Our footsteps echoed, and Mal's claws kept scraping on rock. I was certain someone would hear us. My pulse throbbed in anticipation, and I kept a steady grip on the pommel of my sword, prepared for an ogre to jump out and attack us.

When we reached the bottom, lanterns lit the way, revealing a wide-mouthed tunnel within a cave. The air smelled of blood and ogre.

And in the distance, Aurelia's scream echoed again.

I lunged, prepared to sprint down the hall toward her voice, but Mal growled and snatched my tunic with his teeth, halting me. The fabric ripped, but the restraint gave me pause, my steps faltering. Gasping for breath, I stared down the tunnel, red creeping into my vision.

They were hurting her. Torturing her. Killing her. How could I stand by and do nothing?

Mal's golden eyes glinted, his uninjured eye narrowing with intensity. *Be smart about this,* his expression seemed to say.

Still panting, I nodded, but the rage continued to simmer in my blood.

Those beasts would pay. I would slaughter them all.

Mal and I crept forward, our steps slow and careful as we made our way down the passage. In the distance, low chanting echoed, and I frowned. Were those the ogres? I strained to hear what they were saying, but it was in a language I didn't understand.

I didn't know the ogres could speak at all. They were so feral, so animalistic, that I assumed they were nothing more than wild beasts.

I had underestimated them. And now, Aurelia was suffering for it.

Swallowing around the lump in my throat, I focused on the chanting, concentrating on the voices of each ogre to try to estimate how many were there.

It had to be more than a dozen. Perhaps two.

Unease curled within me, but I focused on my fury, letting it fuel me as I continued down the tunnel. Beside me, Mal huffed, his large nostrils flaring as his sharp white teeth flashed in the lantern light.

He was enraged, too. I knew without a doubt he would show the ogres no mercy. We would destroy them together.

When we reached the end of the passage, I raised a hand to signal Mal should stop. I leaned forward, peering around the corner. Aurelia's muffled protests filled the air—the ogres must have gagged her. Meanwhile, the chanting continued. I made out the shapes of more than twenty ogres surrounding a slab of concrete on which Aurelia was tied, thrashing against the ropes tethering her.

My blood ran cold. Oh, gods. They were going to sacrifice her.

I'd heard rumors of dark ogre rituals, but I had assumed they were merely tall tales meant to frighten us, to keep us out of the woods.

But this meant ogres possessed *magic.* And that changed everything.

My palm was slick with sweat as I gripped my sword, steeling my nerves with my sharp breaths. I could do this. Sure, I was still weak, and I only had one weapon. And I was severely outnumbered.

But I had a dragon at my side. And once Aurelia was freed, she could help, too.

We could do this.

And even if the odds were against us, I would die before leaving

Aurelia to this fate. The knowledge pulsed through me with quivering intensity. The conviction, the truth of my feelings for her, startled me.

I was in love with her. Desperately and hopelessly. I would do anything for her.

My grip on my sword tightened. I nodded once at Mal, who inclined his head, his golden eyes glittering with malice.

Together, we stepped into the room.

THE SUMMER PRINCESS

TEARS STREAMED DOWN MY FACE AS I HOPELESSLY THRASHED AGAINST THE ropes. Blood ran down my arms and legs from the restraints cutting into me.

I tried summoning my dark powers to no avail. I thought of the rage that had consumed me before I'd set the goblins on fire, or the burning sensation that swept over me when Fenn had marked me with the rune.

But nothing happened. I felt nothing but hollow inside. It was as if the air here stifled my magic.

I was powerless.

Awareness crept into the corners of my mind, and I froze, sensing a new presence. A presence I knew better than anyone.

The faint smell of sulfur met my nose, and I drew in a sharp gasp.

Mal.

I glanced around, unable to believe it. It was impossible; Mal *couldn't* be here.

But as I twisted my head around, I made out a dark shape looming near the entrance of the cave. The gleaming dark scales were unmistakable.

A surprised breath whooshed from me, and I almost laughed with relief. But Mal's movements were slow as he crept forward, no doubt hoping to surprise the ogres.

"Hey!" I shouted before I could stop myself. The fabric in my mouth muffled my outburst, but several ogres stiffened from the sound nonetheless. I wriggled on the stone slab, trying to spit the fabric out, pushing it with my tongue. It slid down to my chin, and I shouted, "*Stop!* You have to stop this, or you all will die!"

A few ogres exchanged wary looks. The one in front who had spoken to me continued chanting, his eyes narrowing at me in suspicion.

"My power will obliterate you *all!*" I roared, my voice echoing and bouncing off the cavern walls. "I will destroy you! All of you! This place will burn, and I will only watch as the flames consume you."

Two ogres shifted their weight on their feet, clearly uncomfortable. It made me wonder if they could understand my words, or if the shrill volume of my voice distressed them.

It didn't matter. It was only a distraction.

Mal's claws scraped on stone, and an ogre in the back turned at the sound.

I unleashed a scream, the sound ripping from my throat and splitting the air. The circle of ogres scattered, some diving for the ground, and others clamping their meaty fists over their ears. A few roared in agony. The leader surged toward me, eyes blazing as he tried to shove the fabric back into my mouth.

I only continued screaming, turning my head away from him. He slammed his fist into my jaw, and I groaned, my scream cutting off as pain split through my head.

Before he could shove the gag into my mouth, a dark shape barreled into him, tackling him to the ground.

Mal.

The dragon gnashed his teeth, snapping and snarling as the ogre's thick hands clamped around his mouth to stop him from tearing off his face.

The remaining ogres sprang into action, rushing to their leader's aid. I struggled uselessly against my restraints, desperate to help.

With a loud squelching sound, one ogre lost its head, and I froze, eyes wide. The creature's headless corpse fell to the ground, revealing Fenn wielding his short sword, his expression twisted and murderous.

My breath caught in my throat. *Fenn had come for me.*

Fenn moved with lethal grace, his blade singing with each stroke, each powerful thrust. Black blood sprayed, pooling along the floor from the ogres' demise. I had never seen the Midnight Prince like this before, deadly and unhinged, his eyes slightly crazed with bloodlust.

He was like a beast himself, terrible and magnificent.

A horrifying shriek filled the air, the sound of anguish and torment. It cut off abruptly, and I glanced around to find Mal had won the fight, his jaws closing over the ogre's head. With great force, he clamped down, black blood exploding from the ogre as Mal ripped his head clean off.

The dragon immediately bounded toward me, using his claws to tear the ropes free. When they were loosened, I sat up, my back throbbing, and the wounds on my wrists and ankles still bleeding freely.

"Mal, what the hell are you doing here?" I hissed, sliding off the rock and wrapping my arms around him. Gods, it was so good to see him. Even though I knew he should be home, defending the palace, I was secretly glad he was here.

The dragons *never* flew outside our borders for fear of being attacked. The protective wards of our court kept them safe. This was the first time I had ever heard of a dragon breaching those wards on their own.

Mal had come for me. He'd cared for me enough to risk that flight, to risk his own life.

Gratitude swelled within me, so intense that tears pricked my eyes. I pressed my cheek to the top of Mal's head, inhaling his familiar scent and warmth for a brief moment before drawing my dagger and joining the fray.

My limbs were weak and my body frail, but my blade was sharp, and deadly fury fueled my movements. I gutted an ogre, then slit the throat of another. I ducked to avoid a large fist swinging my way, then sliced my blade into the ogre's thighs, bringing it to its knees.

More ogres poured into the entrance, rallying together and blocking our escape. There were too many of them, and unlike the forest, this was their dwelling.

We wouldn't make it out of here.

Still, I continued slashing and stabbing, refusing to give up, not after Mal and Fenn had sacrificed everything to free me. I would die by their sides before giving up.

An ogre's claws ripped into my side, and I hunched over, groaning in pain as blood bloomed, staining my already filthy shift. The creature's closed fist collided with my skull, slamming me backward.

I fell to the ground, my head throbbing as darkness clouded my vision. I shook my head, trying to clear it, trying to see through the fog before the ogre gutted me.

I swung my dagger wildly, and when it met flesh, I shoved it deep, dragging it downward. Blood and intestines spilled out, putrid and hot, and the ogre fell. But one grabbed me from behind, his hand closing around my neck, thumbs digging into my throat and cutting off my airway.

My eyes bulged, and I tried to scream, to draw in a breath, but I couldn't. My lungs were on fire. I waved my dagger, but the ogre was behind me, and I couldn't reach him. Fire burned in my throat, scorching my insides.

Suddenly, the ogre's grip released, and dark blood splattered my front. I gasped, the sound rattling and painful, but blessed air filled my lungs. I breathed in again and again, ignoring the white-hot knives in my throat with each inhale. Slowly, I raised my head to find Fenn decapitating the ogre who had nearly killed me. The Midnight Prince turned to me, extending his hand. I took it, and he hoisted me up.

"You came for me," I wheezed, massaging my throat.

"Of course I did," he said, his voice low and rough. His brows knitted together, as if the notion that he had rescued me was so obvious, so expected.

As if he would *always* come for me. No matter what.

Warmth filled my chest, blotting out the pain of my injuries, drowning out the screams and cries around us. For a moment, it was only me and Fenn, his emerald eyes locked onto mine, drinking me in completely as if trying to memorize my features. It felt like he was feasting on me, devouring me with his eyes, unwilling to ever let me go.

It only lasted for a moment. An ogre slammed into me, and suddenly, we were battling once more, grappling for survival. Fenn and I moved together, covering each other, intervening when the other needed assistance. We were a deadly pair, wreaking havoc and destruction.

But we were only two people. And the horde of ogres never stopped coming.

Fatigue and agony slowed my movements. Another ogre managed to impale its claws on me, slicing deep. I fell to my knees, my head spinning.

I was going to die. Fenn and Mal were going to die.

A brilliant white light filled the cave, burning against my eyes. Startled, I blocked my face with my hands to ward off the intensity of it, but the light continued to burn, searing into me, practically melting off my flesh. The ogres' piercing screams made my eardrums rattle. I was torn between covering my eyes and covering my ears. Blood trickled down my neck, and I realized the sound of their screams was so powerful it was making my ears bleed.

I fell to the ground, crying out, the sound lost in the chaos of the ogres' deaths. Tears ran down my cheeks, the pain so severe, I was sure I would die along with the creatures.

Then, quite suddenly, it stopped. The light vanished, but the echo of it still flashed in my eyes. I squinted, the glare making it impossible to see.

The air filled with a strange and foreign smell, and yet, I *knew it*. It was sage and lavender and cool mist. I had never encountered it before, but a deeper part of me knew this scent. It felt like a past life. Like an echo of a memory I once had.

Squinting through the haze still clouding my vision, I made out three distinct figures at the entrance of the cave. All around us, the bodies of the ogres twitched violently, black blood oozing from their now empty eye sockets. I stared in horror at the carnage, marveling at how something so brief yet so powerful had managed to affect every single ogre.

My eyes locked onto Fenn, who was on all fours, gasping for breath, gazing in wonder at the three figures. Beside me, Mal nudged my arm with his snout, and relief filled me. He was alive. Fenn was alive.

But… how?

Slowly, I turned to the three figures, who lowered their crimson hoods. I knew at once that they were witches. One had short black hair, the other had long, gray locks, and the other had a shock of wispy white hair surrounding her face. All three stared at me with wide, all-seeing eyes the color of lilacs.

"Dragon queen," the white-haired witch said to me, spreading her arms wide. "Welcome home."

The Midnight Prince

Dragon queen.

Welcome home.

The words echoed in my head, and I glanced from the three witches to Aurelia and back again. The witches were unfamiliar to me, but their red cloaks signified they belonged to the witch clans of the Star Court.

"What are you talking about?" Aurelia demanded, her voice ringing with authority despite her bloodied state. Her body was so covered in blood and grime that only small splotches of her freckled ivory skin was visible.

"We have waited so long for your return," said the white-haired witch, her lavender eyes glowing with power.

"Return?" Aurelia sputtered. "I've never been here before. You must have me confused with someone else."

"She is not ready, sister," hissed the black-haired witch, her eyes narrowing.

"She is *here*," protested the first.

"But she is not here for us," said the gray-haired witch, her voice lower than the others.

Aurelia shook her head, striding toward them. I flung out a hand to stop her, and she looked at me with a mixture of alarm and confusion. Slowly, I shook my head. A single look from these witches could kill us all. To cross them would be foolish.

"Thank you for saving us," Aurelia said stiffly. "Now please, let us pass. We mean you no harm."

"We know," the three witches said in unison.

Unease prickled along my skin. I didn't like this. Something wasn't right.

For a long, tense moment, the five of us—and Mal—stood there, unmoving, watching each other. It felt like I was sizing up an opponent, preparing for another battle.

A battle I would not win.

"Please," I said, my voice soft. "Please let us pass. We need to see a healer. We need—"

"You need nothing," the white-haired witch snapped. "Be silent, foolish boy."

My head jerked back in surprise. I had never seen these witches before, but the few I had encountered had been nothing but respectful to me.

Aurelia stiffened, her fists curling tightly at her sides. "This *foolish boy* just saved my ass from being sacrificed by those ogres. Show him some respect."

"We never would have let them continue the ritual," said the white-haired witch, waving a hand idly. "His intervention was unnecessary."

"So you let those ogres cut us down? You *let* them fight us?" Aurelia's voice was full of outrage.

"We only intervene when necessary," said the gray-haired witch in that low, soothing voice.

"Who are you?" Aurelia demanded, her voice shrill and ringing.

"Ruby," said the black-haired witch.

"Jade," said the gray-haired witch.

"Sapphire," murmured the last.

The air rippled with the power of their names, and I swallowed hard. Though the witches regarded us with a stoic calmness, every nerve in my body told me we were in grave danger.

"Again, we thank you for *intervening*," Aurelia said, sneering at the word. "But please either tell us why you are here, or let us pass."

A deadly silence followed. My arms began to tremble. I couldn't tear my eyes from the three witches as I waited for them to lash out, to obliterate us all. It would be quick and easy. Of that I was certain.

At long last, the white-haired witch—Sapphire—stepped forward, drawing something from the folds of her cloak. I almost lunged for Aurelia, certain the witch was about to stab her with a poisoned blade.

But she only withdrew a small, glass vial. It was tinted lavender, the same shade as the witches' eyes, and it was completely empty.

"When you start to remember, shatter this," the witch said softly, pressing the vial into Aurelia's hands. "We will come."

Aurelia frowned, but she took the glass, inspecting it thoughtfully. Before any of us could react, another blinding flash of light illuminated the cave, and then the witches were gone.

When you start to remember... What the hell did that mean?

I looked at Aurelia, who was still running her finger along the hard edges of the glass vial, her expression contemplative.

"Aurelia?" I asked, gently gripping her elbow.

She looked up at me, her blue eyes wild with a riot of emotions— anger, confusion, and pain. I wondered what she was thinking. What burdensome thoughts filled her mind right now?

Did she know what those witches were talking about?

After a long moment, she shuddered, then swayed. I caught her by the shoulders before she fainted, then realized just how much blood was flowing from her wounds.

Stars above, it was a miracle she hadn't lost consciousness already.

I quickly shed my cloak and wrapped it around her before hoisting her into my arms. My body screamed in protest, but I ignored it, cradling her against my chest.

"Don't worry," I whispered, pressing a kiss to the top of her matted hair. "I'll get you to safety. The Court of Twilight isn't far from here. Mal can fly us there."

Mal grunted his agreement, and together, we left the godsforsaken room where the ogres had almost sacrificed the woman I loved. We made our way down the passageway and climbed the winding steps that led to the trapdoor. Our steps were slower than before; carrying Aurelia's weight while enduring my own injuries made me see stars, and there were moments when I thought I would topple down the staircase. But Mal was at my back, his head nudging me forward.

When we reached the top, I threw open the trapdoor and gasped, breathing in the familiar midnight spruce scent of the forest. I gently set Aurelia on the forest floor before climbing out after her.

I meant to kneel by her side, to tend to the most pressing of her wounds, but I froze at the sight that awaited us.

A squadron of my mother's soldiers stood before us, weapons

drawn. In front was a man I recognized: Gorrick, my guard captain. He removed his helmet and bowed low.

"Welcome home, Your Highness. The queen has sent us to escort you to the palace."

I gaped at the men standing before me. Never before had I led soldiers into this forest. It was suicide. Yet here they stood, ready to protect us, ready to guide us home.

A mixture of confusion and gratitude swelled in my chest.

"Gorrick," I said breathlessly, stepping forward to clasp his hand in mine. "Stars above, it's good to see you. We are in desperate need of assistance."

"There are horses waiting for you just outside the forest," Gorrick said. "Come, I can lead you there."

My grip tightened on his arm, stopping him. "We—We intend to visit the Twilight Court first."

Gorrick frowned, then looked me over, no doubt taking in my thin shirtsleeves, stained and torn, and my extensive injuries. "Sire, you are in no shape to make such a visit."

"The matter is quite urgent." I *had* to see King Marek. The fate of Aurelia's kingdom was at stake. If I could only get a word with Queen Adira, then I could find out where the Dream Mage was.

Gorrick's face twisted in an apologetic grimace. "I am sorry, sire. But my orders come directly from the queen. I am sure that once your injuries are tended to, you will be able to make your visit."

I closed my eyes in frustration. Mother outranked me, so Gorrick would be disobeying a direct order from his queen by catering to my request. Damn it all. I scrubbed a hand down my face and sighed. "Very well. Do you have a healer with you?"

"We do. He can tend to you once we leave the forest."

"And Aurelia as well." I gestured to the Summer Princess, who was sitting up and watching the interaction with a dazed expression. I was shocked she was still conscious, but it was clear she was fading fast.

Gorrick glanced down at the princess as if just now noticing she was there. "I—Who—" He cleared his throat in uncertainty. "I did not realize you had a traveling companion."

"Yes. My fiancée."

Gorrick blanched but quickly masked his surprise. "I—I see. This will be interesting news for the queen indeed."

I'm sure it will be, I thought bitterly. I had sent word ahead of our visit to break the news to Mother, but I was certain she believed it to be a joke of some kind.

There would be no softening this blow. She would have my head for making this arrangement without her consent or blessing.

But it meant we could have a dragon. Surely, that would be a good enough reason for her.

At the thought of dragons, I glanced around in alarm, scanning the forest for Mal. What would Gorrick and the soldiers do if they found a *dragon* with us?

But the black dragon was nowhere to be found. He must have noticed the crowd awaiting us and kept himself hidden below the trapdoor.

Smart creature.

With a deep breath, I crouched low and gathered Aurelia into my arms once more. Gorrick immediately stepped forward and said, "Sire, please. Let me carry her."

"No." My protest was sharper than I intended. I softened my tone and added, "I will do it. I am well enough."

Gorrick's mouth formed a thin line but he made no further objections. His soldiers led the way, marching us out of the wretched forest and toward the safety of my home.

THE SUMMER PRINCESS

At first, I sat in the tea room with Gigi. She clutched her tea with trembling hands, and dark circles lined her eyes. When I spoke to her, she flinched, then gasped.

"Aurelia! You cannot be here. You must wake up!" She gripped my arm, her fingernails digging into my skin as if trying to awaken me with pain.

I shook my head. "I want to be with you, Gigi."

Gigi leaned close, her blue eyes wild. "If you want to be with me, you must break this curse. *Save us.*"

I opened my mouth to speak, but suddenly, the scene changed, and I was standing in the nesting grounds of the Summer Court. Instead of the clan of dragons surrounding me, the forest was empty, save for me and Mal. He looked at me, his brilliant gold eye gleaming while the other remained milky and scarred. Even my dream couldn't erase that.

"Mal, do you know what's going on?" I asked.

I only know bits and pieces, Aurelia, his voice resonated in my head.

"How do I do this?" I asked, desperation pulsing through me. "How do I break this curse?"

You must unlock your power.

"You've said that before!" I said, growling in frustration. "How do I *do* that?"

Mal inched closer to me, his eyes shrewd as he surveyed me. *You must remember.*

. . .

My eyes flew open, my pulse racing. My chest heaved with panicked breaths.

I sat up quickly, my head spinning. In my mind, I was still in that forest with Mal. My stomach coiled in dread as I frantically glanced around the room for him.

But I was alone. Not only that, but I was lying in a strange bed in a place I'd never been before. It was some kind of ornate bedchamber with a plush fur rug, several narrow bookcases, and a warm fire crackling in the hearth opposite the bed. Floor-to-ceiling windows revealed slivers of a starry night sky behind the silver drapes.

The Star Court. Of course. I had no idea what time it was, since this kingdom rarely saw the sun. The thought made me feel strangely alone. I missed the sun. I wrapped my arms around myself as if I could hold the fragile pieces of my soul together.

But I was here, and there was no turning back.

My breathing sharpened as I recalled the events from earlier. The ogres. The stone slab. The chanting and the ritual I was almost sacrificed for.

Fenn, in his unholy fury, cutting down the ogres to save me.

And… those three strange witches and their all-seeing eyes.

Welcome home.

We have waited so long for your return.

I shuddered, rubbing my arms to ward off the chill that had nothing to do with the temperature. My gaze fell on the small lavender vial resting on the little table beside my bed.

When you start to remember, we will come.

Those witches had to have been mistaken. Or they were speaking in riddles, as witches often did.

No amount of rationalization could ward off the prickles spreading along my arms. With a sigh, I shoved off the blankets and padded across the room to the wardrobe opposite the wide window.

Only then did I stop and glance up and down my body. I had gotten slashed by ogre claws and sliced with the tight restraints on my wrists and ankles, not the mention sustaining several head injuries. But my flesh was smooth and unblemished; not even a scar marred my freckled skin. While I was unconscious, it seemed someone had bathed and changed me into a clean shift, though I couldn't be too upset; I had been filthy.

I raised my hands in front of my face, running my fingers along each wrist. Not a single mark. Not even a dull throb of pain.

It was as if the entire incident with the ogres hadn't happened at all.

Of course, no amount of healing could erase the memories permanently seared into my mind. I closed my eyes, rubbing my temples as I tried to rid my thoughts of that otherworldly chant, of the tall ogre leader and the words he spoke to me.

I shook my head, throwing open the wardrobe doors so loudly one of them banged against the wall, making me flinch. I had to dress, had to get out of this room…

I frowned, glancing out the window again. Where was I? Was this the Court of Twilight, or the Court of Midnight? Fenn had mentioned we would be stopping to visit the Twilight King and Queen first, as they had information about the Dream Mage. But I didn't think they had magic healers in their court, as half their population was human.

I made my way across the room to the massive window. Millions of stars glittered from the midnight sky, and a glowing crescent moon illuminated the scene below. I was at least three stories high, perhaps more. I could make out a grand courtyard below as well as a vast forest and a sparkling silver river. My breath caught in my throat at the way the water rippled, shimmering in the starlight.

This had to be the Celestial River that Fenn had told me about. Which meant we were in his court.

I swallowed around a lump in my throat, my stomach coiling with unease. We were supposed to announce our presence formally, to share the news of our engagement with the whole kingdom. Not be dragged in, half-dead, with the future Midnight Queen covered in blood and gashes, unable to even greet her people.

I shook my head. I would *not* be the Midnight Queen. It was all a ruse.

Even so, it gave us a bad image and tainted the facade we were desperately trying to maintain. I had to right this.

I found a rope dangling near the bed and pulled lightly. Within minutes, a handmaid arrived, and I let her into the room. She was a faint, slight figure with black wispy hair and pale green eyes. Her skin was tan, perhaps a shade lighter than Fenn's. She bobbed a quick curtsy, her eyes darting from me to the floor and back again.

"What can I help you with, miss?" She wrung her hands together and bit on her lip, clearly uncomfortable in my presence.

I didn't blame her. For centuries, our people had been sworn enemies. I yearned to put her at ease, to comfort her, but I needed to appear the future queen of her kingdom, not her friend.

I had to wear my mask again.

Lifting my chin, I said in a firm voice, "I wish to dress."

"Of course, miss." She bobbed another curtsy and bustled over to the open wardrobe. I glanced over her shoulder as she sifted through silver, navy, black, and violet fabrics, so very different from the bright and vibrant colors of the Summer Court. I was accustomed to wearing turquoise and cerulean and forest green.

The maid looked over the silk fabrics, then shot me an uncertain look, no doubt wondering which color would go best with my orange hair, myriad freckles, and rosy complexion.

"What's your name?" I asked abruptly. I hadn't planned on saying it, but I couldn't stand the blatant terror shining in the girl's eyes.

The maid gaped at me for a moment before squeaking, "Cela."

I offered a small smile. "My name is Princess Aurelia."

"I know, miss."

"Well, Cela, I know this is… a unique opportunity for us both. But I swear I mean you and your people no harm while I am here. I wish to experience the culture of your kingdom and learn more about your customs. Do you think you can help me with that?"

Cela blinked once, then nodded quickly. "Yes, miss."

"Excellent. I think for now, we should try the navy dress. In the meantime, can I send for a modiste or seamstress to make me a custom gown for the fete tonight?"

Cela's eyes flared wide. "The… The Summer Princess wishes to attend our fete?"

I frowned, unsure why this was so shocking. Perhaps Fenn hadn't yet formally announced our engagement. Choosing my words carefully, I said, "Yes. Prince Fenn has invited me, and I'm most eager to attend. I've heard nothing but delightful things about it."

Cela cleared her throat, wringing her hands together once more. "It is only… Well, begging your pardon, miss, but we have not had our fete in a few weeks now because of the attacks."

My stomach dropped. Yes, of course, Fenn had mentioned as much.

How could I have forgotten? I found myself nodding and saying, "Of course, of course. Forgive me for the presumption. Even so, I would like to get a gown ordered for this evening, if possible. Can you arrange this for me?"

Cela nodded again, pulling out the navy dress and draping it over her arm. "Of course, miss. What color would you like?"

I glanced over the remaining fabric in the wardrobe, considering this. "Something warmer in tone, perhaps?"

Cela nodded, her eyes brightening. "I was thinking as much, miss. Perhaps a soft rose gold, to complement our silvers but also to go with your features as well."

I beamed at her. "That sounds perfect." I stepped around her, fingering the soft silk of a silver gown. As I pulled it loose, I looked over the simple design. Two long swaths of fabric covered the bodice, leaving a large space between the breasts and the back completely exposed. There was no corset or petticoats. The skirt seemed to shimmer in the light as I moved it.

I smiled. "Something like this one would do."

Cela curtsied once more. "Of course, miss. Let me help you out of your shift."

It took the better part of an hour for Cela to prepare me. The gown itself had been simple to put on; the fabric was light and soft against my skin, with a low-cut neckline, leaving my collarbone bare. The lacy cape sleeves covered my arms, the sparkling fabric extending past my elbows and falling nearly to my feet. Small gaps in the fabric allowed my arms to move freely. The diamond-studded skirt was thin and shifted with every movement, making the gown sparkle.

But my hair took the most amount of time. Cela worked through my tangles, her movements patient and tender. When my hair fell in soft, clean waves down my back, she pinned it up in chunks, securing each curl with a diamond pin until my hair formed an elegant knot at the top of my head. She loosened a few, letting them rest against my cheeks, and then placed a diamond tiara on my head. The final touch was a simple necklace with a long row of diamonds that trailed from my collarbone to the top of my breasts.

It was a bit excessive. I seemed more like a shiny butterfly than anything. But I did indeed look like a queen.

Cela stepped back to admire her work, all unease and uncertainty gone, her hands resting casually at her sides. "A vision, miss. You look like you belong in our court."

I turned my head from side to side, the diamond earrings swaying as I did so. I looked… almost unrecognizable. I didn't think the silver and diamonds would suit my skin tone, but with the powder Cela applied to my cheeks, softening the rosiness, it did seem to bring the ensemble together.

"You have done fabulous work, Cela," I breathed, trying to ignore the knots of anxiety tightening in my chest. "Truly marvelous."

Cela blushed and curtsied. "Thank you, miss. Shall I show you to the dining hall? I believe a spread of lunch is being served now."

I rose from the stool, smoothing my hands along my skirts. "Is Prince Fenn there?"

Cela frowned. "I don't believe so. Last I heard, he and the queen were speaking privately in the throne room."

My blood ran cold at that. *Shit.* Queen Sonara was known for her brutal and unforgivable nature. If she and Fenn were speaking privately, that couldn't be good.

I lifted my chin. "Then, take me to the throne room, please."

Cela balked. "M-miss, I cannot! There are guards keeping the doors closed to avoid interruptions."

"All you must do is guide me to the throne room," I assured her. "I will take it from there. If the guards turn me away, then so be it. I only ask that you show me the way, and then you can go about your day."

Cela gnawed on her lower lip as she considered this. After a moment, she nodded once. "Very well, miss. I will show you the way."

THE MIDNIGHT PRINCE

MOTHER HAD NOT BEEN PLEASED UPON OUR ARRIVAL. BUT THIS WASN'T entirely surprising, given the state of us. Aurelia had passed out from her injuries, and I had burst into the castle, demanding for our healer. No pleasantries. No welcome. Certainly not what Aurelia and I had planned.

But none of that mattered. I needed her safe. I needed her cared for. We could smooth things over later.

The following day, that was exactly what I was doing, standing in the throne room as my mother paced before me, berating me for my actions. Her inky black skirts swished with each step, her dark eyes flaring with rage. "Careless," she hissed. "Reckless. Foolish! What in the stars' name were you thinking?"

"I was thinking we needed assistance," I said calmly. "And we received it."

She scoffed. "We received nothing but a loathsome princess who despises our people and would rather die than help us."

"Do not speak of my fiancée in that way," I said sharply.

Mother stopped her pacing to stare at me, eyes wide. I didn't often use a tone like that with her. Generally, it was the opposite. But I wouldn't have her sullying Aurelia's name based on gossip alone. "You have not met her," I went on. "Aurelia is lovely, and she is willing to put aside our differences to forge on with this alliance. I was hoping you would do the same."

Mother's expression twisted into a disgusted grimace. "She has deceived you, Fennick. You cannot trust her."

I said nothing, because her words were far too close to the truth. It *was*, in fact, a deception. But she couldn't know that. "I sent word ahead of our arrival. Did you not believe my message?"

"Of course I didn't! You have been in the bed of practically every female courtier in our kingdom. Never in a thousand years did I expect you to settle down, let alone with an *enemy princess.* I thought it was some rather hideous joke on your part."

I sighed. "I have made a bargain with her, Mother. She will give us a dragon."

Mother froze, looking me over, her eyes narrowing in suspicion. "She swore it in blood?"

"Yes. Whatever dragon possesses the most powerful fire. She will give us what we need."

Her eyes narrowed further still. "And in exchange?"

"We grant her access to stardust."

Mother's lips grew thin. "Foolish boy. You can't offer something like that. Our stores are low enough as it is."

"Yes, but with Dragonfire, we can secure our people's safety. We can increase our coffers with trade once the roads are clear and the unseelie have stopped their attacks. Commerce will flow smoothly once more."

Mother frowned, her eyes shrewd and calculating as she considered this. "You swore in blood as well?"

"Of course I did. The Summer Princess is many things, but she is no fool. She would not have sworn in blood if I had not done the same."

Mother sighed, then resumed her pacing. "This is still disastrous. You should have consulted me first."

"There was not time. We need the dragon *now*, Mother. To cease negotiations for me to run home and get permission from dear Mama first would have been ridiculous."

Mother sniffed in disapproval, her nose wrinkling. "I suppose."

"You needn't have sent a squadron for us," I said, rubbing the back of my neck. "We were meant to visit the Court of Twilight before coming here."

"My mages sensed you crossing the border, and with the unseelie tribes rampaging through the kingdom, I couldn't take any chances."

"I need to speak with Marek."

"You shall do no such thing," she snapped. "You are needed *here*,

Fennick, not only to clean up the mess of your engagement, but to put the people's minds at ease. You can visit your friend later."

"The matter is urgent, Mother. I *must* speak with him."

"Speak with him another time." Her tone was firm and gave no room for argument.

I bit my lip, remaining silent. Perhaps I could slip away after the fete, while the kingdom was sleeping off the alcohol and merriment. It was less than a day's ride to the Twilight Palace, and by the time Mother realized I was gone, it would be too late.

But would Aurelia come with me? And if she did, what if we were caught? For me to sneak off in the middle of the night was one thing, but if I was with the Summer Princess, my betrothed, whom the people already suspected of duplicity, that would reflect poorly on her. And we couldn't afford that.

I frowned as I considered my options. Marek and I both possessed contact runes to reach each other in case of emergency. But it did not allow us to speak to one another; only to send an emergency flare, so to speak.

But what if I could find a rune that *could* allow us to speak across long distances? I was sure I had encountered one in the books I'd borrowed from the witch clans.

If I couldn't go to Marek, then I would find a way to speak with him through magic. If he or his wife knew anything about the Dream Mage, I had to try.

It wasn't just Aurelia's kingdom at stake anymore. The Winter assassin had told us the Dream Mage had already seized the Lunar Court. It was only a matter of time before she reached our court as well.

"Did you hear me?" Mother barked.

I blinked, realizing she had asked me a question. "I'm sorry, what did you say?"

She sighed, casting her gaze toward the vaulted ceiling as if praying for strength. "You are impossible, Fennick. I was asking if you know what breed of dragon she has promised."

I frowned. "What does that matter?"

"Not every dragon can produce Dragonfire."

My eyes narrowed as I scrutinized her. The pinch of her lips was a telltale sign she was hiding something. "How do you know this?"

She sighed. "We have a dragon in custody. But it is unable to produce any fire, whether from injuries or some other ailment, I do not know."

I blinked, uncomprehending. "You have a—*What?*"

"We captured a dragon," Mother said, her words slow and measured, as if I were daft. "We procured it a few weeks ago. It's in the dungeon now."

I felt the blood drain from my face. *Oh, gods...* "Mother, what have you done?" I breathed. I remembered the rumors I'd heard of how we had captured a dragon. When I had asked Mother, she'd dismissed it. But she hadn't outright said the rumors weren't true.

I covered my face with one hand, my heart seizing in my chest. Gods, Aurelia would be *furious.* How could I tell her?

"I did what was necessary for our people," Mother said in a clipped tone. "But it was all for nothing, as the beast is useless."

"You cannot do things like this!" I bellowed, dropping my hands and glaring at her. "I am trying to forge alliances and foster trusting relationships with other kingdoms, but when you send soldiers into other kingdoms to steal from them, it undermines everything I've been working toward!"

"Well perhaps if you had told me of your plan to strike a bargain with the Summer Court, I could have acted appropriately," Mother said with a sniff.

Gods, she was impossible! I wanted to keep shouting at her, but I knew it wouldn't do any good. My blood boiled with anger at what she'd done. And now...

"After everything that's happened, I don't think we can smooth things over with our people if you are to announce your engagement to their enemy," Mother said, as if the matter of her stealing a dragon had been settled. "Perhaps it would be best to wait until we have received a dragon with proper Dragonfire first."

I was shaking my head, prepared to argue, when shouts echoed from the other side of the closed doors. I stiffened, turning toward the commotion. The muffled voices rose in volume, and I made out Aurelia's loud voice.

"I said let me through!" she cried.

Oh, shit. I hastened to the doors and threw them open, ignoring my mother's protests. There stood Aurelia, dressed in a glittering silver gown, her body adorned with diamonds that made her whole figure sparkle. Beside her were the two soldiers tasked with guarding the throne room. Aurelia's cheeks were pink, her eyes flashing with anger and irritation.

For a moment, all thoughts fled from my mind as I was wholly and completely consumed by her stunning appearance.

"Beloved," I said softly, unable to keep myself from looking over her beautiful figure once more. "I didn't realize you were awake."

"These imbeciles are trying to keep me from you." Her chin lifted, and I bit back a smile at the haughty royal mask she wore. Oh, she would be a formidable presence in our court, that was for sure. I couldn't wait to see how she fared against my mother.

My good spirits faltered when I remembered what my mother had just confessed to me. Our people had snuck into the Summer Court and stolen a dragon. Stars, how could I tell Aurelia? It would have to wait until we were in private; if I told her now, it would shatter her carefully crafted mask.

"Let her through," I told the guards, waving my hand at them. "She may enter."

The men nodded, though one of them shot Aurelia a glare before they returned to their station. I took Aurelia's elbow and guided her forward, leaning close to whisper in her ear, "You look radiant."

She shivered slightly, and judging by the way her cheeks reddened, it wasn't from the cold, but from the way my breath tickled her ear. I offered a crooked smile.

"Aurelia, I'd like you to meet my mother, Queen Sonara of the Midnight Court," I said loudly, still clasping Aurelia's arm as I presented her to my mother. The queen had made her way to the throne on the dais and was now perched on it, her chin high and her eyes sharp as steel as she surveyed us both.

Aurelia sank into a low curtsy, her head bowed. "It is an honor to meet you, Your Highness."

"I find that hard to believe, since you barged your way into a private conversation with me and my son," Mother said coldly.

I sighed. "Mother—"

But Aurelia cut me off. "All due respect, Your Highness, but I sought out my betrothed immediately upon waking, knowing we had fires to put out after our chaotic entrance yesterday. I thought it best to get started right away, beginning with a formal introduction to the great queen of this court." She sank into another curtsy. "So, Queen Sonara, it is a deep honor and pleasure to finally meet you. I hope this introduction is the beginning of an amicable relationship between our two kingdoms."

I raised my eyebrows, impressed by her boldness and flattery, even as my stomach twisted into knots at the words *amicable relationship.* There was nothing amicable about our relationship. Not once she found out that Mother had stolen a dragon.

Mother only offered a single slow blink; other than that, her fierce expression remained unchanged. "I want to know why you two entered into this agreement," she said.

"Mother, I've explained this to you," I said.

"I want to hear it from *her.*" The queen kept her gaze pinned on Aurelia.

The Summer Princess was unfazed. Her blue eyes sharpened as she said calmly, "Fenn and I entered into an agreement that would benefit both our kingdoms. He needs dragons. I need stardust. We both need the appearance of a strong alliance to signify to the realm that we are a powerful force to be reckoned with."

Mother chuckled, the sound low and full of ire. "I seriously doubt you were willing to put to rest the centuries of turmoil between our kingdoms simply because you needed stardust. I'm surprised your people didn't invade my land to just take it for yourselves."

Aurelia's nostrils flared, her face turning pink with anger. I bit down on the inside of my cheek to keep from intervening. Aurelia would need to prove herself to my mother one way or another. But could she keep her anger in check? Or would this encounter turn volatile?

A few tense seconds passed before Aurelia responded, "Fenn is the first representative of your court who was even willing to negotiate with me. Now, I cannot speak for my parents. If they were unwilling to smooth relations with you, then I apologize. I do not know their thinking or their reasons. But I am different, and I hope to lead my court differently. I do not hold petty grudges simply because my ancestors did."

Mother's thin eyebrows lifted. "Is that so?"

"It is, Your Highness."

"Well, if it is only an alliance with my *court* that you need, then may I suggest marrying my nephew, Sir Cordon? Or Lord Halsburg, a wealthy noble in my court? Anyone will do. Just not my son."

My stomach hollowed. Shit, what was she doing?

Aurelia's face paled. "Forgive me, Your Highness, but our bargain has already been struck."

"You and I both know that any party of a faerie bargain can dissolve the terms if they only speak the words. Even with a blood bargain. As long as the bargain has not been fulfilled, it can be annulled in the same way it was contracted: by blood."

Aurelia exhaled in frustration. "I am next in line to my throne, and Fenn is next in line to his. It is a fair match."

"And I am asking for a show of good faith. If your intentions are as pure as you say, then marry someone else. Make that first step, Princess Aurelia."

My heart slammed against my ribcage, my pulse roaring in my ears. This was falling apart. We needed to salvage the situation, and quickly.

"That will not do," I said loudly.

Aurelia and Mother both looked at me, the former with alarm, the latter with annoyance.

"And why not?" Mother demanded.

"Because you and I both know you don't give a damn if Cordon or Halsburg live or die. Neither of them would provide enough leverage to ensure this court keeps our side of the bargain. But I do."

Mother opened her mouth to object, but I spoke over her, my stomach fluttering from the prospect of what I was about to do. "Furthermore, to arrange a marriage between Aurelia and another man would be devastating to me, because—you see—I am utterly and hopelessly in love with her."

The Summer Princess

The world seemed to stop from the force of those words.

I am utterly and hopelessly in love with her.

Gods above. Fenn couldn't lie.

He… was in love with me.

The Midnight Prince was *in love* with me.

My heart seized with violent intensity as I tried to find a reason, an explanation for this lie. Because surely it was only part of our ruse. Surely he couldn't mean—

"Blazing stars, Fennick, you cannot be serious!" Queen Sonara bellowed, her voice ringing in the throne room. She stood from her perch, her magnificent gown sweeping behind her like a cape as she strode down the steps of the dais toward her son. "You are confused. You are wearied and wounded from your ordeal. I must insist you rest and put your mind at ease. There is no need for you to make such rash declarations when you are not of sound mind."

"I *am* of sound mind," Fenn said, his emerald eyes burning as he stared his mother down. I willed him to look my way so I could read his expression to determine if he was being earnest or not. But his gaze on the queen never once faltered. "I am in love with her. She is strong and bold and the perfect candidate for our next queen. She will defend us to the very end. There is no one in the entire Realm of Valora that I would rather marry."

My chest tightened, and a roaring sound filled my ears. Burning suns, I couldn't breathe. I couldn't even process this declaration.

Oh gods. What was Fenn doing? He was about to ruin everything.

This was no longer a bargain for him. He had just announced that he wanted to marry me. It was a lie neither of us could have told during our ruse because it was not the truth.

Except… that had changed.

And worse—I could not reciprocate his words. I could not say, *Yes, I love Fenn, too, and we will marry as two heart-struck lovers should!* I could not say those words, as much as I longed to be able to, because I didn't know what I felt. I had feelings for him, yes, but I hadn't been able to examine them, to see how deeply they ran. I was so consumed by fear of my strange powers and concern for my family and my kingdom that I hadn't had the time to inspect my feelings for the prince.

It certainly wasn't love. It *couldn't* be. Could it?

My throat thickened, and I struggled to take my next breath, to remain composed. My mask cracked and faltered under the strain of this turn of events. I had to keep my royal persona in place. I could not crumble, not in front of the queen.

I stared at the reflection of the moon that gleamed on the marble floors, losing myself in the way the pearly glow illuminated that particular spot, the way the shadows parted around that sliver of light. As I kept my gaze pinned on this one section of the floor, I counted in my head to ten, ever so slowly, inhaling deeply and exhaling steadily.

I repeated this twice until my pulse evened out, until I could force myself to look at Fenn and the queen without losing my mind.

Fenn was speaking, and it took all my restraint not to grab him by the shoulders and shake him, to demand what the hell he was doing right now. Instead, I plastered a look of calm interest on my face and focused on his words.

"…you would not have me watch the woman I love marry another, would you? Would you deprive me of a happy marriage?"

"You were never intended to marry happily," the queen argued. "You knew from the beginning that your marriage would be an arrangement for the good of the kingdom."

"And it is. Can you not see the good that will come of this? We need dragons. And Aurelia—"

"Aurelia has not provided *proof* of the dragons she will give us." Queen Sonara fixed her steely gaze on me, her eyebrows lowering in accusation.

"Mother, she swore a blood bargain," Fenn objected.

"I do not care!" the queen shouted. "You are my son. This is *my kingdom.* And I am not taking chances on this girl and her duplicitous family, not after our history. I am sorry, Fennick, but I—"

"What if I could give you proof?" I asked, the words bursting from my lips before I could think better of it.

Fenn went perfectly still, his gaze flicking to me at last. I tried to decipher the emotions in his eyes, but his own mask was in place, cutting me off.

The queen's eyes narrowed. "I am listening."

I stepped forward, encouraged by this response. "A dragon came here with me. A show of good faith, as you would put it. What if we could use his Dragonfire to resume your Nightfire fete tonight? It would be a sign to the people that this union can bring joy, that together, Fenn and I can make the kingdom safe."

Queen Sonara's eyes glittered with a savage hunger that made my stomach roil. In a flash, the look was gone, replaced by an expression of cold disinterest. But I couldn't shake that look from my mind, the look of a smiling predator closing in on its prey... It was so unlike the warm gaze I was accustomed to from her son.

"You brought a dragon here with you?" Her voice was low and intense. I had the distinct impression that I was in danger. The hairs on my arms stood up from the lethal edge to her voice.

I swallowed hard. "He will only come when I call him. As you can imagine, he does not feel comfortable in this land."

"Aurelia," Fenn said quietly, his voice pained, but I ignored him.

"Is that proof enough for you?" I asked the queen. "I am earnest with my intentions with Fenn. I wish to bring safety and prosperity to your people and mine. Let me prove that to you tonight. Send a decree to your people that they shall prepare for a fete tonight. Let Fenn and me introduce ourselves as a couple to be wed, to end this centuries-long feud between our kingdoms. Let tonight be a time for joy amidst all the trials your people have faced."

Fenn's head reared back, his eyebrows lifting as he gave me an impressed smirk. I couldn't resist smiling back at him, though it was weak; I was still wracked with guilt and confusion over his confession.

Queen Sonara lifted her chin, her eyes calculating as she looked me over. I held my ground, meeting her gaze head-on, refusing to back down from my claims or from her scrutiny.

At long last, she said, "Very well," and I released a heavy breath. "But understand that I will be watching very closely, princess. If you double-cross the Court of Midnight, we will show you no mercy."

I forced a bland smile. "I would expect nothing less, Your Highness."

The queen left the throne room after that, claiming she had a dozen tasks to see to if we were to host the fete tonight. In a blur of motion, she exited the throne room, and suddenly, Fenn and I were alone. The doors remained open, however, and I was painfully aware of the guards who stood outside the doors.

My skin felt itchy and far too tight. I resisted the urge to fidget and squirm, but I couldn't bring myself to look at him, either. I was afraid of what I might see. Or perhaps I was afraid of what I *wouldn't* see.

I wasn't certain what terrified me more—the notion that he *did* love me, or the possibility that it was all an act, that he would laugh and give me that signature smirk, his eyes full of mirth as he said, *I can't believe she fell for it!*

"Aurelia," he murmured.

My eyes closed, and in that moment, I knew. I knew he spoke the truth.

He drew closer to me, his warm hand at my elbow, and gods help me, but I wanted to lean into his touch, to envelop myself in his scent, in the strength of his arms.

But I didn't. I *couldn't*. I didn't know what it was I felt for him.

But he did. He loved me.

And this changed everything.

"I cannot believe you said those things," I whispered, opening my eyes to peer up at him. His gaze shone with unrestrained desire. Gods, it was so intense and pure. I had never seen anything written so plainly on his face. The adoration, the longing, the despair, the *truth*.

It made my chest ache.

"This changes nothing," Fenn murmured, trailing his fingers up my arm. I suppressed a shiver of pleasure from the lightness of his touch. "Our bargain is still intact, and I fully intend for us to part ways after this is all over. I have no interest in holding you to something you did not promise. You will be free from me, Aurelia."

I shook my head, my eyes welling with tears. "You can't say those things and then say you will release me. You can't make me the villain who steals your heart and then shatters it, leaving you to sweep up the pieces alone."

Fenn exhaled a sharp laugh. "I think you have mistaken me for a weak, fragile thing. I will be *fine*, Aurelia. I—I may have feelings for you. But I uttered those words *only* to convince my mother. Nothing more. Not to beg for your love or to persuade you to marry me."

"Fenn—"

He drew closer, clasping my hands in both of his. I gazed up at him, a single tear streaking down my cheek.

"Don't," he breathed, catching the tear with his thumb and sweeping it away. "Don't cry for me, little firebird. Once my people see the fete and the Dragonfire that will protect them, all will be well. But I think… I think it would be best if you left immediately after the fete."

My stomach dropped. "What? Why?"

"You have been away from your court for too long, and we can't visit the Court of Twilight to seek answers about the Dream Mage. If she is as powerful as the hunter says, then your people are in danger. After the fete, I will get you your supply of stardust, and you can be on your way."

Alarm pulsed through me. He couldn't be serious. "Fenn, I can't just leave! We are putting *everything* into this ruse. If I vanish like a thief in the night, everyone will know it was a sham. And they will be livid when I take Mal with me. He was supposed to be a show of good faith."

"I will smooth things over," he assured me, though I sensed the uncertainty in his tone. I had met his mother; she did not seem like the forgiving type. I wouldn't be surprised if she waged war immediately after my departure.

Fenn seemed to read the doubt on my face. "Aurelia, it will be fine. I swear it. Don't worry about my court. Your people need you. Once you've broken the curse, we can mend things here. But we can't risk leaving your palace undefended for much longer. You know this."

My throat tightened. As much as I wanted to insist on staying, on helping Fenn with his own court issues, I knew he was right. Kade, our biggest dragon, would need to return to her hibernation soon, and with Mal here, the palace would be practically defenseless.

I looked up at Fenn, at the somber certainty in his eyes. Was he insisting I leave because of my people? Or because he couldn't bear to keep up our pretense any longer, knowing I did not return his feelings?

"When our engagement dissolves, I will assure them our alliance remains intact, and they will know we can keep them safe," he went on. "*That* is what matters. Our people. The safety of our kingdoms. Not my silly feelings. Do not worry for me, Aurelia."

I swallowed thickly and nodded, though I did not believe it. How could I part ways from him, knowing what I knew? How could he do that to me? How could he put that burden on my shoulders?

To my surprise, Fenn chuckled. "Well, this won't do. Should I return to my flippant and dastardly persona? Would it be more suitable if I went to a brothel to secure a bedmate for the night, per my usual standards?"

"No," I said, my voice far sharper than I intended. Fenn's eyebrows lifted, and my stomach churned with a foreign anxiety. I didn't know why I said that. But the idea of Fenn sharing someone else's bed filled me with rage.

Before I could scrutinize this emotion further, I cleared my throat and said, "Tell me how I can help prepare for the fete tonight."

Fenn smiled, linking my arm with his as we strode from the throne room. "I'd be delighted to."

THE MIDNIGHT PRINCE

I KNEW I HAD MADE A TERRIBLE MISTAKE IN CONFESSING MY FEELINGS FOR Aurelia. The instant that look of shock and confusion flitted over her features, I knew.

She did not love me.

But I couldn't take it back now. And my plan had worked. We had secured Mother's approval—for now.

All we had to do was host the greatest fete the court had ever seen.

I knew I needed to pull Aurelia aside and tell her about the captured dragon. But I also knew that as soon as she found out, she would drop everything and try to free it, even risking her own life to do so.

No, it would have to wait until after the fete. We couldn't afford for this to go badly. Afterwards, I vowed I would tell her everything. I would even help her free the dragon myself.

For the rest of the day, Aurelia and I worked together, overseeing all the preparations for the fete. To my surprise, the castle staff took kindly to Aurelia, ever polite and courteous, a few even offering tentative smiles. It wasn't until I caught sight of Cela, Aurelia's handmaid, whispering excitedly with her fellow maids as she glanced at Aurelia and back again, that I realized why. Cela was the castle's biggest gossip, and the most influential of the maids, as she and her mother, Donna, had been with us the longest.

I knew Mother had assigned Cela to Aurelia to dig up any dirty secrets and report back to her. But in truth, Mother had done us a favor. Aurelia had clearly made a positive impression on Cela, and she was now sharing this impression with her colleagues.

I couldn't keep the smile from my face as Cela curtsied to Aurelia, who grinned broadly at the maid and thanked her for her hard work. The Summer Princess was indeed a queen in the making.

The nobles of the Midnight Court, however, were another thing entirely. When we summoned the court to announce the fete, several courtiers cast hostile looks toward Aurelia. And when we shared our courtship and arrangement, several nobles rose to their feet, raising their voices with vehement objections. It wasn't until I informed them a dragon would provide us with Nightfire for the fete that the court fell silent. Some still scowled, obviously displeased with the arrangement, but no one voiced any further qualms. Even they weren't stupid enough to refuse what we so desperately needed to protect our people.

Mother was nowhere to be found, of course. She had claimed important fete preparations required her attention. But I had a sneaking suspicion that she wanted me to handle the objections. Perhaps she hoped that if enough of our court voiced their concerns about the union, that we would call it off.

She didn't know her wish would come true. This time tomorrow, Aurelia would be gone, and I would be making excuses for her. Mother would be pleased on that front, but when she discovered Aurelia had taken the dragon as well, she would go blind with fury.

It would be a miracle if we could hold this alliance intact. After Aurelia's departure, I wasn't sure if even I could smooth things over with the court.

But I didn't need to tell the princess that. Her kingdom needed help. She shouldn't stay here on my account. Hopefully, I would find a way to put out the fires we would start after this bargain ended.

Gods, what a mess.

To be honest, I was grateful for the distractions. They kept us busy, preventing us from addressing the grievous blunder I'd committed which had driven a tangible wedge between us. I felt it in every glance she threw my way, in her stiff posture as she stood alongside me, in the way her hands clasped in front of her, wringing together as if she was afraid to even touch me.

Stars, I had really mucked things up.

I told myself it didn't matter. As we sampled pastries and sparkling fire wine, oversaw the setting up of faerie lights and bonfires, checked the stores of stardust and the protective wards, and dispatched royal decrees with each of our nobles to announce the fete to all the districts, I reminded myself this would end soon. After tonight, it would be over. We needed to ensure we had enough stardust to keep the Dragonfire burning, but after that, I would give Aurelia a generous amount for her needs. She and Mal would return to the Summer Court to break her curse, and we would part ways.

I was a coward. In truth, maintaining this facade of our betrothal, of the love we claimed to share, was too painful for me. Over the past few days, with the way Aurelia seemed around me, I had thought...

Well, it didn't matter what I thought. If she seemed enamored with me, it had to be merely a part of her act. She was just a good actress. That was all. Or perhaps she found me maddeningly attractive. It wasn't hard to succumb to the charm of my good looks and flirtations.

But I couldn't force her to love me. And I didn't want to. I didn't want her to feel obligated to feel something for me. I couldn't bear to see the pity in her eyes.

No. She needed to leave. We both knew it.

Despite how we both desired to uncover the mystery behind the Dream Mage, it was more important for Aurelia's kingdom to be protected against any threats. We could focus on the Dream Mage later.

But this didn't mean I wouldn't try to reach Marek. While Aurelia was busy working with the castle staff, ensuring the courtyard was properly prepped, I snuck away to my chambers and bolted the door, then pulled the loose stone from the hearth that hid my book of witch runes. After looking over the page on portal communication, I etched the chalk markings in a circle on the floor, then painted a charcoal rune on the back of my hand. I didn't have time to light candles.

To my surprise, the runes on the floor started to glow. I didn't expect the spell to work the first time. My chest lightened, and I stared as the floor within the circle of runes began to ripple like the surface of a lake. I stepped outside the circle, envisioning me falling through the liquid floor into some otherworldly witch dimension. Probably best if I kept a safe distance.

Squinting, I watched the floor turn smoky, like the contents of a crystal ball. The fog churned and floated, and I frowned as I tried to make out shapes or objects.

But nothing happened. The smoke continued to roil, but no objects or people appeared.

"Marek?" I called uncertainly.

No answer.

I waited a few more moments, even dared to poke the rippling surface. It felt like cold, solid marble to my fingers.

Perhaps I had drawn the runes incorrectly. Or perhaps my magic wasn't strong enough. After vowing to try again later tonight, I replaced my rune book in its hiding spot along with my chalk, then wiped the floors clean and returned to preparing for the fete with Aurelia.

Aurelia and I barely had time to scarf down a rather late lunch before we had to get ourselves ready for the fete. It was of paramount importance that we make an elegant and prompt appearance, as this event was directly tethered to the success of our alliance. If anything went amiss tonight, it would reflect poorly on us.

Aurelia would call for Mal as soon as the guests were assembled in the outer courtyard. Witnessing a dragon's landing would be a sight to behold and a fabulous way to begin the festivities.

My manservant, Hayworth, dressed me in my finest black suit, with intricate silver detailing on the vest. I fumbled with my diamond cufflinks, trying to steady my nerves. Gods, I had never been nervous before a fete.

"Allow me, Your Highness," Hayworth said gently, and I huffed, surrendering my wrists to have him secure the cufflinks.

"Will you be attending the fete, Hayworth?" I asked, trying to distract myself from the anxiety roiling through me.

Hayworth, with his fraying white hair and wrinkly smile, offered me a baleful look. "I am far too old for the merriment, Your Highness."

"Nonsense. I'm not asking you to partake of the strongest fire wine. But you can still observe the festivities. It will be an extraordinary event, I assure you."

He smiled. "Perhaps I will look on for a bit before retiring for the night."

"Good man." I clapped him on the shoulder. "You won't regret it."

His eyes seemed to twinkle as he stood back to survey my appearance. My hair had been slicked back, but all it would take was one dance to pull the unruly chestnut waves free again.

"Would you like me to have Gorrick run interference on the ladies for you tonight?" Hayworth asked.

I frowned, and it took me a moment to realize what he was referring to. "Ah. Right. Interference."

Ordinarily, during the Nightfire fete, I had several eager dance partners for the night. The women of the court knew my reputation well, and many expressed their interest. But in cases like this, on an evening where more important matters needed to be tended to, I had Gorrick discourage the ladies from their pursuit so I could focus on my responsibilities.

I considered this for a moment, then shook my head. "No. That won't be necessary."

"You are sure?"

"Yes." I would save a few dances for Aurelia, which would be enough to appease the crowd. But I didn't want to anger the court any more than we already had. I wanted to show them I could still be the same Prince Fenn they knew. I had not so fully changed.

Besides, once Aurelia left, I would need a way to distract myself. Perhaps I could find someone tonight who *would* return my affections. Someone I could lose myself in.

It was impossible, of course. There was no one like Aurelia. And there never would be.

But I could still pretend. I could tell myself I would find someone to fall desperately in love with. Someone who would help me move on.

Hayworth nodded once. "As you say, Your Highness. Is there anything else you need from me?"

"No, that is all. Thank you, Hayworth."

He bowed and left the room, leaving me standing before my mirror, staring at this face I no longer recognized. Gone were the smarmy smiles and twinkling eyes. Gone were the smirks and looks of superiority and smugness. This man here looked like a fool. A coward. A man who didn't know where his life was going. A man who was lost in his love for a woman who did not care for him.

This will all change when Aurelia leaves, I assured myself. *Once she leaves, everything will go back to the way it was.*

I rehearsed this lie in my head until I almost believed it. Then, I drew in a steady breath, lifted my chin, and donned my most secure court mask—an expression of haughty apathy and confidence.

When I was satisfied with my appearance, I strode for the door, vowing to make this night a stunning success.

THE SUMMER PRINCESS

Once again, Cela had outdone herself. I made sure to compliment her often, realizing this pleased her the most. I had certainly noticed the way the rest of the castle staff had taken kindly to me, and I attributed this largely to her. Any allies I could secure while I was here would help, and Cela was proving to be a valuable ally.

She had procured me a gown of glittering rose gold, with gold lace sewn into the bodice. The fabric swept over my breasts in two long streaks of fabric, tying together behind my neck and leaving my back completely bare. The skirt fanned out, flaring wide, with gold sparkles that shimmered as it moved. Cela completed the ensemble with teardrop-shaped rose gold earrings that hung low from my earlobes. She curled my hair, leaving it down per my suggestion. I wasn't sure why I wanted it that way. But I couldn't shake the sound of Fenn's low voice as he told me how much he loved my hair when it was wild and free. And a small, embarrassed part of me hoped he would plunge his fingers into my curls like he had the night he'd kissed me.

Warmth spread over my skin, making my blood heat. What was I doing? I did not love Fenn, and it was cruel of me to expect anything to happen between us. He knew how I felt.

Which was… what? What did I feel for him? Not love, no. But… something. Definitely something.

Even so, it didn't matter. After tonight, I would leave. Our bargain would come to an end. We would never have to see each other again.

The thought should have brought me relief. After all, I would finally be able to return home to forests and sunshine. I would be able to break the curse on my kingdom. All would be well.

I swallowed down my uncertainty and forced a smile as Cela stood back to allow me to look over my appearance. She had painted rouge on my lips and cheeks, bringing out the rosiness of my complexion. With the rose gold dress, and my natural flushed skin tone, my whole appearance seemed more pink. Even my hair seemed to shine with a more coral tint than its usual pale orange.

The final touch was a smattering of some kind of sparkling gel that Cela dabbed all over my skin, explaining that it was customary to adorn one's body to look like the stars. When my arms moved, the faint glitter particles shimmered in the light.

"You look radiant, miss," Cela breathed, her eyes wide with awe. "A vision. Truly."

"It's all thanks to you, Cela. You are a miracle worker! I never could have managed this on my own. Thank you."

She curtsied, her face turning crimson, but her expression pleased.

"Fenn tells me the entire kingdom, regardless of their station, is invited to the fete," I said. "Will you be attending?"

She grinned. "Yes, miss. I never miss it!"

I smiled. "I'm glad. I will see you there. You should go and get yourself ready. I have everything I need."

"Are you certain, miss?"

"Absolutely. Thank you again."

She bobbed another curtsy before leaving the room. I took a deep, steadying breath. I could do this. My stomach knotted at the idea of facing Fenn after… after everything. And the thought of summoning Mal, bringing him here among a crowd of hostile enemies? Would he even answer my call?

I knew he would. Mal never failed to come when I called, no matter the danger. He would lay down his life for me.

But that was exactly what I was afraid of. I envisioned the courtiers going wild with rage at the sight of a dragon, wielding swords and daggers as they tried to take his life.

But no. This was foolish. The kingdom *needed* Dragonfire. They needed Mal alive.

I tried to be comforted by this, but the knots in my stomach only tightened. My breath was shaky as I left my bedchamber, the soft silk of my skirt whispering with my steps. My sandals were light and comfortable, which was unexpected. In the Summer Court, I was always expected to wear tight contraptions that scrunched my toes and made me ache for days.

Then again, this court was already proving to be different. Looser, more revealing clothing, more cavalier behaviors, and a fete that brought the entire kingdom together. My court did nothing like that. All our balls and festivals were only for a certain group of people—balls for the courtiers, and festivals for the commoners. We never mingled.

But perhaps, with this alliance, that could change. I loved the idea of bringing our people together, regardless of class or social status. What a beautiful way to unite a kingdom.

It was so unexpected, so surprising, coming from a court that had a reputation for being brutal and deadly, full of darkness and despair. How had I been so wrong about the Midnight Court for so long?

I made my way down the hall and descended the staircase. Already, a low babble of voices echoed from below. I was reminded of my time in the Autumn Court, of the nerves that twisted through my body for an entirely different reason as I faced the brute who assaulted me.

But already, this was proving to be so very different. The lights in the sconces glowed a silvery blue, and they barely illuminated the staircase and foyer. A dome-shaped window was built into the vaulted ceiling, through which a glittering sky full of stars shone. The crescent moon gleamed, and with the low light in the palace, it allowed the moon to be the brightest source of light. I knew this was done intentionally. Halfway down the stairs, I paused to gaze up at the starry sky through the ceiling, my chest swelling with awe and wonder.

It was breathtaking. I couldn't deny it.

A small smile lit my face as I descended the final steps, weaving through various figures to make my way to the outer courtyard. Most of the people here were eager nobility or castle staff, the bulk of the guests having not arrived yet. I recognized one of the maids as a friend of Cela's and nodded politely at her.

I also swept past Lord Northall, who wrinkled his nose as I passed. He had been one of the lords vehemently opposed to my union with Fenn. I kept my head held high as I passed, not even bothering to acknowledge him.

After tonight, everything would change. He would probably despise me, yes. But tonight, Fenn and I would prove just how much this alliance could change things for the better.

When I stepped through the open double doors leading to the courtyard, the chill of night swept over me, raising the hairs on my arms. I rubbed them to ward it off, then sucked in a sharp breath as I took in the scene before me.

The courtyard opened up to a vast and expansive field surrounded by trees, with faerie lights stringing from branch to branch, glowing with that same light blue ethereal glow. Across the field was the brilliant silver river, which seemed to shine even brighter than the moon. Sparkling lights glistened from within the churning water, which I knew now to be the stardust embedded in the sediment below. Several braziers lined the river bank, but they were empty, waiting for the fire of a dragon to fuel them. Fenn told me the magic of the faerie lights would ward off attacks from the unseelie, but the lights only lasted an hour.

The soothing sounds of the river mingled with the sweeping melody pouring from the courtyard balcony where the musicians played, all of them wearing elegant finery. Some would lay their instruments down to join the dancers in the field, pausing their playing to participate in the revelry without a care in the world.

I found myself grinning at the sight. This fete was so informal, so inclusive, that even the musicians could stop their playing to enjoy themselves. I watched as a courtier downed a glass of sparkling fire wine, laughing as she climbed the steps to the balcony, and picked up a lute to join in the music.

Raucous laughter filled the air, echoing in the open space. There were people *everywhere*. They spread from the courtyard to the field and across the bridge that spanned the river. The crowd was so vibrant, so full of life, so carefree. It was no wonder Fenn behaved in such a flippant and easygoing manner, when he was accustomed to revelry such as this. Men and women of all shapes and sizes danced together, drinking fire wine and singing along with the music. A circle of dancers had large, gossamer wings spreading from their backs as they joined hands. I recognized the red cloaks of a few witches, and my heart lurched until I realized they weren't Ruby, Jade, or Sapphire, but witches I did not know.

I had tucked the lavender glass vial they had given me into the bodice of my gown. Just in case. I was sure I wouldn't use it, though.

On the other end of the field, I caught sight of a pair of figures spread on the ground under the cover of a tree. The man's hand was up the woman's skirt as she writhed in pleasure.

My face heated at the sight, and I inexplicably thought of Fenn with his hand in a similar place while I moaned, urging him onward.

I averted my gaze from the sight, suddenly feeling flushed. My eyes scanned the crowd, searching for the familiar messy chestnut waves and cocky smile. Was Fenn here yet? My stomach fluttered as I looked for him.

Just when I had decided he must still be getting ready, I turned back to the palace doors and found him standing there, one arm casually propped against the door frame. My throat tightened as I gazed over his trim, muscular form. His midnight suit was fit to perfection, particularly tight around the muscles of his bicep as he leaned into it, watching the merriment from afar, a small smile on his lips. His waistcoat had an intricate silver design sewn into it, and his vest was decorated with gleaming silver swirls that sparkled in the moonlight. Sparkles shone on his cheekbones and neck, likely from the same gel Cela had put on me.

Gods, he was a masterpiece, standing there with perfect nonchalance, his expression soft. I could drink in this scene all day and never tire of it.

In that moment, his eyes locked onto mine, and he straightened, his jaw going slack. He, too, looked me over, his emerald eyes gliding slowly from my head to my feet. I stood there, feeling a restless energy swell within me as he scrutinized me. Slowly, we made our way toward each other. I wasn't sure who moved first, but after a few steps, we closed the gap between us, standing on the steps of the courtyard.

"I—" He swallowed, his throat bobbing. His eyes darkened with desire and lust as he stared at me. He huffed a breathless laugh and leaned close to me, his breath tickling my ear. "That dress is a far more dangerous weapon than any dagger you've threatened me with." His voice was low and sultry and made my toes curl.

I laughed, too, my face flushing. I tried not to focus on his cheek so close to mine, or the way his cool mint and pine scent enveloped me. "You cut a fine figure yourself, Fenn."

He bowed, then offered me his hand. "Shall we announce ourselves to the public?"

My heart fluttered in my chest for an entirely new reason now, but I nodded and took his hand. It was time.

340

THE MIDNIGHT PRINCE

 courtyard to where we could better be seen. After sharing a nod with her, I bellowed, "Good people of the Midnight Court! May I have your attention please?"

The laughter and music faded, and the couples stopped dancing to gaze up at us, smiles on their faces. Just seeing my people so full of joy and life only confirmed that this was the right choice. There was nothing better we could have done for them than give them this fete they loved so much.

Yes, this alliance would do great things for all of us.

I offered a wide smile and said loudly, "I would like to formally announce my engagement to this beautiful creature beside me, Princess Aurelia Perdis of the Summer Court!"

Murmurs and whispers met my words, several people frowning or casting curious looks at Aurelia. No one was smiling anymore.

I pushed on. "To celebrate this joyous occasion, we have hosted this Nightfire fete once more. You have probably noticed an absence of Nightfire, but not to worry. The fae lights have been sufficient until now, but we have another exciting element to our evening to share with you. To keep the merriment going all night, Aurelia has provided a dragon to grant us the fire we need to keep us safe!"

Gasps echoed around us, and I turned to Aurelia, who took a shaky breath before bringing her fingers to her lips and whistling loudly. The shrill sound rang, piercing the air, and my head reared back in surprise.

I didn't realize she could whistle like that. It was a strong, resounding note that even those across the bridge would be able to hear.

The crowd seemed to hold its breath in anticipation. I scanned the area, waiting for Mal's black figure to bound forward.

A roar echoed in the distance, and several people cried out in alarm. Then, a dark form cut through the sky, wings spread wide as it flapped toward us. I found myself grinning as Mal swooped into view, arcing over the crowd with a graceful turn that made many of them gasp in awe. He landed on the terrace opposite where the musicians had been playing, his clawed fleet slamming into the stone and making the ground tremble.

He certainly knew how to make an entrance. And judging by the smirk on Aurelia's face, it was all intentional. Mal knew exactly what he was doing. The thought made me chuckle. What a clever beast he was.

"May I present Malvolio of the Darkener species!" I said, waving a hand toward Mal. "He will be providing our Dragonfire for the evening."

Cheers erupted from the crowd, and I beamed, knowing we'd won them over. No one could resist a dragon, after all. Aurelia had rushed to Mal's side and was stroking his snout, murmuring something incoherent. Mal twitched one ear, then inclined his head, and she smiled, her whole face lighting up. I found myself entranced by that smile, the way her eyes crinkled and her cheeks flushed.

Stars, she was beautiful. Absolutely breathtaking.

And she could never be mine.

Swallowing hard, I took a breath and said, "Aurelia, dearest, if you wouldn't mind?"

Aurelia nodded and strode down the steps with Mal behind her. The crowd immediately parted to let them pass. When she reached the riverbank, she paused, glancing expectantly at Mal. He inhaled deeply, the sound raspy, and then unleashed a stream of blue flames toward the river. Flecks of stardust floated from the water, coiling around the Dragonfire. The flames spread, catching each brazier along the riverbank as the stardust we'd placed inside ignited.

One by one, each brazier was lit with the magical fire, glowing brightly and illuminating the forest with a light just as brilliant as the sun. I hadn't realized just how dark it was outside until I saw how much *brighter* everything was with the Dragonfire.

Screams of delight filled the air, following by raucous applause. The people were laughing and grinning once more, overjoyed with our announcement.

I raised my arms jubilantly and shouted, "This is a sign of better times to come, thanks to our union with the Summer Court! So please, enjoy yourselves, and let the fete commence!"

Whoops and shouts of joy followed my words as I clambered down the steps to Aurelia's side. She was saying something to Mal, who huffed in disapproval before taking off to the sky. Aurelia watched him go, her brows tightening with worry.

"He'll be all right," I assured her.

"He wanted to stay close to me, just in case," she said, her eyes not leaving the sky. "But I fear for him in this strange place."

I laced my fingers through hers. "I know."

She squeezed my hand, finally looking at me, her eyes shining. "That was quite an announcement."

I offered her a roguish grin. "Yes, I was rather charming, wasn't I?"

She laughed, then glanced behind me. The music and dancing had resumed, and Aurelia's expression turned soft, her eyes full of awe as she watched.

"Shall we?" I asked.

She beamed. "Yes please." But when she strode for the crowd, I stopped her, tugging on her hand. She looked at me in confusion. "We are dancing, aren't we?"

"Yes. But I told you before that one of my favorite spots to dance is in the forest. I'd like to take you there, if you like." My stomach twisted with nerves. Perhaps she didn't want to. Perhaps she would give me that pitying look that had crossed her face so often since my declaration in front of my mother.

Instead, a slow, surprised smile spread across her face, and she nodded eagerly.

With her hand still in mine, I guided her across the bridge, weaving past dancing couples and guests downing glasses of fire wine. On the other side of the bridge was a much thinner crowd, but they were enjoying themselves just the same. Women spun, their skirts twirling, and men leaned close, arms wrapped around their partners, their bodies pressing together.

When we reached the edge of the Crescent Glade, the small forest on the other side of the river, I faced Aurelia, standing up straight and offering her my hand with my most princely smile. She laughed and accepted it. My arm came around her waist, bringing her chest flush against mine. Her rain and jasmine scent filled my nose, and it took all my restraint to keep from leaning in and pressing my mouth to her neck to breathe her fully in.

Her breath was shaky as she drew closer, her arm against mine, and her other hand resting along the back of my neck. I felt her fingers toying with the edge of my hair, almost unconsciously, as if she didn't realize she was doing it.

I smiled down at her, at the way her eyes shone in the moonlight and her lips parted ever so slightly.

Then, I glided us into movement, and she fell into step with me. At first our movements were slow and careful as we found our rhythm together, but after a few moments, our moves became more elaborate. I twirled her, and her hair whipped around as she spun once then came back into my chest.

Our steps took us backward, toward the river. Her leg came up, the slit in her gown revealing an enticing amount of her thigh. Then, I pushed her backward, toward the forest, our steps bringing us left, then right. I lifted my arm, twirling her again, then placed my hands on her waist and lifted her, spinning her in a circle. Her arms came out, spreading wide as if in flight as she laughed loudly.

When I placed her on her feet once more, I dipped her low, hovering with my face a breath away from hers. The music faded, coming to a stop, but we remained suspended like that, both of us panting and grinning widely. My hand braced her back, keeping her from falling as I leaned over her. I knew I should bring her back up, should step away from her now, but I couldn't bring myself to do it just yet.

Aurelia's eyes glittered with delight, her cheeks flushed from the dance. She offered a breathless laugh and murmured, "You're right. There's nothing quite like dancing in the forest."

"There's nothing quite like dancing with *you*," I whispered.

Her smile faded as she looked at me with earnest intensity. My eyes darted down to those carefully parted lips. Gods, I remembered how delicious that mouth tasted...

Aurelia cleared her throat, and I immediately lifted her, setting her on her feet once more. I took a healthy step away from her, putting distance between us. Her expression was guarded and uncertain, and I knew I'd gone too far again.

Damn it all.

With a heavy exhale, I bowed low to her. "Thank you for the dance, my lady. If you'll excuse me, I'm going to make the rounds and ensure everything is running smoothly."

"Fenn—" She stepped toward me, her expression anguished.

Stars above, I couldn't take it. I couldn't bear to see her pity, her damn sorrow for not feeling what I did. It was unbearable. More than anything, I yearned to go back to before, before she knew how I felt, before I had ruined everything between us.

I forced a smile. "All is well, Aurelia. I just need space right now."

Her mouth clamped shut, and she nodded, her eyes full of regret. "Of course."

I turned from her, striding across the bridge and wishing more than anything that I could push this infuriating woman from my thoughts for good.

THE SUMMER PRINCESS

I STOOD BY THE RIVERBANK FOR A LONG MOMENT, STARING AFTER THE space where Fenn had vanished. My heart twisted into a painful knot as I battled between chasing after him and fleeing into the forest.

So, instead, I lingered in between, my feet rooted to the spot. My chest heaved with heavy breaths, my face on fire from our dance and from--

From Fenn. He elicited such an intoxicating heat from me. The way his hands held my hips, guiding me in our dance, and the way his nose brushed my cheek as he whispered in my ear...

Why couldn't I go after him? What was stopping me?

I huffed a laugh at that. *Everything* was stopping me. This bargain between us. The situation with my kingdom. His volatile mother.

There were a hundred reasons why I should let him go.

Then why was I staring after him, longing for him to come back to me?

I rubbed my arms to ward off the chill that tingled along my skin as the heat finally left my body. The dancing couples around me slowly glided away, leaving me alone at the edge of the forest. The soothing sounds of the river mingled with the muffled music floating across the water.

It was strangely calming, this sense of solitude. I gazed upward at the glittering stars in the sky and the inviting crescent moon. With the braziers lit, casting a bluish glow on the grass, it was hard to believe it was the middle of the night. When I had pictured the Midnight Court, I had envisioned utter darkness. Not... *this.*

I found myself smiling as I drew closer to the sparkling waters. The stardust sediments glimmered under the surface. I recalled what Fenn had said when I'd shown him Kellen Falls: *I felt a sense of peace while I was there. Something I've only ever felt next to the Celestial River.*

A startling realization hit me: I felt the same sense of peace here, too. This place, this river, was as comforting to me as the rushing waters of Kellen Falls.

A surprised laugh bubbled up in my throat, and I found myself unable to stop smiling. Fenn and I, we were the same. Two souls bound to one another irrevocably, despite our differences, despite our warring kingdoms.

I had never felt this way with Tyrone or even Callan. Never had I felt so drawn to another soul, so inexplicably tethered.

My feet moved of their own accord, guiding me across the bridge and toward the crowd dancing just beyond the courtyard. I had to find Fenn, to tell him...

Tell him what?

I wasn't quite sure. I just knew I needed to find him.

I strode past dancing courtiers and laughing ladies, a pair of women locked in a passionate embrace, and a couple making love along the riverbank. Echoes of the upbeat and vibrant music floated through the air, growing louder as I drew closer to the mass of people.

When I reached the courtyard, I climbed the steps to get a better look at those dancing in the field, my eyes scanning for a sign of Fenn.

Be with me, I wanted to say to him. *Love me. Touch me. I want all of you, Fennick. All of you.*

I was breathless, my heart drumming an erratic rhythm in time to the music around me. When a servant offered a tray of sparkling fire water, I took a flute and downed it in one gulp. The drink quite literally burned my throat, and I belched. Smoke unfurled from within my mouth, and I gasped, choking slightly.

The servant chuckled. "It gets easier the second time." He offered me another.

It was probably unwise of me to take it, but I did. As I downed the wine, this time, it didn't burn as much. But that was probably because the inside of my throat was completely past feeling. The drink spread warmth through my entire body, all the way down to my toes. Courage and confidence swelled in my chest, and I suddenly felt the urge to join in, to dance with these strangers, to share in their merriment.

But no. I needed to find *Fenn.* I could dance with him. I could push myself up along his body, writhing against his hips, and—

My thoughts stuttered as my eyes latched onto a pair of dancers in the center of the field. The woman was thin and wore a black slip-of-a dress that barely covered any skin. The skirt came just above her rear, exposing most of her thighs, and the neckline plunged low, all the way to her stomach, the thin strips of silk barely containing her large breasts.

And her dance partner was Fenn.

He was laughing, his smile wide, revealing his teeth as he swayed with the woman, guiding her hips to his as they moved to the rhythm of the music. The woman draped her arms around his neck, her face close to his as she whispered something in his ear that only made his grin broaden.

The sight of them made something roar inside of me. Heat and rage and bloodlust surged, coiling so tightly in my chest I wanted to scream. No, I wanted to plunge my dagger into the woman's throat.

I wanted to plunge my dagger into *Fenn's* throat. What the hell was he thinking? Wasn't this fete meant to celebrate our engagement? And here he was, dancing with someone else. I wasn't sure who she was, but she certainly didn't look like a courtier.

I was striding down the steps of the courtyard before I realized what I was doing. My gaze never strayed from Fenn and the woman as I weaved through the crowd, making my way across the field to the dancing couple.

Fenn noticed me first, his eyes meeting mine over the woman's shoulder. And he winked at me. The bastard actually *winked.*

The woman turned, a lazy smile on her face, her eyes glassy. "Join us!" she cried out, waving a hand toward me.

I ignored her, focusing all my wrath on Fenn. "No thank you. I need a word with my *fiancé.*" I spat the word.

How could I ever think we could be together or that he could change? He was nothing more than the arrogant asshole I always believed him to be.

"Aurelia—" Fenn said, but I was already tugging his arm, pulling him away from the crowd. He stumbled but quickly righted himself as he followed me.

When we reached the bridge, I whirled to face him, snarling, "What the *hell* are you doing?"

He exhaled a short laugh, running his hand through his hair. "What does it look like I'm doing? I'm enjoying the fete."

"With another woman?"

He sighed. "Really, Aurelia, does that bother you?"

"Yes!" I blurted out without thinking.

He arched a single eyebrow, his eyes flaring with irritation. "Let me get this straight. You do not love me. You do not intend to marry me. And yet, you have some claim on me that is meant to prevent me from dancing with other women. Is that right?"

I let my arms fall on my thighs, the wine making my head cloudy. "I don't—That's not—How do you think it looks to everyone, to see you grinding up against another woman's ass? When, moments ago, you announced your engagement to *me*."

"I think it looks like I'm a very typical courtier," he said, his tone thick with amusement.

I shoved his shoulders hard. "This is not a *joke*, you bastard!"

My voice rang out, and several people turned to look at us in alarm.

Fenn's smile vanished, and his nostrils flared. "You are making a scene," he said in a low voice.

"Oh, you've already done that on your own with that sickening display." I waved my hand toward the field of dancers.

Fenn grabbed my hand and tugged me across the bridge toward the Crescent Glade where we had danced. It seemed like ages ago, and yet it hadn't even been an hour. Less than an hour since he'd held me close, making me feel like the only woman he saw, the only woman in the entire realm.

What a fool I'd been.

We reached the other side of the bridge, where only a few couples remained, lost in their own dance. Fenn led me into the Crescent Glade, away from any potential eavesdroppers, then turned to face me, his arms crossed. "Care to tell me what this is really about? Because I guarantee I'm not the only royal to be seen dancing with someone other than his betrothed."

I rubbed my forehead, struggling to think clearly. "We had an image to uphold. Wasn't it you who suggested we show the entire realm how madly in love we are with each other? Who is to believe that now?"

He shrugged. "Aren't you leaving this court in a few hours? By the time gossip reaches anyone's ears, our bargain will be fulfilled."

I shook my head. "It isn't fair that you can make demands of *me*, like I must share a room and a bed with you, but you aren't expected to do the same."

His brows knitted together. "What about this is unfair? Didn't *you* dance with another man at the Equinox Ball?"

"Yes, but that was the *king*, not—"

"So, how is this any different?"

"When I danced with the king, you made a show of kissing me on the dance floor to steer gossip away from it."

"Is that so?" He inched closer, his mouth curling into that despicable smirk. "So, what will you do to me now, to fix the mess I've made?"

I groaned in frustration, turning away from him. "Everything is a game to you. You're being ridiculous."

"No, *you* are being ridiculous." His voice rose as he trailed after me, wrenching my arm and whirling me to face him once more. His eyes blazed with intensity. "You turned me away, Aurelia. I offered you everything—my heart, my soul, my body—and you said *no*."

"You didn't offer me anything!" I yelled. "You said those words to your damn mother, not to me."

"Would it have made a difference? You would still have rejected me, looked at me with that sickening pity in your eyes as if I'm a forlorn puppy starving to death in the street, a helpless creature you can't save."

Rage boiled my blood. "That is not—"

"And now, when I'm trying to rid my mind of your infuriating presence, when I seek distraction, you still manage to insert yourself, blustering your way into my life."

"This bargain was *your* idea! I'm not inserting myself anywhere."

"Yes, the bargain was my idea, but falling in love with you was not!" he roared. "You latched your claws onto me and pulled me to you, and I was powerless to resist. And now, when I try to escape, you *will not let me go*."

I stared at him, chest heaving with my breaths, the fury spreading through me, making me see nothing but red. How dare he fling these accusations at me? As if I had a choice in the matter. As if I intentionally seduced him and took away his free will.

He was abhorrent. And I was ready to be done with him at last.

"Fine," I hissed through clenched teeth. "You want to be rid of me? I'll leave now. Just give me my stardust. I'll send for Mal, and we'll fly away within minutes, leaving you to as many waiting women as your heart desires."

"Aurelia—"

I jerked my arm free from his grasp and stepped away from him. "Just give me the stardust, Fenn."

A muscle worked in his jaw. "I can't. I need to ensure the fire burns all night. We may have to add more stardust before the fete is over."

I wanted to scream. I wanted to slap his smug face, to ram my dagger in his heart, to—

I turned from him and let out a frustrated cry that echoed in the forest. "Now it's *you* who won't let me go, Fenn!" I faced him once more, wild with anger. "I didn't ask for any of this. I thought I would have to pretend with you, wear a mask, and then it would be over. But you worked your way into my heart and you teased me, taunted me, made a game of it. I was nothing more than your conquest."

"What the hell are you talking about?" He stomped toward me, his eyes blazing. "I *love* you, Aurelia. This isn't some sick game to me. My feelings are real. I don't want them, but they are real. I'm not pretending anymore."

"Well, neither am I!" I shouted.

He blinked at me, his head rearing back. "What?"

"I love you, Fenn!" I cried, tears filling my eyes. "And to see you like that with *her*, when all I want to do is—"

I didn't get to finish. In a swift movement, he raised his hands, cupped my face, and brought his mouth to mine.

The Midnight Prince

I couldn't stop myself. The moment she said she loved me, I had to taste her, to breathe in her words and her confession.

She loved me.

She *loved* me.

When I kissed her, Aurelia uttered a startled sound that I inhaled, my mouth covering hers. My tongue slid between her lips, prying them apart, and she sighed, opening for me completely. My tongue swept in her mouth, twining with hers, tasting her thoroughly. Gods, she tasted like perfection. Like the heady air just before a rainstorm.

I guided her backward until her back pressed into a tree trunk, pinning her there with my chest, my mouth still on hers. She caught my lower lip between her teeth and pulled, eliciting a feral growl from me. My mouth moved to her neck, where I swept my tongue in a circle at the base of her throat. She moaned and writhed against me, hips bucking in silent demand. I bit down on the exposed part of her shoulder, my teeth holding her in place, and she cried out.

Her hands fumbled with my waistcoat before discarding it on the forest floor. Then she worked at the buttons of my vest.

"Aurelia," I gasped. "Aurelia, we don't—"

She looked up at me, her eyes wild and her mouth swollen from our desperate kisses. "I want you, Fenn. Will you give yourself to me?"

I groaned in part need, part agony. "Of course I will."

"Then make love to me. Right here. Right now."

Gods, I would do anything this woman said. With one hand on her waist and the other along her back, I eased her backward until she lay her on the grass, careful to avoid any roots. With my arms braced on either side of her, I hovered just above her, gazing at her breathless form. I kissed her throat again, moving my lips lower until I reached the fabric of her dress. Sliding the strap aside, I bared her breast before capturing it with my mouth.

"Oh. *Oh.*" Her voice was ragged as she thrust her hips. My teeth clamped down on her nipple, and she uttered a strangled gasp.

Her hands were tugging on my trousers now. She pulled my shirt-sleeves free, then plunged her hand underneath, grasping my length firmly.

I jerked, my body spasming from the feel of her. Stars above, I needed to be inside her. I needed her *now.*

I ripped my vest off, popping several buttons in the process. Aurelia rolled up my shirt, and I lifted it over my head, tossing it to the ground. Her hands worked at my belt. I tugged it free before sliding the trousers off, leaving me naked before her. Her eyes roved over me with a hungry look that made my hardened length twitch in anticipation.

I hiked up her skirts, thanking all the gods I could name that she wasn't wearing undergarments. She spread her legs for me, and I marveled at her slick center, so moist and ready for me.

"Gods, you look divine," I groaned.

"Please, Fenn," she begged, and damn it all if that didn't undo me right there.

But instead of thrusting inside her like I yearned to do, I hoisted her up, settling her on my lap. "Not yet," I murmured, pressing another kiss to her mouth. "I want to look at you when you come. I want to claim you with my mouth when I claim you with my cock."

Her eyes closed as her legs clenched around me, pressing directly into my arousal. I angled myself, then slid into her.

She cried out, throwing her head back in rapture. I thrust again, deeper this time.

"Oh, *gods.*" Aurelia's thighs clenched around me, burrowing me further inside her. She rocked against me, guiding me deeper until I had filled her completely. And for a moment, we held there, suspended, with me wholly inside her, our bodies twined. Her mouth was open in part shock, part pleasure, her wide eyes fixed on me.

"Aurelia," I moaned, my legs quivering with need. But I held still, focusing on the pulsing and throbbing of my length inside her, the way it felt as it trembled with her body, the way she tightened around me.

I would never forget this moment, when our bodies fit together perfectly, her legs wrapped around me as I quivered inside her.

When the ache between my legs was almost unbearable, I lifted my hips, pushing with more force. She whimpered, then dug her heels into my back, urging me onward. She continued pushing with her legs, making a rocking motion.

I followed her lead, thrusting, driving deeper. When I withdrew, she hissed, making a frustrated noise in her throat. I only grinned, panting, as I slammed into her with violent fervor.

A ragged sound burst from her lips, her eyes closing as her mouth fell open. Her throat worked as she unleashed another rough cry when I plunged in a third time.

With each movement, our rhythm became more brutal, more uncontrollable. I gripped her ass, my fingernails digging into her flesh. She raked her nails along my shoulder blade and back, then bit down on my neck. Her moans turned into shouts and screams and I pounded into her, my grunts feral and unhinged. The sound of our skin slapping together mingled with our animalistic noises. I tangled my fingers in her hair, jerking her head back so I could drag my tongue up her throat.

Pressure built within me, an unbearable heat burning between my legs, my length pulsing inside her. Stars, it felt so good, to feel her stretch to fit me inside her, to taste the sweat on her neck, to smell her musky scent. The sounds of her as she came undone. Her limbs around me, bringing me even closer.

I dragged my thumb along her bottom lip and demanded, "Look at me."

She lowered her head, her eyes dark and manic, practically unrecognizable as she met my gaze. My hands pressed into her back, and she cried out again. My mouth crashed into hers, swallowing her outburst, my tongue ravaging her. I was so close, so close to that edge. But I wanted her to tumble over it with me.

I thrust again, and she moaned in my mouth. I shoved my tongue deeper, and she met it with her own, pushing against me with savage delight. As I drove between her legs, my tongue plunged into her mouth, the movements synchronizing. In, out, in, out. Faster and faster.

Harder and harder. I stroked my tongue within her just as I jerked my hips, driving myself into her body in every way I could.

She bit my tongue, but the flash of pain only stoked the flames inside me until I nearly exploded.

Oh gods, I would topple over that edge at any moment...

She withdrew to stare at me, pupils dilated and face covered in sweat. A clump of her hair stuck to her forehead, and gods above, she was the most beautiful thing I'd ever seen, all wild fury and untamed power.

As we stared at each other, still moving against one another, still keeping up that rhythm, I pressed my hand to her cheek, then slid down to her throat, dragging a finger down, down, down, until I reached her breast. I cupped one, then brought my mouth to the other, biting down hard. With my hand, I rolled her nipple between my thumb and forefinger, then pinched it.

That was all it took.

Her head rolled back as a guttural scream burst from her. With one final thrust, I spilled into her, my body seizing and quivering, my moans strangled as I came. Stars burst in my vision, and all I knew was sweet release, the chaos of pleasure and passion driving me over that edge with her.

She continued her movements, writhing against me even long after I'd finished. Her voice was hoarse and strained when we slowed and stopped, our bodies still joined together.

Burning stars, there was nothing else like it. Never before had I experienced such intense lovemaking before. Such a brutally addicting and all-consuming collision. I wanted nothing more than to stay inside her, to let myself get hard so we could start all over again.

I wanted more of her. And I would never get enough.

"Gods, Aurelia." My voice was merely a rasp as I buried my face in her neck, breathing hard. "Gods..."

She stroked my hair, pushing the sweaty strands out of my face. "I know. Me too." She rested her head on my shoulder. "You still infuriate me to no end."

I huffed a weak laugh. "I seem to remember you saying you loathed me more intensely than a thousand burning suns."

She chuckled hoarsely. "That is still true."

"But... you love me." I said the words tentatively, as if unsure if she truly meant it. Perhaps she was confused. Or mistaken. If she was drunk on fire wine, she could have said *anything* without meaning it.

She lifted her head to look me in the eye. Her expression was worn from exertion, but the light in her gaze was brighter than ever. Clarity burned in those magnificent blue irises. "I love you, Fenn."

I shook my head, a slow smile spreading across my face. I still could hardly believe it. "So, were you merely toying with me before?"

She snorted. "You would deserve nothing less."

"True."

"No, Fenn. I… I did not know. I knew I felt *something* for you. But I didn't realize how strong my feelings were until I saw you dancing with another woman. Until I saw what it would look like if I walked away from you. Until… I imagined you spending your life with someone else. Someone who wasn't me."

I cocked my head at her, grinning wolfishly. "You were jealous?"

She whacked my arm. "You are *such* an ass! Did you dance with someone else on purpose, to make me jealous?"

With a laugh, I said, "No, not at all. I was truly just looking for a distraction. But no one comes close to you, Aurelia. I knew no one ever would. Everything I tried to drown myself in to forget about you only paled in comparison." I ran my knuckles down her cheek, and she leaned into my touch.

"I still must leave in a few hours," she whispered, her voice almost inaudible, as if she thought if the words were soft enough, they wouldn't be true.

An ache filled my chest at the thought. I wanted to go with her. Desperately. But if we both vanished like thieves in the night, Mother would riot. She would likely invade the Summer Court. I needed to stay and smooth things over with her.

With a sigh, I said, "I know."

"You have ruined me, Fennick Mardion. Ruined me completely."

I nuzzled her neck. "Good."

"How can I leave, when you make me feel this way?" She tilted her head back, letting me roam my lips up and down her throat. "Why do you do this to me? You worked your way into my heart, and now, I cannot exist without you haunting me. My love for you burns hotter than my hatred ever did. It burns *brighter* than a thousand suns. Forever drawing me into its orbit."

I exhaled against her neck, my chest quivering from the way her words struck me to the core. When I withdrew, I brought her mouth to mine in a slow, sensual kiss. I ran my tongue along the seam of her mouth before pulling away a few inches, our noses still touching.

My voice was thick with emotion as I said, "Aurelia Perdis, my love for you shines brighter than the stars in the heavens. Even when the stars go dark, still I will burn for you, filling the night sky to guide you back home to me."

Tears sparkled in her eyes, and she swallowed hard, nodding slowly. "I will come home to you, Fenn. When I free my family and my people, when my kingdom is safe, I *will* come back for you."

Her mouth collided with mine, her tongue filling me, stroking and tasting. She angled her head, and my fingers wound in her hair, pulling her ever closer. I felt myself grow hard once more, and I almost thrust again, prepared to take her a second time.

"I will have you again," I growled against her lips. "We are not finished here."

"Oh, I hope not. You promised to unravel me repeatedly, remember? I intend to hold you to that." A coy smile lit her features, and I laughed in surprise.

"My beautiful firebird." I leaned her backward until she was reclined on the grass, then kissed her thoroughly, my lips memorizing her, capturing her fully.

Soon, I would let her go. Soon, we would part ways with the promise of reuniting later.

But not yet.

THE SUMMER PRINCESS

My legs ached, the tender space between my thighs sore and throbbing from Fenn's thorough claiming of my body in the forest. But the lightness in my head from the fire wine and the pure, unfettered delight of being in love made me oblivious to the pain.

It softened the blow of my departure, knowing I would return. I wasn't sure if we would reside in his court or mine, but I knew we would be together. That was all that mattered.

I found myself drifting to sleep against his chest, our legs still tangled together, my mind sleepy and content.

A flash of distorted images seared through my mind. Blurry faerie lights. Dancers with butterfly wings. Green-faced ogres leering at me.

Then, one scene came into focus with stark clarity: a circle of red-cloaked witches, hands clasped as they chanted in an ancient tongue.

The witch in the center stepped forward, lowering her hood. She dragged a blade down the center of her own palm. Blood dripped to the ground. In a powerful, echoing tone, she said, "I give my blood to the earth and stars. Let it seal this spell forevermore."

Her face was mine. Her *voice* was mine.

The witch was me.

I jerked awake, my eyes flying open. My heart pounded painfully in my chest as I glanced around the darkened forest, searching for that circle of witches.

But Fenn and I were alone. His slow breaths filled my ears as he continued to sleep, blissfully unaware of my vivid nightmare.

How long had we been asleep? Was the fete over? I couldn't hear the music anymore, but we were deep enough into the forest where the sounds of the river could be drowning out the echoing strains of music.

Slowly, I extracted myself from Fenn's embrace, despite how I yearned to curl into him, to burrow my face into his bare chest and chase away my fears and worries.

As I eased away from him, I hastily adjusted my bodice and skirt. It was rumpled and damp in a few places, but there was nothing to be done about it. I found the lavender glass vial from the three witches resting in the grass nearby, and I quickly slid it back into my bodice.

After patting down my hair and tucking the wild strands behind my ears, I looked at Fenn one last time. I knew I should wake him. I still needed stardust from him. And if he found I had slipped away without saying goodbye, he would be livid.

But if he looked at me with that dark, sensuous expression again, if he kissed me once more, if he gathered me into his arms, I knew for certain I would be unable to leave.

Besides, I could scoop up a handful of stardust from the Celestial River. Surely, I wouldn't need more than that.

I blew Fenn a kiss and murmured, "You have my heart, Fenn. Guard it well."

Then I turned and walked away before the sight of him pulled me back. Tears streaked down my face, and I impatiently wiped them away. This was silly. We *would* be together. This parting was only temporary.

Then why did my chest constrict so tightly that I couldn't breathe? Why did a chill of foreboding ripple along my spine, warning me this would be the last time we ever saw each other?

Shaking these irrational thoughts from my mind, I made my way through the forest, emerging to find the bridge empty. I frowned. Perhaps the fete *had* ended. I wasn't sure how long I had slept.

The air was eerily silent as I crossed the bridge. Even the river seemed quieter than usual, the babble soft and ominous.

When I reached the other side of the river, I scanned the empty field and courtyard. No music. No dancers. The faerie lights had dimmed.

Something was wrong.

My blood ran cold as I realized what it was. The braziers along the river were no longer lit. The strong Nightfire that Mal had provided must have burnt out.

Panic pulsed in my chest as I whirled toward the bridge, prepared to dash across it and rouse Fenn.

I found myself face-to-face with a huge, four-legged beast. It leered at me with a dozen milky white eyes, large fangs protruding from a wide mouth. Each leg was thin and hairy like a giant spider as it inched toward me. Foam dripped from its open maw.

I scrambled backward with a terrified yelp. The creature scuttled toward me with frightening speed, its legs completely silent on the grass. That was how I hadn't heard it approach. It didn't make a single sound as it closed the distance between us, filling my nose with the scent of cobwebs and decay.

Panic surged through my veins, spurring me into action. I spun and fled, my feet scrambling up the steps of the courtyard. Before I could make it to the castle doors, two more beasts appeared in my path, one with large pincers that snapped at me hungrily.

I felt the blood drain from my face. *Oh, gods.* I glanced behind the beasts, thinking perhaps if I screamed, someone from the castle would come to my rescue.

The doors were sealed shut.

Dread coiled in my chest. Did the staff think Fenn and I were inside? Or had these beasts devoured everyone while Fenn and I had been sleeping?

Fenn.

I inhaled a deep breath and unleashed a piercing scream that echoed in the night. The creatures shuddered, scuttling away from me. It seemed they, like the ogres, were repelled by loud sounds.

I could use that in my favor.

When my scream died, the creatures scurried closer to me. I bellowed loudly, my throat raw from the intensity of my shout.

Once more, they recoiled from the noise, giving me the opening I needed. I ran down the steps, sidestepping the approaching monsters. My bare feet burned with each stride as I sprinted for the bridge.

Get to Fenn. Get to Fenn. I repeated the words in my head as a chant.

But when I reached the bridge, I stopped short. An entire horde of the spider-like creatures waited for me.

Shit. Perhaps I shouldn't have screamed so loudly. Now every unseelie beast within a one-mile radius knew I was here.

I had no dagger. No weapon. I was alone and severely outnumbered.

Suddenly remembering, I pulled the lavender vial from my bodice and smashed it on the wooden beams of the bridge. It shattered, and an eerie violet smoke poured from it, coiling in the air.

I wasn't sure what I expected—perhaps the witches to appear instantly and rescue me?—but the unseelie beasts only continued to advance.

The witches were not coming. I was on my own.

Even so, I bared my teeth, refusing to cower in fear.

You are the most powerful fae in this kingdom, I reminded myself. *Perhaps the most powerful fae in all of Valora.*

Unbidden, Mal's voice from my dreams echoed in my mind. *You have more control than you think, Aurelia. Think of the level of control you exercise when we are flying through the sky. You put your trust in me to keep you safe, and you must do the same with your magic. Let it go. Let go of the reins, Aurelia.*

Had that conversation been real, or merely a nonsensical scenario conjured by my subconscious?

In this moment, it didn't matter. Though my arms trembled with terror, my heart seizing in my chest, I held myself still and forced a steady breath. The creatures drew nearer, closing in around me, cutting off any hope of escape.

Still, I focused on my deep breaths. My eyes closed, and I thought of riding atop Mal, soaring through the sky. I thought of the one night we had sailed across the stars, gliding among the heavens. The stars shone just like tonight, guiding us along.

I thought of the way my arms had stretched wide as if I, too, had wings. I had leaned back, hands spread, the cool night air whipping at me. The freedom. The release. The sensation of all my restraints snapping, my cage shattering, my wings carrying me away…

A burst of energy flowed from my chest, igniting something powerful within me. I threw my head back and roared into the night, but the sound wasn't my voice; it was the voice of a deadly beast within me.

Two of the unseelie creatures scuttled away, their quivering forms vanishing into the forest. But the rest approached with wary interest, their legs twitching.

I roared again, and smoke poured from my mouth. My teeth elongated into fangs, and my forked tongue darted out, tasted the air, tasting their *fear.*

I would devour these vermin. I would crush their bodies, feasting on them as if they were nothing. I inched closer to them, my back arching. Somehow, my body felt longer. Larger. Something slithered behind me, and I glanced over my shoulder, alarmed to find a scaly black tail extending from my rear, swishing along the grass.

But I was too enraged to register my shock. Nothing had felt so right in my entire life. This was me. This was the power locked inside me.

I threw my head back and screamed, a feral and monstrous sound. Blue flames poured from my mouth, igniting the air.

A creature lunged for me, barbed mouth open wide. I swiped a clawed hand, my arms now black and scaled. My talons tore into the beast's flesh, and hot green pus poured from within, forming a steaming heap on the ground. I whirled, gutting another creature. Then another. Two more rushed me, but the rest had fled, wisely taking cover in the forest, knowing they would not defeat me.

I inhaled deeply, then breathed more flames that engulfed the creatures. Their piercing shrieks filled the air as my fire consumed them, burning their flesh. The rotting stench stung my nostrils, but I poured more fire, burning and burning until they were nothing more than ash. My vision was tinged green, but I could see more acutely than ever, the broken bodies of the creatures crisp and clear, even in the darkness.

When the last of the beasts dissolved into a pile of ash, I spread my wings wide, unleashing an almighty roar of triumph. I was unstoppable. Powerful. Lethal.

Nothing could stop me.

"Aurelia?" cried a familiar voice.

I turned, my large dragon's body lumbering awkwardly, my long neck craning to see who approached. Across the bridge, I made out a figure, dressed in only his trousers, his bare chest gleaming in the moonlight.

It was Fenn, his face pale and his mouth open in horror.

THE SUMMER PRINCESS

Awareness rushed over me like a bucket of ice water had been dumped over my head. I shuddered, my body quivering as I shifted. My limbs shrunk, my tail vanished, and my fangs receded. My tongue returned to its normal size, and my vision darkened once more. Instead of black scales, my pale skin returned, covered by the rose gold dress I'd worn before.

My tender flesh felt cold and clammy, and I shivered, collapsing to the ground as violent tremors wracked my body.

"Aurelia!" Fenn shouted again. His footsteps pounded as he sprinted across the bridge. When he reached me, he knelt to my side, peeling sweaty hair off my forehead.

"W-What's wrong with m-me?" I whispered, my teeth chattering.

"You—You were a dragon," Fenn said weakly. "Aurelia, how is that possible? How were you a *dragon*?"

"At last, you remember," said a cool voice nearby.

I slowly turned my head, my body still jerking uncontrollably. Three figures materialized from nowhere, and I knew immediately who they were.

Ruby, Jade, and Sapphire. The three witches who held the key to my identity.

They had come after all.

A surge of hot fury swept through me, momentarily blotting out the cold nausea roiling within me. I pushed myself up on my arms and bared my teeth at them. "Explain," I demanded, my arms trembling.

Sapphire, the witch with white hair, cocked her head at me in calm indifference. "You have the answers within you. All you must do is unlock them."

I was so damn tired of people telling me that. "I can't unlock anything! I have no control over this!"

"You do," said Ruby, her black hair billowing as a breeze swept over us. "Look deeper, Dragon Queen. The truth is there."

"I don't—I don't—" I faltered as I remembered the scene of the red-robed witches, the dark ritual coming to life in my mind.

And me, stepping forward to seal the power of our spell.

Horror churned in my gut. *Oh gods, no.*

"I—I did this," I whispered. "Didn't I?"

The witches looked at me with a solemnness that only confirmed my suspicions.

"What are you talking about?" Fenn snapped. "You didn't do this, Aurelia. *They* did." He gestured angrily at the three witches.

"Bite your tongue, foolish boy," Sapphire snapped.

"No, you bite *your* tongue before I bite your head off," I growled. "You will not speak to him in that way."

Sapphire smiled, as if my violent response only pleased her.

"Explain," I said again, my voice raspy. The short burst of strength was fading fast, and I slumped to the ground, unable to hold myself up anymore. Fenn was at my side in an instant, pulling me against him, tucking my back into his chest. His warm and solid presence filled me with confidence as I said, "I only recall bits and pieces. Fill in the gaps, please. I beg of you. You said when I was ready, you would answer my call. I am asking now."

The three witches exchanged grim looks, their eyes flashing as they wordlessly communicated with one another. Then, as one, they nodded and stepped closer to me, their lavender eyes glowing like orbs.

"Your given name was Aurora Briarcliffe Gaelania," Sapphire said. "And you were the most powerful witch of us all."

My mouth fell open, but I didn't interrupt. Even though I had suspected I possessed witch blood, it still came as a shock. Within me, recognition and confusion warred against each other, struggling for dominance. The resulting chaos was making my stomach roil, and I was sure I would be ill.

"You ruled the witches of the Star Court many generations ago," Ruby said, "until a prophecy emerged, stating that your power would become so great that you would either destroy or unite the Realm of Valora."

A chill skittered over my flesh from the resonance of her words. I closed my eyes, and in my mind, I saw that towering, powerful figure. *Me.* With a red cloak surrounding me, a blade poised in my hand.

"At first, we all believed you would be the savior of Valora," said Jade in her low, steady voice. "How could you not? Your power had protected us for so long."

"But then, your inner beast emerged," Ruby said. "And we feared the worst."

I shook my head. "I don't understand. Witches—Witches are not unseelie. They cannot shift. This is impossible."

"We all possess a modicum of unseelie blood," said Sapphire. "Yours must have come from the shifter line. Occasionally, it is possible. Rare, but possible."

Oh gods, I was truly going to be sick. This couldn't be happening.

"It was your idea to cast the spell," Ruby continued. "You were our leader. We could not refuse."

"Each of us contributed a gift to make the spell come to life," said Sapphire. "Mine was the gift of forgetting. I knew it would destroy you, to knowingly give up your powers, and it would be better if you did not know the truth. So I blessed you with blissful ignorance."

"My gift was the suppression of your powers," said Ruby. "To protect the realm from your wrath."

"And my gift was the blood of the Summer fae," said Jade, "where the sun would help mask your Night Fae blood."

Night Fae blood. I belonged to the Night Fae.

No. *No.* This could not be true.

"We did not fully understand the consequences of such gifts," Ruby went on, her voice full of sorrow. "When you departed for the Summer Court, the dragons went with you. The Midnight Court accused Summer of thievery, claiming they stole the dragons. This ignited the war between the two kingdoms."

I shook my head, tasting bile in my throat. No. This was a lie. A vicious lie. These insane witches thought *I* was the cause of the feud with the Midnight Court? No. It was ludicrous.

"You were smuggled into the Summer Court, disguised as a royal and entrusted to the king and queen for safekeeping," said Sapphire. "We wanted to provide you with as comfortable a life as we could. A life away from magic, so your powers would not be awakened. When the king and queen realized they had access to powerful dragons, they were more than willing to protect you and conceal your identity in exchange."

I closed my eyes. Suddenly, I didn't want to hear anymore. This was a cruel joke. I couldn't bear it...

"Despite the power of the spell, your memories kept returning," Jade continued, oblivious to my turmoil. "One generation after the next, the royal family contacted us, begging us to suppress your powers again. We would cast the spell, wipe your memories once more, and you would begin your life anew, oblivious to your past. To avoid suspicion, the king and queen kept you confined to the Summer Court, claiming you were a distant cousin of the royal family, so none of the other kingdoms would see your face."

"But after many years, we knew this could not go on," said Ruby. "We pleaded with the Summer witches for help. They had just discovered a powerful runic magic that could help. With a binding rune, they were able to permanently entrap your magic, only to be unlocked by the magic of your ancestral home. The Star Court."

I thought of how Fenn and I passed through the mist protecting the Star Court. Not because I was traveling with Fenn, but because I possessed Night Fae blood.

The visions of my past life hadn't begun until I'd entered the Star Court.

And my inner dragon—she could only come to life here.

"We swore the Summer witches to secrecy," Ruby said. "And we left you to live out your life, confident this time the magic would hold you. And from the rumors we've heard, it seems the king and queen became more lax, claiming you as their daughter, allowing you to travel to other courts, and even making plans to abdicate the throne to you. It seemed our plan was working, and you had truly become a daughter of the Summer Court."

"Why?" I bit out, unable to contain my rage. "Why did you want me to come back here? Why unlock my powers at all?"

"Because of the Dream Mage." Sapphire's voice was low and solemn, and the air seemed to ripple around her. "She is gaining power. She has overcome our clan. We need you to return, to save this realm as you were born to do."

I barked out a harsh laugh, surprising even myself. Laughing was the last thing I should be doing right now. Even so, it was so ridiculous, so *foolish*, that I couldn't help myself. "So you cage me for hundreds of years, wiping my memories again and again, forcing me to live a new life every time, clueless about what's happening to me… only to beg me to return and save your sorry asses from this stupid Dream Mage? I don't believe it."

"Aurelia," Fenn murmured. Only then did I realize he was trembling, his arms still wrapped around me. But the fear in his voice was stark.

He believed them.

I whirled to face him with a look of incredulity. "Don't tell me you're swallowing this delirious tale. It cannot be true!"

"What's your explanation?" he challenged. "Your magic is volatile and unexplainable. You have a connection with the dragons. Your dragon form looks *just like Mal*. You share a kinship with him. It explains this terrible feud between our kingdoms, why the Dream Mage would go after your kingdom, go after *you* specifically—"

"No!" I roared, jumping to my feet, ignoring the dizziness that swelled, making me teeter. Fenn rose, reaching to steady me, but I pushed him away. "If this is true, then I—I—" My voice broke as the realization crashed into me.

I was not my parents' daughter.

I was not Gigi's sister.

I did not truly belong in the Summer Court.

Tears stung my eyes, and I shook my head in denial. "No," I said again, my voice thick with emotion.

"We will leave you to process this," Sapphire said slowly, backing away from me. "When you are ready, call upon us, and we will march into battle for you. Together, we will defeat the Dream Mage."

"*No!*" I screamed, balling my hands into fists. "*You* did this to me. You broke me! You think I want you by my side? Leave this place, and never return! I never want to see you again."

They continued to retreat toward the woods, their expressions full of pity. It only made me want to scream louder. Gradually, they faded into the forest until they finally disappeared from view.

I crumpled, anguished sobs ripping through me. Fenn wrapped his arms around me, stroking my back. He said nothing as he held me. What was there to say?

If this was true, it changed everything. I was dangerous. Deadly. The only reason I was here was because there was a threat I needed to eliminate.

And after this, those wretched witches would bind me once more, erasing me from existence. I would be nothing but a helpless shell of who I once was.

I clung to Fenn's tunic, weeping openly, unable to comprehend the horrors of this convoluted tale.

Please, I begged the gods. *Please don't let it be true.*

From behind me, a cold voice shouted, "Guards! Seize her."

I whirled, panic rising in my chest. The castle doors were wide open, and Queen Sonara stood on the steps of the courtyard, a cruel, triumphant smile on her face. Behind her stood a squadron of soldiers. At her command, they rushed toward me, swords drawn.

THE MIDNIGHT PRINCE

My head still reeling from the witches' tale, it took all my remaining strength to keep my hold on Aurelia's arms as the soldiers surged toward us.

"Mother, *no*!" I bellowed, stepping in front of Aurelia. "You cannot do this. She is—"

"She is a monster!" Mother cried, waving her hand toward Aurelia. "You saw the creature she changed into. You heard what the witches said!"

My blood ran cold, and I gaped at her in horror. "How long were you watching?"

Her eyes glinted with triumph, and that was all the confirmation I needed. She had been watching the entire time. Waiting for this particular moment.

How much had she known? Had she figured out who Aurelia really was, even before the fete? I pictured her peering out the window, waiting for Aurelia's true form to be revealed.

Rage burned within me. "Mother, what the hell did you do?"

"I did what I had to to save my court," she said. "To save my *son*. And not a moment too soon, it seems. Imagine if you had married that creature." Her face twisted with disgust.

A roar of fury burst from my lips, and I reached for my sword, only to remember my belt and weapon had been abandoned in the forest when I'd come chasing after Aurelia. I wasn't even wearing a shirt.

Mother's soldiers would cut right through me.

"Gorrick, please," I said, my eyes landing on my captain.

Gorrick's face sagged with regret from behind his helmet. "I'm sorry, Your Highness. The queen outranks you."

"Fenn," Aurelia murmured, her voice eerily calm. "Step away from me."

I glanced at her. She gazed at my mother with lethal intensity. For a moment, her eyes flashed green, her pupils turning into narrow slits.

I released my hold on her arms as Aurelia's body began to shift. She hunched over on all fours, her body elongating and sprouting scales and claws. A black tail formed, and she rose in height until she towered over the approaching soldiers.

Gods! She was going to kill them all.

My men. My people.

I sprinted forward, raising my hands to stop her. But the dragon looked down on me without recognition or warmth, its animal eyes surveying me as its prey.

"Aurelia!" I cried out, trying to reach the woman who knew me, the one who knew compassion and sympathy. That woman wouldn't do this. "Aurelia, please! I will stop this, I swear it."

"No," Mother said loudly. "I will." She nodded to someone in the distance, and a faint shriek filled the air.

I stilled, my heart sinking with dread as a pair of soldiers brought out a familiar black creature. Mal. A muzzle was clamped tightly over his snout, and his limbs were bound. A thick net was draped over him, trapping his wings.

Aurelia's dragon froze, and a guttural moan burst from her.

"Come quietly," Mother said, her voice ringing with authority, "and we will not harm the beast."

My eyes grew wide. No. She couldn't do this. She *couldn't*—

Aurelia held perfectly still for a long, tense moment. My heart thundered madly against my ribcage. I wanted to sprint forward, to tear at Mal's restraints and set him free.

But the line of soldiers standing in my way would cut me down. Mother would order my execution without another thought. I stared at the woman who had raised me. She was unrecognizable now. How much had she plotted without me realizing it? How much of this had she orchestrated behind my back, even as I was enraptured with the idea of marrying the woman I loved?

Energy filled the air, and in a flash, Aurelia had shifted to her fae form once more, trembling in her wrinkled pink dress. I raced to her side, but Mother snapped, "Restrain him."

Two soldiers gripped me under the arms and hauled me backward, away from Aurelia. "No!" I bellowed. "No, don't! *Aurelia!*"

Aurelia's shoulders shook with sobs, her voice breaking as she cried, "Release him! Release my dragon. Please, I beg you."

"Not yet," Mother said, her mouth curling with satisfaction. "I think you'll find he'll remain right here with you. You two are bound, are you not?"

Aurelia's face twisted with rage, even as more tears poured down her face. "I will tear you apart. You think your soldiers can hold me?"

But Mother's smile only grew, and my chest hollowed with dread. I knew that look. Mother had won. She had one last trick to reveal... I braced myself for the blow.

She withdrew a small pouch from inside her cloak and tossed it. It landed at Aurelia's feet, spilling open to reveal a smattering of stardust.

My stomach dropped with realization.

"The bargain is now complete," Mother said, gliding down the courtyard steps, her black gown swishing with her confident strides. "You belong to me now, princess. The bargain you struck with my son demands it."

I shook my head. "No. You're wrong."

"Oh, am I?" Mother's head whipped toward me. "Tell me again the terms of your bargain. We owed her stardust. She now owes us a dragon, does she not? A dragon with—"

"The strongest fire," I finished in a horrified whisper, turning my stunned gaze to Aurelia. Her eyes locked onto mine, wide with confusion, terror, and... betrayal.

"You told her?" she whispered. "You told her the terms of our bargain."

"Aurelia—"

"Of course he did," Mother said. "I'm his mother. And you are nothing more than a beautiful woman he thought he was in love with. His ties to me are far stronger than his ties to you, dragon wench."

The light in Aurelia's eyes shuddered and died, replaced by something dark and full of despair. When her eyes closed, more tears poured from her eyes.

"Aurelia, it's not true!" I shouted, but she didn't seem to hear me.

"I suppose I should be grateful," Mother went on, grinning widely. "Without this bargain, we never would have acquired a dragon as powerful as you. Because *you* possess the strongest fire." She pointed a long finger at Aurelia, then turned to smirk at me. "Very clever of you to word the bargain like that, my darling."

"No!" I shouted. "No, I release you from our bargain. Aurelia, I *release you!*"

Mother laughed. "It's too late for that, Fennick. The terms of the bargain have been met. She has her stardust. And we have our dragon."

Aurelia unleashed an almighty scream that rang through the forest, echoing in the vast space. A trio of soldiers surrounded her, gripping her arms tightly to keep her in place.

I struggled against the men holding me, desperation flooding my veins. I had to do something. I couldn't let them take her.

Digging deep within myself, I summoned my power, drawing up every last drop of strength within me. I held nothing back as I bellowed, *"You will release her!"* The words sounded deep and animalistic and not at all like my own voice. The sound of my shout echoed around us, piercing the air. *"Step away from Aurelia and the dragon."*

The soldiers went completely still. Even Mother froze, staring at me.

Then, slowly, the guards lowered their arms, releasing Aurelia and Mal. They took several steps away from them. Mal was still tied up and muzzled. Aurelia was gaping for breath, her eyes rimmed in red and tears staining her cheeks. She stared at me with disbelief.

"Aurelia, run!" I urged. "Get Mal out of here!"

"No!" Mother roared. "Guards, stop them!"

"Do nothing!" I bellowed, infusing more power into my words. My vision swam, and my head swayed as fatigue overtook me, but I would not let her win. I refused. "Let her go!"

"Gag my son, *now,*" Mother ordered, her face twisted with rage as she stormed toward me.

"Do not—" Before I could finish speaking, a filthy piece of cloth was shoved into my mouth. I choked, trying to spit it out, but the guard shoved it hard, blocking my voice completely. I wriggled against his grip, but my limbs were weak. I had overexerted myself.

I looked at Aurelia, who had hurried to Mal's side, fumbling with his restraints. My eyes burned as I mentally pleaded with her to go, to *run.*

"Seize her," Mother said, pointing to Aurelia.

I screamed against the gag in my mouth, thrashing and fighting, but the soldiers held me back, keeping me from running to Aurelia's side.

Aurelia had managed to untie Mal's legs when two soldiers approached. I was powerful, but my command couldn't span the entire squadron of soldiers, especially if none of them were inclined to obey. Judging by the sour looks of these two soldiers, they were on my mother's side. I would never have been able to persuade them anyway.

"Mal, get out of here!" Aurelia sobbed as the soldiers pinned her arms in place. "Please! You have to leave."

Mal's legs were free. He could take off into the forest. He could be free. But the dragon let out a muffled whimper, shaking his head slowly.

He would not leave Aurelia. Even I knew that much.

Aurelia sobbed harder, her legs giving out. Were it not for the soldiers' hold on her, she would have collapsed to the ground.

"Don't worry, my dear," Mother said with a savage smile. "He won't be alone. He can keep the blue one company."

Aurelia sucked in a sharp gasp, her gaze sliding to the queen. "What are you talking about?"

"We have one of your dragons already. Or didn't you know?" Mother's catlike smile widened. "She was weak after giving birth. Snatching her was so easy... No one even noticed. Not even her little hatchling."

Oh gods, no. My chest seized, tightening until I couldn't breathe.

"A shame, really," Mother said. "The beast was too injured when we captured her. She doesn't produce any fire at all. So it's a good thing you struck this bargain, Fennick, otherwise we would have still had no Dragonfire."

My eyes closed. I was going to be sick.

"I'm surprised you didn't tell her, darling," she went on. "You seemed so taken with her, I thought for certain the first thing you would do was free that dragon."

No. *No!* Aurelia looked at me, her eyes full of that darkness, that wretched, haunting agony. "Fenn," she said slowly. "Tell me it isn't true. Tell me you didn't know about this."

I shouted against the gag, but I couldn't form any words. And even if I could, what would I say? I couldn't lie to her. I *had* known about it. And I hadn't told her.

But now I knew for certain that it was the Blue Amethyst. The mother of the dying dragon that could save Aurelia's people.

"You bastard." Aurelia shook her head, her eyes full of rage. "You— You—" She broke off with another cry of anguish as she wept.

I moaned, trying to speak her name, but the gag stifled my words.

"Lock her up," Mother ordered. "And if my son resists, tie him up in his rooms." Her eyes were cold as she surveyed me. "You could not do what was necessary to protect our people, so I will. Do not stand in my way. I will not hesitate to cut you down."

With that, she turned on her heel and strode into the castle. Aurelia screamed as the soldiers dragged her away. I struggled against the men holding me, desperate to get to her, to free her, but there were too many guardsmen. It was useless.

I cried out for her once more, my throat burning, but her screams drowned me out. They echoed around me, even long after she disappeared from view.

THE MIDNIGHT PRINCE

My mind was numb and unfeeling. Cold and empty. I knew nothing but darkness. My insides were hollow as I allowed the soldiers to escort me to my rooms. They would stand guard outside my door, no doubt, ensuring I wouldn't sneak off to the dungeons to free Aurelia.

What was the point? The moment she was free, she would burn me to a crisp. And it would mean nothing, because our bargain was fulfilled. She had to remain here. Once a bargain's terms were met, it could not be undone.

She was trapped here. The dragon within her now belonged to the Midnight Court.

As long as my mother still lived, it would remain that way. Aurelia was bound to serve the sovereign of the Midnight Court. And Mother would never let her go.

A sickening dread filled my chest. How had I not seen this coming? How had I not realized how cruel and vicious Mother could be? I had known her to be brutal, yes, but she was my *mother*. I believed her love for me to be stronger than all else.

I'd been wrong. She didn't give a damn about me or my happiness. She had just chained up the woman I loved with a gleeful look on her face.

I sat on the edge of my bed, staring into nothingness, my gaze fixed on the stone wall in front of me. On the outside, I felt nothing. My expression was blank, my eyes open but unseeing. Inside me, a riot of

I had to do something. I couldn't just sit here and let Aurelia rot in the dungeon.

But I would need to be smart about this. Fighting Mother would do no good. I had to make her believe I was on her side, that I could be trusted.

After thinking over the words I would say, I rose from my bed and strode to my door. When I threw it open, sure enough, a pair of guards turned to face me.

"I wish to see my mother," I said, my voice cold and detached.

"Your Highness, we've been instructed to keep you to your rooms."

"Am I to be a prisoner in my own home?" I demanded. "Take me to see her. She can tell me to my face that I'm confined to my quarters." I pushed as much authority as I could muster in my tone.

When they continued to stare at me, unmoved, I layered my magic into my voice and said, *"Take me to the queen."*

The guards stiffened, then nodded and said in unison, "Yes, Your Highness."

They led me down the hall, and we descended the winding staircase until we reached the second floor. I trailed after the guards, my mind elsewhere as they led me to the throne room.

When the doors opened, I found Mother poring over a stack of scrolls on a long, narrow table in front of the dais. She glanced up at me, her eyes narrowing into slits as she appraised me.

"What is this?" she demanded. "Your orders were clear. I'll have your heads."

"Don't blame them, Mother," I said, my voice barbed. "I coerced them. I need to speak with you."

Mother sighed and waved a hand at the guards, who left, shutting the doors behind them. "I'm quite busy. We have much to prepare for, if we are to utilize the Dragonfire of our two newest weapons."

I resisted the urge to flinch at her words. She eyed me, as if waiting for that exact reaction. But I kept my cool, indifferent mask in place.

"Why are you here, Fennick?" Mother asked, crossing her arms and facing me, her expression rigid and unyielding. Not a drop of affection or remorse. It was as if she had no feelings at all. No emotion.

Did she even love me?

I pushed the thought from my mind, focusing instead on my plan. But first, I had to test the strength of my magic. I poured only a few drops of power into my voice, so as not to alarm her, as I said, *"You need to stop this, Mother."* The air rippled from the energy behind my words.

Mother went completely still, her expression going slack. Then, her nostrils flared, and rage burned in her eyes. "You dare try to use your power on me, boy? That has never worked on me before, and it certainly won't work on me now. Get out."

Dammit. I stepped toward her. "We need to provide comfortable accommodations for the princess." I couldn't bring myself to say her name.

Mother huffed a laugh, turning back to her scrolls. "I don't think so."

"It was part of the bargain," I said loudly, and she faced me once more, her eyes sparking with irritation. "I vowed to give the most comfortable life our kingdom can offer. Unless you want the fae magic to claim my life, you will do this."

Mother stared at me for a long moment before sighing. "Stars above why did you offer that to her, Fenn?"

"So she would trust me. You know she cares deeply for the dragons. It was the only way."

She rubbed her temples. "You are making this impossible."

"Well, if you had told me your plan, perhaps I could have done better," I bit out.

She glanced at me, her eyes sharpening. "What are you saying, Fennick? Do you expect me to believe you would have gone along with this? You were professing your love for the girl only yesterday."

"That was before I saw her monstrous form." My face twisted with disgust. "Do you honestly think I could love someone like that?"

"You were fighting for her," Mother argued. "When I arrested her, you were fighting to free her."

"I had to. I needed her trust."

"Why?" Her voice was laced with suspicion.

"I'm the only one who can calm her. I know her better than anyone. You heard what those witches said. Aurelia can either be our savior or our doom. Which would you prefer? If you keep her locked away like this, it will only enrage her further, and I guarantee that beast of hers will tear the entire castle down, even if it kills her, too."

Mother's eyes grew distant as she considered this. After a moment, she shook her head. "No. I'm not worried about this."

I frowned. "Why not?"

"I have measures in place to protect us from that," she said vaguely, turning back to the scrolls on the table.

I groaned in frustration. "There you go keeping secrets from me again."

"What do you expect, Fennick?" she snapped. "You have never taken your duty to the crown seriously, and I honestly don't believe that's changed even now. Your feelings have clouded your judgment. If you truly want to earn my trust back, it will take time. Now, leave me while I make these preparations."

"Mother, the bargain—"

"Yes, yes, I swear I will provide better accommodations for the wretched princess." She waved me off with a lazy flick of her hand. "Leave. Now."

Biting back my frustration, I stormed from the throne room, my hands balling into fists. What was I to do now? I couldn't persuade her with my fae magic, and I couldn't convince her to trust me, either.

There could only be one thing left to do. The thought left me with a sickening sense of horror. I couldn't—No, I couldn't.

Something warm seared into my palm, and I hissed in pain, lifting my hand. A slow, black circle formed in the center of my hand, getting hotter and hotter until it took all my restraint not to cry out in pain.

I knew what this was. Runic magic.

Alarm raced through me, and I sprinted down the hall and up the stairs, gritting my teeth against the pain throbbing in my hand. It scorched my flesh, piercing through skin and bone, driving white-hot knives right through me. Gods, the pain was unbearable. I had to—I had to—

I staggered to my room, cradling my hand against my chest. My movements were clumsy as I pulled the brick free from the hearth and withdrew my chalk, drawing sloppy symbols on the stone floor.

When the circle was complete, the pain in my hand vanished, and the runes on the floor began to glow. A fog formed within the circle, and after a moment, the picture cleared to reveal a face I hadn't seen in years.

"Fenn?" said a familiar voice.

My face broke into a relieve smile. "Marek! Thank the gods."

Marek frowned, squinting at me through the haze of our portal communicator. His black hair was longer than I'd ever seen it, curling at the nape of his neck. "What kind of dangerous runes are you experimenting with? Your summons interrupted a meeting with the council. Everyone thought a clan of witches was attacking. It took us the entire day to quell the chaos."

I flinched. "Sorry. It was an act of desperation. I didn't mean to cause any harm. I have to ask you if you know where the Dream Mage is."

Marek's expression darkened. "Is this a joke? Because it isn't funny in the slightest."

My eyes grew wide. "Marek, no! I'm being earnest."

"If you are, then you're a fool. Don't you know what's been going on in your own kingdom?"

Dread twisted in my gut. "I haven't been here in weeks, Marek. Speak plainly. Please."

"The Dream Mage has allied with Queen Sonara. They have declared war on us and plan to seize the Court of Twilight by force."

THE SUMMER PRINCESS

Betrayed.

Broken.

Deceived.

I was such a fool. I deserved this, for trusting someone as deceitful as the Midnight Prince. Just like Tyrone, Fenn had used me for what he wanted. I was an object to be possessed. Nothing more.

When would I learn?

And now, my entire court would perish for it. I was the only one who could save them, and I was trapped in this godsforsaken dungeon. The air reeked of excrement, and the bench I sat on was stained with all manner of unpleasant fluids.

But I couldn't bring myself to care. It was over. All of it. Mal was captured. And so was I.

I was a slave to Fenn and his despicable mother.

Fenn. Gods, I ached for him. Not the true Fenn, but the man I'd fallen in love with. The man I thought I knew.

How much of it had been real, and how much had been a lie? Was he even a full blooded fae? Perhaps he had some unseelie blood, which allowed him to lie. It was the only explanation. He did not truly love me. Not if he had captured the Blue Amethyst behind my back. And it was awfully convenient that the terms of his bargain had been precisely the right language to keep me trapped here.

I could feel the power within me stirring to life, eager to be released. But I knew guards were stationed near Mal. The instant I transformed or unleashed my magic, they would hurt him. Possibly even kill him.

"

My instincts had been right. From the beginning, I had suspected him of duplicity. From the moment he'd shown up in my court.

He and his mother had planned this entire bargain. The shrewd cunning in Queen Sonara's eyes told me she could have easily concocted a scheme like this.

But Fenn? Never in a thousand years would I have expected him to betray me.

He fought for you, said a small voice in my head. *He tried to help you escape.*

I shut off that voice, ignoring the words. It didn't matter anyway. Even if I could forgive him, it was over. I was enslaved. And he would never overthrow his mother. As long as that woman lived and breathed, I would be trapped here.

A loud, metallic creak rang through the dungeon. I stiffened, gazing upward as footsteps scuffed on the stone steps. A torchlight bobbed into view, revealing the sour face of a guard. He fumbled with a ring of keys before unlocking my cell door. I briefly thought about attacking him, but he wore a complete set of armor, including a helmet, and I had no weapons.

Besides, they would kill Mal. I couldn't risk it.

"What's going on?" My voice was hoarse and ragged from my sobs.

"Come with me," the guard said, his voice deep and gruff.

I crossed my arms, my eyes narrowing. "You'll have to drag me from this cell if you don't tell me what's going on."

The guard stepped closer to me, but I held my ground, glaring at him. It would be undignified to be tossed over his shoulder. And I knew it would be easy for him. He was more than a head taller than me, and twice as thick.

But to haul me up those stairs would be no easy feat, especially if I put up a fight.

The guard looked me over, clearly considering this. After a long moment, he said, "The queen wishes to speak with you."

I scoffed. "I will not see her. She can come down here in this disgusting pit and talk to me here."

"It's in regards to your family."

My blood chilled, and I dropped my arms, my jaw going slack. No. *No.*

Sonara had found out. She must have discovered the sleeping curse.

Had she captured them? Killed them?

Oh gods.

"All right then." I forced my tone to remain steady, even as chaos and panic erupted in my chest.

The guard led me up several sets of stairs until we emerged into a narrow passageway. I was gasping for breath, my legs screaming in pain. I was weak, sleep-deprived, and starving. Not to mention the power of shifting into my dragon form had completely drained me.

I still couldn't believe it. I had this entire *dragon* living within me.

And yet here I was, powerless to stop Sonara from enslaving me and Mal.

We reached the main hall, and the guard led me up another set of stairs, taking me through the corridor where my bedchambers had been. I frowned in confusion. The queen was meeting me here?

The guard took me past the bedchamber where I'd woken up only yesterday after the ogre attack—gods, that felt like an entire lifetime ago. We reached the chamber at the very end, and the guard stood back, jerking his head toward the door in silent command.

Steeling myself, I opened the door.

The room was small. Much smaller than my previous bedchamber, though I was certain that was intentional. Only a small, narrow bed took up one end, though it was decorated elaborately, with plush silver pillows and lavender drapes. Matching lavender curtains covered a wide, floor-to-ceiling window that boasted a view of the glittering stars and crescent moon.

On the opposite end of the room was an empty fireplace, a pair of bookshelves, and a large spinning wheel. Frowning at the latter, I made my way into the room, only to find Queen Sonara sitting in the armchair facing the empty fireplace. Her gaze was also fixed on the spinning wheel, her dark eyes full of contemplation as I entered the room.

"What is this?" I bit out, not bothering with propriety or manners. Neither would do me any good with this viper.

Sonara rose from her feet, sweeping her arms in a wide, grand gesture. "These are your new accommodations."

I snorted. "I don't believe you."

"Believe what you will," she said, sweeping toward me, her sparkling violet gown trailing behind her. "Fennick has made it clear the terms of your bargain demand better sleeping arrangements. So, I have provided this suite for you."

Fennick has made it clear... My stomach soured. So, instead of coming to the dungeons to speak to me himself, he was making arrangements with his mother, letting her do the talking.

What a coward.

I was right. There was no love between us at all. It had all been a ruse to bring me here.

"No, thank you," I said in a hollow voice. "I would prefer the dungeons."

The queen laughed, though there was no joy in the sound. "Don't be impossible about this, my dear. You cannot tell me you prefer to sleep in that filthy vermin-filled hole, do you?"

"It serves as a reminder of what I am," I said, lifting my chin. "A prisoner. A slave. Not even the most ornate of bedchambers will change that fact."

"You are right." The queen's smile turned serpentine, and the look she gave me made my insides wriggle with discomfort. It was the knowing look of an opponent who had just won the game. "But these accommodations come with something else. A gift, if you will."

I gave her a wary look. "And what is that?"

"Freedom for your family."

I straightened, my chest tightening. "What do you mean?" My voice was laced with panic.

"I know a sleeping curse has befallen your people." Sonara moved toward the spinning wheel, running a long finger against the mahogany finish of the drive wheel. Her hand stopped at the front of the device where a long, thin needle protruded from where the bobbin was usually kept.

I shifted my weight but said nothing. I couldn't confirm this information. Instead, I watched the queen, waiting.

"I imagine you would want to free them from this curse," she went on, turning to face me with a wide smile. "Is that so?"

I swallowed hard, choosing my next words carefully. "Should this be true and something *has* befallen my people, then yes, I would be... interested in seeking an opportunity to free them."

She hummed a soft laugh at that. "Clever wording, my dear. But there is no need for that. You see, it was I who arranged the sleeping curse."

My stomach hollowed, and nausea roiled in my gut. It shouldn't surprise me. Not in the slightest. Of course Sonara was behind all of this. She was likely working with the Dream Mage.

But Fenn had sworn to me he had nothing to do with the sleeping curse. He had sworn with his blood…

Had his mother deceived him? I found it hard to believe he hadn't suspected *anything*. Fenn was many things, but he wasn't stupid.

"The Dream Mage is a powerful witch," Sonara went on, continuing to admire the spinning wheel. "She has infused a spell into this needle here." She gestured to the long, sharp point of the wheel. "If you so desire, you can free your kingdom from the enchantment… if you take their place."

I froze, my body going utterly still as I processed her words. My eyes flicked over the sharp point of the needle, and my stomach clenched with unease.

"Why?" I demanded. "Why would you offer this?"

"Well, a kingdom is no good without its subjects," Sonara said. "If I wish to conquer your court, I can't very well do that if the entire castle staff and army are asleep."

My blood chilled, and I shook my head. "No. I won't do it if you're just going to enslave my people."

Sonara sighed. "I'm going to conquer your kingdom either way, Aurelia. It would be easier if you made this exchange. But, if you prefer, I can simply kill your sleeping citizens and bring in my own army. The choice is yours."

My eyes narrowed. "Why don't you just ask the Dream Mage to end the curse? Surely, that is the easier way."

Sonara's lips pinched, forming a tight line. "It is… difficult to negotiate with her. She cannot leave the Dream Realm."

I scrutinized the irritation creasing her brow, then chuckled, the sound harsh. "She won't do it, will she? You can't control her." I laughed again. "Well, that's fitting, isn't it?"

"She wants *you*," Sonara snapped. "She's wanted you the whole time. Once she gets what she wants, I can be done with her. But she will not let your people go unless she has you."

Horror washed over me, making my skin prickle and my hands tremble. "Why does she want me?"

She leveled a flat look at me. "Because you're the Dragon Queen."

"And she wants my dragons."

Sonara sighed impatiently. "Everyone wants your dragons, child."

I paused, conflict warring within me. "What will happen to my dragons if I agree?"

"Does it matter?" She arched an eyebrow at me. "Which would you choose to save, your kingdom, or your dragons?"

I hated myself for even hesitating. I really did. But my gut wrenched with despair at the thought of my dragons being slaughtered and enslaved.

And yet… my kingdom was more important. They always would be. Even if I didn't truly belong to the Summer Court. Even if my parents weren't actually my parents. I still loved them. I loved Gigi. I would wager she didn't know about any of this deception. She was innocent, and she didn't deserve this fate. No one in my kingdom did.

I owed it to them to protect them. Even if I couldn't save them from Sonara, at least I could keep them alive.

After a long moment, I nodded, my throat tight with emotion and my eyes burning. "I'll do it." My voice was strained, but full of resolve.

"I knew you would." Sonara's smile widened. "All you must do is prick your finger on the spindle and draw your blood. Then, the exchange will be complete."

I stared at the spinning wheel with a mixture of dread and apprehension. "I need you to swear—"

"Yes, yes, I swear on my life and my blood that this needle is enchanted to put you in a magical sleep, and those in your kingdom will be freed from the curse once you offer yourself freely." The queen's voice was bored, but her words were thorough. I quickly sifted through them, trying to find a loophole or a trick.

Then again, Fenn had already destroyed my life with the way he'd worded his bargain. And I hadn't suspected a thing. My judgment wasn't exactly foolproof.

My heart felt like lead in my chest as I stepped forward, wondering why the Dream Mage had used a spinning wheel, of all things.

Perhaps I could ask her. I imagined she was waiting for me in the dream world.

With a deep breath, I extended my hand, pressing my finger into the sharpened point of the needle. It pierced my flesh, drawing blood. A crimson droplet fell to the floor, and I hissed, withdrawing my hand instantly. The room became fuzzy, my vision swimming as I teetered and fell into darkness.

"You're certain of this?" I asked Gorrick, whose eyes had glazed over from the pressure of my magic.

"Yes." The captain's voice was slow and measured, his expression slack.

I rubbed my jaw. "Very well. *You will forget this encounter the second you leave my room.*" My voice was layered with fae magic, which was getting easier and easier to do. I had been so afraid of it before, but now, none of that mattered. I would use whatever weapons I had at my disposal, and with my reluctance no longer hindering my powers, they rushed forward with unstoppable fervor.

"Yes," Gorrick repeated, then turned and left my chambers. When the door shut behind him, I braced my arms against the window, glaring in the distance. The information Gorrick had given me hadn't necessarily changed anything; but it was unsettling nonetheless.

And it only made me more aware of the many ways I had failed my people. I'd failed to keep them safe from the dangers of the unseelie… and the dangers of my mother.

I still had much to do. After my interrogation with Gorrick, I went to the stables, where the witch Priscilla awaited me. I found her standing next to the stall of a white stallion, dressed in her signature crimson cloak. She turned at my approach, her dark brows pulled together in concern.

"I told you never to summon me," she hissed, glancing around the stable. But we were completely alone.

"I know," I lifted my palms placatingly. Priscilla and I had a strict agreement. She was willing to teach me runic magic, but only on her own terms, and only when she was available. This was the first time I had ever reached out to her on my own. "I'm sorry. But it's urgent. Do you know how to contact the witches Ruby, Sapphire, and Jade?"

Priscilla's face paled. "How do you know them?"

"It's a long story. Can you reach them?"

She shook her head. "Those three operate under their own rules. They always have. They are separate from the rest of us."

I swore under my breath. "Can you gather as many witches as you can? The kingdom is in danger."

Priscilla's dark eyes flared wide as I filled her in on the situation as best I could, leaving out particular details about Aurelia's identity.

"If we don't do something, my mother will allow the Dream Mage to take over the entire realm," I finished. "Will you help me?"

Priscilla's expression turned wary. "What is it you need from us?"

"I'll need your support when I challenge my mother."

Priscilla stilled, her lips growing thin. "The royal family has never been civil toward witches. It will be difficult to persuade them to support you."

"I'm prepared to swear right now that I will change that once I take the throne," I said in a firm voice. "It's something I should have done long ago."

Priscilla took a step back, her mouth falling open. "My lord, that is quite a bold promise."

"I know. But I need the witches' allegiance, and time is of the essence. Please deliver this message to them."

Priscilla scrutinized my solemn expression before nodding once. "Very well. I agree. And, at the very least, I swear that you will have *my* allegiance, my lord." She pressed her fist to her heart and inclined her head.

I offered her a small smile. It was all I could manage, given the circumstances. Without preamble, I murmured, "I, Prince Fennick Mardion of the Midnight Court, swear to you, Priscilla of the witch clans, that I will grant all witches in my kingdom freedom, respect, and a voice in my court as soon as I take the throne." I closed my fingers into tight fists, biting back a groan as the heat of my vow seared through me.

I looked at Priscilla expectantly. Her eyes were shining. "You have no idea how long we have waited for this, my lord."

"I'm just sorry it's taken so long." My voice was heavy, and the words didn't seem nearly enough.

"I suspect many of the witches will come to your aid, if not all," Priscilla said. "I cannot say for sure, but I will do my best to convince them."

"Thank you, Priscilla."

She nodded and gave me an encouraging smile before I turned and left the stable.

I hadn't tried to visit Aurelia yet. I knew Mother was waiting for me to do it, to try to sneak into that prison cell and free the woman I loved.

My chest ached, cinching tighter and tighter with every passing minute. My mind was constantly on Aurelia and how she fared. I knew she must despise me. But that didn't matter. If, after this was all over, she wanted to part from me forever, I would let her.

But I had to free her first. I owed her that much. Then, she could live her life as she pleased.

"Why have you summoned us, Your Highness?" demanded Lord Northall, his bushy gray beard twitching with displeasure.

I had quietly summoned the nobles of our court, and we stood in the council room. The twelve nobles were seated at a long, rectangular table with me at the head—in Mother's place.

My insides coiled tightly with nerves. If this didn't work…

I cleared my throat, shoving aside my unease. Next to me stood Brannon, a servant from the kitchens. Several nobles cast him wary looks, but the servant stood next to me, silent and serene, his expression almost bored.

I gestured to the servant and said, "I've invited Brannon here with us today because his fae magic can counteract another person's powers. Lord Halsburg, could you please demonstrate your abilities for us?"

Lord Halsburg, a broad-shouldered blond man with vibrant green eyes, nodded, and rose to his feet. He flexed his fingers, and long, leafy vines sprang forth, slithering across the table like snakes.

"Brannon, if you wouldn't mind?" I asked.

Brannon nodded, then closed his eyes. The air thrummed with

power, and in an instant, Lord Halsburg's vines receded, sliding off the table and vanishing. Lord Halsburg continued to stretch his hand and fingers, trying to summon his powers, but nothing happened.

Every noble stared at me with wide, fearful eyes.

I swallowed hard. "Brannon is here to guarantee to all of you that I will not use my magic against you. I will not take away your choice."

Twelve pairs of eyes watched me solemnly in response.

I resisted the urge to twist my fingers together, instead focusing on my determination. In my heart, I knew this had to be done.

But that didn't make this any easier.

After a deep breath, I said, "I have brought you here to discuss deposing Queen Sonara from the throne."

Gasps and frantic whispers met my words, the nobles muttering to one another in shock and alarm.

I waited another moment before continuing, "She seeks to overtake the Court of Twilight as well as the Summer Court. She plans to drag us through unnecessary wars, submitting our people to the horrors of battle, not to mention heavy taxes to fund her army. I am here to tell you we do *not* need to go to war. And I refuse to stand by and let her do this to our kingdom."

More hushed comments drifted down the table, and, once again, I waited, my insides jittering in anticipation.

At long last, Lord Northall said, "Our people have been suffering, Your Highness. You cannot deny that something needs to be done about it."

"We *have* done something about it," I argued. "The Summer Princess and her dragon are currently in our custody. That dragon could supply us with enough Nightfire to keep our people safe for the foreseeable future." I didn't point out that I planned to release the Summer Princess as soon as the crown was mine. They didn't need to know that just yet.

"And what of your… complicated involvement with the princess?" asked Lady Flora, her tall, bony fingers steepled together atop the table. Her beady eyes appraised me with keen awareness.

"That is between me and the Summer Princess," I said stiffly. "I had hoped to strike an amicable alliance with her, but my mother ruined that with her deception. My top priority is preventing war. If my mother is deposed, it's possible I can still salvage an alliance with Summer. But if not, their dragons are sure to tear us apart."

"But we could win," argued Lord Northall.

"At what cost?" I said, my voice rising. "Do you want to sacrifice thousands of lives? For nothing? We *have* Dragonfire. There is no need to invade the Summer Court."

"We have Dragonfire *now*," said Lord Vincent, his large and beefy frame extending past his chair. "But what about the future? How can we guarantee enough Nightfire to protect our people after the dragon dies?"

I pushed away the horrifying thought of Mal's death and instead focused on a logical answer. "One step at a time. First, we must keep the unseelie tribes at bay, holding off further attacks. From there, I am confident that it won't take long for our commerce to return to normal, for our revenue to rise once more. That includes our stores of stardust. If we can increase the production of stardust, we can make the Dragonfire last longer. In addition, if I can salvage relations with the Summer Princess, then perhaps we can utilize her other dragons and keep the Dragonfire burning."

Lord Northall snorted. "I highly doubt she'll do *anything* for you, after we've imprisoned her and captured her dragon."

My lips grew thin, and I had to fight to keep my hands from shaking. "A valid point. But I know Aurelia well. She doesn't want our kingdom to suffer. If we can stop treating her like an enemy and start treating her like an ally, I have every belief that she will honor the original terms of our arrangement."

My chest tightened from my words. I did, in fact, believe that Aurelia would still help us after she was free. In a perfect world, she would forgive me and rule by my side as Queen of the Midnight Court.

But I knew that could never be.

"You must forgive us, Your Highness," said Lady Windsor, a slim, blond figure with a robust voice that was surprising, given her stature. "You have never taken court matters seriously before now. It is… difficult to believe you are in earnest."

Several other nobles murmured their agreement.

I sighed, closing my eyes briefly. "I know. And I understand your hesitation. It *has* taken me too long to accept my responsibilities to this kingdom, and for that, I deeply apologize. But I am ready now. The events of the past few days have shown me that I can no longer sit idly by while our court suffers. I am here. I am ready. And, with your help, I can save our people.

"To prove how serious I am, I would like to introduce the allies I have secured us in protecting our borders from the unseelie, at least until we can get a more stable supply of Nightfire."

A pair of guards obediently opened the council room doors to reveal a crowd of red-robed witches, with Priscilla standing in the front, tall and regal, a satisfied smile on her face.

Shouts sounded among the council. Several nobles jumped to their feet in alarm. Lord Northall bellowed, "What is this?"

"Our Nightfire fete brings people of all classes together," I said, practically yelling over the commotion. "That is the heart of our kingdom and our people! We are united. My mother has harbored prejudices against the witch clans for too long. We should have sought their help sooner. They possess powerful magic that can help us, if only we grant them the freedoms they rightfully deserve. My first step as king will be to strike an alliance with the witch clans so we can cast protective wards around our kingdom and prevent any further unseelie attacks.

"Furthermore, if you do *not* give me your support for the throne... you will have them to answer to." My teeth flashed in a feral smile as I stared down each and every noble at the table. "Under my mother's rule, they have no freedom. They are cast out as pariahs of society, only to be seen during our fete alongside the lower class citizens. It is in their best interest that I take the throne. So, consider your next words carefully."

I clasped my hands together on top of the table, drumming my fingers along my knuckles as I plastered a pleasant smile on my face. Inside, my stomach was churning violently, but I maintained my calm demeanor and patiently watched the nobles whisper among each other.

It was a risk. But I had to believe it would pay off. I had to believe the council would choose to do the right thing.

"Is he—" Lord Halsburg began, with a fearful glance at Brannon. "Is he using his magic?"

Brannon closed his eyes for a moment, then shook his head. "No. I do not sense any magic coming from him."

Halsburg met my gaze for a long moment, then gave a sure nod, his eyes full of sincerity.

He was on my side.

"This is absurd," blustered Lord Northall, waving a hand toward me. "He is threatening us! The witches will kill us if we don't do what they want."

"And what do you think my mother will do?" I snapped. "She has done *far* worse. I know for a fact she has threatened the families of our guards in order to coerce them to do her bidding. I also know she arranged to have the braziers drained of stardust during the fete so the unseelie tribes would attack. She cannot be trusted to keep us safe. Not anymore."

Gorrick had confessed as much, but only after I had used my magic on him. Mother had a tight hold on him, threatening to have him arrested and imprisoned if he did not comply. Gorrick had a wife and children to support, and he couldn't afford the risk.

Lady Windsor gasped loudly, raising a hand to her mouth. Halsburg paled, and Lady Flora pressed a hand to her chest, her eyes flaring wide. Even Lord Northall's thick eyebrows lowered in dismay, his beard twitching again.

"She is willing to risk innocent lives to get what she wants," I said, my words slow and forceful. "But I am not. Give me your support, and I will swear it. Please."

I held my breath, waiting for someone to speak. Several nobles glanced at each other, communicating wordlessly with widened eyes and significant looks. A few gazed at me with solemn contemplation.

I wanted to shout, to shake the shoulders of each noble. I wanted to unleash my magic and force them all to agree.

But I couldn't. I needed their trust. And I didn't want to start my rule on deception. That was my mother's way. Not mine.

This was it. If my plan failed, all was lost. Mother would march us into war. And Aurelia would rot in our prison cell.

There were no other options.

So, with my hands still clasped together, I sat at the head of the table, my eyes on the council, and I waited.

After what felt like an eternity, the council looked at me with expectant gazes. My pulse roared in my ears.

Halsburg spoke first. "You have my vote."

"And mine," said Lady Flora.

"Mine, too," said Lord Vincent.

One by one, each noble gave me their support. With each vote, something loosened in my chest, and my heart soared with gratitude.

The last one was Lord Northall, who was scowling, his brows still lowered. "I do not like it," he grumbled. Then, he heaved a sigh. "But I like what the queen has done even less. Begrudgingly, Your Highness, you have my vote."

I resisted the urge to bark out a laugh at that. Instead I grinned broadly and nodded my thanks to each noble individually.

King of the Midnight Court. A title I had never wanted for myself. Yet today, it made me feel more complete than I'd ever felt in my life.

THE MIDNIGHT PRINCE

I stood, poised and erect on the dais of the throne room. Guards formed an aisle before me, and the council was on either side. My heartbeat hammered loudly inside me as I waited.

At long last, the throne room doors opened, and a pair of soldiers escorted Mother inside. Her expression was twisted in fury, but when she caught sight of me—standing in front of *her* throne and wearing my crown—her face slackened in shock.

"Fennick," she hissed, glancing around the room. "What is this?"

"This is a formal declaration that you have officially been deposed," I said. My insides rumbled with unease, but my voice remained firm. "As of this moment, you no longer hold the right to rule the kingdom of the Midnight Court. The council has unanimously voted me to take your place."

Mother's face drained of color, and she staggered back a step. Her eyes swept around the room as if searching for someone to tell her this was a joke. But everyone watched her with a stony expression.

"You—You cannot do this," she breathed. "Fennick, you *cannot* do this!"

"It's already done, Mother." I stared at her, my expression stoic and impassive.

She held my gaze, eyes wide, for a long moment. Then, her features contorted with fury. "I have sacrificed *everything* for this crown! And you think you can take it from me so easily?" She elbowed the soldier next to her in the throat. He doubled over, and Mother drew his sword, advancing toward me with the blade aimed at my chest.

The crowd gasped. Someone shouted something, but I couldn't make out the words. I held perfectly still, panic and fear coursing through me.

All our blades were infused with iron. It was the only way to ensure we could kill the unseelie who attacked us. A normal blade wouldn't deal me a fatal blow. But this one would.

She wouldn't… Would she? Would she murder her own son?

I had once believed her to love me. To love her people. But these past few days had shown me how wrong I was. I wasn't sure what to believe anymore.

"Mother," I said softly, "you are surrounded. Even if you strike me down, these guards will arrest you immediately. Be rational."

"Rational?" She laughed, the sound high and slightly crazed. "Nothing about this is rational! You are a *child*. You've been so busy cavorting with women that you don't know the first thing about ruling a kingdom. And you expect me to believe our people willingly chose to follow you over me?" She huffed another dry laugh. "It's clear you've used your persuasive powers to turn the council against me. And it won't work, Fennick! They will come out of the spell soon, and when they do, I will have *you* arrested."

She inched forward, and the guards closest to her shifted as if to intervene.

"Don't," I told them, raising a hand. "Do nothing."

The council's frightened murmurs grew louder. But still, Mother drew closer. With each step, an alarm blared louder and louder in my ears, drowning out all other sounds.

When the sword tip touched the fabric of my tunic, I lunged, drawing my short sword until the blades clashed with a metallic *clang*.

A noblewoman shrieked in surprise. Mother's eyes widened. It was clear she hadn't expected me to fight back.

Did she think I would just let her attack me?

I swung again, pressing my advantage. She parried and dodged, backing up to keep me from running her through.

I had no intention of killing her. But I had to remind her I was the better swordsman. I always had been.

She struck, and I blocked. I swung wide on purpose, and when she fell for the bait, I jabbed her in the gut, then wrenched the sword from her hands. She stumbled, barely catching herself before she fell, then glared up at me, panting.

"Yield, Mother," I said, my voice cold.

"Never," she growled, then lunged again.

I swung without thinking. My blade struck her chest, but she didn't stop. With a roar of anguish, she grabbed the hilt of my sword, burrowing it further into her until the blade protruded from her back.

One of the courtiers cried out, making a strangled, horrified sound. My mouth fell open in horror, and I dropped the sword, but it was too late. It was lodged straight through her chest. Blood bloomed on her dress, spreading until the silver fabric turned crimson. She choked, blood bubbling from her lips.

"Mother," I breathed. "W-What have you done?"

She fell to her knees, a stream of scarlet now pouring from her lips. "I would… rather die… than lose this… crown," she choked. "And y-you did this… to me… Fennick. *You…*" She wheezed, spitting up more droplets of blood. Her eyes grew unfocused as she murmured, "At least… the work… is done."

She slumped over, blood pooling from her form as she jerked once, then went still.

I could do nothing but stare, shock numbing my entire body as I watched the life leave her eyes.

Mother was dead. And I had killed her.

Soldiers gathered up Mother's body. It didn't take long for the council to spring into action, peppering me with questions about a funeral and a formal coronation ceremony. I didn't remember speaking at all, but somehow, I answered their questions and made it through the day.

Only when I was alone in my chambers did I allow myself to feel. And I felt all of it. The regret. The rage. The shame. Pain and sorrow exploded within me, and I fell to my knees, sobbing so hard my throat ached and my chest burned. Tears streamed down my face, but I let them come, furious and ashamed with myself for feeling *anything* for the savage woman who had once been my mother.

She was a monster. Deep down, I knew she deserved to die.

But she was still my mother. And, as much as I didn't want to, I mourned that loss. I mourned the mother she could have been; the mother I had always believed her to be.

And I mourned the Fennick who had died with her—the version of myself who thought he could let her rule forever, who believed he never needed to assume her responsibilities or play this role.

Those days were over. I would never be the same again.

And for that, I wept.

I only took a moment to grieve. After that, there was no time. There was too much to be done.

My thoughts were constantly on Aurelia. As soon as I could get away, I raced downstairs to the dungeons to search for her. The guards immediately turned over the keys to me.

"Aurelia!" I cried out, peering into every cell as I ran past.

But she wasn't there.

With each stride, panic built up more and more in my chest. Had Mother moved her? Had she had her killed?

And I would never know, because my mother was dead.

Shit, shit, *shit...*

The final cell, our largest one, held a very cramped and restless Mal. He thrashed against the metal bars when he saw me, the loud clangs bouncing off the dank walls.

"Mal!" I drew closer, and he fixed his golden eyes on me, grumbling something I couldn't understand. "Mal, where is she? *Where is she?*"

He roared, pushing more fervently against the bars.

I fumbled with the keys, trying three different ones before I was able to unlock the cell. The metal door groaned as it slid open, and Mal immediately bounded forward. It was only thanks to his massive size that I was able to follow him; he had to wriggle and squeeze to make it through the dungeon, which slowed him down.

As soon as we were up the stairs and in the courtyard, he took off, his wings spreading wide as he rose several feet in the air. Several people screamed, cowering and covering their heads with their arms. The guards swarmed, swords drawn, but I threw up a hand to stop them.

"No!" I shouted. "It's fine. He won't hurt anyone." I gazed up at the sky, following Mal's dark shape. "Mal!" I shouted, waving my arms frantically. "Mal, *wait!*"

But he was in a frenzy, desperate to find Aurelia, and it was as if he couldn't hear me. He soared higher and higher, but he lingered by the stone walls of the castle. I frowned, squinting at him, until he drew closer to a window on the fourth floor, his wings beating to keep him hovering in the air.

He growled, baring his teeth, his eyes flashing. As his head swiveled down so he could glance at me, I understood. My heart gave a painful jolt in my chest, and I was running before I knew what I was doing, legs pumping furiously as I bolted up the flights of stairs, barely pausing to catch my breath. I flew down the hallway, counting doors until I reached the one with the window facing the courtyard. The one Mal had been looking into when he'd been flying.

When I reached the door, I found it locked. With an angry roar, I aimed a high kick and slammed my foot into the door repeatedly. On the third blow, the wood splintered, and it banged open.

I raced inside, stopping short at the sight before me. Aurelia was lying motionless on the bed, her hands clasped demurely before her and her eyes closed. Her face was paler than death, making the freckles stand out against her skin. She was so still, it didn't even look like she was breathing.

I hurried to her side, taking one of her hands in mine. It was ice cold. "Aurelia?" I whispered.

She did not respond.

Swearing, I turned away from her, then jumped back with a startled yelp.

Sapphire stood in the doorway, her eerie lavender eyes fixed on Aurelia.

"Forgive me," she said softly, her white hair seeming to float around her as if underwater. "I should not be here, but..." She trailed off, her eyes turning somber as she stared at Aurelia. "My sisters believe it is too late for her. That we cannot help. " Her gaze shifted to me. "But *you* can. And I will do what I can to help you."

"There—There is a way to bring her back?" Hope bloomed in my chest.

"Yes. If you enter the Dream Realm and retrieve her, you can bring her back."

"How do I do that?"

"The spinning wheel." Sapphire gestured to the large contraption by the fireplace. I hadn't noticed it there before. "The Dream Mage has enchanted it. Whoever pricks their finger on the spindle will be transported there." She leveled a stern gaze at me. "But if you do not have an anchor tethering you to this realm, then you will be stuck there just like her."

I swallowed. "And... I suppose you'll be providing this anchor for me?"

Sapphire sniffed in response, as if bestowing such a gift was beneath me because I was a man.

"Why are you helping me?" I asked. "I know you despise me. You've made that abundantly clear." Of the three witches, she had always been the one to reprimand me just for speaking.

"My sisters are far more accepting of what Fate deals us than I am," Sapphire said. "I, however, enjoy tempting Fate now and again. They would believe that Aurelia is doomed. That there is no hope for her." Her eyes took on a steely edge as she looked at me with fierce determination. "I do not agree. And although I cannot go into the Dream Realm to revive her, I know there is no one who loves her as you do. No one else who is more fit for this task than you."

My eyebrows lifted at her praise. "Well... Thank you."

"It was not a compliment, you foolish boy," she snapped, then waved at the spinning wheel. "Come. We must hurry. There isn't much time left."

"What about my kingdom? The court, the council—"

"My sisters and I will manage things here for you," Sapphire promised. "Besides, if this works, it will be as if no time passed at all. That is why she is looking so ill now. She has been there for far too long."

Concern wrenched in my gut. Gods, I'd been so busy planning my ascension to the throne while Aurelia had been stuck in this dream world, suffering. I felt so foolish. How could I have believed Mother would leave her alone? Of course the wretched woman would torment Aurelia further. As if kidnapping her dragon and imprisoning her hadn't been enough.

I suddenly straightened, turning to face Sapphire with wide eyes. "Can I bring a dragon with me?"

Sapphire barely reacted as she said, "You mean the dragon in the hall?"

My mouth opened and closed as I glanced over her shoulder. In the hall, Mal's familiar grumble echoed.

He was making his way to Aurelia. His size was likely slowing him down again.

I nodded. "Yes. She is bonded to Mal. If I can't bring her back, then her dragon certainly can."

Sapphire was silent as she considered this. Then, she nodded once. "Yes. You can bring the dragon with you. I will tether him to myself as well to anchor him here. It should be easier for him, as a beast."

I frowned. "But you won't come?"

"I cannot. The Dream Realm is warded against us witches. All I can do is serve as your anchor."

"All right then." I drew my short sword and held it above my wrist. "How much blood do you need?"

Sapphire reached into the pockets of her cloak and withdrew a vial. "Fill that please."

I nodded, slicing into my wrist and letting the blood droplets poor into the vial. When it was full, I handed it back to Sapphire. She corked it, then lifted it, inspected it closely. "I think I was wrong about you, child." She offered me a wry smile. "You are not as useless as I believed."

"What a glowing compliment," I said with a chuckle. Then, I glanced at the witch. "And the dragon?"

"I will get his blood after this so he can join you. Do not worry. Dragons trust witches."

I edged closer to the spinning wheel. I rolled up my shirtsleeves and took a steadying breath, unsure how to prepare myself for something like this. "Are you ready?"

"I am."

Before I could talk myself out of it, I stretched out my hand, pricking my finger on the sharpened point of the needle. The room around me went blurry, and I felt myself falling, falling, falling into utter darkness.

THE SUMMER PRINCESS

I was floating in a sea of memories, sifting through them one at a time. I saw the moment Aurora Briarcliffe Gaelania was born into this world, a babe among the witch clans, sired by a soldier passing through the kingdom. She had pale orange hair and freckles covering her entire body. When she first opened her eyes, they were a vibrant green with vertical black slits, marking her as the first dragon shifter the clan had seen in over a thousand years.

The next memory I fell into was the moment Aurora's powers came into fruition. She was able to call blue flames at will and direct them as she wished. Her aim and level of concentration was impeccable. The sage declared she would be the most powerful weapon the clan had ever seen.

After that, hundreds of years passed as Aurora Briarcliffe Gaelania's powers grew. She became a healer in her clan, using her knowledge of herbs to help her fellow sisters. But when a tribe of witch hunters came, slaughtering half her sisters—her mother included—she unleashed all the horrors of her magic and wiped out the entire tribe without another thought. This was the first sign of her dangerous and deadly power.

The next memory was her journey to become the sage of the witch clan. Several witches objected to this, as Aurora's gifts were volatile and dangerous, but overall, she gained her sisters' approval and was granted the gift of Sight.

Decades later, a prophecy came to her mind. It revealed the true nature of her powers, and the two sides of the coin that was her soul. If she mastered her powers, they could be used to unite the realm. But if she did not, she would be the cause of the realm's destruction.

At first, Aurora kept this prophecy to herself, knowing her sisters would oust her if they discovered it. But when she came across a village in desperate need of assistance, her dragon unwittingly took over, and she accidentally set the hamlet ablaze. Nearly every soul in the village perished from the accident.

After that, Aurora confessed to her closest sisters, Ruby, Jade, and Sapphire. She asked for their help. Together, they concocted a plan to bind Aurora's powers but to let her live another life. A safer life.

One witch in the clan was opposed to this idea. She wanted to harness Aurora's powers and use them to destroy their enemies, to conquer other witch clans and expand their territory. Her name was Rosalina.

After much discussion, the clan decided to bind Aurora's powers instead of utilize them. Rosalina lashed out, attacking her fellow sisters until she was cast out from the clan, never to be seen again. The clan heard rumors that she had disguised herself as a human, living among royals and keeping her identity a secret. But no one knew for sure what became of her.

Ruby, Jade, and Sapphire helped Aurora initiate the spell, but it was Aurora's blood that finally sealed it, bringing it to life. After this, her life as a sage, a healer, and a witch was no more.

A blinding light overtook me, blotting out the memories I'd been enveloped in only moments before. I found myself sitting in the tea room at the Emerald Palace in the Summer Court. A cup of mint tea was in my hands, warming me to the bone. I looked around, confused at finding myself alone. I could have sworn that, only moments ago, I'd been speaking with Gigi.

But she wasn't here.

Humming to myself in thought, I sipped at the tea, thinking perhaps my sister would join me shortly. My gaze fixed on the window, through which I could barely make out the forest where the nesting grounds were. I missed my dragons. Perhaps, after tea, I would venture that way and take one of them for a ride. Perhaps I could check in on—

My thoughts faltered at that, and an unusual stab of unease worked its way into my gut. I swallowed, blinking rapidly to clear my mind. I wasn't sure why, but the thought of my dragons and—and—

Which dragon was I thinking of? He had black scales and golden eyes, but the more I thought of him, the more the details flitted away like petals in the wind.

Another slice of pain, and I hunched over, groaning. Burning suns, what was this? Was something in my tea? I set the cup on the table, then rubbed my temples.

Perhaps I needed to retire early tonight. My nightmares of witches and spells and prophecies had plagued me for far too long. If I sought out our healer for a sleeping tonic, I was sure to have a dreamless sleep tonight.

I rose to my feet, smoothing my palms along my skirts before turning to leave, only to find a figure standing in the doorway. He had wavy brown locks and vibrant green eyes, and the look on his face was so intense with longing and grief that it brought back that familiar ache in my stomach. I tilted my head at him, wondering why he was here.

"Aurelia," he breathed, the sound a low rasp.

I blinked. "Who are you?"

He drew closer until his large form was only a few inches away, warming the space between us. I found my throat dry, though I wasn't sure why. I had never seen this man before.

"You must remember," he murmured, taking my hand in his. His palm was so warm and familiar, and when he laced his fingers through mine, it felt like an echo of a past memory. A past life.

My brows knitted together, and I jerked my hand away. "What— What are you doing to me?"

"I've come to bring you back."

"Bring me back *where*?" My voice was shrill. "I'm already home."

"Aurelia, this isn't real. You've been trapped here for too long. If you don't come with me, it will be too late for you."

I laughed. This man was clearly insane. "I'm sorry, but I don't know you, and I'm not going anywhere with you."

I tried to step around him, but I froze at the sight of the black dragon in the hall. His wings were spread wide, making him too large to fit through the doorway. As he looked at me with one golden eye and one milky eye, I felt my breath shudder within me.

"Oh gods," I whispered. "*Mal!*"

Within seconds, I had fled from the tea room to throw my arms around my dragon, clinging to him tightly in the hallway. He nuzzled my shoulder, his body rumbling as he purred and wrapped his wings around me as if in a loving embrace. Tears rolled down my cheeks, and his familiar earthy and ember scent filled me with memories of home and flight and the open sky.

Home.

My body jerked as if pulled in motion, though I remained rooted to the spot. Awareness burst in my mind with searing intensity, and suddenly I remembered. Not just the life of Aurora Briarcliffe Gaelania, but *my life*—the life of Aurelia Perdis, Princess of the Summer Court.

The sleeping curse.

My bargain with Fenn.

Our journey through the Autumn Court.

His lips on mine, his hands roaming my body.

The Mistwood Hills.

The ogre attack.

The Midnight Court and the Nightfire fete and—

I glanced up at the man, who had followed me to the hall. But he wasn't just a man. He was Prince Fennick of the Midnight Court. The man I had fallen in love with.

And the man who had betrayed me.

"*You!*" I roared, jumping to my feet and baring my teeth at him. "You have some nerve coming here, you bastard. Get out of my castle!"

"I can't do that, Aurelia. I have to bring you back, or you'll die." His eyes were full of pain.

"I don't believe you!" I shouted in his face. "You've done nothing but deceive me from the start. I'm done with you. Come on, Mal, let's go for a ride."

I stormed down the hallway with Mal at my side. I didn't bother looking back to see if Fenn followed us. Part of me hoped he didn't.

But another much smaller part of me hoped he did.

When we rounded the corner, Mal nudged my hand with his snout. My steps faltered, and I cast him a questioning look. "What?"

Mal jerked his head back toward where we'd come.

I scoffed. "I'm not speaking with him."

Mal's ear twitched. Then both ears folded backward.

He was scared. And my brave dragon wasn't easily scared.

I took a shaky breath. "Mal, I can't trust him."

Mal huffed as if in agreement, and I found myself smiling.

"Do you believe he's here to help me?" I asked quietly.

Slowly, Mal inclined his head in agreement.

"So, you're saying I should trust him?" My tone was full of doubt.

Mal's ears perked up, and he tilted his head to the side, letting his tongue loll out. I laughed, interpreting his response as, *Maybe. Maybe not. It's up to you.*

With a sigh, I turned back to the tea room. "Fine. I'll speak to him. But don't go far, just in case I need you to bite his head off for me."

Mal huffed again as I strode back down the hall. Fenn was right where we'd left him, pacing the small space in front of the tea room. He looked up at my approach, his eyes wide with desperation and hope.

When I faced him, my eyes narrowed into slits. "You have until I finish my cup of tea to convince me to believe you." Then, I pushed past him, returning to my seat on the sofa and taking another sip of tea. When he didn't move from the doorway, I said lightly, "Tick tock."

With a groan of frustration, Fenn stepped into the room, sitting on the sofa opposite me. He clasped his hands over his knees and looked at me with an intensity that made my stomach flutter.

After a moment, he said, "I killed my mother."

My hand froze halfway to bringing my teacup to my lips. Then, I laughed. "You would never."

"But I did."

I stared at him, trying to figure out if he was joking or not. Sometimes, with Fenn, it was impossible to tell. "How did you do it?"

"I deposed her. She was so enraged she attacked me with a sword. And I—I—" He broke off, his eyes full of anguish.

I shook my head, taking another sip of my tea. "Sorry. I don't believe you. You let your mother cage me. You let her steal my dragon. You worded our bargain so I would be trapped to stay in your court. I have no reason to trust you're telling me the truth."

"None of that was intentional, Aurelia." His face was stricken and full of despair. "Yes, I knew she'd stolen a dragon, but I wanted to wait until after the fete to tell you."

"You *knew* I was looking for that Blue Amethyst's mother," I snarled. "You *knew* I suspected someone had captured or killed her. How could you have kept this from me?"

His eyes closed, and he nodded, his mouth pressing into a thin line. "Yes. You're right. I'm sorry. I should have told you right away. But the bargain… I was only looking out for my kingdom. I had no idea about your shifting abilities, Aurelia. I thought for sure it would be Jorey who would come with me to the Midnight Court. I was looking forward to it, actually." A slow smile lit his face, making him look like the normal Fenn for the first time since he'd shown up here. His gaze turned distant as he no doubt thought of the happy silver dragon who had warmed up to him so quickly.

I was torn between affection for the man who cared about a dragon as much as I did, and defensiveness that anyone dared to try to take Jorey away from me.

"I didn't know what she was planning," Fenn said, his eyes pleading. "I know that's no excuse. You're right—It *is* my fault. Because I should have seen this sooner. I should have paid more attention. By the time she'd imprisoned you, it was too late for me to do anything. The bargain was fulfilled."

"How convenient." I took another sip of tea.

"Dammit, Aurelia!" Fenn slammed his fist on the table between us, making the teapot and saucer rattle. "I am *in love* with you. And it's been tearing me apart, finding a way to get back to you. If you never want to see me again, that's perfectly fine. But you *must* return with me before this place kills you. If you don't believe me, then believe Mal. He's here for you, too."

"Don't you dare drag him into this." I set my teacup on the table so hard it sloshed, spilling onto the saucer. "He was captured because of you. He lost his eye because of your soldiers. That alone should have kept me from trusting you. But I was a fool. I won't be making that mistake again."

I rose to my feet. "Sorry. Your time is up." I didn't care that there was still tea in my cup. I was done speaking with this arrogant ass.

"Wait!" Fenn caught my arm before I could stride for the door. "I—I'm going to kiss you now."

I stiffened, my body heating from those words. The very same words he uttered before he kissed me at the Equinox Ball. My mouth went dry as I stared at him. "What?" My voice was shaky.

Fenn stepped around the table until he faced me, our chests touching, our bodies sharing the same space. "I'm going to kiss you. And if you feel nothing, then I will leave you alone and never bother you again. But if you feel *anything* at all, then I'll know I'm right."

"Right about what?" I tried to make my tone sharp, but the tremor in my voice betrayed my fear.

"Right about your feelings for me." He gave me a crooked half-smile that both infuriated and aroused me all at once. "You love me. Admit it."

"Never," I growled.

"Fine. Then this test should be easy for you." He drew closer, his mouth hovering over mine as he waited for me to object.

I wanted to shove him away. To scream. To throw the teapot at him.

But if I refused, I would have to explain *why*. And I couldn't do that.

So, in answer, I grabbed his collar and pulled his mouth to mine.

THE SUMMER PRINCESS

FENN'S SOFT MOUTH CLAIMED MINE, HIS TONGUE SWEEPING OVER MY LIPS, eliciting a moan from me. Powerful and explosive emotions flooded within me, and heat scorched my blood and veins. I pulled away, startled by the intensity of it. As soon as I did, my mouth ached for more, yearning for Fenn to come closer so I could taste him better.

My eyes were still closed when I withdrew. I was too afraid to open them. He was panting, his hands on my waist, and I didn't even have the strength to push him away.

"Aurelia," he groaned, the sound low and husky.

I kissed him again, unaware of what I was doing. My hands, my mouth, moved of their own accord. My fingers threaded through his hair, his tongue filled my mouth, and my chest pressed against his. His hands were gliding down my back until they cupped my rear and squeezed.

"You bastard," I breathed before his mouth claimed mine again. In and out, our tongues collided, stroking and licking until my lips were numb.

"Do you remember now?" he murmured against my mouth.

"Remember what? Your betrayal?" I bit down on his lip, and he made a soft, strangled sound.

"No." He moved his mouth to my ear, nipping the lobe. I shivered with pleasure, heat pooling between my legs. "Remember the home you have to come back to. A sister. A mother. A father. A *dragon*. A man who will marry you without hesitation."

My hands tugged at his tunic, pulling it free from his trousers. "Yes, and that same man will stab me in the back and keep dozens of secret lovers, I'd wager." I plunged my hand into his trousers and gripped his firm length, squeezing hard.

"*Shit.*" His hips bucked, and he threw his head backward. The veins along his neck stood out, and his jaw went slack. "Oh *gods*, Aurelia."

"Am I wrong?"

"Y-Yes. You're wrong. Dead wrong. I would never—I *could* never." His eyes were still closed as I pumped my hand up and down, from tip to shaft. His groans became more feral with each of my movements.

"Then swear it," I breathed, the heat between my thighs becoming nearly unbearable. "Swear you're mine and only mine."

"I—I am yours, Aurelia. Always. Yours alone."

I squeezed again, and he cried out, the sound desperate and pleading. "Prove it to me."

"I—I will do anything. Gods, Aurelia, *anything*. It's only you. Even if you leave me and never return, I swear I will never love again. I—"

I sank to my knees, working my fingers along the waistband of his trousers. With slow, deliberate movements, I pulled, bringing them down until they fell to his ankles, exposing just how hard he was for me. I smirked knowingly up at him as he panted, his breathing ragged.

"Do what you want with me, Aurelia," he whispered.

I inched closer before closing my mouth around his tip and sucking gently.

A strangled growl escaped him, and his body quivered. I ran my tongue along his tip once more, tasting the small droplet of moisture that had already collected there.

Fenn gasped, thrusting toward me, his eyebrows raised and his face a mixture of torment and pleasure.

"Promise me," I commanded, my mouth hovering just over his arousal.

"I promise," he rasped. "Aurelia, I promise I belong to you. You own me. I am yours to command."

I swept my tongue over him again, and he shuddered violently. "Tell me again."

"I am yours. Yours." His voice was strained, and his hips rocked, urging me onward.

But still I taunted him. Drawing it out. "Give yourself to me, Fenn. Surrender. If you are mine, then show me. I want all of you."

"You can have it," he groaned. "All of me, Aurelia. Take it. It's yours. Just, *gods*, take it, please."

I finally obliged, taking him fully in my mouth. His hips jerked, and he moaned loudly, thrusting into my mouth. His hand fisted in my hair, tangling the strands and tilting my head backward to plunge himself deeper inside me.

"Please, Aurelia," he begged. "Gods, please."

Never before had I had such power over a man. Tyrone, Callan… Neither of them had ever given me this much control over their bodies. Some small bolt of clarity speared through my mind, along with the realization that Fenn *was* different. He was not Callan. He was not Tyrone.

He was *mine.*

I dragged my tongue along his tip, then my teeth followed the same path. He shoved harder, tickling the back of my throat, but I held fast, clamping down on him.

He pushed and pushed, driving into me, his body trembling as he approached that sweet release. I licked and sucked, drawing circles around him with my tongue.

"Stars above," he choked, thrusting harder.

I took all of him, even as he slid so deep inside I thought I might retch. I held him there in my mouth, devouring him fully, claiming him as thoroughly as he had claimed me.

His frantic gasps were faster now, his body pulsing to the same rhythm as his breaths. His sounds were more wild and uncontrollable until he sounded like a feral creature instead of the calm and collected prince I knew so well.

And a savage part of me loved that, that I was able to make him come undone. I was able to shed that mask, that skin he wore to protect himself. He was completely bare and vulnerable here with me now.

"Oh. *Oh.*" He thrust again, and I dragged my teeth along that sensitive flesh, closing my lips around him.

"No—No—I can't—" His body spasmed as he came, filling my mouth. I gulped it all down, letting it burn my throat, letting it pour into me one drop at a time. Gods, he tasted delicious. I found myself gripping his thighs, his ass, bringing him closer to me. He panted, his hips still moving, even when there was nothing left. My touch alone had consumed him, had driven him to madness.

He was mine. Only mine. No one else's. In this moment, I owned him, and he was proving it to me, letting me take utter and complete control.

The Fenn I knew would never surrender that control to anyone else. He loved me.

I licked him once more for good measure, tasting that delicious part of him that was now mine and only mine.

When he was finished, I drew back, releasing him from my mouth. I stood, wiping my lips with the back of my hand and facing him, a look of smug superiority on my face. He was panting, leaning against the wall, his expression wary and exhausted.

"You're cruel," he rasped.

My smile only grew. "You love me."

"I do. Desperately. More intensely than a thousand burning suns."

"Even when the stars go dark," I whispered, remembering our declarations to each other in the Crescent Glade during the fete.

"My love will shine through the night, guiding you home to me," he breathed, bringing his hand to my cheek and brushing his fingers along my jaw.

I sighed softly, my breath shaky and ragged. I wanted to lose myself in this moment, in this place between us where I knew he loved me, and he knew I loved him.

"Do you believe me now?" he asked.

I didn't want to. I wanted to stay here forever, where it was safe. Where I would never be betrayed again.

Instead, I nodded, my eyes filling with tears. "I trust you, Fenn. Against my better judgment."

He laughed hoarsely. "I'll take whatever you can give me. And I'll spend the rest of my existence earning your trust back." He hoisted up his trousers and fastened his belt before shooting me a coy look. "You're filthier than I thought, little firebird. I've never come so quickly in all my life."

My eyebrows lifted. "Gods, you think so highly of yourself, don't you?"

His grin turned feral. "You have no idea how long I can last. How much I can make you scream. We've only scratched the surface."

In spite of the situation, fresh heat bloomed in my core, and my toes curled from the sultry promise of his words.

He chuckled. "Let's find your dragon and go home."

We left the tea room, making our way down the hall where I'd last left Mal. My face heated as I realized he must have given us privacy for our intimacy. How embarrassingly thoughtful of him.

But as we wound through various corridors and descended several staircases, panic took root in my chest, and I exchanged a worried look with Fenn. "Where is he?" I asked.

He shook his head, his gaze dark and intent. "I don't know."

My eyes lit up. "The nesting grounds."

We took off down the stairs, racing out the double entrance doors and into the blindingly bright sun. My feet followed the familiar path leading to the forest, a habit from years of visiting my precious dragons.

But when we reached the cover of trees, none of the dragons were there, save for one: Mal. He was galloping around the clearing, wings bounding with each movement as he leapt and darted this way and that. It would seem playful—he often behaved this way when he had too much energy to get out—were it not for the figure standing on the opposite end of the clearing, her hand raised as wisps of white magic darted from her fingertips to Mal.

She was controlling him.

Rage filled me as I stormed toward the figure. "Release him! *Now!*"

To my surprise, the woman obliged, dropping her hand and gliding forward with a smile on her face. Only then did I realize I had seen her before. She had long, curly blond hair and wore a crimson gown with layers of fringe cascading down the skirt. Her cold blue eyes surveyed me with familiarity and distrust.

I had seen her once before, in memories—she belonged to the witch clan of Aurora Briarcliffe Gaelania. She was the witch opposed to the spell, the one who had been cast out for rebelling against the clan.

Rosalina.

The Dream Mage.

Terror froze me in my tracks, with several yards between us. In the center of the clearing, Mal had stopped his movements, crouching on all fours and placing his head on the ground, ears folded back, his wings trembling.

He was frightened. I had never seen him so frightened in all my life.

The thought sent a bolt of fury churning in my blood, and I bared my teeth at the witch. "Your quarrel is with me, Rosalina. Not the dragon. Leave him be."

Rosalina's cruel smile widened. "It was the only way to get your attention. And forcing him to do my bidding is *such fun*." Her gaze slid to Fenn, and her expression brightened. "Ah, you brought a friend! This must be the handsome Midnight Prince I've heard so much about."

My blood chilled. *Oh gods, no.* She couldn't have Fenn. Not him, and certainly not Mal. She was only here for me.

"Rosalina," I said, my voice thundering. "What do you want from me?"

Rosalina looked at me once more, her expression turning smug. "I want your dragons."

My eyes narrowed. "How do you expect to take them when you're in the Dream Realm?"

She tilted her head at me, giving me a mocking smile. "I thought your memories had returned. Surely you aren't *that* daft."

I sifted through Aurora's memories, searching for any information that might help. After a long moment, I sucked in a sharp breath. "Damn it all."

Rosalina's eyes glinted. "You understand now."

My body began to tremble, and I curled my hands into fists. Beside me, Fenn whispered, "Aurelia, what is it?"

Without taking my eyes off Rosalina, I said, "There is only one Dragon Queen in the Realm of Valora. Once she dies, another is called to take her place so the line continues."

"If the Dragon Queen dies, so do the dragons bonded to her," Rosalina continued, her smile wide enough to show teeth. "The only way a dragon bond can be transferred is if the Dragon Queen is rendered unable to protect her dragons. Then, the duty is assigned to the next powerful witch in line. Which is me."

"But you're trapped here," I argued. "You can't leave the Dream Realm."

"With the magic of the dragons behind me, I can." Rosalina's chin lifted in triumph. "Ordinarily, witches can't come here. But it seems *you* are the exception. Your magic is strong enough to overpower whatever wards are surrounding me here. It will be all the power I need to travel between realms at will."

Cold dread sank in my stomach like a block of ice. How much time did I have left before the transfer was made? How long had I been in the Dream Realm?

As if Sonara's plotting hadn't been bad enough… Now things were much, much worse. I had no doubt Rosalina had cursed other kingdoms into an enchanted sleep—like the Lunar Court. When the Winter assassin told us she had taken over the Lunar Court, I assumed she had taken their throne.

But she couldn't. Not yet.

Because she was stuck here.

All that was about to change, thanks to me.

Fury coursed through me, swift and powerful. I tried to summon my power, to let it surge within me. I focused on my flight through the midnight sky atop my dragon, my arms spread wide as if I had wings of my own.

But nothing happened. I felt no strong presence within me. My eyes grew wide with horror as Rosalina gave me a knowing smirk.

"Sorry, Aurora," she said. "Your magic doesn't work in my domain."

No. *No*! I tried again, my fists quivering as I strained and pushed, but still, nothing happened.

My magic was gone.

Oh gods. My eyes closed against the onslaught of grief and despair. She'd won. She had *won*.

And I couldn't stop her.

The Midnight Prince

I had never met the Dream Mage before—I only knew Rosalina from how Marek had described her.

But it seemed Aurelia *did* know her.

It also seemed she had gotten her witch memories back.

I wasn't sure how I felt about this. On the one hand, I was grateful she knew more about her past and her abilities. But on the other hand, did this mean she was a different person? Did her past memories, her past *life,* affect her future? Would she rejoin the witches of the Star Court?

The entire time she was conversing with Rosalina, I was digging into my well of power, trying to summon any bit of fae magic I could manage. But Rosalina seemed to be telling the truth; I could not access my powers in this realm.

Which meant we were powerless.

"Fenn and the dragon have nothing to do with this," Aurelia was saying. Her voice was firm, her posture rigid as if preparing for battle. I could detect the hint of a tremor in her voice that betrayed her fear, but only because I knew her so well. "Please let them leave, and then you can keep me here as your prisoner."

I stepped forward, grabbing her arm. "Aurelia, no."

"You are my prisoner either way," Rosalina said, eyes narrowing. "I will not relinquish the leverage I have to keep you in line. Should you make a move against me, I can use these delightful pets of yours to coerce you into behaving." She smiled at Mal, then stroked her hand along his snout. Mal shuddered, burying his face deeper beneath his wing.

"*Don't touch him!*" Aurelia roared, surging forward. Before she could reach Rosalina, the Dream Mage flexed her hand toward Mal, who stiffened, wings going rigid as he began marching back and forth across the clearing.

Aurelia froze, and Rosalina's expression turned smug.

"Don't come any closer or I'll have him claw out his other eye," Rosalina said.

Aurelia's shoulders shook, her hands curling into tight fists. "You monster," she hissed.

Rosalina's smile only grew. "I do what I must to protect myself."

Strange whispers filled the air, brushing against my ears. I frowned, glancing around, wondering where the sound was coming from. The words were unintelligible to me, as if they were a foreign language.

"What are you doing?" I asked Rosalina sharply.

She cocked her head at me, her brows knitting together. "I'm doing nothing to *you*, prince. Although I could, if you want me to." Her voice turned sultry.

The whispers grew more intense, swelling around me, hissing with intensity. The hair on my arms stood on end. "I—I hear something. Don't you hear that?"

Aurelia and Rosalina were silent. But the whispers had increased in volume, now forming a low murmur. It was chanting, not unlike the chanting of the ogres when they had tried to sacrifice Aurelia.

Rosalina's eyes widened. "You are tethered to an anchor."

I stilled, remaining completely silent, watching as comprehension spread across her features.

"Ah, it all makes sense now." Rosalina sighed, dropping her arm. Mal stopped his marching and immediately covered his head once more, his body trembling. "That's why you seemed so unaffected by my dreamscape." She shook her head, clicking her tongue. "Dear Aurora, it seems you'll be getting your wish after all. The strength of the prince's anchor is fading."

My blood ran cold. Only then did I notice that the murmurs surrounding me sounded like Sapphire's voice. She was chanting, trying to keep up the spell that linked us together.

But the spell was failing. I was out of time.

"No. *No!*" I drew closer to Aurelia, taking her wrist and lacing my fingers with hers. "Aurelia, you can come with me. Please."

Sudden pain took hold of me, making me crumple. My back arched, my legs failing me as I sank to the ground. Fire erupted in my blood, coursing through me with swift agony. My scream was lost in the chaotic torment that had taken over my body.

Distantly, I registered Aurelia's shouts and Rosalina's sharp demands.

Then, just as suddenly, the pain left me wheezing on the ground, my body aching. Gasping for breath, I staggered to my feet, every ounce of my body throbbing from the lingering pain.

"I swear it," Aurelia was saying, her voice tainted with tears. "I swear if you leave him be—and my dragon—that I will remain here."

"Aurelia," I groaned, struggling to rise. "Don't… do this…"

She crouched beside me, her warm hands against my cheeks. "You have to go without me. Your kingdom needs you, Fenn." Her soft lips brushed against mine. "It's already done. She wants *me.* I'm trapped here, but I'm not condemning you and Mal to the same fate." As my vision cleared, I made out her red-rimmed eyes and pink nose, the tears glistening in those beautiful blue eyes. She blinked rapidly, and more tears spilled down her face.

I tried to pull her toward me, to hold her tightly, but Rosalina barked, "Step away from him, Aurora. Now."

Aurelia's breath shuddered as she straightened, stepping obediently toward Rosalina. The back of her dress had slid to one side, revealing the top of the rune etched into her shoulder blade.

I froze, staring at the marking on her skin.

Witch runes. Of course!

If Aurelia's magic was strong enough to cross realms, then surely it was strong enough to overpower the magic warding this place. The very magic that kept her from accessing her powers.

All she needed was the right rune to unlock it.

"Let me say goodbye," I said quickly. "Please."

Rosalina's expression was stony as she looked at me, not a flicker of sympathy on her face.

"I will go!" I promised. "I'll leave without a fight. Just please let me say goodbye to her one last time."

After a long moment, Rosalina offered a stiff nod.

Aurelia slowly turned to face me. Her lower lip quivered, and she took a shuddering breath.

I closed the distance between us, cupping her face in my hands. I pressed a firm kiss to her lips, telling myself it would not be our last.

She could do this, I knew she could.

In a soft whisper, I said, "Remember where your power comes from. Remember the first time it ignited."

Her brows pinched slightly in confusion. I pulled her to me, wrapping my arms around her and holding the back of her head with one hand. My voice was barely more than a breath as I said in her ear, "The rune you used when Shay died. Remember it."

Her body went tense in my grasp, but I stroked her hair, shushing her as if trying to soothe her cries. I pressed a kiss to her cheek and withdrew, leveling a significant look at her. Her eyes were wide with realization, and she nodded once.

Around me, Sapphire's voice rose in volume until it drowned out all other sounds. A fierce wind whipped around me, tousling my hair and sending leaves and dirt flying. I shielded my eyes against the onslaught, shouting for Aurelia.

I hadn't told her I loved her.

I hadn't promised to see her again

Gods, it was too soon. *Too soon.*

"No!" I roared.

Then, the wind dissipated, and I found myself standing in the bedchamber with the spinning wheel. Across from me, Sapphire was gasping for breath, one arm braced on the stone wall as if it were the only thing keeping her upright. Her face was covered in a thin sheen of sweat, and her face was pale.

"Stars, no," I whispered, rushing over to the spinning wheel.

"Do not touch it," Sapphire growled. Her voice was hoarse, but it still rang with authority. "If you go back there, I cannot stay linked to you. I have already spent my energy. It is too late, boy."

I shook my head, whirling to face her. "She can't use her magic there. The Dream Mage won't let her go."

Sapphire shook her head, her eyes closing. "Then there is nothing more we can do for her."

"I have to go back and fight with her!"

"And what will you do, that she cannot do herself?" Sapphire snapped. "Use your brain, foolish boy. If she is powerless, then so are you, and you are a liability that the Dream Mage can use against her."

Dread sank in my chest, dragging me down. "So, my going to the Dream Realm did nothing."

"Perhaps. Perhaps not. You awakened her from the dreamscape, did you not?"

I frowned. "The dreamscape?"

"Yes. Everyone who travels to the Dream Realm is trapped within a dreamscape of her making. It makes them believe they are only dreaming."

I thought of Aurelia in the tea room, her confusion upon first seeing me. "Yes," I said slowly. "I awakened her. But it did nothing. It only made her aware of her imprisonment. She still can't be freed."

Sapphire was nodding. "That is the first step, boy. You must trust that she can deliver herself from her predicament. Somehow." But even her own words sounded feeble, as if she didn't quite believe it.

I swallowed thickly before sinking to the chair next to the spinning wheel, sudden exhaustion clouding my head. In my mind, I saw Aurelia's broken expression. I saw my mother's face, eyes wide and empty as the life left her. As my sword punctured her chest.

Gods, it was all too much. Agony twisted through me, sharp and merciless. I scrubbed a hand down my face and glanced around the room, searching for a distraction. Aurelia's sleeping form still rested on the bed. She seemed even paler than before.

"Mal? The dragon?" I asked Sapphire.

"He is still in the hall," she assured me. "He returned when you did. When I cast the tethering spell, he couldn't fit in the doorway. So I got a vial of his blood instead, and was able to tether him that way. When you both went to the Dream Realm, it was as if you two had merely fallen asleep. No one would have noticed."

I laughed. "Except for the massive sleeping dragon in the hallway."

Sapphire's lips twitched, and I almost died of shock at the sight.

A thunderous knocking rattled the door. I jumped to my feet, heart pounding as I raced to open it.

It was Gorrick, and he was out of breath, his face taut with panic. "Forgive me for the interruption, Your Highness, but we just received word of movement of the Autumn Court's army."

My spine straightened as dread pooled in my stomach. "Are they coming here?"

He shook his head. "No, sire. They are invading the Summer Court. The Autumn King has just declared war."

THE SUMMER PRINCESS

Fenn's words echoed in my mind, circling over and over again as I faced Rosalina, the two of us now alone in the clearing in the forest. I was simultaneously relieved and devastated that Fenn and Mal were gone. Their presence had given me strength, but it had also added to my panic and turmoil, knowing Rosalina could hurt them with a mere wave of her hand.

I faced Rosalina, my chin lifting. "So, now what? Will you put me in chains? Force me to relive my worst memories?"

"There's no need for that," she said. "All I need to do is wait for your energy to drain and the bond between you and your dragons to snap. I don't need to resort to any unpleasantness as long as you can remain civil."

The rune you used when Shay died. Remember it. My mind strained to recall the specific image the witch had drawn on me when my magic first awakened in the witches' encampment. It was… a circle of some kind. With lines protruding from the center. But how many lines? Runic magic had to be very specific, and I couldn't risk getting this wrong.

Rosalina was watching me, waiting for a response, so I forced a laugh. "I find it hard to believe you don't want any *unpleasantness.*"

She sighed. "Think what you will about me. I said it before: I do what is necessary to protect myself. No more, no less."

The Awakening Rune, Shay had said as she'd painted the rune on the back of my hand. *The circle represents your magic. The lines extending from it represent your body and your soul.*

Two lines. There had been two lines on the rune. I was certain of it.

I started pacing the length of the clearing, keeping my steps slow and casual, as if I didn't care where my feet took me. "I'm curious," I said. "Why a spinning wheel?"

For a moment, Rosalina blinked at me. Then, she said, "Do you not recall what my role was within our clan?"

I halted and sifted through the memories that had only recently returned to me. After a moment, my eyes widened in surprise. "Ah. You were a weaver."

"Yes. Weavers can create powerful spells. I found I was able to create the most powerful ones using a spinning wheel. The intricate workings of the machine helped weave the layers of magic perfectly." Her tone became wistful, and I knew she was remembering her past life, just like I had been.

"Am I allowed to roam?" I asked. "I want to know what else is here in this dreamscape."

Rosalina's eyebrows narrowed. "No one here can help you, Aurora."

"I know that," I snapped. "But I would like to pretend I am home once more. Before my strength fails me."

"If you wish, I can pull you back under my influence. Make you believe you are dreaming once more."

"No," I said quickly. "I—I want to be lucid for this part. When my connection to the dragons is lost, I won't be myself anymore, will I?"

"No," Rosalina said, her tone cold and indifferent.

I nodded, forcing my face to crumple in grief as if I were fighting back tears. I turned away as if to cry, when really I was trying to scan the area for some kind of substance I could use to paint the rune. If this was all just an illusion, would something like dirt even work?

A rune is most powerful when blood is used, Fenn had told me.

I surveyed my hands, thinking hard. "You… probably have better things to do than watch me waste away," I said.

Rosalina chuckled without humor. "I'm not leaving your side until the transfer is complete, Aurora."

"Aurelia. My name is Aurelia."

"I refuse to refer to you by a false name. Your given name was Aurora Briarcliffe Gaelania. That is who you were when you and my other sisters cast me out. Nothing will ever change that." Her words were clipped and full of malice.

I turned to face her, nostrils flaring. "You attacked our people. Can you blame us for retaliating?"

"You would not see reason!" she seethed, drawing closer to me. "You were squandering a powerful energy that could have been useful to us."

I shook my head, turning away from her. *Something sharp. I need something sharp.* I rubbed my hands down my face, then lifted my fingers, pretending to scratch just above my ear. My fingers met a long pin still holding some of my curls in place. I turned, continuing my pacing, waiting until I fully faced Rosalina before I slowly removed the pin from the back of my head and closed my fist around it.

"Did you think I was lying when I revealed the prophecy to you?" I asked, trying to keep her distracted.

"I believe you could have been the savior of the realm," she said.

"Really? Even after I destroyed that village?"

"It was a minor setback."

I turned away from her once more, my feet continuing the same path up and down the clearing. With my back to her, I glanced down at the pin in my palm, then dug the sharpened point deep into my finger. Blood welled, but I kept digging. I would need more than just a few drops to paint this rune.

"I don't consider the loss of hundreds of lives to be a *setback*," I said.

"That's why you never should have had this power," Rosalina said, her tone harsh. "You are *weak*. You refuse to do what is necessary for the good of the realm. For the good of the witches."

More blood flowed until it was dripping down my finger. I coated the fingers of my other hand in the blood, then painted the marking on the back of my palm, just as Shay had.

A circle... and two lines... My hand shook as I drew.

"What are you doing?" Rosalina demanded, finally noticing my attention was elsewhere.

I finished the final line, completing the rune. The moment I lifted my hand, the rune glowed white, searing into my hand. A blast of energy exploded from within my chest, sending me flying. But instead of careening into a thick tree trunk, I floated, hovering in the air, my feet dangling just above the ground. My arms spread wide, and I threw my head back as a burst of power flooded my veins, my blood, my very soul.

Rosalina screamed something unintelligible, but I paid her no attention. Power swarmed inside me as if a dam had broken, gushing and flowing without restraint.

It was so similar to that day in the witch encampment. The day Shay had died. My arms trembled, and I drew in a sharp breath, trying not to think of those screams and shouts, of the horrors of that day.

No, right now, I *needed* that power and devastation. Right now, it was just me and Rosalina.

So I let it all go. I unleashed everything I'd been holding back. With an almighty roar, I poured every drop of power and strength into the air, letting it encircle me. White sparks shot from my fingertips. And from deep within, a low, rumbling growl resonated.

My dragon had returned.

Rosalina was rushing toward me, but it was too late. As the rune's magic faded, I gently sank to the ground once more. The moment Rosalina reached me, her hand whipping toward me as if to strike, I shifted.

My body elongated. Wings sprouted from my back. Claws extended from my hands and feet. Sharp scales coated my body, and my teeth sharpened into fangs.

The transition was seamless. Effortless. In mere seconds, I stood before Rosalina as a dragon, intercepting her blow with a swipe of my claws. I tore through her sleeve, cutting into her flesh. She fell, cradling her arm as it bled freely. Her murderous gaze fixed on me, her eyes blazing. With her uninjured hand, she flicked her fingers toward me, and a blast of purple magic speared into my chest.

I folded my wings around me, but the impact still sent me staggering, crashing into trunks and branches. Branches and twigs broke my fall, and my impenetrable scales protected me from any pain.

She couldn't stop me. I was too powerful. Too indestructible.

"You cannot defeat me!" she screeched, standing tall before me. "Not in my domain!"

She seemed taller than before. No—She *was* taller. Her body grew in height, lengthening and stretching until she resembled a giant before me, towering over even my bulky dragon form. She was a mighty beast, her eyes glowing red as she advanced, each footstep making the ground rumble.

I ducked to dodge a swipe of her massive hand, then clamped my fangs down on her ankle. She cried out, the sound reverberating around me, making my ears fold back. Using my wings for momentum, I darted behind her, just out of reach as she grabbed for me. She might be a giant, but I was quicker. Faster.

I could also breathe fire.

I inhaled deeply, then unleashed the blue flames, scorching the backs of her legs. She bellowed in agony, crashing to her knees. The ground shook again, and I teetered, unable to keep my balance. My wings stretched wide, allowing me to float instead of fall alongside her.

But I was so distracted from losing balance that I didn't notice her fist until it collided with my left side. With a howl of pain, I was sent toppling, rolling and crashing among the brush. When I finally stopped, I tried to rise, but a fresh wave of pain held me down. My left wing wouldn't move. Only then did I notice it was bent at an unnatural angle.

It was broken.

Growling, I staggered to my feet, pushing past the agony throbbing in my wing as I made my way toward Rosalina again. She grinned widely, her expression demonic with those glowing red eyes.

"Your strength is failing," she said, her voice echoing. "You won't be able to fight me for long."

She was right. Already, I felt too weak to continue.

But I had to try. This was the only way.

I had to strike her where she couldn't reach me. Slowly, a plan formed in my mind. Digging my claws into the earth, I pressed down and launched myself forward.

Rosalina was ready for me, arms spread, prepared to strike me once more.

But instead of aiming for her chest, which was what I wanted her to think, I turned at the last moment, diving between her legs and circling around. Using my claws, I dug into the backs of her legs, making her shriek in pain. I continued climbing, making my way up her legs until I was clinging to her lower back. My claws pushed deeper into her flesh, drawing blood.

She thrashed, arms swiping blindly, trying to remove me from her back, but she couldn't reach me.

I opened my jaws wide and clamped down on a piece of flesh, tearing, tearing, tearing...

Her screams made my ears throb, but I continued biting, ripping her apart piece by piece, until a mess of mangled flesh and blood surrounded me.

At last, she fell, careening to the ground, her body spasming. I continued climbing up her back until I reached the back of her neck. With a deep inhale, I unleashed my blue flames, igniting her hair and setting her head ablaze. Her body twitched, but she was in too much pain to even scream.

I pounced off her, landing hard on the ground, winded and gasping for breath, my tongue lolling and my throat dry. But I wasn't finished yet. As long as she still breathed, she would be drawing strength from me. This wasn't over until she was dead.

Using my snout, I pushed underneath her massive body, straining until I had rolled her onto her back. Then, I leapt onto her chest, climbing until I reached her throat. Her pulse was faint, but it was still there.

With a swift motion, I dragged a claw deep in her throat, sliding from one end to the next. A fresh river of blood flowed, dripping onto the ground and staining her dress. I jumped off her just as the enchantment on her body wore off, making her shrink down to her normal size once more. Her body jerked violently as she choked on her own blood, her face pale as death.

I shifted to my normal form as well, massaging my left shoulder, which was bruised and bleeding from her attack. Slowly, I approached her, my expression stony and unyielding as I watched her die. Her wide, vacant eyes fixed on me.

I could have taunted her. Said something fierce about how I had won and she would never take what belonged to me.

But instead, I looked on with pity. This woman, this witch, had been so consumed by her thirst for power, that she hadn't loved anyone other than herself. And for that, I was sad. I was sad for her loneliness, for all the lives she had already destroyed, and for how the world would not mourn her passing.

Her eyes eventually glazed over, and she took one last wet, ragged breath before going completely still.

When I was certain she was dead, my strength gave out, and I sank to my knees in the dirt, my head spinning. I didn't know how to get back to the mortal realm, but I had nothing left to give. I fell backward, my head meeting the hard ground as oblivion took me.

THE MIDNIGHT PRINCE

I had thought the greatest threat to the Summer Court had been my own kingdom. Foolishly, I had believed that with Mother's death, the Summer Court would be safe.

Stars help me, but I was so very wrong.

As soon as Gorrick told me the news, I was flying down the hall until I reached Mal. He was leaning against the wall with his wings curled up. When I reached him, he stumbled forward and licked my face in an uncharacteristic show of affection.

It almost made me smile. But the circumstances were too dire for me to appreciate it.

"Your home is in danger," I told him. "Aurelia needs us. Can you fly me over there? Are you well enough?"

Mal's nostrils flared, and he uttered a low growl before inclining his head in confirmation.

We emerged into the courtyard, and several courtiers and servants cried out in alarm at the sight of the great dragon. Like before, I had to call off the guards before they surrounded him. Mal's back arched, his wings flaring in warning.

It didn't take long for Gorrick to join us. He had my armor and weapons, as requested. He glanced at Mal with a dubious expression.

"Sire, I must advise against this," he said. "You are our sovereign, and you have no heirs. If something should happen to you—"

"I'm the only one who can get to the border fast enough," I said, donning my armor as I spoke. Gorrick obediently came behind me to fasten the breastplate. "Mal will trust no one else to ride him. And I know once I arrive, I can convince the Autumn Court to back down."

"How?" Gorrick asked, his voice full of doubt. "How will you convince them?"

When my armor was in place, I turned to face Gorrick and offered him a grim smile. "With my charm. And if that doesn't work, I'll use my magic."

Gorrick's face paled. "Are you certain it will work?"

"No. But I have to try."

I turned toward Mal, but Gorrick grabbed my arm, stopping me. "Are you sure this is worth it? The princess is not here. Your bargain to her is fulfilled. You don't owe her anything."

I stared at him, nostrils flared, gritting my teeth so hard it made my head throb. In a low voice, I said, "Yes, I do." I faced Mal, who was crouched low to the ground, ready for me to mount. I climbed atop his back, satisfied to note that the sharp scales did not bother me when I was wearing so much steel. "Send our forces to the border. Ride all night if you have to. I don't know how long I can hold them off."

Gorrick nodded, his expression tight with dismay. But he bowed to me and said, "Yes, Your Highness. Please be safe."

"I will."

Mal didn't wait for my command before taking off, galloping down the steps and through the trees. When we reached the open plains, he spread his wings and shot forward, lifting us above the ground and into the air. My stomach dipped as we arced through the sky, floating above the treetops and among the clouds. I struggled to hold on, keeping my arms wrapped around his neck. My armor and swords made me so damn heavy that I was sure I would slide right off him.

But Mal was an expert flyer and knew how to keep his rider mounted. When he sensed me slipping, he leaned the other direction until I settled back into place. The wind whipped at me, stinging my eyes even through the visor of my helmet. I found myself laughing as the open sky lay before us. Mal arced and curved, gliding with perfect precision. His wings pumped furiously, pushing us forward with more speed than I had ever known.

It's no wonder Aurelia loves this so much, I thought, my chest aching for her. I hoped and prayed to all the gods I could think of that she was safe and that she had unlocked her magic.

If anyone could do it, she could.

And in the meantime, I had to protect her kingdom for her. She would have done the same for me if our roles were reversed.

Once we passed the mist that separated the Star and Autumn Courts, the sun filtered through the clouds around me, making my eyes burn for an entirely different reason.

Gods, I hated the sun.

But as the burn intensified, the air began to shift. Power thrummed, tickling my ears, and beneath me, Mal went tense.

"What is that?" I cried over the rushing wind.

Mal jerked sideways, and I yelped, scrambling for purchase, my arms tightening around his neck.

An explosion of purple magic burst in front of us, and Mal swooped low to avoid it. Power rippled in the air, and I sucked in a horrified breath as realization hit me.

Aurelia had said her dragons were protected by the land of her kingdom. But once they crossed the border, they were no longer safe.

Some other power was reaching for us here. And with Autumn marching on Summer, I had no doubt their mages were on the hunt for the dragons as well. The witches of *my* realm could be trusted, but here?

We were definitely in danger.

I gripped Mal tightly and said to him, "Do what you have to. I know you can get us through this, you clever beast."

Mal grunted in acknowledgement, and then started spinning. I clung to him with every ounce of desperation as my body spun with him, suspending in mid-air for one terrifying moment. More jets of light soared through the sky, aiming for us, but Mal dodged them all, his wings pumping hard, a deep and menacing growl rumbling his body.

The amber and gold leaves were a blur beneath us as we soared over the forests lining the Autumn Court. As the magic continued assaulting us, Mal dipped lower, able to use the cover of the trees to protect us. We were so close now... Sweat dripped down my neck, and my armor suddenly felt too heavy and stifling. I glanced behind us, searching the skies for more magic. But the sky was clear.

In what felt like no time at all, we reached the Summer border. As we descended lower and lower, I made out the Autumn forces marching toward Aurelia's home, their metal armor glinting in the sunlight. There had to be more than ten thousand of them. The standard-bearer in front wielded the orange and crimson banner of the Autumn Court. They were only a few miles from Kellen Falls, where Aurelia and I had been attacked by goblins.

"Let's head them off, shall we?" I asked Mal, who grunted in agreement. He dived, and it took all my strength to maintain my grip around his neck, barely keeping myself atop him. He weaved, spinning to avoid trees and branches before landing hard in a clearing just north of Kellen Falls.

The ensign was barely visible in the distance, nothing but an orange and red blob. Mal and I galloped toward it. When we drew closer, shouts of alarm filled the air as the soldiers no doubt noticed a lone soldier atop a dragon racing toward them. A jet of purple magic speared toward us, confirming my suspicions that the Autumn army had mages with them, intent on bringing us down.

But Mal expertly dodged the attacks, and he didn't slow, not until we were right on top of the lines of soldiers. He careened to a halt only inches from the standard-bearer leading the forces. The man staggered back with a yelp, no doubt expecting Mal to crash straight into him.

I dismounted and removed my helmet, panting as I surveyed the crowd of soldiers. "I must speak with your king. Immediately."

"You are in *our* kingdom," said the man on the other side of the standard-bearer. The eyes visible from beneath his visor were wrinkled with age, and the deep authority ringing from his voice told me he held a high rank. Captain, perhaps.

"I'm here to stop you from needlessly killing thousands of your soldiers!" I shouted. "On behalf of Princess Aurelia of the Summer Court, I demand to speak with your king."

"Who are you to demand anything?" the man spat.

"I am her betrothed, King Fennick of the Midnight Court." I spoke the words with firmness and strength, even as my stomach twisted as I recalled the way my sword had skewered my mother, her blood pooling on the floor. I was only King because I had ended her life…

No, I chided myself. Now was not the time for such thoughts. I needed to focus.

A hushed silence followed my words as several soldiers exchanged worried glances. At long last, the man I presumed to be captain said quietly, "King?"

"Yes, that's right. Queen Sonara only recently passed." I paused, swallowing around the lump in my throat. "The kingdom has fallen to me now."

More silence met my words. I took the opportunity to drive the point home.

"My forces are on their way to you now. Unless you want to risk fighting a battle on both fronts, you will grant me an audience with your king immediately."

The captain stiffened, his eyes narrowing. He whispered something to the soldier behind him, who darted away, weaving through bodies until he vanished from sight. I merely stood there, staring down the soldiers before me, pretending I possessed more courage than I did. Beside me, Mal growled low, his back arching and his wings flaring. He, too, was trying to appear intimidating.

And it was working. Several soldiers shifted their weight uncomfortably. But they had stopped their march. If anything, I was buying Aurelia more time.

And I hadn't had to use my magic yet. I wanted to avoid that at all costs. If there was any way to lose trust in a negotiation, it was to reveal that I could persuade people to do my will.

But I would do what I had to do to stop this war.

After what felt like an hour, the soldier returned and whispered something into the captain's ear. He nodded once and turned to me. "The king will see you. Follow me."

"The dragon comes with me," I said.

The captain glared. "That beast cannot—"

"Either let him through, or he will tear out your throats," I snarled. To prove my point, Mal bared his fangs, his wings spreading even wider. "I could have landed directly in front of your king, even let this creature slash his guts open with his claws. Instead, I came to you to request a formal appearance before the king. Don't make this any more uncivilized than it needs to be."

The captain stared me down, his eyes full of venom, but he nodded again, the motion stiff, before turning and disappearing into the crowd. Mal and I trailed after him, pushing past swords and breast plates, shields and helmets, and the unyielding rows of soldiers who were reluctant to let us pass.

When we reached the cavalry, with their mighty steeds and massive spears, my eyes fell on the biggest and grandest stallion in front, the rider's sword drawn and shield at the ready. It was Callan, the new king of the Autumn Court.

The captain led us straight to the king, who removed his helmet, his eyes blazing with intensity. He dismounted from his horse and strode toward us, each step purposeful and commanding. He oozed authority, even more than his brother had, which was surprising. Callan had seemed unassuming and feeble, but perhaps that was just a mask he had worn—something I was all too familiar with.

When we faced each other, Callan raised an eyebrow at Mal, who growled again.

"Your Highness." I bowed.

"King Fennick," he said coldly. "I was surprised when Captain Reynolds informed me of your mother's demise."

I said nothing at that. Instead, I gestured to the row of soldiers waiting behind him. "What is this, Callan? What the hell are you doing?"

He stiffened at the informality. "I am invading an enemy court."

"Summer is not your enemy. For years, they were your ally."

"Not anymore." His tone was harsh, but he gave no further explanation.

I sighed. "On behalf of my betrothed, I implore you to elaborate. Was there a breach of contract? Did Summer commit an act of war against your people?"

Callan was silent for so long, I wasn't sure he would respond. At long last, he said in a low, broken voice, "The Dream Mage commands it."

My blood chilled. "Y-You are here under her orders?"

He nodded once.

Oh, shit. The Winter assassin had been right. Autumn had aligned themselves with the Dream Mage.

"Dammit, Callan, *why*?" I hissed.

"I had no choice!" he barked. "Tyrone was in league with her, and now I'm left to clean up his mess. I tried to refuse her. But she enchanted my mother. Said the only way she'd let her go was if we invaded the Summer Court."

"So you would condemn your entire court to war just to protect one person?"

"She's my mother," Callan growled.

I snorted. "Don't talk to me about loyalty to one's mother. I was loyal to my mother for years. My entire life. And she still threw it all away for the good of her people. She may have been a manipulative monster, but at least she was willing to do whatever it took to protect her people." *And I sacrificed her in the name of peace. In the name of keeping my kingdom safe.*

But gods, killing her had nearly destroyed me. The ache of it still ripped through me, fresh and festering. Could I really ask Callan to do what I had done? To destroy his soul and carry that weight with him forever?

A muscle feathered in Callan's jaw as he stared at me. "Would you refuse? If it was Aurelia's life on the line?"

I froze at that. The devastation in the king's eyes told me just how much he still cared for the Summer Princess.

Eliminating my mother had been one thing. But could I have made the same choice, if it was Aurelia?

I was surprised by how quickly the answer came to me. "As much as I love Aurelia," I said in a low voice, "I would never subject my people or hers to the brutality of unnecessary war. She wouldn't want that. Is that what your mother would want?"

Callan went perfectly still, his dark gaze betraying nothing.

I opened my senses, unleashing a mere tendril of my power. I didn't want to alarm him, just in case he could sense the presence of fae magic. *"Don't do this, Callan."*

He only watched me, blinking once.

I added more power into my voice. *"Take your armies back. Turn around, before you do something that cannot be undone."*

Callan stood straighter, his nostrils flaring. "I—I don't—" He broke off, his brow furrowing in confusion.

"Leave," I said, pouring more strength into my voice. *"Turn around and leave."*

His arms began to shake, and his breathing turned ragged. "What— What are you doing to me?"

"I'm offering you a taste of what I can do with words alone," I hissed, baring my teeth at him. Then, I unleashed the full force of my magic as I bellowed, *"Fall to your knees!"*

Callan's legs gave out, and he knelt before me, crying out in pain. "Stop. *Stop!*"

A few soldiers rushed to his aid, but I turned on them, too. *"Stop. Do not move."*

They froze in their tracks, limbs stiff as if they had become nothing more than statues.

"Do you want me to decimate your army with a single word?" I asked Callan, cocking my head at him in consideration. "Because I would destroy every single one of them if it meant keeping Aurelia's home safe."

I was bluffing. Already, my insides were quivering with fatigue from pushing so much power into my commands.

But Callan didn't need to know that.

The Autumn King gazed up at me, his eyes watering. "You wouldn't." His voice trembled.

"Between me and the dragon, we could certainly do some damage," I said with a cruel smirk. "And my armies are on their way to you now. Do you really want to have your forces torn apart before you even cross the border?"

"Fennick… The Dream Mage…"

"Aurelia is battling the Dream Mage as we speak," I said. "I think she has more important things to worry about than you and your mother."

Callan blinked, his eyes flaring wide. "What?"

"Aurelia is saving your sorry ass," I said. "She's saving all of us. Now, this is your last chance." I drew my sword. "Leave, or I'll cut you down right now. Or, better yet, I'll order you to fall on your own sword."

Callan glanced at the three soldiers who still remained frozen, unable to come to his aid. Then, he looked at me. His eyes flicked to the slight tremor in my hand as I held my sword.

Dammit. *Dammit.*

Callan sucked in a breath, then rose to his feet as if suddenly realizing I couldn't hold him there any longer. After a long, tense moment, he said, "No. I'm not going anywhere."

I raised my sword, and Mal growled, baring his sharp teeth.

"Reynolds," Callan said, addressing his captain. "Arrest King Fennick. Use excessive force if you must."

Panic and fatigue throbbed through my body, but I brandished my sword, glaring as Reynolds approached me. I would cut him down. I wouldn't last long, but I would take out as many men as I could.

Reynolds did not falter. He didn't even blink, clearly unfazed by my bravado.

When he was close enough, I swung my sword high. Too high. He met it with his own, and the clang echoed around us.

Taking advantage of his position, I kicked him hard in the shin, then rammed my knee into his groin. He sank to his knees with a strangled groan.

With one swift motion, I cracked the pommel of my sword against his skull, and he fell to the ground, motionless.

Panting, I raised my eyebrows at Callan, who scowled at me. "Is that all?"

With a growl, Callan pointed his sword at me. "Take him down!"

Shouts rang out. As one, the soldiers surged toward us, swords drawn.

My hand was sweaty as I gripped the hilt of my sword. I shared one last somber look with Mal before we both dived into battle.

THE SUMMER PRINCESS

I AWOKE IN THE VERY ROOM WHERE I HAD PRICKED MY FINGER ON THE spindle—only this time, Queen Sonara was nowhere to be found.

Exhaustion settled deep into my bones, dragging my body down even as I struggled to rise. With a groan, I forced my body upright, trying to shake off the drowsiness of my enchanted slumber.

All I wanted to do was sink back against the pillows and sleep.

Instead, I swung my legs around and tried to stand. My legs wobbled like a newborn calf, and I hissed in pain, gripping the bedpost for support. I helplessly cast another look around the empty room.

No one was here.

Where was Fenn? And Mal?

"Dammit all, Aurelia," I growled at myself. "You are the Dragon Queen. If you can't shake off a little sleepiness, then what the hell are you good for?"

I summoned my power—just a kernel of it. I let it glow in my chest, spreading warmth and energy across my body. Flames coiled low in my belly as magic sizzled in my blood.

With a gasp, I straightened, all fatigue and sluggishness leaving me in an instant. I vaguely remembered Rosalina wounding me during our battle, but I felt no pain. There were no lingering injuries. Somehow, I had been healed.

My fingers twitched, eager for me to shift into my dragon form.

But I couldn't. Not yet. If I did that here, I would destroy the castle.

With renewed energy, I burst out of the room. A passing servant yelped when she saw me, and I frantically asked where I could find Cela. With a shaky finger, the maid pointed down the hall.

I found my handmaid changing the linens in my old bedchamber. When I entered, she dropped the wadded up sheets with a sharp gasp, then rushed toward me, arms out, as she pulled me to her in a tight embrace. Startled, I held her, touched by her show of affection.

"My lady!" Cela withdrew to look me over, eyes wide and cheeks pink. "Are you well?"

"I am. Can you tell me where my dragon is? And where is Fenn?"

Cela's face paled. "You have not heard?"

"Heard what?" I asked impatiently.

She quickly filled me in on what had happened. Sonara's death. Autumn's army.

And Fenn, racing to head them off.

I didn't hesitate. In seconds, I was taking off down the hall, flying down the staircase and out into the courtyard. Several servants stared in alarm as I sprinted, trying to put as much distance between myself and the castle as possible.

My heart slammed against my ribcage, my breaths coming in short spurts as I turned back to stare up at the towering turrets of Fenn's home.

In the Dream Realm, things had been different; there was no risk when I shifted. It was all an illusion. If I damaged anything, there were no consequences.

But here and now, there were people I might hurt. Buildings I might crush.

Sweat trickled down my brow as I assessed my surroundings. A servant drew closer, a question in his eyes, but I waved him away.

"Get back!" I cried. "All of, you get back!"

He had the good sense to flee, drawing other servants with him until I stood alone in the middle of the courtyard.

Part of me knew that the only reason I'd been able to unlock my dragon form was because of the Dream Realm. I hadn't held anything back. That release, that trust in my magic, was precisely what I had needed.

It was exactly what Mal had told me. To trust my magic, like I trusted him when we flew.

With this in mind, I closed my eyes, and unleashed it all. I spread my arms wide, freeing my dragon from her restraints.

Be free, I thought.

Power exploded from me. Fire roared in my chest, spreading through my body and heating me down to the tips of my toes. With an almighty cry, I released a jet of blue flames that ignited along my arms. My body lifted and grew in size, just like during my fight with Rosalina. A tail swished behind me, and wings spread from my shoulder blades. More, more, more, my body continued to grow until I was heavy and massive and powerful.

In moments, I stood in my dragon form, towering over the courtyard. Screams echoed nearby, but they were distant enough to reassure me no one stood within striking range.

Unlike when I had shifted to attack the unseelie, I felt in complete control. I remembered who I was and why I was here.

Fenn. I needed to find Fenn.

I took stock of my body, gazing down at my midnight black scales. So much like Mal… My dragon form must have been part of the Darkener species, just like him.

I wriggled my clawed feet, breaking concrete with my heavy steps. My barbed tail swung to the left and right. I exhaled a puff of ash and tried to spread my wings.

Nothing happened.

With a growl of frustration, I tried again, focusing on where I thought my shoulder blades were. One shoulder rolled. Then, I felt it. The muscle connecting my right wing. Gingerly, I flexed it.

My right wing spread wide, casting a large shadow over the courtyard as it blocked the light of the moon. Triumph raced through me, and I spread the other wing as well. Once I located those muscles, it was as easy as breathing.

I flapped both wings, and a gust of wind billowed from the motion. With a roar, I took to the skies, wings beating as I floated higher and higher. Delight raced through me from the feeling of flying freely. Completely on my own. The wind whistled past me as I arced through the sky. I curved to the right, away from the castle, and put on a burst of speed, flapping my wings with more force. My scales protected me from the moisture and the wind, and I felt nothing but freedom, the weightlessness of gliding through the sky.

A hum of delight burned in my throat, and I released a stream of blue fire into the air. Burning suns, there was nothing like it!

I soared higher until I could make out the tips of the Mistwood Hills. The sight of it sobered me, reminding me of the task at hand.

Fenn and Mal were in trouble. I had to get to them.

Sudden awareness rippled through me, and I looked around in alarm, trying to find the source of it. After a moment, I realized it sounded like... *voices.*

I closed my eyes, concentrating. Then—

Aurelia?

My heart lurched. I *knew* that voice!

Mal? I thought.

You have done it. You have unlocked your power. There was pride in his voice.

I tried to laugh, but in my dragon form, it came out as a low huff. *Yes, I have. Thanks to you. Where are you?*

Just south of the Autumn Palace. Fenn and I are in danger.

I'm coming.

Aurelia... You might need to summon the others.

I faltered. *Others?*

The other dragons. You are their queen, after all.

Uncertainty bubbled in my chest at the thought. Could I do this? I had only just unlocked my powers.

Put your trust in your magic, Aurelia.

I took a deep breath and searched within myself, trying to isolate another voice from inside me. They were merging together, mingling to form an incomprehensible babble, like a churning river.

When I focused on one, I called out, *Jorey?*

I wasn't sure how I knew it was him, but I did.

His voice fell silent, just before he exploded with delight.

Aurelia! Is it really you? Have you done it? I knew you could! You were always so capable, so strong. I knew you had it in you. This is wonderful! The kingdom is saved! Now we can—

Jorey, I said, cutting him off. *I need your help. Can you gather some dragons and meet me in the Autumn Court?*

Yes, of course, my queen. Right away. I will do this for you immediately. You can count on me. I will—

I tuned out his eager voice, relief and amusement coursing through me.

I could speak to the dragons. We could *communicate*.

Gods, it was almost too much for me to process. All these abilities, all this power...

But no. I could focus on it later. For now, Fenn needed me.

I pumped my wings again and took off toward the hills. With ease, I burst through the strange mist surrounding the Star Court. A stream of sunlight burned against my eyes, but I put on more speed, my wings beating even faster.

A tingle of awareness shivered past me, and I slowed, my eyes surveying the skies. Something else was here. Was it one of my dragons? Had they already reached me?

But this presence felt different. Foreign. It was not a form of dragon magic, that much I knew.

A blast of power shot toward me, and I spun, narrowly avoiding getting struck. I growled and flew lower, my clawed feet brushing against the treetops. More magic flashed, and I ducked and dodged, weaving my way through the trees and using the branches as cover for whatever magic was after me.

I had just flown past the Autumn Palace when I caught sight of the massive army heading toward my kingdom. A snarl built up in my throat when I spotted Mal and Fenn, standing amidst a crowd of soldiers, swords swinging. Mal leapt on one soldier, tearing out his throat before moving on to another. Next to him, Fenn struck with lithe grace, but his ashen complexion and hooded eyes betrayed his exhaustion.

He wouldn't last much longer.

A roar burst from me, and the fighting halted as everyone froze to stare at my mighty form approaching. The ground shook when I landed next to Fenn and Mal. Several soldiers dived out of the way, afraid of being crushed by my landing.

I could hardly blame them. In my dragon form, I was more than twice Mal's size, and I towered over the army easily. It wouldn't take much to wipe them out. My blue fire alone could melt the flesh off their bones.

The soldiers withdrew, swords still raised, but fear apparent on their faces.

And there was Callan, cowering behind his horse. His wide eyes flicked from Fenn to me and back again. "Fennick, what is this?"

"A reminder of who you're facing," Fenn panted, wiping sweat from his brow. Despite his fatigue, he offered a cruel smile. "May I present, Aurelia Perdis, sovereign of the Summer Court, and the Dragon Queen of the Realm of Valora."

My chin lifted at the pride in his voice, and I fixed a steely stare on Callan, who had gone paler than death.

"Dragon Queen?" he repeated weakly. "*Aurelia*? You—You cannot be serious."

I pulled on the power within me and shifted to my mortal form, appearing in the same blue dress I had worn in the dreamscape. Callan stumbled backward, practically falling over in his shock.

I offered him a simpering smile. "You're lucky I haven't turned you into ash, Callan. I have control over the dragons, and I have already summoned them here. You know you cannot win this. Turn back now. Before I end you."

He swallowed, his throat bobbing as he glanced over my shoulder as if expecting my army of dragons to descend at any moment. He then looked at the rows of soldiers behind him The horses were still rearing, pawing at the ground in agitation. The few riders who had been thrown from their mounts were scrambling backward, away from me and Mal.

Callan had lost the courage of his men. He had lost their respect. There was nothing left for him now.

"The Dream Mage is dead," I said firmly. "You do not need to fear her retribution."

Callan's head swung to face me. "How can you be sure?"

"Because I killed her," I said icily. "And I will kill you, too, if you bring your armies onto my soil."

Callan's jaw went rigid, and he rubbed the back of his neck. "Aurelia... I had no choice."

"Save it, Callan."

He flinched from the harshness of my tone. "Aurelia, please—"

"Our alliance will remain intact, but only if you take your forces and *go.*" This was more mercy than he deserved. Fire burned within me, begging for me to slice open his throat for attacking Fenn.

But I needed to be diplomatic. And Fenn had been right—my court needed allies.

Callan nodded stiffly, then turned to a soldier and muttered something. The soldier shouted orders through the cavalry, and row by row, the forces began retreating, turning back toward their castle.

I stood, watching them go with a stony expression. Callan looked at me, his mouth opening as if to say something. But my glare had him closing his mouth and turning away from me without a word.

Together, Mal, Fenn, and I remained standing in the grass, our eyes never leaving the retreating army. Even long after they vanished from view, we stood there, unmoving.

At long last, I let my shoulders droop, overcome with fatigue. In seconds, Fenn had me gathered against his chest, crushing me in a tight embrace.

"Gods above, Aurelia," he murmured, stroking my hair, his hand cradling the back of my head as he held me. "I love you. I love you with all my heart. I should have said it before."

I sagged against him, letting him hold me as if he could piece together every part of my shattered soul. I inhaled his delicious cool mint scent, memorizing the warmth of him, the feel of his hands on me.

"I love you, too," I whispered, feeling fresh tears drip down my face.

He withdrew to look me over, his eyes full of concern. "Are you hurt? Did she hurt you?"

"My shoulder was injured, but when I awoke from the dreamscape, it had healed. I think passing through the realms brought some of the witches' healing magic with me. Or it was my dragon magic."

"So, she is really dead? The Dream Mage?"

I nodded. "I watched the life leave her eyes, Fenn. It's done."

He laughed in amazement, then drew me in again, bringing my lips to his. His mouth claimed me, his tongue pressing between my lips as he infused all his desperation and emotions into that singular, bruising kiss.

When he withdrew, he pressed his forehead to mine, and I focused on the feel of his breath, his heartbeat pulsing in time with mine.

A cacophony of roars filled the air, and we broke apart to find Jorey and four other dragons flying toward us. I grinned widely, waving them toward us.

As soon as Jorey landed, he pounced on Fenn. Fenn yelped, falling to the earth as Jorey licked his cheek.

A delighted laugh burst from me as I surveyed the others—the twins, a pair of auburn dragons named Calliope and Desdemona, a crimson dragon named Leo, and a tall bronze dragon named Raddigan.

I surged toward my dragons, arms spread wide as they nudged closer to me. Calliope pressed her snout into my shoulder, and Desdemona tenderly licked my ear. Tears pricked at my eyes as I embraced them. Part of me hadn't believed I'd really communicated with them. Part of me feared I had imagined the whole thing.

But they were here. They had heard my call and come to my aid.

"The army has left," I told them. "We are safe. Thank you for coming to assist us."

Calliope purred, nuzzling further into me. For a moment, I did nothing but hold my dragons, reassuring myself that they were here, they were unharmed, and we had saved the kingdom. Just for this moment, I needed that peace.

"What happens now?" Fenn asked. He had risen to his feet and was scratching under Jorey's chin.

I turned to look at him in confusion. "What do you mean?"

"You got your memories back. Your kingdom is safe. What will you do?" A rare note of vulnerability laced his tone.

I drew closer to him and pressed the flat of my palm against his cheek, feeling the prickle of stubble on his face. "Now, we return to my court and ensure the curse is broken. I'll introduce you to my family as my betrothed. And then, we plan our wedding."

A slow smile spread on his face. "You—You wish to marry me? Even after everything?"

I kissed him again, long and sensuous, my tongue sliding along his lower lip with agonizing slowness. He shuddered, a growl building in his throat as his hands came around my waist, gripping me firmly.

"Yes," I whispered against his lips. "I will marry you, Fenn. If you'll have me."

He answered by nipping at my lip, and I laughed. He kissed me again and again, bringing his mouth to my throat, my jaw, my collarbone. For what felt like hours, we stood there, holding each other and making up for lost time while the dragons chased each other in the grass. We still had foes to face and conflicts to resolve, but here in this moment, we were simply two people in love, eager to spend the rest of eternity together.

THE SUMMER PRINCESS

Fenn and I returned to my court to find Kade on the brink of succumbing to her hibernation. The remaining dragons flanked her like soldiers, prepared to defend her if necessary.

We brought a pouch of stardust with us to break the curse. But by the time we reached the castle, I could already tell the enchantment had broken with Rosalina's death. Servants bustled about, and shouts of concern and distress echoed throughout the castle.

Before I faced my people, I sprinkled a smattering of stardust around Azure, the dying Blue Amethyst. Fenn and I had already put plans in place to bring back her mother, whom Sonara had chained up in her dungeon. She was too wounded to fly, but once she had healed, she could be reunited with her youngling.

But for now, the stardust would heal Azure. Already, I could see her tiny form wriggling toward the stardust, sniffing around with interest. Her tongue lapped up a few of the crystal flakes, and color was already brightening her eyes.

With a small smile, I left Mal in charge of the pouch of stardust, indicating he needed to knock over a few more piles of it whenever Azure looked like she needed more. Then, Fenn and I made our way to the castle.

I went to the tea room first. As I made my way down the hall, trying to shove back the memories of when I was here in Rosalina's dreamscape, the echoes of tearful shouts met my ears. When I reached the doorway, I stood there for a moment, taking in the scene before me.

Gigi and Mother sat on the sofa, embracing one another tightly, both of them weeping. They looked up at my approach, their mouths falling open in shock.

For a long, tense moment, we only stared at each other. I stood there, enduring their scrutiny, waiting for them to send me away, to shudder at the monster they knew me to be. My powers were no longer bound; I was the Dragon Queen, and I was dangerous and deadly.

Gigi reacted first. She jumped to her feet and flew toward me, barreling into me with a fierce embrace. Her arms wrapped around me, and she sobbed into my dress, her shoulders trembling.

"I knew you could do it," she said, her voice muffled as she cried. "I knew it!"

I held her, my own eyes pricking with tears. Gods, I had missed her! We clung to each other with all the desperation of two sisters who had almost lost one another. Though we were not connected by blood, she would always be my sister.

My grip on her relaxed as Mother approached, her eyes moist and full of hesitation.

"You—You know everything, then?" she asked in a solemn voice.

I withdrew, and Gigi positioned herself next to me, clutching my hand in hers. "Yes," I said softly.

Mother nodded once, a single tear racing down her cheek. She sniffed, then released a shuddering sob. "Oh, *Aurelia.*"

Then, she was holding me, cradling my head against her chest. Gigi joined us, and Mother's arms gathered both of us close to her as if we were both her children. As if she had raised us both from the womb.

Gigi was her flesh and blood. And I was not.

But in this moment, I felt as loved, as cherished as if I had been born into this family. As if we had lived and loved together.

And that feeling of intense joy and love and relief blossomed within me until I felt as if the broken remains of my memories and past lives could be healed in this singular moment.

I didn't bring up our plans for the future. Not yet. The time for that would come later.

Mother and I saw to the needs of our people, sending the healer to inspect those who had been under the curse, and reaching out to the nobles in the outer cities who hadn't been affected by the enchantment to assure them all was well in the castle. There had been riots and skirmishes, and it would take a while to quell the unrest that had risen from the ordeal. But for the most part, the kingdom was safe.

I had been avoiding my father. I let Mother bring him up to speed, knowing I was not yet ready to face him.

When I could put it off no longer, I sent word to the witch clans, politely requesting Samiria's presence. I wasn't sure if she would come, after everything that had happened. But, to my surprise, she did—and so did Ruby, Jade, and Sapphire. Together, we met with my parents and sister in the throne room and outlined everything that had happened. The three Midnight witches lifted the spell that had bound Samiria, finally allowing her to speak about it. And for hours, we discussed what had happened and what to expect from my newfound power.

"My great-grandparents thought your power would protect us," Father said to me, his voice stoic and as unfeeling as ever. "It was the only reason they took you in. The only reason we continued to keep your secret from generation to generation."

"But," Mother interjected, shooting him a worried glance, "we came to love you, Aurelia. We still do. When it was clear your memories wouldn't come back, we began to see you as part of our family, not —not—"

"A weapon," I finished in a hollow voice.

Mother flinched, but Father met my stare.

"We did what we had to do," he said softly. "For the good of our kingdom."

"And promising my dragons to Tyrone?" I asked, unable to keep the bite from my voice. "Was that for the good of the kingdom, too?"

Father's eyes widened slightly—the only sign of his surprise. After a moment, he said, "That was to clean up your mess. It was the only way to maintain our alliance with them, after you ended the engagement so abruptly."

"Because he *violated* me," I growled. "Tyrone was a monster. And I refused to bind myself to a man who would force me into his bed without my consent."

A hushed silence fell around us. Mother's face turned ghostly pale, and Gigi looked like she might vomit. Even Father had the good sense to look shocked, his expression stricken with horror.

"Aurelia," Father said, his voice strained. "I—I did not know. I—"

I shook my head. "Because I did not tell you." Perhaps if I had, things would have been different. But I supposed it didn't matter anymore. With Tyrone dead, the bargain had been nullified. All that remained were my traumatized memories and the betrayal of knowing my father had made such a bargain in the first place.

I swallowed around the lump in my throat and forced myself to ask, "So, what now? Will you send me away?"

Father's head reared back. "What?"

Mother's hand went to her chest, and Gigi stepped forward, her eyes full of panic. "Aurie, what are you talking about?"

"With the Dream Mage dead, you all don't need me anymore," I said, my voice thick as I struggled to hold back my tears. "My powers are too dangerous."

Father stared at me, but his expression was stoic, giving away nothing. Mother gripped his arm tightly. "Stefan..." Her voice was pleading.

"But—But Aurie isn't dangerous anymore!" Gigi sputtered. "Right?" She looked at me beseechingly.

I wrung my hands together, trying to stifle the anxiety coursing through me. When it had just been Mother, Gigi, and me in that tea room, things had seemed so much simpler. But with Father here, knowing he hadn't abdicated to me yet, things were complicated.

Before I could answer, Sapphire spoke. "Aurelia has unlocked her magic. She did it in the safety of the Dream Realm. We believe that, because of this, her powers are less volatile and explosive. The reason why they were uncontrollable before was because she was trying too hard to quash them."

"It is different," I agreed. "I have my memories back, and never in the six hundred years of my existence have I known such... inner peace with my magic. I was always deathly afraid of unleashing too much, of releasing my devastation and hurting people." I paused, thinking of how Mal had compared my magic to the trust between a dragon and his rider in flight. "But instead of leashing my magic, I let it free. It is no longer bottled up inside me. It is no longer a threat."

"So you say," said Father.

"*Stefan*," Mother chided.

I shook my head, unable to keep the tears from leaking, tracking down my cheeks and dripping onto the floor. "It's all right. If you all will feel safer if I leave, I understand. I cannot blame you, not after everything that's happened. We aren't truly family, after all."

"Aurelia, you *are* our family," Mother said, stepping toward me, her arm outstretched. Father raised a hand to silence her, but to everyone's surprise, she shoved his hand away. "*No*, Stefan. I will not be silenced. Aurelia is our daughter. I don't care what you say or what her past is. She has proven herself to us again and again. She was the *only* one unaffected by the sleeping curse, and she saved us all. If you send her away, I will go with her."

"So will I." Gigi's chin lifted with her words, her eyes glinting with a fierce determination I had never seen in her before.

My heart swelled and knotted all at once, torn between relief, gratitude, and fear for my family being ripped apart. I cast a frightened look at my father, whose face had paled, his beard twitching with his frown.

"You were planning to abdicate to me before all this," I said, my voice tentative. "Was that all a ruse? A lie?"

"Of course not!" Mother said hastily. "We love you and trust you to protect our people, Aurelia."

But my eyes were on Father. I believed Mother loved me. But Father?

After a long moment Father sighed. "When—When my father's health was failing, he told me the truth about you. I believed you to be an estranged cousin, kept away in our manor in the country. But after he died, leaving the kingdom to me, I didn't want to shut you up in that old house any longer. The witch clans here had successfully bound your magic, so we thought it best to claim you as our daughter. We thought that no kingdom would ever dare to challenge us if we had the Dragon Queen within these very walls. And the witches assured us the binding spell would hold.

"But as more years passed, we started to think of you as more than just a defense tactic. You became a family member. Especially after Gigi was born. All we had to do was pretend there were enough years between you two so that she didn't notice that you did not age. After that, it was easy for you two to become sisters. You were—You were so good with her. You were the only one who could calm her down when she was upset."

My heart swelled in my chest, and my eyes suddenly felt hot. Mother sniffed, and I found tears streaming down her face. Gigi's eyes were wet, too, as she gazed at me with love and affection.

"It—It was hard for me to see past your true identity," Father admitted, his gaze fixed on the stone floor. "Your mother and Gigi loved you so easily, but it was harder for me. I was scared. And when the witches checked in on you, assuring us that it was unlikely your powers would *ever* manifest… I saw an opportunity. We had a powerful connection to the witches because of you. And a powerful connection to the dragons as well. Not only that, but you loved the Summer Court so much. It was clear the block on your memories wasn't affecting your life at all. And I thought that, if you became queen of this court, you could keep our people safe. You were loyal to us. You believed you belonged here."

Father took a deep breath before continuing, "Your mother is right. We *did* come to care for you and trusted you to look after this kingdom. We still do. But things are different now. Your powers have been unlocked. And you have your memories back. You know who you are now. I—I'm afraid this changes everything."

I straightened to my full height, forcing myself to meet his gaze. Though everything in me wilted, and I yearned to flee from this situation, to throw myself onto my bed and sob until I had nothing left, I lifted my chin. I gathered the courage within me, projecting strength I didn't think I was capable of.

"Yes," I said, my voice even and firm, despite the raging emotions within me. "I know who I am. I am the Dragon Queen. I am the Summer Princess. I am a daughter of Midnight and a daughter of Summer. I belong to *both courts,* Father." I fought to take a steadying breath. "Will you let me prove that to you? Now that I am myself, now that my memories and my magic have been freed, let me show you I can be trusted. Let me prove to you that I can be the fearless protector our kingdom deserves. I won't ask you to abdicate to me unless you know with complete certainty that I can keep our people safe."

The entire room fell silent from the promise of my words. Gigi watched me, her eyes shining with admiration. Mother had her hands pressed to her chest, tears spilling down her face as she glanced from me to Father and back again.

Even the witches remained silent and somber. Ruby, Jade, and Sapphire stood side-by-side, while Samiria remained on the opposite side of the room. It was clear from her stiff posture that she wasn't happy to be in the same room as the other witches. I couldn't blame her.

At long last, Father cleared his throat and said in a strained voice, "Yes, Aurelia. Of course. I—I will grant you that opportunity."

"Thank you." My words were strained, my throat tight with emotion. "Now, if you'll excuse me, I have wedding preparations to take care of."

Father blinked. "Wedding? You—You and the Midnight Prince—"

"Yes," I said, a soft smile lighting my face. For the first time since I entered the room, the tightness in my chest eased at the thought of my marriage to Fenn. "It is a mutually beneficial arrangement for both kingdoms. I would… love to have your blessing, Father, but even if I don't, nothing will keep me from marrying him. I love Fennick with my entire soul. I want to bind myself to him for eternity. If you have ever felt love for me in your life, you would grant me that much."

Father's eyes flared wide, his mouth opening slightly. My words clearly caught him off guard. I wasn't sure if it was my intense declaration of love, or the fact that it was the prince of a former enemy kingdom that shocked him. But for a long moment, he only stared at me, his eyes flickering as he processed this.

At long last, he nodded stiffly, and that was all I needed.

One by one, we filed out of the room, starting with Mother and Gigi.

"Give him time," Mother whispered to me, swiping a tear from her face. "He just needs time."

I nodded, unsure if this was true. Mother clearly believed it, but I didn't know if Father could ever love a monster like me.

But this was a start. I was not afraid.

After all, I had the soul of a dragon living inside me.

Mother left the room, followed by Gigi, who swept me into a tight embrace, murmuring assurances that nothing had changed for her and we would always be sisters. I thanked her, tears rolling down my face from the promise of her words.

When she left, it was only me and the witches remaining.

Sapphire spoke first. "So, you intend to remain here."

"I do," I said. "I may have my memories back, but my life is here. But, with the union of our courts and the freedoms Fenn is granting to your clans, I will be visiting often."

The three witches only looked at me somberly. Ruby said, "You cannot have both, Dragon Queen. You cannot be a part of our clan if you serve the seelie courts."

I found myself smiling. "I don't want to be a part of your clan."

For the first time since I'd known them, Sapphire, Ruby, and Jade looked confused, exchanging bewildered looks with one another. Across the room, Samiria was smiling.

"I was meant to unite the realm," I went on, my voice full of conviction. "And that is what I plan to do. Not by spinning prophecies and practicing runic magic, but by serving the people of this land and protecting them to the best of my ability. *That* is the true meaning behind the prophecy that started it all."

Samiria pressed a fist to her chest and bowed low. "Well said, my queen."

I turned to face her, my eyes softening. "Samiria, if you accept, I would be honored to have you as the Keeper of the Dragons in my absence."

Samiria bowed again. "The honor is mine, Your Highness."

I smiled at the formality, then turned to the three witches of the Midnight Court. Their expressions had been wiped clean once more as they gazed at me, their wide lavender eyes blinking slowly. I inclined my head in reverence to all three of them, then paused when I met Sapphire's gaze.

"Thank you for everything," I whispered to her, pressing my hand to my chest as a sign of respect.

Sapphire reached out, taking my hand in hers. Her skin was cool against mine, and she squeezed once. "Take care, Dragon Queen."

After parting from the witches, my body was spent. I found Fenn waiting for me in my chambers, wearing nothing but his shirtsleeves and trousers, the loose fabric hanging from his lean body. He lounged on my bed with a book in his hand, though his gaze was fixed on the window. An unusually solemn expression was on his face, his eyes somber.

I knew he was thinking of his mother. Every day, her death haunted him. I wasn't sure if he would ever forgive himself.

After a moment, he looked up to see me standing in the doorway, a crooked smile playing on his lips. That smile told me he wasn't ready to talk about it yet. And I would respect that. I would give him as much space as he needed.

We had both been through an ordeal. It would be a long journey for us to fully recover from it. I wasn't completely certain we ever would.

"You look rather comfortable in my bed," I commented lightly, already pulling pins from my hair and letting the curls cascade down my back.

Fenn watched me let my hair down, a dark, hungry look brimming in his eyes. He set his book down, rising to his feet and closing the distance between us.

"I'll be much more comfortable if you join me," he murmured, pressing kisses against my hair. His hands came around my back as he began pulling at the strings of my dress. "Gods, I can't believe these dresses you Summer folk wear. They are impossible."

I sighed. "One step at a time, Fenn. Let's quiet the unrest in the realm before we make decrees on fashion changes."

He laughed, his breath tickling my neck. When the bodice was loosened, he tugged at my dress until it pooled at my feet, leaving me in nothing but my shift. His mouth was on my throat, working his way down. I sucked in a sharp breath when his lips grazed the top of my breast. My head rolled back, my eyes closing as the heat of his mouth warmed my body and soul.

I needed this. All day, I had yearned to be in his arms, especially knowing he would have to return to his court tomorrow morning. We hadn't worked out the details yet, but for now, we had decided to split our time between our two kingdoms. We both had responsibilities to our courts and our people. And luckily, with my shifter abilities, traveling between kingdoms was effortless in my dragon form. I could even fly to the Star Court and bring Fenn back to my court in less than half a day's time.

Eventually, I would want to start training Gigi in court politics, the economy, and the safety of our kingdom. The hope was that one day, she could take my place as queen and I could live with Fenn in the Star Court.

But that was far in the future and not something to worry about tonight.

"Do you want to talk about it?" Fenn asked between kisses.

My mind already felt tired just thinking about the whole ordeal with Father. When Fenn withdrew to peer into my eyes, his expression earnest, I shook my head. "Not right now. But soon."

I walked him backward until we collapsed on the bed in a tangle of limbs. I brought my mouth to his once more, tasting him fully, losing myself in the feel of his skin against mine.

"For now, just hold me," I murmured against his lips. "Tomorrow, we can conquer the world, but tonight is ours." I rolled, straddling him, grinding my hips against his.

He groaned, his fingers clenching around my thighs. "As the Dragon Queen commands."

As we shed our clothes and lost ourselves in the passion and collision of our bodies, I felt a certainty grow within me, igniting a powerful flame that could never be doused. I knew that together, Fenn and I could face anything. Together, with the strength of our love and magic, the support of our people and kingdoms, we could shine brighter than the stars.

And so we did.

Want to know what happens to Azure, the Blue Amethyst dragon with magical powers? Read the next Crowns of the Fae book, *Crown of Briars*, a Beauty and the Beast retelling!

ACKNOWLEDGMENTS

This story would not have been possible without the many individuals who worked so hard to help me bring it to life.

Amy, Zoe, Jenni, and Sara, my beta readers, who read the rough draft version and helped me make it into a polished story.

artjake, teviense, Anastasia Subbotina, and Samaiya Art for the gorgeous character art for this series.

Blue Raven Book Covers for the covers and formatting.

The gorgeous special editions of this book are thanks to the many Kickstarter backers who brought the project to life! Thank you to everyone who supported the campaign. And thank you to the Kickstarter for Authors group, who provided valuable feedback on my campaign, helping me improve it and make it the best it can be.

I wouldn't be anywhere without my fabulous ARC team! Thank you so much to all of you lovely ARC readers who read early versions of the story. Your enthusiasm and support is such a gift!

The Tuesday Tribe, who gave me advice and suggestions to make the story better. Thank you for letting me vent and complain when the characters were misbehaving and deviating from my original plan!

A big thank you to my FSFA group, who helped me brainstorm when I'd gotten myself stuck. Talking it out really helped me find the right way to finish off the story!

And above all, thank you to my devoted husband and beautiful sweet children, for your patience and understanding while I try to meet deadlines and get this book out into the world.

ABOUT THE AUTHOR

R.L. Perez is an author, wife, mother, reader, writer, and teacher. She lives in Florida with her husband and three kids. On a regular basis, she can usually be found napping, reading, feverishly writing, revising, or watching an abundance of Netflix. More than anything, she loves spending time with her family. Her greatest joys are her children, nature, literature, and chocolate.

Subscribe to her newsletter for new releases, promotions, giveaways, and book recommendations! Get a FREE eBook when you sign up at subscribe.rlperez.com.